BORDERTOWN TROUBLE

Snake and the Dog-Man Book 1

JOHNNY GUNN

WOLFPACK
PUBLISHING
— EST 2013 —

WOLFPACK
PUBLISHING
— EST 2013 —

Published in the United States by Wolfpack Publishing, Las Vegas

Wolfpack Publishing
6032 Wheat Penny Avenue
Las Vegas, NV 89122

wolfpackpublishing.com

Paperback ISBN 978-1-64734-868-7
eBook ISBN 978-1-64734-867-0

BORDERTOWN TROUBLE

1

"The big one calls himself Snake. Looks more like a mangy coyote to me." The burly deputy held the helpless man called Snake by the back of his heavy coat. "The other one's called Dog-man. Been in town two or three days. Tried to sell a mine they don't own. Lock 'em up or escort 'em out of town?"

"They do anything else? Hell, everyone sells mines they don't have. It's a way of life in these parts." Deadwood's sheriff, Seth Bullock laughed. "I got maps showing bonanza diggin's to make the Denver Mint jealous." The deputy shook his head no. "If they can sit a horse, lead 'em out of town. Head 'em south, that way we won't get 'em back at first snow."

Deadwood, in the Black Hills, was where many a prospector headed when the winter storms covered the north country, and when their pokes ran out or low, became burdensome to the community. Many became thieves, some worse, and Bullock wasn't going to set these two up for an easy winter.

Two deputies managed to get the drifters on

their horses, their mules were already packed. "These two were lookin' to hightail it anyway. How much did they take old Zeke for?'

"Zeke said two hundred but the one called Snake only had fifty on him."

"Zeke's good at that."

They reached the road south, swatted the drifters' horses and rode back to town. "You hear what that guy said? Said we took two hundred from that drunk." Snake waited until the deputies were well out of sight before sitting upright in the saddle. "We never talked to anyone named Zeke."

"Weren't us what conned old Zeke," the one called Dog-man laughed. "Better keep ridin', though. When Peterson wakes up and finds he paid us five hundred for that map, well, they just might come lookin'."

"What that sheriff said about runnin' out of money in the winter is a fact. My Uncle Zebediah was in Kansas after a fall drive, didn't leave back for Texas, ran out of money. Tough winter," Snake said.

"What'd he do?"

"Walked right up to the sheriff and punched him in the groin. Sentenced to six months. Warm and well fed for the winter," Snake laughed.

Snake was long and lean, near thirty, and was a fine Texas cowboy who came north with a herd a couple of years ago and decided it was time to retire.

"I don't like workin' for someone," Dog-man said. "You worked for anyone?"

"Worked for a widow lady but she fired me." Snake shook his head, remembering the experience.

"Was she pretty?"

"I might have made a different decision if she had been," Snake chuckled. "I caught one of the hands, pilfering, you know, and shot him. Couldn't let him take her silver cuz he would have been taking from a widow." He was shaking his big head back and forth.

"Life gets all confusing, Dog-man. We sold a mine we didn't own and I shot a man for takin' from a widow. Them deputies thought we were outlaws and that sheriff laughed it off. The widow was upset cuz I shot one of her best men, not know-in' why I shot him."

"Life has twists and turns no mountain trail could compete with," Dog-man said. "I kissed a girl when I was fourteen and her father, along with a shotgun, was gonna force me to marry her. Let's just stay on our own path, Snake, and let the rest of the world have theirs."

He met up with Dog-man some time that year and the two had been roaming through wild coun-try. Not a care in the world if their poke was more than a quarter full. It was sellin' that mine that filled it out this time. They rode for a ranch for a month or two, tried cutting timber for the army and rejected that without heavy discussion.

"Colorado's sounding pretty good right about now. We got enough money to make Mexico? There's easy pickins along the border. Met a feller in St. Loo once. Said them Mexican banditos were real mean." Snake chuckled, biting off a chunk of chew. "Like to fight with knives."

"Got involved in a knife fight once," Dog-man said.

"Must have won since we be ridin' together."

"He was in a knife fight. I was in a gun fight. He lost." He looked behind to make sure they weren't being followed. "If that sheriff went through our packs on the mules we probably ain't got a dollar, but if he only took what was in your pocket, we can ride high to Denver. Might sign on at a diggins or maybe join a drive south."

Dog-man was about the same age as Snake but looked almost like a youngster. His blondish hair blew about even if there wasn't any wind, his bright blue eyes were as clear as any virgin's, and he had a little boy smile that devastated the girls. He was also a wonderful liar and a brilliant poker player if he was using his cards.

"Only diggins I want is one with my name on it. Our name," he chortled. "Partner."

They shook hands. "My partner, Snake," Dog-man said. Where'd you get that name?"

"I whacked a big old diamond back several years ago. Chopped its head right off, and when I reached down to pick up the carcass, the head bit me. Made me so mad I ate the whole thing in one setting, turned the skin into a hat band, and I've carried the head as a fob for all these years."

"We go on south to Mexico and we can have a diggins with our names on it," Dog-man said. They rode well into the sunset hours and found a grove of trees near a stream to set up camp and find out if old Seth Bullock left them any money in their packs.

"You know anything about minin'?" Snake asked.

"I've watched them fellers splashin' around in

the creeks. Then spending what they found in the saloon. Don't look to be too hard." They were well off the main road and hoped out of sight just in case those deputies decided to follow.

"These are my knots, Snake. Guess we got lucky. Looks like a couple of hundred left. Course, you lost us that fifty and we did buy some victuals and whiskey."

"There is a difference between them taking and me losing," Snake growled, getting a chuckle back from Dog-man. "This road leads to Cheyenne, I do believe. Nasty little town. Course Denver ain't much better. Everybody's got a game. Let's by-pass Cheyenne and head for Denver. Might get a drive south."

"We'd have to do something other than push cows to go south. All the drives come north," Dog-man said. He had a distinctive chuckle that was contagious. "We've never done nothin' like that map sellin', Snake. I didn't like bein' hassled by them deputies and called those ugly names. Coulda woke up tomorrow morning behind iron bars for something as silly as selling a piece of paper. Don't want to do that."

"Your ma did a lot of your raisin', eh? I didn't have a good one of those. Ma was a rascal at heart, but bein' behind iron bars ain't good. It ain't the bars so much as those you have to spend your hours with. Nasty fellers, mostly. Yup, not for me, either, Pardner."

"Let's make Denver, then, stir up some dust, fill out the poke if we can, and head for the border. Got to be gold in them mountains down there."

"They said that about California, too. My ma

and pa run like the deer when they heard about the California strike back in '49. I was nine year old and I still ain't never seen a speck in a pan," Snake laughed right out. "I was fourteen when we got back to Texas where we belonged."

"Closest I come to being near gold was when we was back there in Deadwood just a couple of hours ago, Snake. Even though, we should go for the border and make our own gold." The two laughed their way into the night and were on the trail early the next morning for Denver.

***

They found a couple of young doe mule-deer the next day and shot one of them, skinned her out and spent the next two days smoking the meat. "We're good for a week, anyway, Dog. Ever worked on a farm? I did once. Back breakin' work. Was a tater farm and the old boy didn't have a piece of equipment that didn't have to be worked by hand. Pa sold me off to the old man."

"Sold you? Like a slave or somethin? Damn." Dog rode his horse like a cowman would, sitting straight in the saddle, balanced and with weight in the stirrups. Snake, on the other hand, rode with one leg wrapped around the horn, slouched back, and often resting an elbow behind the saddle. "You'll get throwed one day ridin' like that. Don't understand your own father sellin' you, though."

"Spent a whole season hoein' them taters, diggin' 'em out, gettin' a dollar a week for my efforts. Left out, the old bastard sent the sheriff after me, and he was the onliest man I ever kilt with reason. Ain't never been back in that country, and don't want to ever have to kill another man. It ain't a good feelin', Dog. Let's fill our poke in Denver and make for the border."

"Does that mean you've killed someone without having a reason?"

"That all come out wrong, Dog. The sheriff was a bull headed fool and that farmer paid him to bring me back. I said no, the sheriff went for his gun, and I shot him. Dead."

"Sounds to me like you had reason."

"That's what I was tryin' to say. See you're the mean one. I'm the nice one. I shouldn't be goin' around shootin' people."

It was a long slow ride to Denver and Snake and Dog-man found themselves in the middle of a town seized by gold fever. "Ain't gonna pay those prices for a damn flea infested bed," Snake said when they left the Borealis Hotel. "Let's make up a camp on the south side of town and see what's really going on."

They found a creek boiling down out of the Rocky Mountains, wending its way through a copse of pine, spruce, and aspen that was tucked well back from the main road. "We'll spend a day or two, re-fill our poke and make for the border."

"Everyone we talked to had some kind of game, Snake. Ain't a straight man in this town."

They had a lean-to strung up, a fire pit dug out and lined with rocks, when two men on horses rode into their site. "You boys are on Y bar L land," the scrawny one said. "Gonna have to leave."

"Just gonna be here for a day or two. Get our bearings and head south. Won't be eatin' much of your Y bar L grass," Snake drawled out in the best Texas talk he could gather. Even standing straight up he appeared to be slouched some.

The second rider moved his horse a step or two closer to Snake. Dog-man was on the other side of the lean-to. "You boys lookin' to head south, eh? Your pockets full?" He was big, full muscled, and dressed as a cattleman not a line rider.

"Not quite," Dog-man said. He had a little boy's smile on his face but his right hand was close to the Colt hanging from his waist. Everybody has a game. This feller gonna pull on me? Doesn't look like an outlaw, but that skinny one does. "That's why we will only be here for a day or two. Get that poke filled out."

The big man looked over at Dog-man and smiled. "You good with that iron?" Snake laughed right out. "I could use a couple of guns right now. You heard of Ben Townsley?" Both men shook their heads. "Well, his place neighbors mine and he's tr-yin' hard to make my beef his. That's why Bo and I were checkin' on you two. I'm Chet Hamilton, owner of the Y bar L."

"Glad to meetcha, Hamilton. My name's Snake, that there's Dog-man, and we're riding to stake our claim near the border. If you're lookin' for herd protection, we be your men. If you're lookin' for killers, well, maybe we be ridin' on in the morning."

"Herd protecting might mean killing," Hamilton said.

"Wouldn't be murder," Snake replied. He had the slightest smile dancing about in his eyes and mouth.

"Ranch is one mile due west. Follow the creek

and be there at sunrise. Pay's a dollar a day and found. You sign on for no less than a month. Bring your gear."

Hamilton and his skinny rider rode up stream without another word. "Between what we make as herd protectors, not murderers, and what we make in the bunkhouse with your deck of cards, we'll have a full poke to get us to the border, Dog-man."

2

They had their personals and packs stashed in a barn, the pack mules in a corral, and Snake and Dog-man were standing on the bunkhouse porch with half a dozen cowboys when Hamilton rode up from the main house. The morning was clear and the Rocky Mountains were etched in bright sunlight, glorious peaks stretching higher than the sky. "Just look at that," Snake said. "Makes it obvious a big man ain't very big."

"You got a way with words, Snake. Last time I was really high up in the mountains, I damn near froze to death and couldn't breathe either."

"You have a hard time with beauty, Dog."

"I like my beauty standing on two legs," Dog-man chuckled.

"Right on time," Hamilton said, looking straight into Dog-man's eyes. "You two will ride with Bo today and get a lay of the land. The rest of you, bring those pairs down from the north quarter. Grass is better down lower."

"Townsley claims that north quarter, Chet," a rider spoke up.

"So do I, and I have for ten years. And the Rocky Mountain Cattlemen's Association agrees with me. Bring the beef down from the north quarter and don't take no gruff from Ben Townsley." He turned his horse and rode back toward the ranch. He met up with another rider coming down.

"Who's that?" Snake asked.

"His brat of a daughter," Bo said. "Name's Shawna. Mount up. Let's get started. It's gonna be a long day." Bo Stanley was about five-eight, maybe one forty, but swaggered like he was the circus strongman. Snake watched him walk down off the porch and to his horse.

"Man ain't got a friendly hair on his head," Snake said quietly. "Might have to prod him some, make him smile. Probably break his face."

Dog-man stood silent at the comment. He was shading his eyes, looking down the trail to where Hamilton and the girl were talking. "Shawna's a rather well developed brat, I'd say," he chuckled.

"Hands off, saddle bum," Bo said.

"You better watch your mouth, Bo. I don't much cotton to that kind of talk. I'm a man who appreciates a beautiful woman, and a man who will stand up to being called ugly names. Don't do it again." Dog-man said. He turned to face the Y bar L cowboy, his legs slightly apart, his right hand dangerously close to that big Colt.

Bo spun his horse and found himself looking into the long barrel of the weapon. He had reins in his left hand and a coiled lasso in his right. Dog-man slowly eased the Colt back in its holster and mounted his horse. "Don't never talk to me like that again."

Bo never said a word during the entire time, but never let his anger lift either. They rode north and west off the main ranch toward some rolling hills with higher and meaner mountains stretched out behind.

***

"You hire some new men, Daddy?" Shawna saw Snake and Dog-man standing next to the mounted ranch foreman. "Bo will run them off just like the others."

"I need Bo and his guns, Shawna. You know that. These two are trail bums, drifters, but appear capable of taking care of themselves. We need men out there to protect the herd, girl. Townsley has hired actual gunmen to claim his territory."

"Maybe you should, too," the pretty girl said, riding out to the ridge to watch the men ride off to the herds. Ben Hamilton rode alongside. Shawna was seventeen, head-strong, selfish, and gorgeous. She was close to five feet ten inches, one thirty at the most, with blond hair and blue eyes. She wasn't close enough to note that the one called Dog-man was looking back at her.

"They're gonna start bringing the north herd down today, and we'll need to move that west herd down next week. And, keep Townsley off our range at the same time. Bo knows what we need to do."

"The way he acts when you hire new men, I'd believe he works for Townsley," she said. "Bet those men don't make two days, Daddy." She turned her horse to ride back to the ranch and made up her mind that as soon as her father got busy on something, she would ride out and watch the men work the cattle. It always fascinated her the way they could bring cattle down out of the high country, cattle that didn't necessarily want to come down.

***

"I noticed Chet used the term north quarter, Bo. Just how does he have this place laid out?" Snake rode for more than one brand in Texas and was sincerely interested. "We don't have mountains like this in Texas."

"Ain't really none of your concern how Mr. Hamilton runs his ranch. Just do as you're told and you'll get your dollar."

"Got yourself a real attitude, cowboy. The way I see it, Chet wants us to know these things. We were hired to protect the herd, I do believe." Snake took his time saying all that. He slouched back in the saddle, pulled his knife, and started cleaning his fingernails. Dog-man was riding slightly behind, chuckling quietly.

"Don't get smart with me or you'll find yourself back on the trail south," Bo said. "I'm the foreman here and you'd be best keeping that in mind."

"Way I heard it, Chet told you to give us a tour of the place. So far, we've rode in a straight line and we've heard a mean mouth. Now, where are these herds we were hired to protect at the kingly price of a dollar a day and found." Snake looked back at Dog-man and got a thumb's up and a dirty grin.

Bo pulled his horse up, turned to the two trail bums, and scowled. "You're fired. Gather your gear and get off the Y bar L."

"Don't think you have that power, but we will ride back to the ranch and have a chat with old man Hamilton." Snake nodded to Dog-man and the two turned their horses and rode off without another word spoken.

"Notice how he always has his hands filled with something?" Dog-man was snickering as they rode off. "Can't shoot a man what can't get at his gun, now, can we."

"Well, even if he could, he'd be safe going up against you. You ain't never hit what you be shootin' at, anyway," Snake chuckled. "He's staying about two hundred yards behind us, Dog-man. If he pulls a rifle, hit the dirt."

"I'm better with a rifle," Dog-man chuckled. They had their horses at a comfortable lope and crested a hill in time to see Shawna Hamilton ride toward a small gathering of steers. "That is one fine looking young lady, Snake. Think she needs company?"

"No, I don't," Snake said. "Let's go find Chet Hamilton, get our dollar, and clear out for the border. I might just want to kill that Bo feller if I have to see him again."

"I kinda hope we all meet up one day soon, then."

As was the practice in mountain country, Hamilton let his beef run with their horns. Wolves, bears, and mountain lions tended to dislike being gored and his losses to predators were low. Heifers running with their young can be aggressive when the young ones are threatened. "She's gonna ride right into that bunch, Snake," Dog-man said. He was pointing at the girl riding at a fast rate toward the small herd of maybe twelve animals.

'She needs to slow that horse to a walk. Those

big old cows have young ones with 'em. Damn, can you get her attention?" Snake was sitting tall in the saddle, his eyes shaded by his floppy sombrero.

The cattle started to scatter but one was a mama cow with a young one standing near. Shawna rode, almost casually between the mama cow and her baby, and mama took umbrage with the girl's behavior. That big mountain-raised cow whirled around, lowered her head, and sunk a horn deep into the horse's side.

"Girl's about as dumb as she is beautiful, Snake. Let's ride." They raced to where the horse was floundering its last and Shawna was on her hands and knees about to be gored by an angry mama cow. Snake got his lariat ready, built a quick loop, and heeled the calf, dragging it away. Mama, quick as a fox, followed while Dog-man rode to the girl, dropping low in the stirrups and grabbing her on the first pass.

He lifted and whipped her around behind him, settled his horse down some, and trotted off a short distance. Snake dragged the calf away, let off on the rope and the loop fell away, letting and animal loose. Two quick shots from his pistol sent the small herd off at a run. Snake rode to where Shawna's horse was still thrashing in the dust and put a bullet in its head. "We'll come back for the gear," he said.

"You okay, Miss Hamilton?" Dog-man was half turned in the saddle, smiling into her frightened face. "That old girl was about to have you for lunch. Didn't your daddy tell you that you shouldn't ride up to a group like that? Well, you're safe now," he said, spurring the horse into a lope and heading back to the ranch house. She had her arms tight around the man.

"You killed my horse," Shawna screamed at Snake as he rode up alongside.

"No, 'fraid not, missy. Believe your horse was gored some. Wouldn't never let a horse suffer like that. But, your welcome, anyway."

"What for?" She demanded.

"I do believe we saved your pretty little … ," and he let it end there. Dog-man was howling in laughter as they rode into the big yard between the corrals and the ranch house. "Put her down gently, Dog. Don't want to hurt her tender little … ," and again, let the sentence end.

Chet Hamilton came out of the house at a run. "What's going on here? What happened?"

"These saddle tramps killed my horse." Shawna bawled. She was glaring at Snake, moving away from Dog-man as quickly as she could, and put her arms around her father.

"That ain't quite the entire story, Chet," Snake said. Dog-man was smiling into Shawna's face, his hat in his hand, his unruly hair flying about. "Interesting ranch you got going here." Snake stepped down from his horse and took the lead rope from Dog-man as he stepped off, too.

"Your daughter rode up on a rangy old mama and calf that got riled and gored her horse. She was flung to the ground and that big old heifer was about to have her way with her when Dog-man pulled her onto his horse.

"I, in turn, killed the young lady's horse to take it out of its misery. Your daughter ain't the most grateful person in these parts." He tied the two horses off and squared up in front of Chet Hamilton.

"On top of all that, Chet, you owe us a dollar each. Bo don't like us much, neither. Fired our skinny butts just before your daughter pulled her stunt."

Hamilton eased Shawna back and looked into her face. "That the way it went down?" She didn't say anything, tried to wrap her arms around the older man, but he pushed her back. "Is it? Don't lie to me, girl."

She kicked some dirt, and looking first at Snake, then at Dog-man, said, "Mostly."

"Then you boys deserve my thanks for saving my daughter's life. What do you mean, Bo fired you? Hell, you ain't been on the payroll long enough to do something to get fired." He paced around, glared at his daughter who was looking more at Dog-man than him, and drummed his clenched fist into an open hand. "Just damn that man."

"Told you he would," Shawna said. "You ain't had a new man stay on since the day you hired Bo Stanley, Daddy. I swear he works for Ben Townsley."

"Quiet, girl. Let me think," Hamilton said. "Come on, boys, let's go to the cook shack and get some coffee. Might even find a splash of whiskey if we look about. Go get cleaned up, Shawna." Hamilton was quiet on the short walk to the cook shack and they found chairs around the long table. Dog-man found the coffee and Chet found the whiskey.

"She might just be right about that man," Chet Hamilton murmured. "Well, tell me what happened that made him fire you."

3

"Hamilton's bringing 'em down off the north quarter. Tell Townsley that now would be the right time to move a herd into that area." Bo Stanley was talking to a Townsley drover, turned his horse, and rode off to join up with the Hamilton crew that was bringing Y bar L cattle down. The strain of what he was doing was evident in his face and actions. They were on an exposed flank of the mountain, but he had to get the word to Townsley.

"I hate these meetings in the middle of the day. Sure as hell somebody's gonna see me one of these days." Bo Stanley wasn't the sharpest rock on the shelf but did understand the danger he was putting himself in. It wasn't that many years ago that he was a fine cattleman, before he discovered the game of faro. Bucking the tiger, they called it. Now, he rode for any brand that will get him close to a faro table.

Stanley had been working for Townsley all along. It was Townsley's idea to get him hired on not expecting Hamilton to make him foreman. Young Hefty Jackson watched the conversation from hundreds of yards away and rode back to the Hamilton ranch house. Hefty and Shawna had been having their time together late at night and she told him there would be something special for him if he kept an eye on Bo Stanley.

After telling her what he'd seen, she walked him over to the cook shack. "Now, you'll believe me, Daddy," she said. "Tell him what you saw, Hefty," she said.

Hefty hemmed and hawed some, put his weight on one foot, then the other, and after a couple of seconds, Chet thumped the table with his fist. "Do it now," he all but shouted.

"Saw Bo talking to a Townsley hand," Hefty Jackson said. "Off, alone like."

"Thank you, Hefty. Ride back to your crew." He smiled. "No need to tell anyone else." Chet Hamilton stood up and walked all the way around the table, stopped at the cook stove and poured another cup of coffee, and finally sat back down. "We got a burr in the blankets now," he grumbled. "Did Bo point out where the north quarter is to you boys?"

"When Snake asked where it was is when he fired us," Dog-man said. He said it to Shawna even if it was meant for Chet. It was obvious the two were talking to each other with their eyes and Chet Hamilton didn't want that to continue.

"All right, then. Let me get my horse saddled and we four will take a little ride. We'll come in from the rocky front, not the meadows, and I'll put a cartwheel on us finding Townsley cattle moving in."

Hamilton ran to the barn to saddle up two horses for he and Shawna while Snake and Dog-man walked back to theirs. "We riding into a range war, Snake? Don't much care for that. Dollar a day and found to protect some cattle is one thing."

"He's bringing his daughter so I doubt we're looking for a fight here. We'll ride up with him, maybe run into Bo and shoot him," and he laughed, trying to choke it back. "Then, my friend, let's just chuck it and head for the border. Ain't filled the poke, but it ain't empty either."

The ride to what Chet Hamilton called the north quarter took a good hour, crossed several streams of icy water, and climbed high into timber country. There was excellent grass and brush, abundant water, and both men wished they had a herd to pasture up there. "Fine summer range, Chet." Snake tried to compare what he was riding through to what his pa called their range back in Texas.

"You got more grass in half an acre than we had in a section back home," Snake chuckled.

"Yeah, and I gotta protect it from scoundrels like Ben Townsley. When we ride around that terrible rock face ahead of us, we'll be in the heart of the north quarter."

"I don't mean to interfere with your working plans, Chet, but we didn't hire on to get in the middle of a range war. We ain't gunmen, just a couple of good drovers what knows cattle some." Snake took a long time to get it all out, with Dog-man smiling at Shawna the whole time.

"Us cattlemen have organized and have range riders to keep order, Snake," Chet said. "I just need to remind that bastard Townsley that this is my range, duly registered. Will you back me up?"

Chet Hamilton was quick to note the looks

back and forth between the men and caught their thoughts. "There would be extra money involved."

"We'll back you up, but only this one time, Chet," Dog-man said. "We ain't much for staying on after that, though. Won't work around Bo, and we need to keep moving toward the border, get our claims staked out before winter."

"I plan to fire Bo Stanley as soon as we return to the ranch, but I understand how things have changed since we talked last night." Was he talking about the Townsley situation or that between his daughter and Dog-man?

Interesting, Dog-man thought. Every time to I try to catch a sneak peak at the lovely girl, she's looking right at me. He gave her a big smile, which was returned, and rode on with even more interesting thoughts roaming through his active mind.

The rock bluff was a good two miles long with deep grass, brush, and timber at its base and around its far left end, on the south. The grassland extended around the south end and considerably farther up the mountainside. As the four riders came around the base of the bluff they saw the dust of a small herd of about a hundred cattle moving down the slope.

"Yup, there he is," Chet said, pointing. "He must have had them cattle in position, just waiting for Bo to tell them when it would be clear to come."

The herd was controlled by four Townsley riders and Snake pointed out three other men on horseback riding in from the south. "Who are those men?"

"I hope they are Denver Range Riders," Chet said. They rode toward the moving herd and Chet waved the lead drover over just as the three range riders rode up. "You men are on Y bar L range. Move these animals back to Townsley range now," he commanded.

The Townsley drover pulled his horse up to a sliding stop. "It's now Townsley range and these cattle are staying."

Chet looked over to the lead range rider. "I'm Chet Hamilton, and this is my range."

"I know who you are, Chet. You," he said, pointing at the Townsley man. "Move these cattle now or we will. This is Hamilton range and old man Townsley knows it."

The Townsley man glared at the range rider. "I only take orders from Mr. Townsley and he said bring the cattle here, and here is where they stay. He don't belong to your association, range rider."

"Belong or not, this is Hamilton range." He looked around, saw his men in position to move the cattle back to where they came from. "All right, men, let's get 'em moving." He touched his spurs and whirled his horse around, loping off to work the cattle.

"Oh, no you don't," the Townsley man said, pulling his sidearm. Dog-man saw it coming and slammed his quirt down on the man's arm, ripping his shirt sleeve and drawing blood, but not knocking the gun loose. He whirled in pain, brought the gun up and fired, almost point blank.

The bullet nicked Dog-man's arm and buried itself in Shawna's leg, knocking her from her horse. Dog-man jumped down and raced to her side. "You bastard," he cried out, pulling his Colt and firing. The Townsley man fell to the ground, mortally wounded.

"Well, I'll be damned," Snake laughed. "Ain't never seen the likes. You actually hit the man with just one shot." The other Townsley riders made moves for their weapons but three range riders, Chet Hamilton, and Snake all had theirs in hand.

"It's over boys. Take your dead and your cattle and clear off this range." The head range rider now held a Winchester aimed at one of the drovers. "Tell Ben Townsley to stay off this range. We'll be patrolling it regularly."

"So will I," Chet growled. He was off his horse and running toward his daughter. "If she dies, I'm holding Ben Townsley responsible. You tell him that."

"Come on girl, I'm not gettin' fresh, I'm trying to keep you from bleeding to death." Dog-man was trying to rip the lady's riding pants leg open and she was fighting him with fists and teeth. "Damn it, quit," he snarled, pushing her away. He ripped his bandanna off and used it to stop the bleeding just as Chet Hamilton kneeled down.

"How bad is it?"

"Bleeding hard, Chet. Stop her from beating on me and I can get it stopped." Dog-man was fending off blows while trying to get the rag tied tight. "She needs a doctor and I'm sure she can't ride with this kind of wound."

"Why are you fighting him?" Hamilton cried. He knelt down next to Shawna.

"He's trying to take my pants off," she howled.

"I'm trying to save your life, girl. Hit me one more time and I'm gonna let you bleed to death."

"There's a line shack about two miles over there," Chet said, pointing at a stand of spruce and pine. "There's a small wagon and leather. I'll go get it. Stay with her, Dog-man." Chet grabbed the lead rope to Shawna's horse and rode off toward the lone shack.

"I'm gonna help him," Snake said, riding off in a cloud of dust.

"It's just you and me, girl, so if you want to live, quit beating on me. Smack me one more time and I'm gonna hit back. Got it? Good. Now quiet down and let me get you fixed up for the ride back to the barn."

He tore part of his shirt away, ran to a stream and wetted it, came back and was cleaning the wound when he heard a rider approaching. He turned to see Bo Stanley stepping off his horse. "What happened? What have you done to Shawna? You shot Shawna Hamilton? You dirty bastard," Bo screamed, pulling his pistol.

Dog-man rolled away, pulling his Colt as he did, firing two quick shots, hearing one from the other gun. Shawna was screaming in terror, Bo was screaming in pain, and Dog-man was getting back to his feet, a smoking Colt aimed at the ranch foreman. Bo Stanley was holding his side, blood dripping between his fingers, a terrible look of death spread across his filthy face.

Dog-man grabbed Bo's weapon and helped get him laid out in the grass, to die. "Dumb bastard," he grumbled, moving back to Shawna's side. "Now, young lady, let me save your life. No more stupid stuff, I ain't here to hurt you."

He was looking into terror filled eyes but also saw a hint of a smile as he knelt down to work on her leg. "He was going to kill you," she whispered.

"I think that was the plan," Dog-man smiled back

to her. "That bullet messed up some meat in here," he said, "but no broken bones, and the bleeding is mostly stopped now. That wagon'll be here shortly and we'll get you back down the hill."

"But he tried to kill you." She gave him a full on smile this time, took his bloody hand and held it tight. "I'm sorry for fighting you like that."

He sat on the ground, cross-legged near the wounded leg, smiling at the girl. His hair was blowing about and she returned his smile. "I guess I was just scared," she said. "Hope I didn't hit you too hard."

"Just about broke my jaw and blacked my eye," he chuckled, rubbing his jaw. She giggled some then looked the other way, hiding her eyes. "You got a good right cross, girl. Just remember to use it on men trying to hurt you." He couldn't hold back the chuckles and got to his feet when he heard the wagon approaching.

"Let's get you on your feet, sweetie. Use me as a crutch, and we'll get you in the wagon." Snake was right there helping Dog-man, and Chet Hamilton was driving, his horse tethered at the back.

Chet jumped down when he saw Bo Stanley's body in the grass. "We heard shots. What happened?"

"Bo tried to kill us and this man saved us. He was wonderful," Shawna said. The smile she aimed at Dog-man almost knocked him to the ground.

"You were able to hit him? That's two in the same day, Dog. You be careful, boy, you'll get a reputation. What's got into you?" He was laughing and almost dancing, pretending to shoot at Dog-man.

Dog-man and Chet wrapped Bo Stanley's bloody

body in a bedroll blanket and laid him out in the back of the wagon. "I don't want to ride back there with him," Shawna cried out when Dog-man started to walk her to the wagon.

"She's right," he said. He had his arm wrapped around her waist, and gave a little squeeze. "Let's tie the body across his horse and she can ride alone in the back of the wagon."

The ride back to the ranch was a quiet affair. A rider was sent into Denver to bring a doctor back and Chet Hamilton called for a meeting of all the ranch riders and staff to explain what had happened. He did that over supper and called for Dog-man and Snake to join him for brandy in the ranch house after.

The fire was lit and they sat in large leather chairs, eyeing buffalo heads, antelope horns, and great sets of antlers from elk. It was a man's room and Snake asked whether there was a Mrs. Hamilton.

"We lost Colleen to the flu a few years ago. Shawna is exactly like her mother," Chet chuckled. "Even down to being the most selfish individual around these parts." Brandy was poured and Chet's face took on a serious look.

"You boys haven't been with me but one day and have done me some real good. Helped save my north quarter, helped find out my foreman was no good, and saved my daughter twice. I'd like you to stay with me, but I know you don't want to."

"Ain't that we don't like you, Chet," Snake said. "Hell, we like you a lot, but we want to move on south. It's a long ride to the border, and then we gots to find the gold and silver."

Hamilton had to chuckle. "Yup, gots to find the gold and silver," he repeated. "Almost went looking for it myself once. Then I met Colleen and she introduced me to the world of responsibility. Lordy, lordy, did she ever. Never was able to raise enough beef to keep her in her finery." He took a long drink of brandy and poured another for the three of them. He gave Dog-man a long look. "You might want to remember what I just said."

"I think I understand exactly what you said," Dog-man smiled back. "Yes, sir, I think I do." He would gladly spend as much time as he could near that lovely Shawna but seemed to know, almost instinctively, that she would rule the roost if things became permanent.

"About the only way I can thank you boys is to help fill that poke of yours. Think a hundred dollars each would help your journey?"

"Well, now," Snake said. He looked over to Dog-man, took a long drink of brandy, and smiled at Chet. "I do believe it would help us along nicely. Right nicely."

"We'll fill your packs with flour, coffee, sugar, and anything else that will help you to find that gold and silver," the old man laughed. "Do you know where you're going?"

"Heard some good stories about the border country around El Paso. West of El Paso."

"Ride south to Santa Fe and then follow the river to El Paso." Chet poured more brandy and the boys decided the next morning would be the best time to ride out.

"Want to ride out sittin' straight in the saddle and I don't think I can right now," Dog-man chuckled, staggering out the kitchen door toward the bunk house.

4

"Hated to just ride off and leave that darling girl, Snake. She held my hand and smiled at me when I said goodbye."

"Did she say she was sorry for the black eye? You'll get over it. That's one selfish woman and she ain't for the likes of you." They both laughed at that, Dog-man remembering what Chet had said about his wife the night before. "Don't want to get tied up with a woman what can't say thank you. She never did, Dog. Never said thank you."

"Nope, she didn't. Just thinking how I'd enjoy some time with the lovely lady, not a life time of never getting a thank you." Dog-man smiled.

"How far did Chet say it was to Santa Fe?" Snake had been through these little affairs many times. Girls tended to get all swoony around Dog-man and he'd get all fuzzy in the head because of it. "Pull your hat down tight, Dog, she's just a girl."

Dog smiled and shook his head hard. "Mighty pretty girl," he said, "but if she was like the mother Chet described, she wouldn't fit our lifestyle, now, would she." He got a sour look back from Snake.

"Said we could make it in a week if we rode fairly hard. Nice of him to slip all that food into our packs. If it takes two weeks, who cares," Dog-man chuckled. "I think the old man wanted to ride off with us."

"I ain't never seen country like this," Snake said. They were on a well-traveled road winding through great stands of timber, crossing rivers and streams, and fighting off cold late at night and early in the morning. "It's only summer in the daytime," he chuckled.

Late on the second day they were run off the road by a high-balling stage being driven by six strong horses. "Good thing you heard him coming," Dog-man laughed. "Enough dust to choke a griz. At least we know that somewhere in front of us will be a station of some kind."

"Should be. We didn't make much distance yesterday and those stations are usually about twenty miles or so apart. Never forget that one we were at in Dakota country. Snarly old bastard wanted five dollars for a drink of rotten whiskey." Snake was gearing up for a yarn, Dog-man knew, remembered how the story really went, and was anxious to hear a new version.

"His beer was hot and his whiskey was bad," Dog-man said. Their conversation ended with the sound of gun shots off in the distance. "Wonder what that's all about?"

"Somebody don't like somebody," Snake said. "Think we should check it out? One or two shots usually don't mean trouble, but five or six does. Maybe highwaymen after that coach."

"My first choice would be no," Dog-man said. "Then you'd remind me that it would be terrible if we found hurt people that we could have helped, so, I guess we better find out what the ruckus is."

"You're a good man, Dog, even if you don't want to be," Snake chuckled.

The mountain road wound its way through the high foothills of the front range and featured great stands of timber, rocky ridges and escarpments, and limited vision. They put their little train in a trot riding up a long curving and twisting trail to a ridge some miles ahead. As they got nearer they could see the coach and horses standing with people milling about in the middle of the steep grade. "Something wrong for sure, Snake. Let's not just ride up on whatever it is. Let's get these mules tied off and take a sneak peak at what's going on."

"Yup," is all Snake said, turning off the road and into a stand of fir, spruce, and pine. They got the mules tied in good grass and rode slowly through the trees, cross-country, toward the ridge. They were slightly above the road, in trees and stands of granite, and saw two men with rifles aimed at the driver, his messenger, and four passengers. A third man was gathering loot from the assembled crowd.

One of the coach horses was dead in its harness and it looked like the driver may have been injured as well. "Ain't never seen you hit what you aimed at until yesterday, Dog. Think you still got those talents? Looks like those folks need to get acquainted with us."

"Let's tie off and just walk down there and shoot those fools," Dog-man said. They were in country mixed with trees and brush, partially open spaces, but would be able to use trees and rock outcrops to get close to the action if they were on foot. "I'll kind of go off to the right here and you go off to the left. Try not to shoot me, Snake. I know how you are when you get riled."

Snake emptied a saloon one night when someone fired off a round just for fun. Snake started shooting at anything that moved until both his revolvers were empty. It was sheer luck that no one got hit.

"Good plan," Snake said, stepping down and finding a tree to tie his horse to. He eased himself down through a maze of rocks, ducked behind a large spruce and edged up to within thirty feet of the coach group. The man gathering loot held a cloth bag with both hands and became target number one. He had another cloth sack over his head with eye holes cut out. The two men with rifles were dressed the same and had their backs to him. "I think I can get at least two of 'em," he whispered.

Dog-man could help them fill their pokes by way of playing-card manipulations, but it was Snake, putting on shooting demonstrations that got them free drinks in most saloons. He used a large boulder to rest his arm and took a long aim with his Colt at the man gathering loot. Ain't gonna wait for Dog-man. Hope he's ready cuz I am.

The shot blew the man's brains, tied up in a sack, all over a woman who instantly fainted away. One of the men with rifles turned at the shot and took a round through the middle of his chest. The third man was bringing his rifle to bear on Snake when a bullet slammed into his back and he fell to the dust, dead.

"I used my rifle just in case I didn't still have my

shooting talents," Dog-man said, stepping out from behind some rocks. "You folks okay?"

Snake stepped out into the dusty road, tucking his sidearm back in its leather. "That's what you get for driving like a mad man, chasing good people like us off the road," he said to the coach driver. "Let's take a look at that bloody spot on your arm, old man."

"Don't know where you boys come from, but sure glad of your help. Name's Cletus Kilpatrick, driving for Dawson Express. This here's Slippery Jim Lucas, our messenger."

"Have any idea who these fools might be?" Snake snatched the sack mask off one and the driver nodded.

"Yup. That there is Sage Hen Johnny, so the others are probably Louie the Long One and Willie Sanders. Been working this road for several months now."

"I'm going back for the horses and mules, Snake. Keep these folks entertained till I get back." Dog-man loped up the hill to where the horses were tied off.

"That's me, Snake, that other feller's Dog-man," Snake said, getting the driver to slip out of his duster and shirt. "Well, hell, just ripped a little hole there, and, by whackers, another little hole on the other side. You gonna be fine, Cletus, just fine." He looked around at the passengers and the messenger.

"Gather up your belongings, and a couple of you men help old Slippery there get that dead horse off the road."

"You just ride in and shoot up these people and think you have the right to take command, do you?" A gentleman slipping his silver and gold watch back in its vest pocket, sneered his comment right in Snake's face.

Why would someone act like that after me and old Dog just saved his life and all his worldly possessions? Well, I just wonder if this coach is carrying a money box and if this gent might be tied up with the dead ones?

"Right strange way you have of saying thankee there, stranger. Don't believe I caught your name. My friends call me Snake. Others don't. Your choice." Snake didn't offer his hand, instead he left it hanging near that sidearm, fingers twitching just a bit.

The gentleman didn't answer Snake but the driver did. "Said his name was Watkins. Boarded in Denver, heading for Taos."

"What's you game, Mr. Watkins? Don't much care for your attitude, sir." Snake hadn't moved an inch from the time Watkins made his comments. Watkins stood silent, glaring at Snake but taking little side glances at the driver and those moving the dead horse.

Without the slightest warning, Snake's left fist came up from thigh level and smashed into Watkins' jaw, sending man backward five feet and flat on his back in the filth of the road. On the way, Watkins went for the little gambler's pistol he had retrieved from the bandit's white sack. His face, neck, and chest sprung massive leaks of blood when the messenger's shotgun went off.

"How'd you know?" Cletus stood with his mouth open as Watkins bled out.

"Just a good guess," Snake said. He looked around

at all the open faces staring at him. "Got your treasures back? Good, better get this rig on the road,
Cletus. Don't want to be late, now, do you," he said.
Dog-man came riding down the road about then,
trailing Snake's horse and the two mules.

Snake helped get the bodies on top of the rig and
tied off, re-arranged the teams and tied off all the
loose horses behind. Cletus gave a mighty crack of
his whip, calling out, "Hiyah," and they were off in
a cloud of dust. "Station's about ten miles up the
road. Meet us there and we'll get all the paperwork
filled out. You boys have a nice reward coming your
way," Cletus hollered out.

"Did you hear that, Dog? Hell, man, we gonna be
rich before we even find our gold mine." The laughter rolled through the foothills of the front range
for at least five minutes. "We'll camp at the station,
I guess. Let's ride."

"Last time I stayed at one of those stations I was
flea bit for a week, Snake. We'll keep our camp out
and away. Don't know how people can live like that.
I got a cartwheel says our food will be better, too."

"I don't take fool's bets," Snake laughed.

***

It wasn't much of a stage stop. Just a shack doubling
as a kitchen, dining room, and sleeping room.
Outbuildings for supplies and feed, and corrals for
stock. A married couple with a teenage son ran the
operation. The couple, known as Tom and Mary,
were in their forties, filthy dirty, and their son,
Paulie, was as skinny as an alder branch, and even
dirtier.

"We'll be doin our own cooking, Mary. You take care of the passengers." Snake and Dog-man set up their camp well back in the trees, away from the smells and noise of the station. Cletus Kilpatrick came into the circle of fire light to talk to them.

"Have some papers here for you, Snake. Don't know what the reward will be, but you bring these to the Dawson Express Company offices in Santa Fe, and they'll settle up with you. Sure do want to thank you for your work today. Those hombres have been having a field day with our runs for more than a month. Company will take good care of you."

"Well, now, ain't that wonderful," Snake drawled out. "We got some Elk steaks here, if y'awl'd care to join our table."

"Already told Slippery Jim I'd eat with him, boys. Where you heading with your mules all packed solid like."

"Headin' for the Mexican border and stake a gold claim, Cletus," Dog-man said. "Been hearing stories of gold down that way. This road leads right through Santa Fe, does it? Told if we follow the Rio Grande it will take us right to the border. We want to get in those hills west of El Paso."

"There's more outlaws than there is gold in that country," Cletus said. "Stay on this road and it'll take you to Santa Fe, then just ride south."

The boys had elk steaks and fried onions for supper and turned in. "We'll light out before dawn, Dog. I want to see as much of this country as I can. Ain't never seen this much grass, these many trees, and not get bit by a thousand bugs. This ain't Texas," he laughed.

5

Dog-man heard the slightest scrape of a boot and kept as still as an owl, even held his breath until he was sure. He slowly lifted the Colt from under his rolled up jacket, which he used for a pillow, and reared straight up cocking the hammer back and howling, "Stop right there!"

He jumped out from under his blanket and shoved the barrel of his gun into the face of Paulie. Paulie, a skinny, filthy kid, had his hands deep into one of the packs and tried to bolt. Dog-man slammed him across the side of the head with the heavy Colt and watched the slovenly kid go face first in the dirt.

Snake was a little slow getting out of his bedroll, was bleary-eyed from the night's whiskey, and just stood in his long johns looking at the bleeding kid. "Ain't that the way to welcome guests? Snot-nosed little bugger. Take his pants off, Dog-man, I'll cut a switch and mark that boy's back side."

Paulie was fourteen at best, was crying from the pain in his head and from the fright in his heart. "I was just lookin'. Wasn't gonna take nothing."

"A-course you weren't," Dog-man said. "Hell, anybody could see that. Pitch dark, good time to just go lookin'." He grabbed the kid and stood him up, shook his head some, and shoved him at Snake. "If I'd knowed it was him I wouldn't a smashed him like that. Just a dumb kid, but now's a good time for him to be learnin' things."

"It is," Snake said. He walked Paulie over to a young pine tree and told him not to move. He got a rope from one of the packs and tied the kid's hands back around the young tree. Then he tied his feet together and to the tree. Dog-man walked over with arms full of dead limbs, grass, and brush, and spread it out around the kid's feet.

"What are you doin'?" Paulie cried out.

"Gonna cleanse your soul, boy. Send you to the great hereafter with a clean slate. Gonna burn all the evil right out of you," Snake said.

Paulie started screaming louder than a mountain lion in heat and Dog-man watched as lamp after lamp was lit in the station shack. First it was Tom and Mary running outside, then Cletus and Slippery Jim, and finally, the passengers. Some were fully dressed, some needed to go back and get proper.

"What's going on?" Tom demanded. "Why you got my son all trussed up like a hog."

"They're gonna burn me at the stake, Pa," Paulie cried.

"Yup," Snake said, rather quietly. "Been a bad boy. Needs his soul cleansed."

Dog-man was able to hold in his chuckles but Cletus Kilpatrick couldn't. "Cleanse his soul?" He was almost doubled over laughing. "The flames would never get through the dirt to find his soul."

"Well, then, rip his clothes off and we'll bathe him first," Snake said. The lady who got the sack full of bloody brains at the stage hold-up, fainted again and Slippery Jim caught her before she hit the dirt.

"Why you doin this to my boy?" Mary cried out, throwing her arms around Paulie.

"Cuz he was snitching things from our pack, Mary. It ain't right to treat guests that way." Snake was stirring the camp fire, got it burning good, and Mary started untying the ropes holding Paulie.

"No! You won't be burning my boy. Run, Paulie. Run boy," she cried out. Paulie didn't hesitate and was last seen slamming his way through the trees and brush. Mary turned to Tom, glared at him, shook her fist at Snake, and stomped off for the shack, cussing a streak that would embarrass a mule skinner.

Dog-man chuckled along with Cletus, Snake sat in the dirt by the fire watching the spectacle, and Tom just stood with his mouth open. "Got the beginnings of a bad boy, Tom." Snake said. "Better do something about it before it grows to be a bad man. Let's just pack up and leave, Dog-man. I don't like being here."

***

When they crossed a ridge later in the morning they spotted a little lake down in a valley, about five miles away. "Fresh fish, a dip in cold water, and a day's sleep in the warm sun," Snake said, turning into the forest to ride down to the lake. "I just feel dirty after being at that stage stop. Living in the beauty of these mountains like they was filthy hogs, Dog. I'd spend great amounts of time lyin' on my back lookin' at these trees if that was my stage station."

"Let's not get slowed down by all these distractions, Snake." Dog-man had a serious look on his face. "We got to get us south, boy. We flop around in that cold water for an hour or so and then get back on the trail. Santa Fe first, pick up our reward, and then south to the border country."

"You're right. Too easy to just let things happen, and things sure do happen when you're around. Here you are, shootin' people, burning young boys at the stake, and now demanding that we keep on schedule." They were both laughing when they stepped off their horses at lakeside.

"Wish't I could draw," Snake said. "I'd sure like to draw that." The lake was crystal blue, a gentle breeze giving it some life, surrounded by steep, craggy spires of solid rock interspersed with great stands of timber. White clouds were gathering to the north, promising some welcome rain mixed with claps of thunder and flashes of lightning. "I'm an artist at heart, Dog-man. Did you know that?"

"Never once in my life, Snake." There was thick grass along the lake bank and they tied their horses and mules, slipped out of their clothes and walked with tender feet through the rocks toward the shoreline.

"Bet I can beat you to the water," Snake said. He took two quick steps and watched Dog-man run full out into the icy water. Dog-man was howling, sucking in great breaths, trying to get back to shore, listening to guffaws from Snake.

"You got me, Snake. You got me good," Dog-man said. He was knee deep in the bitter cold water as Snake came toward him. He waited, waited just a little bit more, bent down, and threw hands full of cold water to the tall Texan, hearing the yelps, and watching the man dance back.

The surrounding hills echoed with the laughter, and the two travelers splashed and swam in the high mountain lake. They used the sun to dry off and quickly dressed, mounted up, and rode back for the main road. "Next bath I take will be in scalding hot water, attended by some charming wench with fascinating eyes," Dog-man chortled.

"Yup," is all Snake said. It was a full five minutes later when he added. "Maybe in Santa Fe."

***

They rode a full five miles past the next stage stop they came to, decided that wasn't far enough, and rode until it was almost pitch dark. "Wonder why they ain't no railroad run through here?" Snake was seriously interested in railroads. "First one I saw scared me even more than it scared my horse. Screaming monster, it was, billowing great clouds of steam, and sounding like the winds of hades."

"Seen railroad tracks, like we saw leaving Dead-wood, but ain't never seen what moves on them. Heard people talk, like you do, about these things, but ain't never laid my eyes on one." Dog-man traveled north and south through the prairie country, through southern plains, well into Dakota Territory, but had never seen an engine pulling cars on those rails. "Heard you can ride a horse as fast as the train goes, so what's the point?"

"I guess you might could, maybe," Snake said. "Don't think you could for very long. Gotta rest your horse. Don't gotta rest a big old fire-belchin' engine."

It was a long two weeks of inane conversation, no stops at the stage and express stations, that led them into Santa Fe, a bustling city, bigger and busier than the Denver they passed through. "I feel like I'm back home in Texas," Snake said. He pointed at the Spanish colonial buildings, the way the town was laid out, and the people. "They speaking Texas Spanish, Dog-man. I actually understand some of what these people are saying."

Snake pointed at old buildings, at the way some of the people dressed, and breathed the heavily scented air. "Town's been here hundreds of years, Dog. This was all Indian country and the Spanish called it part of New Spain."

"It's a busy town and we got things can be lost." Dog-man didn't have the heart of a poet, Snake always said. "We better set up our camp outside town, Snake. Somewhere we can hide it good, and then find this Dawson Express Company."

Snake nodded. "Looks like some rough customers living along these streets, Dog-man."

The narrow street led them to a central plaza and Snake pointed across at a large sign with Dawson's name in big letters. "Not much huntin' to find our first stop. Let's get the reward and keep right on moving. Don't feel no welcoming in this town."

They rode up to the hitching racks in front of Dawson's freight business and tied their horses and mules. Like the others, it was a long, low, adobe building with large barns visible behind it. A tall, burly man in a serape and sombrero, sitting on a wooden bench in front of the building snarled, "Private hitching racks. Get your scrawny flea-bit animals out of there. For Dawson use only."

"Thanks for your insight, sir, but we're here to see Mr. Dawson," Snake drawled out. He turned to Dog-man. "You goin' in or am I?"

"Think maybe you should. I ain't got in a fight with this here fool yet," he chuckled. "He's got a short barreled shotgun under the blanket he's wearin'."

"Saw it. Called a serape, not a blanket. Be back with that reward money shortly." Snake ducked under the hitch rack and stepped up on the boardwalk in front of the express office. He took just one step and the burly guy stood up, pulled the shotgun out in full view.

"I said, move the animals. Ain't gonna say it again. Got to pay for the use of the hitch rail." He had both hammers pulled all the way back and had it aimed at Snake's belly when a heavy voice called out.

"Lower the gun or die." The burly man must have recognized the voice because he didn't turn or anything, just lowered the scatter gun. "Now ease back on that bench and keep your damn mouth shut."

"Just lookin' to make a dollar or two," the big man said.

Snake and Dog-man turned to see a tall, thin man in a black duster walking down the boardwalk, his own shotgun held at the ready. The wind let the duster blow about some and both men saw the badge hanging on his vest. "You boys got business here? If not, Three-fingers is right. This is private, company hitching."

"Thank you for interrupting Three-finger's game, and, yes we do have business with Mr. Dawson. Who are you?" Dog-man said.

"Name's Eastwood, Deputy United States Marshal Erwin J. Eastwood. What's your business with Dawson? Saddle tramps aren't much welcome around these parts. Bring lots of trouble."

"Appreciate the compliment there, Marshal," Snake said. "We have a letter here for Mr. Dawson, from one of his coach drivers. Now, if you two will excuse me," he looked at the lawman and Three-fingers, "I'll deliver it."

"Let me see the letter," Marshal Eastwood growled.

"Ain't addressed to you," Snake said. He was primed for a fight from Three-fingers' first words, and now the marshal's attitude. Snake looked over at his partner. "Keep care of the animals, and I'll be right back". He was stretched as taught as Red Cloud's bow string as he walked across the boardwalk to the Dawson Company office doors.

I'm gonna get both barrels right in the back, but I'll be a sumbitch if I'll lose that reward. What a dumb-ass place to die. Me and Dog-man gonna die in Santa Fe, not on the open range fightin' dumb cows, not in a mine watching rocks fall on us. Oh, hell no. We're gonna die in a stupid town.

He turned the door knob and walked into a dusty office with three men behind large desks. There were two doors on the other side of the spacious room, one leading into the warehouse, the other, lettered in gold leaf filigree, George Dawson.

"What do you want?" One of the men looked up from a ledger book he was writing in. He had a smile on his face and an open ledger book in front of him.

"Name's Snake. Me and my partner helped out one of your drivers during a robbery a couple of weeks ago, Have a letter here for Mr. Dawson."

"What was this driver's name?"

"Cletus. Cletus Kilpatrick. His messenger's name was Slippery Jim Lucas."

"So, you're the ones, eh? Welcome to Dawson Express Company. Where's this partner of yours?"

"He's doing his best to fend off a marshal and some jerk named Three-fingers, outside there."

All three men jumped up and almost ran to the door. The man talking to Snake got there first. "Eastwood, leave these men alone. Three-fingers, get the hell off my porch." He was an angry man and had his hands on a big Remington hanging from his belt. "You play this game one time too many and blood will flow. Sheriff will hear about this, Eastwood. Now git!"

He turned back to the men with him and saw his workers with drawn guns, Snake with his in hand, and muttered some. "Eastwood's more outlaw than marshal. You," he said, pointing at Dog-man, "are you the one called Dog-man?"

"Yup," Dog-man said.

"Bring your animals around back and settle them in in my corrals. Jake, help him with that, then bring him into the office."

Snake took great pleasure watching Deputy

U.S. Marshal Erwin Eastwood mosey on down the street, and Three-fingers mope alongside. "I take it, then, that you are Mr. Dawson himself."

"Can't stand being locked up in that office back there so I work out front with the boys. Cletus told us some wonderful stories about you two. Been lookin' forward to your arrival. Come on in. I just got a new bottle of Kentucky's best bourbon and it feels the need to be appreciated."

George Dawson was long and thin, had thinning blond hair, blue eyes, and long arms. He had a Remmie hanging on his hip, wore working man's canvas pants, a well-worn wool shirt, and dirty boots. The crinkles around his eyes told everyone he was friendly, enjoyed a good tall tale, and could laugh with the best of them. He could have just jumped down from a long trip driving one of his coaches. "Got those devils, didn't you? Good for you boys."

After the story was told a time or two, the level in the bottle down more than half-way, Dawson got up and walked into his office, coming back with two envelopes. One marked Dog-man, the other, Snake. "Wish old Cletus was here right now. He would have loved being the man to hand these notes out to you."

Snake and Dog-man sat in anticipation, both more than anxious to know how much was in the little vessels. "Cletus was a good man, and I hope my doctoring on him didn't get him hurt more." Snake took the envelope from Dawson, and watched as Dog-man opened his. His partner's eyes were open so far Snake was sure the eyeballs would fall right out on the floor.

"Oh, my goodness," Dog-man said. "This isn't

right, Mr. Dawson."

"It's right, sir. There was more than ten thousand dollars in the strong box on that coach when you broke up the robbery. You saved my company thousands of dollars, boys. You take that money, ride south and stake your claims, and any time you find you need employment, come see me. I need express drivers and guards all the time.

"A word of caution. Don't spend any time around Santa Fe. Eastwood is more outlaw than marshal, and that bruiser Three-fingers has killed more than one. Get on your animals and ride out. Don't stop until it's dark, and camp cold."

"Thanks for the warning, Mr. Dawson. Tell Cletus hello for us." Snake led Dog-man out through the warehouse to the corrals. "Just like I said, Dog-man. Don't feel comfortable in this town."

"Towns ain't for people like us, Snake. Give me a rangy old line of mountains, a broad prairie filled with critters, and I can breathe, but can't do it in a town."

"Yup," is all Snake answered.

"We rode into Santa Fe knowing we were gonna set up a camp and find something to eat before chasing down the Dawson Express Company," Snake drawled out. "Didn't do that, Dog."

"Nope," Dog-man said. "Old stomach's startin' to chat that up with me. Get out of town, Dawson said, eat, my stomach says."

"Mine too. Let's ride out of town and camp early. I could eat half a buf if you help some. Which side you want?"

They laughed all the way out of town.

6

"Haven't seen 'em, Dog-man, but the hairs on the back of my neck are tellin' me there's a skunk or two following along. My envelope had five hundred dollars in it. Yours?"

"Same. Wish I knew where we are or where we're headin'. See something that looks like we could fort up, head for it. I got those same feelings."

Leaving the Dawson Express Co. property, they got back on the road south, riding out of the mountains to lower and flatter country, all the time looking at their back trail. "That marshal feller would kill his mother for what we got in our poke, Snake, and Three Fingers is crazy stupid, the most scary kind."

They had been in high mountains for weeks and those mountains seemed stacked up more to their right than left, and it looked like they were heading for a great valley. "Somewhere out there is a river called the Rio Grande," Snake said. "I've crossed that river many times, but hundreds of miles from where we are right now. It separates Texas from

Mexico, but it don't separate the people, none. River's an invitation for Texans to go to Mexico and for Mexicans to go to Texas," he laughed. "No one wants to stay home."

With two pack mules loaded down, they didn't travel fast and, turning around an outcrop of solid granite, they saw what they were looking for, off to the west half a mile or so off the trail. "We can nest up in those tumbled rocks, Snake."

Dog-man motioned Snake to keep on riding and then turn off and toward where they would camp in fifteen or twenty minutes. Meanwhile, he got off the road and moved cross-country, trying to leave as little sign as he could. Staying in rocky ground most of the way, he threaded through timber, fallen trees and branches, large outcrops, and moved into the huge rock fall. Boulders the size of large cabins were scattered about and Dog-man found an area, almost a cairn, where they could see where the road was, and defend anyone coming from the front and sides.

Snake rode on down the trail watching behind and trying to keep an eye on Dog-man, and after a couple of twists and turns in the road, dropped off in a rock strewn dry wash, and followed it up and back around toward the massive rock fall. "Probably get hit with a thunder storm that will cause another landslide and kill us off," he muttered. It was half an hour later he found Dog-man with a nice camp all set up.

"Ain't nothing come down the trail yet," Dog-man said. "Good thing we filled those gourds with water before leaving Santa Fe. What did Dawson talk to you about while I was packing the mules?"

"He gave me a map that shows several old trails out of these mountains and down to the Rio Grande. Said if we get on one of those, we'd probably be safe from Eastwood and Three Fingers. People been using these road for more than a hundred years, he said."

"Let's do that at first light, then," Dog-man chuckled. "Keep a close eye on the road." Dog-man was going to make a fire well before dark so they could eat and have the fire out before dark.

Snake walked out through the rock field to watch the main road and spotted the deputy marshal and his outlaw side-kick stop in the road. He watched for a minute and dashed back to where Dog-man was.

***

"He saw it. Look, sure as all get out he's comin' our way," Snake chuckled. "You're a dirty old skunk, Dog-man, snaring a fat old killer like that. Remember, no noise. Don't want that outlaw marshal ridin' down on us."

Way back in the rocks, a good solid mile back, Snake pointed out where Eastwood and Three Fingers stopped at the point Dog-man left the road, and continued following Three Fingers as he tried to keep on Dog's trail. They saw the stand of trees he had come through and got there as quickly as possible without making a cloud of dust.

"Best bet is to let him ride past us and then I'll throw a loop and pull him from the horse. We'll jump him and beat him unconscious," Snake continued.

Dog-man was set up with a large rock to smash into Three Fingers' head and Snake shook out a loop and made ready for the catch. "I suppose you'll want to drag him to the fire for the branding," Dog-man chuckled.

"Might at that," Snake said. He was chuckling all the time he worked out his loop, seeing pictures of a naked Three Fingers running through Santa Fe with a big Y bar L brand on his hip.

"You're making too much noise," Dog-man whispered, shushing the tall Texan.

Three Fingers had all of his senses working on trying to follow Dog-man's tracks and followed them out of a rock strewn, brush covered area, into the stand of forest gloom. At a walk, he went right past Dog-man and Snake and was befuddled when the lariat wrapped itself around him and he was jerked from the saddle.

"What the hell?" The air was knocked right out of him when he hit the ground. Dog-man slammed the rock down on Three Fingers' head. Snake was at the man's side immediately, rolled him on his belly and had his hands behind his back and tied off. "Bring his feet up to meet his hands, Dog-man, and we'll truss him like a fat hog for the fire."

They dragged Three Fingers out of the forested area and into the more open country, and left him. "Either the marshal will find him or the wolves will. Let's brush the hell out of our tracks, have supper, and trade watches for the night," Dog-man said.

It was dark when they got back and Snake said he'd take first watch. "I stayed as much as I could in the rocks, so I doubt that old marshal will find us tonight. Better be prepared for a fight in the mornin', though."

Cold meat and cold biscuits washed down with cold water wasn't the best they'd had recently, but Dog-man found sleep came quickly. Snake was perched out a ways from their camp, and could see a broad area. He had tremendous boulders behind him and stayed awake planning their mining operation when they reached border country.

"Water's gonna be the biggest problem," he almost chuckled. "We'll need lots of equipment, though. Dynamite and fuse, picks and shovels, and we gotta build rocker boxes to grab the gold." It was a gleeful several hours and he woke Dog-man for his shift. "We'll have to spend some of this money for equipment, Dog. Can't just go in, you know."

Dog-man was awake, completely confused, and watched Snake crawl under his blanket with a smile on his face. "That man is confusing, sometimes." It was a couple of hours and he found the sky lightening some and woke Snake up.

"If that marshal is still out there, we gotta make our plans, Snake." They wanted great pots of hot coffee and settled for cold biscuits and water.

Snake sat on a rock and spread the map that George Dawson gave him. "Figure we're about here," he said, pointing to where the main highway made a series of turns and twists. "If we go southeast, see, right like this, we should cross this trail here sometime late today. Then, just stay on it.

"Looks to me like it takes us right out of these mountains and connects with the river down below. We're probably gonna have to fight that marshal first, though." They were west of the main north-south highway and would have to cross it to head southeast. "Don't like fightin' a Deputy U.S. Marshal, even if he is half outlaw. They be a mean bunch and back each other up."

"Let's head straight south, cross-country, maybe even a little west, away from the marshal, then turn and find the old trail Dawson pointed out. I don't want to have to fight a marshal either. Remember what we said back in Deadwood about gettin' a reputation of being an outlaw. I ain't no outlaw, Snake."

***

"Keep an eye on that road out of town, Mr. Twombley. If anyone follows those two, get two of your security people to ride with you and follow. Keep those two safe until they are out of the reaches of that bastard Eastwood."

Ed Twombley was the head of security for Dawson Express Company, had several men working for him, most former messengers or drivers. He was behind a building on the south edge of Santa Fe and saw Eastwood and Three Fingers follow Snake and Dog-man out of town. He motioned for his two Dawson men to ride with him and joined the chase. "We'll stay far enough behind to not be seen, but close enough to keep those fools from our people."

It was easy to follow since everyone was on a main road, and easy to keep back far enough to not cause anyone alarm, but when they reached the point where Dog-man left the trail, and then Three Fingers did too, Twombley had to make a decision.

"All right, then," he said. "You follow Three Fingers. Stop him at all costs," he said to Tim Rocha.

Rocha was a large man, worked for years as a messenger, and was trying his best to retire to a small piece of land he bought near Santa Fe.

"I've been looking to take that bastard out for a long time, Mr. Twombley. He won't be hurting our boys."

He rode off at a solid trot and Twombley turned his attention back to following the tracks of Marshal Eastwood. "God help Three Fingers," Jerry Ellison laughed as they rode off. "What do we do if we find Eastwood trying to rob or kill our men, Mr. Twombley? Do we get in a fire fight with a U.S. Marshal?"

"It is an awkward situation, Ellison. We'll just have to play it as it comes. If gun play comes about, Eastwood must die at all costs. We can't have a wounded marshal tellin' lies, now can we." Twombley hid the smile but couldn't hide the twinkle in his eyes.

They were ready to make camp when it got dark and heard a rider coming hard. Tim Rocha pulled up and jumped from his skidding horse, laughing hard. He spent ten minutes telling how he had ridden up on the hog-tied and screaming Three Fingers. "I mended his busted up head the best I could and sent him back to Santa Fe. We had us a good little talk first, though. He didn't want to tell me much until I went to just get on my horse to ride off."

"Is Eastwood involved in an attempted murder and robbery?" Ed Twombley wanted Eastwood out of that position of his as much as George Dawson did.

"Had to prod him some, but yeah, they were off

to get the reward Mr. Dawson gave those boys. Three Fingers said Eastwood wanted both men dead. I put a good fright in the man, threatening to leave him there, but got my answers."

"Good job, Rocha. We'll camp here tonight and find our marshal friend in the morning. "You sent Three Fingers back to Santa Fe? Think he'll actually go?"

"Told him if I saw him on this road anytime in the next five days I would kill him on sight."

***

"You sure they lit out? I was sittin' right there and didn't see nothin'." Three Fingers was riding alongside Deputy Marshal Eastwood on the main road south. "They're probably sittin' in a saloon right now, drinkin' cold beer."

"Shut up and keep your eyes open. They rode out of those stables, just like I said, and are making their way out of town right now. After those stories Cletus Kilpatrick told, Dawson had to give those boys a nice reward. I want that reward. Now, shut up and ride."

It was nearing dusk when Three Fingers saw where Dog-man and one mule left the main road. "Looks like one of them is going off somewhere by himself."

"Interesting." Eastwood looked at the trail Dog-man left and Snake's continuing on the main road. "Must have got in a fight over the reward," Eastwood mused. "Which one has the money? My guess would be the one staying on the main highway."

"Why don't you figure out where that man might

be going and then come join me. I'm staying on the trail south."

Three Fingers did as he was told and rode off across the open country, following Dog-man. He lost the trail several times, realized that he was getting far away from the main road, and was about to turn around and head back when he thought he spotted something. "That looked like something shiny over there in the trees," he muttered.

7

Dark came on quick and Eastwood was still on the main south road following Snake's trail. "Gotta hole up. Why didn't Three Fingers come back? Damn him." Eastwood made a camp, had a good fire, and ate well. "I've got all the food, and that's usually Three Fingers' first thought after whiskey," he snickered. "His loss."

The sun was bright when Eastwood rolled out of his blanket. "This one I'm following is just going south and he'll be gone by now. I gotta catch up with Three Fingers and chase the other one down." Coffee, meat, and biscuits at a hot fire, and Eastwood got back on the trail to find Three Fingers.

"If I can make one or both of those two yahoos make a move on me I can use my federal authority to chase them all the way to Mexico. People like that got no right to belittle a Deputy U.S. Marshal and live to laugh about it. Sure would like one of them to take a shot at me."

He rode around a long uphill curve in the well-travelled highway and came face to face with

Ed Twombley and his two deputies. "Well, well," Twombley said. "Look who we have here. Deputy U.S. Marshal and sometimes outlaw, Erwin Eastwood. Out for a morning's jog, are we?"

"Get out of my way," Eastwood snarled. "You're interfering with a federal officer."

"Might not be a federal officer for long, Eastwood." Twombley had a short, double barrel shotgun aimed at the marshal's belly. "Take his weapons, Mr. Rocha. I'm holding you for Sheriff Cunningham, Eastwood, on a charge of conspiracy to commit murder and robbery."

Tim Rocha had his horse alongside Eastwood's and took a revolver from Eastwood's holster. As he did, Eastwood pulled another from under his coat and fired a shot at Twombley, knocking the security boss out of the saddle. Rocha used Eastwood's own pistol to shoot him dead.

Ellison jumped from his horse and ran to the wounded Twombley. "I'm all right," Twombley said, trying to sit up. "Bullet broke my arm. Let's get it wrapped and get back to town with Eastwood's body. Those two boys will be safe now."

"How much further you figure we gots to go cross-country before we can head east and find that old trail?" Snake was following Dog-man and they had been on the ride for several hours. "Riding in mountains like this just ain't the same as ridin' in Texas. Can't see nothing but the trees in front of us."

"And the rocks," Dog-man laughed. "Let's turn east now and hit the main road for a while, then turn toward that old trail."

When they re-connected with the major high-way they were actually feeling safe enough to stay on it. "I don't know why but I don't think that marshal's followin' us." Dog-man spent some time turning to look at the trail behind. "Damn poor excuse for a marshal, but it is best that we don't get in a fight with him." Snake just nodded, half asleep in the saddle.

They made good time on the main highway, met people coming up toward Santa Fe, were passed by one Dawson Express wagon but it wasn't driven by Cletus Kilpatrick. "Would have been nice to see that old boy." Snake was thinking ahead, too. "We need to stop at one of the stage stations or little villages we come to, Dog.

"We need to get a real lay of the land. We're runnin' out of civilization the farther south we go. Gonna run up against a sign that says Bienvenidoes a Mexico."

"Sayin' what?"

"Welcome to Mexico or something like that. We need to get our minin' stuff, and soon."

Dog-man figured they were a couple of hun-dred miles from Mexico, but laughed and agreed, and they rode downhill toward where the high-way meets up with the Rio Grande. "Looks like a friendly little village," Snake said. "Let's have a cold beer or two, ask some questions, and move on."

"And watch out for a Deputy U.S. Marshal hang-ing around," Dog-man growled.

Tying off in front of a cantina, the two saw a mixture of American cattlemen, frontiersmen, Mexican vaqueros, and Indians. Inside was dark, smoky, and loud with Mexican music. "Two beers,"

Snake had to yell at the barman. He looked around and shook his head. "Ain't gonna get answers in here. Can't even ask the questions."

"There's a big mercantile shop of some kind across the plaza, Snake. Says farm, ranch, and mining supplies. Let's drink up and head over there."

They walked their string of animals across the plaza and entered the Gutierrez Emporium. "Gentlemen, what can I do for you today?"

"Heading south and need some mining supplies," Snake said.

"Workin' your way through bandito country, Apache country, and nasty desert country. Don't mean to get personal, boys, but why?"

"Lookin' to do some prospectin', stakin' a claim or two, and findin' gold," Dog-man said.

"Way south would take you into the Portrillo Mountains, and they never talk about gold in that country." He snickered. "But it's mighty dangerous and a long way from here." The man walked over to a bin full of maps and other papers, rummaged around, and brought a map back, laying it out on the counter. "This here's Albuquerque, and boys, you want to give it a wide spread. Go around, not through, if you be smart. Then just stay on the river for another couple of weeks, and if you still have your hair, you'll see the Portrillo Mountains off to the west. Map's ten cents."

"We'll take it," Snake said. "Last one we saw went for a couple of hundred," he chuckled. Dog-man laughed right out. Snake looked the map over carefully. "Looks like quite a few little villages all the way down. What's this Las Cruces like?"

"Dirty little village like all the others. Best place

to supply up, though."

The boys picked up their supplies, including medicines and clothing, re-packed their mules, and rode out of the little village, along the banks of the Rio Grande. "We been in trouble at just about every place we stopped, Snake. Let's be smart on this journey and do like that man said. Ride all the way around Albuquerque. Just don't need more trouble."

The plan worked but it took them a full two days to work all the way around the spreading community, and the mountains it was nestled in. "Gets cold up here near seven thousand feet," Snake said one morning, breaking ice to make coffee. Let's ride back down in that valley and stick with the river."

The southern Rocky Mountains loomed to their west as they made their way south, always riding through the little villages they came to and camping away from people as much as possible. "We gotta fill the larder, Snake. Almost out of coffee, sugar, flour, and whiskey. Staples, Snake, we're out of staples."

"The next village that's listed on this ten cent map of ours is called Socorro. If it's more than three buildings, we'll stop. If there are only three buildings and one is a cantina, I want something to eat other than biscuits and side meat."

The roadway along the river made for fair travel, but the country was ragged, with deep arroyos, some almost canyon size, open blistering desert, and steep rocky hill sides. There were great plains of white sand and little vegetation. "We're still a hundred miles or more from the border, Dog, so we don't want to make this a long stay."

"Just long enough to slake our thirst, fill the

packs, and smile at the girls," Dog-man said. They rode right down the main street of Socorro and into the central plaza. Music came from upstairs balconies, from cantinas, and from strolling groups. "Hope the food's as friendly as the music."

They tied off in front of a cantina and slipped inside where the music welcomed them. A lovely brown-eyed, well developed young girl got them settled at a table. "Cold beer, just keep bringing us cold beer," Snake said. "And we would like a table full of good food. Whatever you and the cook eat is what we want to eat," he smiled with his eyes, too.

"I learned that, too," Dog-man said. "Was in Saint Loo and the prettiest little girl waitin' tables said I would always get the best food if I remembered that."

"I think that would work everywhere except at the stage stops, Dog. Sure wouldn't have wanted Fat Mary to be cookin' for me," he laughed. "Bet that kid of theirs hasn't stole nothin' since we were there."

"I'd love to see that girl's face at sunrise, peeking out from under my blankets. This might be a good place to hole up for a day or two, Snake. Give the horses and mules a little rest."

"Ain't gonna be so," Snake growled. "Besides, Dog, your spoken for, remember? That selfish little girl up north is waitin' for you." Dog-man scowled and chuckled at the same time.

A mandolin, along with a guitar and trumpet made up the band and the music was lively. Two crazy American drovers were trying to sing but didn't know the words, couldn't keep in tune, and didn't care. As the girl walked by with a tray full of food one of the men tried to grab her to dance.

"Oh, no," Snake yelled. "That's our food and you leave that lovely lady alone, mister." He was half out of his chair and the cow man spun around, grabbed the tray and threw it at Snake. "You miserable sumbitch," Snake howled, jumping all the way up. He fended off the tray of rice and beans, tacos and salsa, and howled like a she wolf at full moon. He took one big step and drove a left, swung from boot top, into the man's groin, doubling the drunk over.

The other cow man, who had been having as much fun as he could, kicked the spilled dishes of food aside and went after Snake. Dog-man, enjoying his first drink of cold beer in a week, watched for another minute. Snake had the one out of the game but the other one was big, mean, and just sober enough to fight good.

After breaking a chair or two, upsetting a table, and drawing blood, Snake got serious when the drunk pulled a knife. "That ain't friendly like," he snarled, throwing a chair in the man's face. The drunk knocked the chair aside and lunged at Snake with the big skinning knife. Snake side stepped the lunge, drew his pistol and whipped the handle across the side of the man's head, opening a gash ten inches long.

The drunk was flopping in a sea of blood when the barman fired his pistol, sending a chunk of lead through the roof. "No more," he shouted, waving the pistol at everyone in the cantina. The man with the aching groin was trying his best to stand up. He saw Snake with a pistol in his hand, his partner on the floor bleeding, and went for his sidearm.

The barman shot him dead. "I said no more."

Snake slowly let his revolver find its way into the holster and settled down at the table. He grabbed a glass of beer and drank it down. The barman walked around the end or the bar and motioned for two men to drag the two drunks out.

"You boys still want to eat?" He nodded at the young girl who was trying to clean up the mess. "Get these men their dinner, Anna. The shootin's sure to draw the sheriff our way, but he won't have nothin' to say to you."

"Very kind," Snake said. "You got a lot of Texas in your talk, barman. Fort Worth's my country."

"Been lookin' for gold north of El Paso. Got a couple of claims in the Portrillo Mountains, but ran out of luck and money. Workin here to make my stake. Come out of San Antonio original. Name's Butters. Jimmie Butters."

Dog-man gave the barman a long look when he mentioned the Portrillo Mountains. That man down the road told them there wasn't much gold in the Portrillos. Dog-man saw more of a gambler in the man than a prospector. He was quick to kill that one feller, but also quick to sidle up to he and Snake.

"Good to meet you, Jimmie Butters. I'm Snake and my partner's called Dog-man. We're looking to stake our claims in the Portrillos. Maybe you could tell us about that country."

"Ain't but two trees per square mile, won't find water ceptin' during thunder storms. Gotta barrel it up when it comes," he laughed. "Gold is there but it fights back fierce like. Don't want to be found."

"We were gonna supply up at Las Cruces."

"You boys ever thought of a third hand? I got

claims, don't got supplies. You gonna have supplies but don't got claims."

"Might be a good idea for some, but we been a two man partnership for a long time. Gonna keep it that way." Snake got a quick scowl back and also noticed just the slightest smile from Dog-man.

"Well, enjoy your meal. I gotta get this mess cleaned up."

"Nice talkin' with you," Snake said.

The girl brought several bowls and platters of food, wouldn't look at either one, probably from fright. Snake's moves on the two drunks were fast and vicious. The boys dug in, getting two or three more glasses of beer to get it washed down.

"Ain't never had food this hot, Snake. I ain't got feelin' one in my mouth right now. How can you just eat it down like that? I got tears in my eyes, sweat on my head, and no feeling in my mouth. I just drank four beers and they had no effect."

"Good food, Jimmie Butters. We be off now. Good luck on gettin' your stake." Snake ignored Dog-man's crying except for soft chuckles and crinkled eyes.

They checked the lines on the pack animals, mounted up and rode toward the general merchandise store a block out of the plaza. "Thought for sure he would offer to sell us one of those claims of his," Dog-man said.

"Yup, could almost hear it comin'." Snake was still chuckling as they filled out their order with the clerk. "This'll get us to Las Cruces, and then we'll need to get serious about supplies for the mine."

They weren't five miles out of town when they saw a rider coming their way fast. "A dollar to ten that's Jimmie Butters," Snake laughed.

8

Butters rode up in a cloud of dust and a face full of smiles. "Sheriff thought I was wrong shootin' that drover and suggested I get out of town. I got a little place about ten miles south I been working on. Figure I'll hole up there for a spell. Mind if I ride along?"

"That'll be fine Jimmie," Snake said. "We'll be ridin' 'till it's too dark to see. What are these Portrillos like?" If Butters had to ride with them the least he could do was feed them the information they needed. That is, if he really had been there, really had claims in those forbidding mountains.

Butters was tough in actions but had the look of a card shark, someone who spent hours doing no physical labor. After all, he shot that man, so toughness was a given, but a miner? Well now, Snake was thinking, this man didn't work two claims. "We ain't never seen the Portrillo Mountains."

"Well, when you leave out of Las Cruces, head kinda southwest, right into the heart of the range. They be steep, great spires of rock, and responsible for many people not coming back. You might run into some Apache ruffians, too," Butters chuckled. Or was it a sneer? "You'll find quartz in the outcrops, but you gotta dig into them rocks to find the gold."

Snake's first thought was the man was lying through that foul mustache of his. "That ain't much of description, Butters." Snake said it quietly but Butters caught the edge.

"Well, truth be told, it's a volcanic hades. Great black cinder cones, bare rock, little gold, and no water. If you asked me to join you right now, I'd say no to mining, yes to joining for the adventure."

Another great lie, Snake thought, looking at the man with his sneaky little grins, shaded eyes, and soft hands. I'd gladly shoot this fool right now. I wonder if we're not the fools, though heading off into nowhere-land?

Butters did as he said and dropped off about ten miles out, leaving the boys to ride on. "If he has two claims he ain't lookin' to sell 'em," Snake said.

"No, he ain't, but he said he ran out of money and supplies so I'd say those claims ain't worth much."

"Now that's good thinkin', Dog. Yup, it sure is. Wouldn't walk away from a filled up stew pot, now would you. Better watch our backs. Something about that man don't fit in right. His hands aren't those of a man that does mining work. We gotta watch our backs, Dog, the whole time. I don't much care for what he said about volcanoes and very little gold."

***

Butters rode in on a seldom used trail and found the little shack he used between jobs in Socorro, had a quick meal and packed up. "Those boys know where they're goin' but don't want to let anyone else know. Bet they got a map, too. I'm gonna let them lead me right to their mine, but if they catch me before we get there, I'll kill 'em and get that map."

Butters waited until morning before leaving. "They've got those pack mules to keep 'em goin' slow. I'm gonna ride out and around them and be waiting for them in Las Cruces to lead me out." He was wearing a light pack and had basics in his saddle bags, had his horse at a solid miles eating trot, seeing pots or gold ingots with his stamp on them.

He made the ride into Las Cruces in two long days and took a room at a drover's hotel. He hadn't shaved but there wasn't really a beard there yet and he needed some way to keep an eye on the boys yet not be seen by them. He found a friendly little cantina along the road leading into Las Cruces and spent time on the veranda drinking beer and toying with the lovely ladies bringing the beer.

"It's only a hundred miles," he fumed three mornings later. "Should have been here yesterday. It was nearing noon when he spotted the four animals and two riders coming in at a slow walk. Butters hustled inside and took a table in the very back, his back to the door, just in case they stopped.

Dog-man and Snake rode on past the cantina and found the general merchandise and mining supply store. "We'll get the heavy stuff first, Dog, then the food and other supplies."

"We're gonna need another mule, Snake. If we're gonna be up in those craggy old mountains for a couple of months, we're gonna need a lot of stuff."

"You're right again, Dog. Go get us another mule

and I'll deal with the mining stuff." They tied off and went into the large, open-air store. "Where can a gent pick up a good mule," Dog-man asked the clerk.

"Got three good ones out back. You lookin' to add to that string or replace one. Those you got look kinda used up."

"Been on the road for a while. We need to add one or two to our string. Working into the Portrillos for the rest of the summer."

"Take your string around back and old Jake will help you. He knows mules. Think his ma may have been one," the clerk said, bursting into gales of laughter. Snake and Dog-man just looked at him.

Dog-man, despite himself, had to chuckle walking out to get the animals. He brought their horses and string around to the back of the building. The mercantile store had quite a corral and equipment yard stretched out. A lovely Mexican girl of about twenty or so walked up to him, with a smile.

"Papa says you're looking for a mule," she said. "Follow me."

"You don't look like someone who might be named Jake. My friends call me Dog-man. What do they call you?"

"I don't know your friends," she teased. It took a moment for him to catch what she said and he laughed. "Papa Calls me Angelina. Jake is my brother, actually my half-brother. Papa was married before."

"I understand," Dog-man said. That's the swipe about Jake's mother being a mule. Dog-man had to chuckle. "Well, let's find Jake and get me a good mule to add to that string. We're gonna be gone for a while. After meeting you, I think I'd rather stick around, though. Do you like to dance?"

"I can break any man's foot in the first half of the first song," she laughed. "Besides that, I'm already asked for," and she flashed a rather large gold ring with a bright diamond. "Tobias Ringwald and I will be married on Sunday, if you're still in town."

"Wouldn't miss it if we're still here." He didn't say that they'd be gone in an hour, but he also didn't say how much he would like to gather her up in his arms and hold her for a long time.

**

Snake walked to the counter with a list of what he thought they would need as far as tools went. "Wouldn't happen to know a man named Jimmie Butters, would you?" Snake drawled it out and laid the list on the counter top. "He had a claim or two in the Portrillos, I think."

"He's a coyote with a wolf's temper," the clerk said. "Hope you're not friends." The clerk was a rough old codger, his hands and knuckles gnarled and scarred, and the muscles in his shoulders and neck more than prominent. "If he had claims they were someone else's," he sneered. "Man ain't worked a pick or shovel, single jack or steel once in his life." The old buzzard mumbled something else, then looked at Snake, hard like.

"If you're looking for gold why would you be going into the Portrillos? Cinder cones, dead volcanos, lava fields, and more barren rock than most men want to see. If there's gold it ain't been found."

"We ran into Butters in Socorro and think he

may be on our tail." Snake was shaking his head, sorry they had ever stopped at that cantina. "If we don't make a strike there, we'll go on further west, I imagine."

"He won't try to befriend you again. He'll sneak up from behind. I'll get this order put together right away. When you ride out, go cross-country, southwest, right into the heart of the craggy old range, and keep right on going. Go south. You'll be in border country. That border has moved several times over the years and many simply don't care where it is or even whether it is," he cackled.

"Mountains to the south have produced, just be wary of Mexican bandits, American outlaws, and mean Apache. Other than that, you'll be fine," he cackled. "You'll have El Paso to your east. If you do strike it good, El Paso's the place to sell your gold." The old man started filling the order and Snake started to walk out back to have a chat with Dog-man. "The Apache are quiet right now. Plundering down south, further into Mexico, I guess."

"Hope so," Snake said. He found Dog-man and the string. "That new mule looks plenty sturdy. Got the low-down on Jimmie Butters. Not a nice man, Dog. Who's the pretty girl? You do have a way of bringin' 'em in."

"Name's Angelina and she's getting married Sunday. Yup, good mule. Hope we don't run into Butters ever again." He was talking in short sentences to Snake but his eyes continued to roam up and down and all around Angelina.

"Did you see those buildings over there when we rode in?" Dog-man was pointing at a compound along the edge of the plaza. "Sign says Dawson Express Company. We might want to remember that."

"Yeah," Snake said. "I liked that man. He had a

way about him that you just knew you could trust him. Not too many like him in these parts."

It was a full hour before they were ready to head out. "Keep your weapons loaded and your fingers loose, boys, and good luck to you," the clerk said, waving them off. Angelina stood next to her father, waving and smiling.

***

Jimmie Butters had watched all the action from a shaded porch across the plaza. They had help from the old man packing the three mules, checking everything over and over. As they rode out from the compound, Butters was sitting on his horse, a pack mule of his own, alongside. He rode around the block, found a rock pile on the edge of Las Cruces, and watched as Snake and Dog-man rode out of town. He watched them leave the main road south and head out across the broad plain toward the Portrillo Mountains. "Lead me to your gold," he whispered.

He gave them a half hour and then followed, planning on staying far back and out of sight until they worked into wherever they had their claim. "Those boys are gonna make me a rich man and New Orleans is gonna make me a happy man," he murmured.

***

"That clerk told me all about Jimmie Butters, Dog. He's a slippery devil. Tell you what, I'm gonna let you lead all three mules and I'm gonna sneak off the trail up here a ways and make a big circle back to be sure we ain't bein' follered."

"Good idea but maybe it should be me doing that. After all, you are too easy on people, always thinking of the other guy. I'm the mean one, remember?"

"No, I'm gonna do it cuz I don't like him more than you don't like him," Snake said, stopping so he could add his mule to the two Dog-man was leading. "There's still lots of daylight so I'll catch up after I'm sure we ain't bein' trailed. Ride a might slow so's I don't have to ride fast."

Dog-man was chuckling as he watched his partner ride off when they hit a rocky patch on the trail. He had been riding in front and let Dog-man and the mules help hide his prints. Snake circled well east letting the natural terrain hide him from view. He came back west and found a jumble of rocks to nest in. "Good view of the trail we made," he muttered. They weren't on a road or trail, just open country, so if there was someone coming the same way, it would have to be on purpose, not by chance.

"They ain't wrong describin' this country," Snake murmured. "All bare rocks and cactus. If it grows, it's got spines. Hope we ain't wastin' our time on this little venture of ours."

In less than half an hour he saw Butters and his pack mule following their trail. "Got that one right, Dog," he muttered. He let Butters get by and rode down from the rocks and out to the trail, put his horse in a lope and rode up on Jimmie Butters. "Hey, there." He called out. "Well, looky here. It's Jimmie Butters," he cried out. "What brings you all the way out here?"

Butters spun in the saddle, startled and frightened. He didn't know what to say, had his reins and mule lead rope in his left hand but was turned that way. He couldn't go for his sidearm and just sat quiet. "Don't look like you're packed for working a claim, Mr. Butters. Looks like you're packed for a nice little camping trip into the mountains, eh?"

"Yeah. I needed to get away. You know, after shooting that man in the cantina. Yeah, get away for a time."

"Well good for you. A nice quiet time around a campfire, fresh trout from the brook. No. Ain't no brooks around these parts. Well, maybe a roasted rabbit, eh? Step it up, Mister Butters. Let's catch up with Dog-man and see what he has to say about all this." Snake smacked Butter's horse and they moved out at a solid trot.

Butters got himself turned back so he could easily pull his gun but Snake knew he might try and kept off at an angle. "Keep it going, Butters," he taunted from just behind the man's left side. Butters would have to pull the gun and then twist all the way around to get off a shot giving Snake all the time in the world to kill him.

"Frustrating, ain't it? We'll work on giving you a chance."

"Don't know what you mean." Butters stuttered but kept his horse and mule at a trot. It wasn't half an hour and they rode up on Dog-man, stopped in the middle of the desert.

"Saw your dust," he said. "By golly, you were right, Snake. Good man. Howdy, Butters. Out for a nice ride?"

"He's on vacation, going camping, Dog. The idea just come on him, quick like. See? No mining equipment. Guess he planned on using ours."

They rode to a stand of brush and Dog-man tied

off his horse and then each of the mules while Snake got Butters and his animals straightened out. Snake had Butters gather enough scattered wood to make a fire and he got a pot of coffee started. "Looks like we have a few things to talk about, Mr. Butters. Let me have your weapon, please."

The whole time, Snake put himself in the hardest position possible for Butters to draw down on him. His taunts finally paid off. Butters started to spin and pull iron and realized that Snake already had his gun in hand. "You're not quite as smart as you think you are. Now, slow, slow, slow, Mr. Butters, pull that cheap little shooter and drop it in the sand."

Dog-man had his weapon in hand, was laughing as he watched Butters slowly pull his gun and drop it. "Man ain't total dumb, Snake. He did as you told him." Dog-man walked over to Butters, without saying a word, drove a long left hook into the man's groin, sending him howling into the dirt. "Been wantin' to do that for some time, Snake. Felt good, too."

"Yup. You are the mean one. My turn next. What do we do now?"

"Let him cry and moan for a minute or two and then have a nice chat. He'll come to see things our way, I'm sure. We be runnin' out of light in an hour or so, so that's our timetable."

Butters was rolling in the desert dirt, curled up like a baby. "Quit that, now," Snake finally said, kicking the man in the butt. "Sit up like a man and talk to us." Snake and Dog-man had tin cups of coffee, even offered one to Butters.

"If you're thinkin' straight you better start

talking straight," Snake said. "We're all through being nice. You ain't got no claims in those mountains over there, you ain't goin' on no camping adventure, and you ain't looking to make friends with us."

"You talk good, Snake." Dog-man looked at Butters, picked up Butters' dirty pistol, blew sand and grit from it, and cocked the hammer back. "Seems to still be working."

"Better try it out," Snake said.

"Yup," Dog-man chuckled. He aimed the gun at Butters' head and slipped his finger over the trigger.

"No!" Butters tried to crawl away and Snake slammed him in the head with his fist. The shark's eyes were huge as he looked into the open barrel of his own gun, saw the cylinders filled with death, and started crying, sobbing, actually. "No," he said again and again.

"I thought he'd be more friendly," Dog-man said. He un-cocked the weapon and tucked it in his belt. "Here's the deal, Butters. We keep your horse, you keep the mule. Start walking. If either one of us ever sees you again, you will die. Go now before I change my mind."

"You can't take my horse," Butters blubbered. "I can't walk all the way back to Las Cruces. I'll die."

"You'll die if you stay here," Snake said. He was laughing, his eyes shining, and pointed the way. "Better get to moving."

They watched Butters take up the lead rope to his mule and start backtracking to Las Cruces. "Let's ride until dark and make a cold camp just in case the fool tries to follow. I'm sure he ain't that stupid, maybe I'm sure, but let's not take any chances." Snake started gathering their mules and got the train put together. "Extra saddle horse never hurt a thing."

"We'll let it go after half an hour or so. Probably head right for town. Might even stop if Butters says please," Dog-man chuckled.

"Should have just shot the bastard."

"There you go, Snake. See, that would make us the outlaws. Lettin' the horse go, we ain't even horse thieves."

The only thing to interrupt their sleep were singing coyotes and the skittering of little desert creatures. There was no moon and the stars were brilliant, lit up the desert. Snake stayed awake for several hours, doing more planning for their mine. He finally woke Dog-man to keep watch and fell asleep when his head hit his saddle.

"Don't wake me 'till the sun's all the way up," he murmured.

9

Snake and Dog-man spent weeks working their way deep into the high and spiny Portrillo range, found a trail that hadn't been used in some time and followed it for another week. "I thought the old man at the mercantile store said we should go southwest," Snake said. "This trail we been on is heading a lot more southeast."

"We've gone south and we've been out of those lava fields for a couple of weeks. I think if we turned around and followed it back, it would lead us right back to Las Cruces. We came in cross country." The trail was old, overgrown and single track in many places. "He sure was right about what we'd see. I ain't never seen a cinder cone before. Sure interesting. Ain't gold country, though."

Without knowing it, the boys had moved well away from the volcanic Portrillo Mountains, crossed a desert like plain, and moved into a more hospitable range. It was a no-man's land, not patrolled by American law or Mexican law, a land of outlaws, banditos, and Apaches.

"Glad we have pack mules instead of a wagon." Snake was following along behind Dog-man, slouched back in the saddle, trying to roll a smoke. They were climbing high into the range, had crossed two razorback ridges, and found water often.

"Look up there," Dog-man said, pointing to some timbers that had been set a long time ago.

"That ain't natural," Snake said. He was shading his eyes from the glaring noon-day sun. "Somebody built that."

They rode another couple of hundred yards and found a single track trail that seemed headed back for whatever had been built. The trail zig-zagged up and down, back and forth, and finally climbed out of a rocky gulch onto a flattened area. "Well, now, Snake, I think we're home."

What they saw from below was the start of a head frame over the start of a shaft. A windless was still in place and the shaft appeared to be about twelve feet deep. There was a small lean-to cabin, a three-sided shed for tools and equipment, and scattered tools, lengths of cut trees, dried out rope, even some rusted cable spread over the site.

"Been some time since anyone has been around this workin's. Did a lot of work before runnin' off, too." Snake was looking into the shaft, saw where a wheel barrow had trucked what was lifted out. A long rocker box was set up and the tailings were sent over the side of the mountain. "Good little one or two man operation, Dog."

Dog-man stepped out of the three sided cabin with a sour look on his face. "Didn't run off, Snake. Got killed off." He motioned and Snake followed him back in. There was a cot off to one side, a stove in the middle, and a table on the other side. In the middle of the rock floor was the remains of whoever did the workin's. Mostly ragged clothing and bones.

"Look at the skull," Dog-man said. Snake saw two holes in the front, just above the eye sockets, and the back of the head didn't exist. "His hands were tied behind his back, too."

"Must have had something somebody wanted real bad," Snake muttered. "Did all this work and lost it to banditos," he muttered again, shaking his head. "He's been dead a long time, Dog, and whoever did this didn't stick around to work the claim. Just bandits taking what he had and killin' him.

"See? That's why I don't want to be an outlaw. Got no feelin's, no heart. Let's give this fine gent a decent burial and clean up our new home, eh?"

"Think there's gold in that hole out there?" Snake had a pick and shovel and was walking off a distance from the workings to start the grave.

"He did and whoever killed him must have, too," Dog-man chuckled. He wrapped the remains in an old wool blanket and tied it together. "This old boy did a lot of work around here, spent considerable money on equipment, so I'd guess he had a return of some kind."

They spent the rest of the day taking inventory of what was there, drew a map of where they thought they might be, and started searching for the claim posts and possible notices. "Hell, Dog, we don't even know which side of the border we might be on. We been going southwest first, and lately southeast, but south all the time. What if we're in Mexico?"

"Ain't no line in the sand I saw. Don't matter none to me. That road we came in on goes back to Las Cruces, I think. I betcha another dollar, Snake, that if we take it in the direction we were going, it would take us to El Paso."

Snake pulled the map they got from George Dawson and compared it to what the guy in Las Cruces sold them, and pointed to El Paso. "You just might be right, Dog. See? Everybody has told us the best place to sell our gold is El Paso, so at least we might be able to find the place."

They were both laughing and Dog-man continued pulling things from their pack animals and getting them sorted. "Do you remember anything that Slippery Jim Lucas told us about using dynamite? I think I got a handle on it, but I might need your help."

Snake had to laugh, remembering how Slippery Jim and Cletus Kilpatrick had spent an evening around the fire talking about using explosives. "I remember Slippery Jim holding up his hand, pretending he only had a thumb and little finger, and sayin' he was ordering five beers. I think that's all we need to remember about blasting."

***

"I tell you, those two outlaws stole my horse, threatened my life, Sheriff. Beat me up and sent me into the desert on foot." Jimmie Butters was sitting on an empty box near Sheriff Warren Baxter's battered old desk, almost crying.

"You're either crazy stupid or crazy drunk, Butters. You came riding into town on your horse, haulin' that mule behind. You ain't got a bruise on you. Go on, get out of here. Ain't nobody beat you up or robbed you or stole your horse. Drunk and disorderly, if you ask me, but I got a full jail, so no room for you, get out."

Butters still had money in his pockets, a mule fully packed, and was riding his horse. The sheriff would have stories to tell about this. Butters was an angry man when he walked into the Las Cruces Golden Globe Saloon and Dance Hall. He put a double eagle on the bar and ordered a bottle.

"You know a rough character or two might be looking for some easy work?" Butters asked the barman. "A couple of tough hombres took advantage of me and I need to get even."

"Probably want to talk with Clint Ayres. Just got out of some Texas jail and needs work. That's him at the table in back. Red shirt, red hair, full beard."

"I see him. Give me another glass." Jimmie Butters brought the bottle and two glasses to Ayres' table and sat down. "Heard you're a tough guy lookin' for a little work. Join me in a drink?"

"You lookin' for trouble? What kind of game is this?" His eyes were narrowed to slits, his right hand had a grip on his weapon, and every muscle in the man's neck was evident. Clint Ayres was about five feet eight inches and squat, not an ounce of fat on his one hundred eighty pound frame.

"No game, Ayres. Two men took advantage of me and I want to get even. They're prospecting in the Portrillos and I want them dead."

"Then shoot 'em," Ayres said. He poured a glass full of whiskey and drank half of it.

"There's two hundred dollars in it for you. Of

course, they might have some gold or a claim when we find them. We'd split that," Butters said, ignoring the slight. His soft hands, lack of strong frame, and pleading eyes made Ayres want to puke in his face.

"Got no gonads of your own, eh? Remind me of a gambler feller I met once. Hid an ace on me. Ripped his head right off, I did. Make it four hundred and no split of gold and claim. It'd be all mine. Four hundred on the table in front of me."

His bushy red eyebrows, ugly grin, and bulging muscles had Butters fully convinced the man would rip another man's head right off. "Four it is," the pasty little man said. "We leave at sunrise. I know where they're going." He pulled a wallet from an inside pocket and counted out four hundred dollars. "I'm trusting you to be there."

"I don't trust you, me, or nobody, but I'll be there. Don't be walkin' off with that bottle. Leave it right there on the table." Ayres was chuckling to himself as he poured a glass full of the rot gut whiskey. Butters slunk away from the table and wondered if he had made yet another mistake.

***

Even though the tracks were almost ancient, they were easy to follow since the trail went cross country. Butters and Ayres had nothing in common, Ayres was the least able to hold a conversation, and the trip was just one day after another. They found where the boys had joined the old trail and started moving southeast. "This road is the old road to El Paso," Ayres said. "Bandit country. If we get hit I'm saving myself. You can go to hell."

Butters didn't try to answer the man, just rode on. It was more important than anything to kill Snake and Dog-man, but Ayres frightened him even more than Dog-man did. He had always been a sneak, always played the safe game, cheated at every chance, but knew he had to play straight with this Ayres brute.

"Doesn't look like the trail is used much," Butters said.

"Bandits," is all Ayres said back.

They were riding through rough country, climbing high into a range of mountains unlike the Portrillos they had come through. There were rocky cuts, over razorback ridges, and around great columns of lava and granite. There were few trees, no game, and little water. The green from a water source stood out like a flag waving, and they stopped at one for the night.

"If I have to kill those men in El Paso, it's gonna cost you another two hundred," Clint Ayres said.

"They have a claim somewhere in this range. Never showed me their map but I know they have one. They ain't goin' to El Paso."

"Neither am I without more money."

They spotted what looked like mining activity two days later. "That's gotta be them," Butters said. "Let's go get 'em"

"Let's find out who it is, how many there are, and whether or not we can attack. You hired me to do this, then from now on, you do as I say or die. Got it?" Butters just nodded his head and slinked away from the angry man. "Now, let's back track and find a place to make a good camp. You make the camp,

I'll find out what's going on up on that ridge."

Butters knew that when Ayres had completed the job he would have to kill him, and he worried about that day and night. He couldn't forget the man bragged about ripping the head right off a man, always talked about how it felt to drive a knife deep into another man's body. Butters winced every time he heard the words.

"I'm gonna have to shoot him six times when he's sleeping," Butters murmured. He had a fire ring made and camp put together in short order.

10

"That old boy was killed a long time ago, Dog. I wonder why nobody has been around to work this claim? It's a good one. Using the rocker boxes dry, like we have, and that hole in the ground has put considerable gold in our poke in just a few weeks."

"I think you had the answer that first day. Banditos, you said. They took nothing but his gold and his life and more than likely, nobody knew he was even here."

"Yeah, kind of like us, eh?" Snake had to snicker when he said it. "Just like us except for one thing, Amigo. He knew where he was. I don't think we do. I think we're a whole bunch further west than we think. And I think we're a whole bunch further south than we think. Sometimes I don't think we think," he chuckled. "Everybody we talked to said we were fools to come into these mountains looking for gold."

"Everyone except Jimmie Butters," Dog-man said.

"Yeah, that. We got trees here. We got quartz

ledges here. We ain't in the Portrillo Mountains, old friend. I got no idea where we are. We get a goodly amount, we will need to make for El Paso, you know. That will catch someone's interest when we sell it, and that's when we find trouble."

"Seems likely. We're following along the edge of that ledge and I wonder if there would be the same thing on the other side of this out crop. Think I'll go take a look."

"I'll run what we dug out today through the rocker box, then. Sure looked pretty down in the hole."

It was what Slippery Jim Lucas had taught the boys that allowed them to keep their claim alive and producing. Hard rock mining wasn't learned from the back of a horse or nestled near a warm campfire. The first several attempts at hand drilling produced lots of bloody knuckles and loud cursing from twelve feet underground. Swinging a four pound hammer onto the top of a chisel bit drill ain't for the light hearted.

"If you hit the top of the steel with the hammer, not your knuckles, it's better," Snake yelled out, getting some filthy language back. "Remember what Slippery Jim said. Hit the steel, give it a twist, and hit it again. Never once said hit your knuckles."

Snake had to climb out of the coyote hole fast, great chunks of rock bouncing off his body, laughing the whole way. It only took a day or two for both boys to become good at single jack drilling. They were always cautious with the explosives and found they were under-loading rather than over-loading, not breaking up the solid granite like they should.

"Cut that fuse the same lengths, Dog, just like old Slippery Jim said." Snake picked up on hard rock mining faster that Dog-man. "That way, when we light the fuses, one at a time, they go off in a sequence. Remember what he said? Break up the rock don't blow up the mine," and he rocked with laughter.

Within two weeks, they had a good operation. They squabbled and cussed, laughed at their mistakes, and made gold. They drilled their blast holes anywhere from two feet to almost four feet, which produced several tons of rock each day for the rocker boxes.

Snake was working the loose sand and gravel first when he caught a glint of sunlight shining off of something about half a mile away. Looked like it might be close to the top of the ridge to their north. "That ain't where Dog was heading," he muttered. He stopped rocking the box and walked back to their cabin, grabbed his rifle and knelt down behind some wooden boxes, watching the side of the hill.

"There it is, again," he muttered, picking up the reflection of something. "Damn bandits coming to take what ain't theirs to take. Well, by damn, they ain't taking what's our'n." He knew whatever it was he saw was way out of range of his rifle, but wondered if he should make an advance on what he was seeing. "Don't know where Dog keeps that telescope of his." He was in the shadows and kept watching.

"No bandito would be working alone," he mused. "So that means somebody is sitting up there watching me while another or two are working their way down toward me. So, Mr. Snake, if I just sit still, they'll come right to me." He settled down behind the boxes and continued keeping track of what was reflecting, and watching for any kind of movement closer.

***

"Butters said there were two men but there's only one." Ayres was muttering, watching Snake work the rocker box. Ayres was the kind of man who did what he was hired to do, no questions asked. He was hired to kill two men who had abused Jimmie Butters and that's what he would do. But this was just one man. Not being head of the class, Ayres was confused.

"Should have brought that stupid Butters up here with me. Don't know what to do." He continued muttering, watched as Snake walked to their cabin. Ayres decided to walk on down and provoke the single man, kill him, kill Butters, and ride on into El Paso with the rest of Butters' money. "I was gonna have to kill that fool anyway," he chuckled.

Snake continued watching the reflection, wishing that Dog-Man would return. "Well, hell, I can't just sit in the cabin and watch something shiny when I got gold in the rocker box out there," he said right out loud. He put the rifle back on its pegs and walked back to his work. "If we had a way to crush these rocks more, we'd sure get more gold," he muttered, his mind back on the job.

He spotted the man slowly advancing on their mine and went back for the rifle. "So," he muttered. "I was right this time. Where the hell are you,

Dog?" He watched this heavy-set man with a wild red beard and long, stringy red hair walk slowly into the work area. "Hold it up right there, stranger. Watcha doin here?"

"Need some water. Don't be gettin' testy. Wouldn't deny a stranger water, would ya?" Ayres didn't seem to care whether or not Snake was carrying a rifle. "There's little water in this country."

"Man don't go walkin' alone in this country, neither," Snake said. "Why don't you slowly unbuckle that gun belt you're wearin' and I'll see to it you get some water."

"You're a pushy bastard, aren't you," Ayres said. He turned just slightly, as if to unbuckle the belt, and pulled his pistol. Snake felt it coming more that saw the move, fired the rifle from his hip and rolled off to the side, levered another round, and fired again. He saw Clint Ayres' revolver hanging loosely in his hand, the man doubled over with a gunshot to his midsection.

Ayres tried to take a step forward and fell to his knees. He looked up, almost with a question in his eyes, and fell forward into the dirt and rocks. Snake got to his feet and walked to the body from behind, kicked the pistol away, and using his rifle and his boot, turned Ayres over.

In just minutes Dog-man came running in. "What's all the shootin'? Who's that?"

"Don't know, Dog. Never seen him before. Just walked in all tough talk and nasty."

"So you just killed him?"

"Yeah," Snake stammered a bit. "Seems he was trying to kill me, so I killed him first. Seemed like the right thing to do. You know, at the time."

Dog-man was laughing. "I think you're right. Man don't just go walkin' around in this country, Snake. Which way did he come in from? Let's back-track him and make sure he was alone, eh?"

They dragged Ayres body off into a pile of rocks and a wad of money fell out of his pockets on the way. "Oh, oh," Snake said. "I don't like what I'm thinkin'." He picked up the wad and counted it out. "Four hundred dollars, Dog. Now, this ain't gonna sound right. A man goes walking in the desert with four hundred dollars in his pocket, finds me and wants to pick a fight over whether I give him some water."

"Yup," Dog-man said. "You're right. Doesn't sound right." They made their way down off their ridge, through stands of towering rocks and almost walked up on Jimmie Butters at the campsite.

"See who that is?" Snake whispered when they ducked back behind a stand of rock. "That's our water hole, too. That bastard paid the dead one to kill us, Dog."

"Do believe you're right, Snake, old man. This puts us in a mighty tough place. We're working a mine that may not be ours, and buried the man that probably owned it. Now we got another dead man we think was hired to kill us, and we're looking at the man that probably hired him. What's really bad, we don't want nobody to know we've got this mine and all that gold."

"Can't just chase Butters off. He's the kind will come back until we kill him," Snake said. "Think he'd be serious missed in Las Cruces?"

"You mean if he didn't come back? Remember what the man at the mercantile store said about him. I think they'd be grateful if we didn't give him that opportunity." They chuckled and Dog continued. "Back me up, old partner, I'm gonna put the fear of the devil in that fool."

Dog-man stepped out from behind the boulders and saw Jimmie Butters about a hundred feet away, pouring a cup of coffee. "Hey, Jimmie Butters. Well, just damn me, what are you doing up here in this neck of the woods? Why, I'll just be. Well, glad you made your little walk out of the desert. How you doin'?"

Butters dropped both the coffee pot and the tin cup and stood straight up. He wanted to grab his Colt and couldn't. He stood, froze to the spot and watched in horror as Dog-man slowly walked toward him, that big rifle cradled and ready, one long slow step at a time, talking up a storm the whole way. "You're supposed to be dead. I heard the shots."

"You want to know something funny, Jimmie? I heard those shot, too. Seems Snake was a whole bunch better than your man. You paid that worn out old man four hundred dollars to kill me and old Snake? Just four hundred? Damn, that really hurts, way down inside, to think that's all you think we're worth. After all we've been through, too."

Butters turned to run and found a pistol shoved in his face. Snake had worked all the way around the camp and came up behind Butters as Dog-man kept his attention continually talking. "Not today, chum." Snake motioned the man over to a log and had him sit down after relieving him of his pistol. He found a knife, too and took it.

"Been looking for one like this," he said, tucking it into his waistband. "What do we do now, Dog?

Think that old horse of his would find its way back to Las Cruces again?"

They tied Jimmie Butters in the saddle and Snake ran up to the mine, saddled his horse, and led Butters down the trail, they thought led back toward Las Cruces. "Leave the trail and get into the mountains somewhere and just leave him. Use your pistol to scare off the horse. Maybe he'll go home, maybe not. Don't come back until tomorrow."

Snake was laughing as he and Butters rode off. "What are you gonna be doing?"

"Gonna bury the big old scary killer," Dog-man laughed.

11

"You can't just ride off and leave me tied up like this," Jimmie Butters cried out. "Please." Snake had gone cross-country for several hours, from one canyon, across a ridge, through little valleys, and was far from any known road or trail.

"You've played your last conniving hand, Jimmie Butters. Me and old Dog-man started out bein' nice with you and you took advantage right from the start. Time to pay the fiddler, Jimmie." Snake pulled the bridle from the horse, slapped its hip hard, and when it trotted off, fired two shots into the air, getting the horse in a lope.

"Saw a monkey tied to a dog, once," Snake muttered, watching Butters bounce in the saddle, his hands tied behind his back. "Didn't think it was funny then, don't think it's funny now."

I wonder why some people have to be like that? Now, if somebody wants to be ignorant and gets fleeced at the card table that ain't the same as what Jimmie Butters was doin'. That's why me and old Dog have vowed not to be outlaws. Hope this is goodbye, Jimmie Butters.

Snake looked at the sun, knew he'd never make it back to the mine before dark, and started back at a leisurely walk. "There are times a man gots to do things that just aren't right," he muttered. "'Course we wouldn't have this here old mine if it weren't for us trying to sell that map back in Deadwood," he laughed right out loud.

The laugh wasn't as sincere as he would have liked it to be. He remembered the humiliation by way of the Deadwood Sheriff and his deputies. "Don't never want to be considered an outlaw again." The thought of what he and Dog-man had just done to Jimmie Butters slipped into his thinking and he tried to brush it off. It wouldn't go away.

"It weren't wrong," he said to his horse. "It weren't. Jimmie Butters was an outlaw, paid money to have us kilt, by damn. We had every right to make him pay for that. By damn, what we should have done is just kilt him ourselves. Ain't no law out here in the desert or the mountains, and we had to protect ourselves." It took just a phrase or two and Snake was fully justified in what the two had done.

The day wasn't cooling off despite the lateness and he rode at a slow walk for another hour, hoping to find someplace cool to camp for the night. He kept thinking about their mine and the man responsible for it. "Man died hard after working hard, and along come old Snake and Dog, finding what that man died for. Well, we didn't kill him and we didn't steal nothin'. Nope, we found it honest and true."

He was fully justified, now, and found a little nest by green trees for the night. "Ain't no way that

Dog-man and I are gonna be outlaws. Sellin' a map to a dummy ain't a big old crime, but what Jimmie Butters did is."

Supper was grouse over hot coals, coffee, and a sip or three of whiskey, and he was on the trail as the sky lightened enough to see. He was at the mine by noon meal. "Get that varmint deep, did you?"

"Deep as I could without using dynamite." Dog-man smiled and held out a rock he found while digging the grave. "Had to pick another gravesite. Just look at this." The specimen of quartz had a worm like thread of gold right through it. "Got several more just like this one. We got us a real problem, now."

Snake stirred the fire alive in the old cookstove in the cabin. "Let's have some bacon and biscuits and talk about this, Dog-man. Winter ain't too far off and we're high enough in these mountains that it'll be snow and ice country for sure." He mixed up a batch of biscuits, fried a pan full of sidemeat, and brewed fresh coffee, humming some kind of Texas gibberish the whole time.

"Don't much care for winter," Dog-man said. He was sitting at the table nursing a glass of whiskey "We got three good mules, an extra horse, now, and no way on earth knowing how far away El Paso is. Gotta get out of these mountains before the snows come." He looked up to Snake. "Whatchew doin' now?"

"Well, seems like we got nothing but good news, so I'm making this meal a celebration." He used the pan full of bacon grease, added a dusting of flour and let it darken some, then added water and made a fine gravy to pour over the biscuits. "Been cravin' some Texas food, Dog-man."

Plans were made to dry wash everything that had been dug up, get the gold bagged, and pack up for El Paso. "We could be on the road in two or three days, Dog. If that fool Jimmie Butters lives through his ordeal and tries to bring another assassin after us, we'll be long gone."

"You're right about that, but the mine will still be here. Sure wouldn't want him to get this place."

"We have our notices posted, that's all we can do." Snake said. "Still don't know what country we're in, though, and with someone like Butters, a little thing like being legal or not don't mean a thing. If we're in Mexico, our notices don't mean nothin' anyways."

They were laughing as they walked out to the large mound of ore that needed to be run through the rockers. "That's about a week's worth of ore, Snake. You rock for a couple of hours and I'll spell you. I'm gonna clean up and get things ready for packing. We're gonna need every one of our animals. That gold's gonna be heavy."

**

It was a full seven days before the boys got on the road. Snake was leading two mules and Dog-man's train was a mule and a horse. The pack animals were loaded heavy and the trek down off their ridge top mine site was slow. "We'll take that road east and it should lead us to El Paso."

"That's what we think," Snake laughed. "Dog, we don't have any idea where our mine is, where Las Cruces is, and now, you're saying you know where

El Paso is."

"I said should. Didn't say would," Dog-man laughed.

The days were long and hot, the road slowly bringing them out of whatever mountains they were in. They were resting, having a mid-day bite to eat. "Looks like this road drops off this ridge and snakes its way down to that valley out there," Snake said. He brought his tin cup up for a drink of coffee when a bullet ripped it right out of his grasp. Hot coffee splashed everywhere.

They hit the dirt, rifles in hand, and rolled, crawled, and scratched their way behind anything handy. Dog-man got behind a rock just as a bullet screamed over his head. I got my rifle, you bastard. Shoot again so I can see where you are. Dog-man had a banged up elbow from rolling around in the rocks, and he was angry about the ripped shirt, too. Come on, show me where you are.

Snake found himself trying to get under a thorny bush that fought back, and instead rolled behind a jumble of rocks. "Stick your head out there again," Snake called out. "Maybe I can see where those shots are coming from." Both men knew there were more men shooting than there were of them.

"You're a funny man," Dog-man yelled back. But the idea stuck, and Dog-man pulled his hat off, stuck it on the end of his rifle barrel, and eased it out from the rock. The bullet ripped the hat right off the barrel and Dog-man watched it roll about in the dirt. "That was my best hat, Snake."

"It was your only hat, Dog." Snake saw where the shot came from, kept a close eye and it wasn't long before someone edged out from behind a puny little tree. Snake had a good aim and fired. The shot was answered by screams in Spanish. "Got him," Snake yelled. "Sneaky devil wrecked my coffee cup, Dog. I got him."

"Yeah, you did. I got a tore up shirt, bloody elbow, and wrecked hat. I don't like whoever it is you shot."

It got very quiet after the commotion of multiple gunshots and finally Snake broke the calm. "Maybe you better go see if that feller is dead."

"Yeah, maybe I'll stroll over and get my good hat first," Dog-man chuckled. "No, it's your turn, Snake."

"Okay, sounds like we need a meeting of the board of directors of this partnership. Compromise. Let's both go see." Snake tried his best to hold in his chuckles, sound sincere as all get out, but of course, couldn't.

As the two slowly made their way to where the wounded bandit should be, they heard horses being ridden off. "There were three of them," Snake murmured. "Be careful, Dog. He might not be dead."

"Yeah. Why don't you walk up on him, then." Dog-man chuckled.

"Naw, you go ahead. I already shot him once." Snake walked over to the edge of the ridge, where the road dropped off to make its long way to the valley. He could see dust well down the trail. "The others are hightailing it, Dog."

Dog-man eased up to what he thought was a wounded Mexican bandito and found a dead Mexican bandito. "He gave it up, Snake. Let's get moving."

"I want you to see this first," Snake answered. He

was standing on the ridge top, pointing down to the valley. "See? Way out there. Two buildings? You got that spyglass handy?"

Dog-man ran to one of the pack mules and found the spy-glass and joined Snake. "Yup," he said. He was braced against a rock, trying to hold the glass steady. "Two buildings. Think one might be a stables. Other one has hitching racks in front. By God, it's a saloon, Snake. We just hit pay dirt again."

Snake grabbed the glass and looked at the buildings and the road leading to it. "There's another road that those buildings are on, not this one. This one crosses that road up this way. The road the buildings are on must be the El Paso road. Bigger, has had more traffic. We're really off from where we thought we would be. Miles off, Dog."

"I wonder how much of the traffic is bandit traffic. We need to go that way, we surely need whatever they be sellin'," he laughed, "and we need to be damn careful." Dog-man walked back toward his horse. "time's a wastin', Snake."

Snake grabbed the dead man's rifle and gun belt and mounted up. "The others went down this road, Dog. Let's ride sharp, old man. Doubt they had any idea what's in these packs. Probably just rode up on us, accidental like."

"Hope they ain't part of a gang. We get to or near the bottom of this road, let's make camp so that we ride in fresh tomorrow, not all beat up like." The single track trail worked around hills and valleys, mostly down, and it was near dark when they found a decent place to set up camp.

"We ever done anything that didn't include trouble, Dog?" Snake spread his bedroll alongside the fire ring and nursed a sip or two from their last bottle. "Even stoppin' for a cold beer and we had to watch a man get shot dead."

"We're just travelers in this long road called life, Snake. Seems like our fellow travelers
are more apt to be trouble makers. Most of our troubles have been when we're in a town or village."

"No, Dog, it's when we run into other people. We gotta learn to stay away from people, that's all."

12

Side meat and biscuits, hot coffee and fresh water from a welcome spring, and the boys were ready to ride back into civilization. "This was a good camp, Snake. Glad you spotted that spring. I'll be looking for cold beer in just a few miles.

When they got to the bottom of the long winding trail and out onto the valley floor, the riding was much easier on all the animals. Dog-man had his elbow patched up, and was wearing his hat with two holes in it. One where the bullet went in, one where it came out. "We'll come to that bigger road in a couple more miles, and then it looked like it was maybe five more to the saloon. Maybe I can buy a new shirt and hat, Snake," he chuckled.

"We surely don't want to be flashing our gold, Dog. Stuff brings out the worst in a man. Just look what it's done to us. We kilt a man was paid to kill us, and maybe kilt the man what did the payin'"

"I love the way you talk, Snake. When we make our way back to the mine, come spring, I mean, we need to bring some kind of machine that breaks up the rock more than we've been doing."

"Man at the mercantile in Las Cruces talked about a rock crusher, but the one he talked about needed power. I met some Mexicans had a silver mine once. They had what they called an arastra, or something like that. Mule did the working. Walked around in a circle all day, dragging a big rock through the ore rocks. Seemed to work."

"Let's find out more about that when we get to El Paso. How come we never saw that saloon?"

"Come in from the other side," Snake said. "Couldn't see it or these other roads from way up where the mine is. We were miles from that ridge where them boys shot your hat. Bet them banditos will be at that saloon. Bet we're deep in Mexico."

"You are a bettin' fool, Snake." They were on the El Paso highway now, probably within a couple of miles of the buildings. "If it's a saloon, I say we walk right in and order cold beer, but if it's a cantina, I say we very carefully walk right in and order cold beer."

"You can't say your name in less than fifty words, can you, Dog?"

The road had sage and many desert spiny plants along its sides, passed through deep arroyos, some with mud in the bottoms. "Looks like at least two horses are traveling in front of us, Dog. Probably the bastard that shot your hat. We'll look for recently used horses when we get there."

"I don't think those bandits know where our mine is. They just lucked up on finding us."

"Sure hope you're right." Snake sat straight up in the saddle, and pointed. "Dust, Dog. Riders coming right at us. Ride for that deep arroyo to your left," he yelled leading his caravan off the highway. The gully was at least twelve feet deep, cut by raging water.

They settled their animals, grabbed rifles and scrambled up to the edge of the embankment so they could see the roadway. There was enough brush along the sides that they were well hidden. "Two riders, Dog," Snake whispered. "One looks to be hurt. Our boys, Dog. Let's get 'em. He shouldered his rifle while Dog-man eased up with his at the ready. Snake fired first and the lead rider flew out of his saddle, landing in a heap.

Dog-man brought the wounded one down hard, and the boys raced to make sure the bandits were dead. They dragged the bodies off the trail, unsaddled the bandit's horses and added them to their train. "Making money on horses when we get to El Paso," Snake chuckled.

"Look at this," Dog-man said. He was holding a crude map. "Writing's in Mexican, but it looks like those boys have been watching us for some time." The map seemed to show the way to their mine from the trail where they were ambushed. "Good thing this is in our hands, now. Help us find our way back," he laughed. He looked at one of the dead men. "Gracias, Señor."

"We got cold beer waiting less than a half hour down the road, Dog. Hope those shots weren't heard by anyone." The bodies and tack were shoved under some brush in the arroyo, newly found 'wild' horses part of the pack train, and they made dust. They were more than two miles out and more than thirsty the whole way.

***

"You first," Snake said after they tied off their strings. "At least we think we're in the U.S." The little shack had a big sign out front and the hitch rack was empty. Georgia's Bordertown Saloon and Stables welcomed travelers on the El Paso route from Mexico. Cottonwood trees gave some relief from the heat, and the main building had half a dozen or more open windows allowing what breeze might be around to pass through.

Snake was looking around, first at the sun, then at the road they came in on, and back at the sun. "We've been minin' in Mexico, my friend. I won't tell nobody if you won't," he laughed. "If that's the road to El Paso, we gotta ride through Juarez and across the river into El Paso. We are way south of where we thought we were."

"Better be gettin' a cold beer, supplies that we can, and be back on the road fast," Dog-man said. "This is bandit country if I ever seen it."

"Gets mighty hot down here in the valley. Feels like it's still summer, Dog," Snake said. "I'll back your play." Dog-man walked in the dirty saloon slow, his rifle in hand. It was a large, dark and smoky room with a short bar along half of one wall. There were two men at a card table near the back, two others stood at the bar, and all eyes were on him.

A short, rather heavy woman with too much lip rouge and enough bracelets and necklaces to give her a list when she walked, said, "Howdy stranger," in a low, whiskey influenced voice. "You must be the one that shot up that Mexican. Well, first drink's on me, cuz that fool has been here for the last time." She grabbed a bottle and handed it to Dog-man.

The men at the table chuckled at the comment but the two at the bar were quiet, looking Dog-man up and down. He saw that each man wore a pistol and large knife, and each had a rifle across the bar. I better remember what Snake said. Every time we run into people we get in trouble. He held back a chuckle.

Dog-man turned and motioned for Snake to come on in. "We got jumped by a couple of road bandits and chased 'em off. How long a ride is it to El Paso?" He took a drink of the hot whiskey Georgia had poured and knew he needed a cold beer. "And a couple of cold beers. Maybe a barrel," he laughed.

"Beer's about as cold as the whiskey," she laughed along with the four other men in the bar. She had a bone-chilling, almost scream of a laugh that made Dog-man and Snake step back a bit. "El Paso, you say? Well, you're on the right road, anyways. Maybe ten days, that way." She nodded toward the north. "Some have made in less. You boys got a big pack string. Been out for a time, I'd guess."

"Came down from Deadwood," Snake said. "Got family in El Paso, at least I do. Better to say I did. Seems I now own a small cattle operation, so Dog, here, and me's goin' home." He drained the glass of whiskey, took the warm beer down, and smiled. "Guess we'd best plan on ten days, Dog-man. We got flour and coffee but ain't had much for meat for some time."

"Since you have the premier location on this

highway," Dog-man said, "I hope you sell trail supplies. Like dried meat for instance." He smiled and Georgia gave another chilling round of laughter.

"And cigars," Snake interjected. Georgia produced a canister or cigars and the boys each took several and had her pour them another glass of beer.

"We offer some good dried and smoked beef," she chuckled. "Had a herd come through a while back and they seemed to have left a beef or two, accidental like," and that horrible screaming laugh rang through the saloon. "Ain't bad if you boil it good before you start chewing."

Snake noticed a couple of the men at the card table were trying to tell him no, shaking their heads. He smiled, knowing it was going to be the worst beef he'd ever had, but needed it none the less. "We'll take ten pounds if you've got it."

He noticed there were far more hats hanging on hat racks around the dirty saloon than there were men. On the way in he spotted several horses in the corrals along with some saddled and hitched at racks. He drank his beer and nudged Dog-man. "Better get moving, old man. Got lots of sunlight left and many miles to go."

Georgia had a well wrapped package of beef for them, a horrible but almost friendly smile, and wished them well. The price she charged for the beef, cigars, whiskey, and beer was reasonable, and the boys sauntered out to their pack string. "There's two bottles of whiskey in that meat bundle, Snake. That'll make ten days go a little easier. Shoulda said thanks to Jimmie Butters for that cash we took from our killer."

"There's more men than we saw, Dog." Snake wasn't laughing. "We got to ride hard, get off the road after dark and make it a cold camp tonight. That's a bandit's camp if I ever seen one." They rode out at a strong trot. "There were at least eight horses and we only saw four men."

"Sure glad you see these things, Snake. I thought we were on the Texas side of the border. Those Mexicans must have been real loud-mouthed and these guys think we're loaded with gold."

"We ain't nowhere near Texas, Dog. It's ten days to Ciudad Juarez on a road that ain't that much used. Those boys will be on our tail soon, you can count on it. They'll want us to get out and away from the cantina, though. Bad for business," he chuckled. "Bet they raid the Mexican ranches for horses and sell them across the border."

They rode well into sunset, keeping a close watch behind, moved off the trail, crossed two deep arroyos and settled under an outcrop for the night. They were probably a half mile or more off the main road.

They gnawed on tough beef and drank water for supper. They were in a patch of sparse grass so the animals fared better than the boys. "Bet we hear hoof beats before long, Dog," Snake chuckled. "You take first watch, but wake me for sure if something comes up."

"Georgia didn't mention that the beef those old boys rode off and left was a ten year old bull, did she? Ain't never had a piece of meat this tough. Sleep good, Snake, cuz we're gonna have to fight our way out of this."

"As long as they don't see where we moved off

the roadway, it'll be fine. That beef just needs a good half hour in boiling water, Dog. Can't say I've had worse, though."

***

The outlaw gang came by at least an hour later and apparently missed where Dog-man and Snake left the road. "Sounded like four or five riders, Snake. Maybe more. I thought it best to wake you up, old man, even though they kept right on going. They were in a lope probably expecting to ride right up on us." Snake wiped the sleep from his eyes and nodded.

"It'll be sunrise before they discover they ain't following nobody," Snake chuckled. "Let's really confuse 'em, Dog. Pack up, and we'll head out but stay off the highway. They'll come high-ballin' back this way when they find there aren't any fresh tracks in the sand."

The animals were packed, horses were saddled, and they were moving in half an hour. The night was bright with stars, there were few trees, and they were able to pick their way cross country with little difficulty. They used arroyos and gullies to stay out of sight, tried to stay a half mile to a mile off the roadway, found a spring on the side of a rocky hill, and watched the sun come up. "Sure could use a cup of coffee," Dog-man said. "We'll need to have some kind of plan if those men find us, Snake. Got any ideas?"

"Yup. Shoot 'em and ride on." He looked around at a wild and beautiful landscape, colored by a rapidly rising sun, and pointed at a stand of rocks several miles in front of them. "Palisades like that are a fortress with our names etched and beckoning," Snake said. "Just look at that. Spires of rock, standing like soldiers on parade, waiting to protect us. We can shelter the string and let 'em come on at us." Snake almost sounded gleeful describing what he saw.

"My friend the poet," Dog-man said. Was it your ma or your pa taught you to talk that way?"

"My old pa weren't worth much when it came to workin', Dog. Didn't like feelin' the hurt in his shoulders and back, didn't much care for dirty hands, but he had a box full of books that he read to us from every night after supper." Snake sounded sad, talking about his family. "Been a long time since I thought much of them. Well, let's get movin', Dog."

"We sure as hell can't outrun anyone with all these pack animals laden with gold." Dog-man led them across the open desert at a trot. The ground was broken and jumbled, rocks of every size scattered about along with nasty vegetation out to scratch the life right out of the boys and their animals.

"And tough bull meat," Snake laughed.

They were within half a mile of their fortress when Dog-man spotted the dust and then riders racing down the highway. "They'll find where we got off the road and come storming after us, Snake. Better step it up some," he said.

"It'll take 'em an hour, Dog. Let's find a good place to take a stand and get the animals settled in. Gotta protect them and what they're carryin'." The ride was fast, the animals arguing some but not that much. They got 'em hobbled or tied off, and the boys spent some time making their fortresses. "This is good, Dog. We can see for miles and they can't see us or shoot through rocks."

He remembered when he felt safe in his rock hide-away west of Penny Station. Those Apaches put a bunch of shots into those rocks and the bullets careened about for what seemed like minutes. "Don't get nested in a cave like area, Dog. Those bullets bounce around like angry bees protecting their queen."

13

"Georgia and her boys must have had an idea of what we're carrying," Dog-man said. They had their rifles and pistols fully loaded, extra ammunition close by, and watched the dust of five riders spread out across the desert, riding slowly toward their fortress. Dust and the mist of desert heat shrouded the far mountains in a curtain of gloom, Snake thought, as he watched the scene unfold.

"Ain't having much trouble following the trail we left for 'em," Dog-man said. "Our six animals leave pretty clear sign."

"Maybe, but I'll bet it was the Mexicans bragging about their damn map and then coming back in all shot up. Then us coming in loaded down and with one of their animals. Hell, Dog, we all but invited these boys to the party."

Dog-man had his spy-glass in hand, watching the line of riders come across the open desert. The morning sun already had the sands heated and it made for waves in the glass's view. "Looks like one of the horses is lame, Snake. Those two guys standing at the bar are leading this group in. Don't recognize the others. That lame horse is being held back some."

Snake pulled a cigar, bit off the end, and got it lit. "Don't matter if there's ten of 'em, Dog. Gonna be death writ in that sand." Snake took a long pull on the cigar and smiled. "You ever been in this position, Dog?"

"Having five men come down on you, bent on killin' you? No, Snake, I ain't never been in this position. I hope this isn't a lead-in to one of your Texas yarns."

"Ain't what I'm talking about," the lean Texan drawled. "I mean, sittin' here in the middle of some desert with more money than you could ever spend. Damn it, son, we're rich and I'm gonna get testy with those boys out there if they try to take it from us."

"First time I've actually let it hit me, Snake. We got gold is all that I've thought. Now you're gettin' me all riled. Ain't gonna let Georgia's boys take our gold, no sir, I ain't." He glared at the five riders spread across in front of them.

"As far as being chased by five killers, nope, ain't never happened. As far as having a string of mules carrying gold that's ours? Nope, never happened." They were laughing at what Dog-man said, and scowling at what they were looking at.

Snake watched as the line of riders spread out wide in their approach. "They don't know where we are but you can bet they think we're in these rocks," he chuckled.

"Let 'em get as close as skeeter bites, Snake. This ain't the time to get riled."

"You just said you was riled." Snake was chuckling and Dog-man turned away from him.

Dog-man watched as four of the riders dismounted, handing the reins to the man on the lame horse. "I guess that means they think they know where we are."

"Well, hell, Dog, they're close enough for my rifle. You still got your good-shootin' eye? You ain't lost that again?" He didn't wait for an answer, fired once and watched one of the outlaws grab his chest and fall to his knees. The other three hit the dirt, scrambling for anything to get under. The one with the bullet in his heart went face first in the sand.

Dog-man fired at one man who was on his hands and knees trying to get under a scrawny and very thorny bush. He saw him stop, then just lay flat, not moving. Two down and one with the horses. Return fire from the two remaining was scattered all over the rocks. "At least they don't know where we are," Dog-man said.

They held back their fire and saw quick glimpses of the outlaws as they tried to find better cover. They weren't able to move forward, only side to side, and exposed themselves to rifle fire with every move. "One of them's is gonna get tired of this and try to move forward," Dog-man whispered.

"One of 'em's by that bush with all the yellow stuff on it," Snake said. "I can see part of his boot sticking out." He took a long slow aim, a long slow squeeze, and heard the bullet slam into the man's foot. "Look at him try to run," Snake was laughing too hard to shoot. "Get him, Dog."

The man was jumping up and down, trying to run, falling in the dirt, and Dog-man took a quick shot, missed, and the sand and rocks being spit up gave the wounded man plenty of reason to keep trying. The man was crying out in pain with every step, not able to duck behind anything and Dog-man squeezed off another round to put him out of his misery.

"One more close by and one with the horses," Dog-man muttered. Keeping track of your enemy during a firefight was important to the man. Dog-man was searching for that fourth man and saw Snake take another long aim. He looked out across the desert at what he might be aiming at and saw the man with the horses about four hundred yards out. That'd be one hell of a shot. He has a good rifle, but that's a long way out there.

The rifle cracked and it was a second or two before Dog-man saw the man's horse rear up, stagger, and fall. "Damn it," Snake said. "Wanted the man, not the horse. Damn it. Well, ain't nobody got hold of any of those horses, now. You're the sharp-shooter, Dog. Kill him."

"Yes, boss," Dog-man chuckled. Don't like shooting a man that ain't shooting back but we can't let him get back to Georgia's bandit camp, either. Dog-man was flat on the ground using a rock to hold the rifle steady, and dropped the man with a shot through his chest. "Got him."

The horses didn't run off, of course. They milled about, grazing, and the boys were concentrating on where that fifth man was. "Man must know he's in a terrible fix, Dog. Ain't got a horse close by, ain't got a friend in the world, and got him two ugly old boys what don't much care for him, lookin' to kill him dead."

"Bad fix, Snake. Stick your head out some. Worked last time," Dog-man chuckled. "It's your turn, partner."

"Got a better idea." Snake picked up a big rock, reared back, and heaved it well out to his right. It banged and clattered in the rocks and sure enough drew a shot from the outlaw.

"I got him," Dog-man said. He snuck down through the rocks, staying low and out of sight until he was about twenty yards or so from the brush the outlaw was trying to hide behind. He signaled Snake to throw another rock. Worked once, why not again? Come on you bad boy, take your shot.

Snake heaved another big rock, the outlaw was on his knees, rifle up and died with a bullet through his head. Dumb as a coot. We're still ten days from El Paso. How long before Georgia sends another crew to take our gold? Kinda wish old Snake hadn't told us we're rich. Ain't never even thought of bein' rich. I ain't gonna act like the rich men I've known. He chuckled. But I am gonna buy a new shirt and hat.

***

"Think there'll be more of 'em coming down on us?" Dog-man couldn't get it out of his head that Snake had seen many more horses than the five carrying the crew that tried to ride them down. "Think she's the boss or just offers a safe place?"

"You got lots of questions, Dog. Need to come up with some of the answers. Cain't be depending on me, like this." They were back on the main road to El Paso after burying the dead ones and scattering their horses. "If I was an outlaw, which I'll never be, we agreed to that, I'd sure be wanting some of this gold."

"I don't much care for the idea of having cold camps for ten days in a row. No biscuits. No coffee. I won't miss that bull meat, though."

Snake laughed and took a quick look down the road behind them. "No, no, no. We'll move well off the road before dark and make camps where they can't be seen from the road. Ain't no more cold camps unless we're fighting off the whole Apache Nation. These arroyos are good for hiding fires."

"They're good for carryin' thousands of gallons of water at a high speed too," Dog-man said. "Don't want to get caught in one during a thunder storm."

"Well, then, we'll just have to be careful," Snake said. "I'll yell if I hear any thunder." Dog-man just shook his head and hid his smile.

After the second night with no sign of outlaws chasing them, they didn't worry too much about the crew from Georgia's, stayed vigilant for anyone else coming up on them, and rode into Ciudad Juarez on the eleventh day. El Paso, Texas sits on one side of the Rio Grande and Ciudad Juarez, Mexico sits on the other. "Looks to be all one town, Snake."

"I've seen about as much of this country as I want. Didn't know just how nice we had it at the mine, Dog. Let's ride on across the river and keep our eyes open for anyone looking like they want what we have."

They made their way to the center of the sprawling Mexican village, walked their string through the plaza and onto the street leading to the Rio Grande and the bridge into El Paso. "Can't tell one town from the other," Snake drawled out. "Just as many Americans in Juarez as Mexicans in El Paso. Let's find an assay office."

"Need to. The sooner we get rid of this gold the safer we gonna be. Ain't exactly a little village we got here." Each had a string of animals but few along the street paid them much attention. "Looks like we're not the only ones packing in or out. I need a bath and a beer."

"Been meanin' to talk to you about that," Snake laughed. "Sittin' down wind's been pitiful." He pointed at a little adobe building with hitching racks out front, sitting off by itself. "I think that sign means food, and I know cerveza means beer. Let's eat."

"Good, cuz I been worrying about something else we need to talk about. Those horses are sure to go back to Georgia's, at least some of 'em, and that means we got a problem as far as us getting back to our mine. We gotta pass by Georgia's and we ain't gonna be much welcome."

They found a table in the crowded little cantina and settled in. "Looks like half the town's in here, Dog. Hope that means the food is good and beer is cold." A little Mexican girl, no more than ten years old came to the table. "You speak English, honey?" Snake gave her a big smile that Dog-man figured scared her half to death.

"Sure, mister. My names Carlita. Whatcha want?"

"I like this kid," Snake said. "Lots of whatever the cook thinks is best and keep bringing us cold beer until we say no more."

"Okay, sure, mister," she said, and ran to the

bar and then into the kitchen just outside the back door. In moments a heavy man with long stringy hair and beard came to the table with two mugs of beer. The beer was almost cool, the welcome was warm.

"You boys been on the trail for some time," he said. "You be nice to my little Carlita."

"This your Cantina?" Dog-man asked. "You don't look like no Mexican I ever saw. Carlita does, though. We might be trail dirty and rough, old man, but we ain't trouble makers or outlaws."

"No, we ain't," Snake said.

"I ain't Mexican but Carlita's mama is. We get some trouble in here sometimes. I'll bring you more beer. Just wave," he said and ambled back toward the bar.

"Straight forward old man," Snake said. "Guess that's best runnin' a joint like this."

The girl emerged with two large bowls of food, one for each of them, buffalo horn spoons, and a stack of tortillas. "Esta muy bueno," she said. "Very good, mister."

"Thank you, Carlita. Muchas gracias, pretty girl." Snake said, and she danced away, laughing. "She won't get much taller than five feet and be a hundred and fifty pounds before she's sixteen, Dog. Make a man a wonderful wife, too. Rode with a feller had a Mexican wife. Got fat, never quit smilin', and raised mules. Good man." Dog-man just chuckled at the commentary.

The food was hotter than anything Dog-man had ever eaten and he watched as Snake shoveled spoons full down. Dog-man drank more beer than he planned just to keep his mouth from catching fire. "How do you eat this stuff?" He asked.

"This is pure Texas, my friend. I'm home." He watched Dog-man wipe tears away, drink an entire mug of beer in one swallow, and laughed. "Better get used to it. We gonna be here for a while." He dipped into his bowl and came out with a whole roasted chili, held it for Dog-man to see. "Just place it in your mouth, so," he said, taking the fiery offering in his mouth. "Chew it good and long to get all the flavor, and swallow it down."

"Not today, Snake. Not today, but I gotta say this is damn good." He sat back laughing. "Sure beats dried bull."

They paid, gave little Carlita a generous tip, and told the barman they'd be back. "Good food is hard to find, Dog-man. I think our best bet is to find a place to camp with all our animals, and find the assay office in the morning. It's gettin' late."

He watched a big wagon come into town with four outriders. The wagon was running with six up and Snake yelled out, "Hey, that's Cletus Kilpatrick driving that rig. Come on, Dog, we got to follow him."

It wasn't hard to know where the big heavy rig was going. Just follow the dust, and the boys found themselves in the center of bustling El Paso. "There he is," Snake pointed. The six-up were stopped in front of Clausen Brothers, Assayers. Gold Bought and Sold. They started to ride up alongside the big rig and one of the outriders stopped them by leveling a double barreled shotgun at them.

"Hold up, gents. That's as close as you get." He was long and thin, wore a white duster like the other outriders, had a long mustache that blew in the wind, and eyes that told the boys he would shoot both of them.

"Just wanted to say hello to your driver. We ain't outlaws." Snake was smiling, held his hands wide away from any weapon. "Old Cletus there is a long-time friend."

The guard turned half way around. "Clete," He yelled. "You know these yahoos. Say the word and I'll drop 'em." He turned back and made sure both hammers were cocked back.

"Don't shoot 'em, Finnegan, they be friends. Hel-lo Snake and to you too, Dog-man. Nice surprise. Park that string of yours and let's have a beer." He climbed down from the high seat of the freight wagon. "You boys just get in town?"

"Been here almost an hour, Cletus," Snake drawled out. "We got a story to tell you. You gonna be here awhile? Got to find a camp and get these animals protected. Looks like you got the same problem."

"I think we share the problem." Cletus yelled out for Ed Twombley to come join him. "These are the boys that tied old Three-fingers to the tree, Ed. Have your men get this wagon in the barn back there, and take their pack train in, too. Same kind of protection. George Dawson wouldn't want anything less. Get that done, come join us at the El Dorado Cantina for a beer."

"Glad to meet you boys. Heard some wonderful stories. Nice pack train you got here. We'll protect it."

"Tell me about this protection," Dog-man said when they got their beer and sat around a table at the El Dorado. "That's a mean bunch you ride with, Mr. Twombley."

"Meanest bunch in the territory," Cletus said.

"Twombley is head of security for Dawson Express. We're moving gold to Clausen Brothers. We have that barn behind the assay office fitted out almost like a hotel. You boys can bunk with us and we'll all protect all the gold."

"Hear anything about Jimmie Butters before you left Las Cruces?" Snake was sure the man died, and it bothered him the way he just rode off, leaving him tied to the saddle.

"Showed up back in town tied to his horse, dying of thirst, claiming he was jumped by you two. Since you'd been gone from town for weeks, the sheriff didn't believe a word the fool said. He got in a brawl at the saloon one night, pulled a gun on a deputy and died with twenty double-O pellets buried in his breast."

"Well," Snake said. "We didn't kill him. We'll unpack tonight, then get that gold into Clausen's in the morning."

"Clausen's an honest man, Snake. He'll treat you right. Tell me about how you came to have four animals packed with gold."

Dog-man laughed, lit a cigar and sat back in his chair. "Only two, Cletus. Have sone enchanting bull meat on one of the others."

Snake took over the conversation and it was well more than an hour before they left the cantina for the barn. Snake told about how they found the mine, being jumped by the bandits, and about Georgia's place.

"Heard stories about her," Twombley said. "She's about a hundred miles in Mexico and thumbs her nose at the Mexican authorities. They'll take her down one day, you can put money on that."

14

"Something we got to talk about, Snake. We can't go back to the mine. Can't."

"I know. We can't be in that part of the country with Georgia's gang never bein' able to forget us. We gonna have a lot of cash come tomorrow morning, Dog. There's gonna be people watching that assay office and they'll know it. We got a couple of rough days coming up." He was sitting on a wooden box near their packs in a large warehouse behind the Clausen Brothers' Assay office.

"We got to make some kind of plan," Dog-man said. "Think we could sell that claim? Can't just let it go after all the work we did."

"Long as we don't tell stories about how we got it or how we come to be here with our scalps intact, we can sell it. I'll work on that," Snake said. "After what Twombley said, ain't no question we were in Mexico, Dog. I think we blew right through the mountains we were supposed to prospect."

"Don't matter none," Dog-man said. "Cletus said George Dawson would give us a job any time we wanted. I think I'd like to travel some, though."

"Me, too. Not north though. Not Deadwood north, anyway." He laughed and whacked Dogman across the shoulders. "Here we are talking about sellin' a mine we don't own and talking about where we got in trouble selling a map about a mine we didn't own. No, sir, Dog. Maybe Kansas, but not Deadwood."

"Ain't never been to Kansas. Lots of cattle sent up there."

Their conversations lasted another half hour and the two slept right through to sunrise and their visit to the assay office with heavy bags of gold embedded rocks.

***

"I seen them come into town, Hank." Irish Pedro pointed out the boys with their strings of pack animals. "Those animals are loaded down. We need to keep track of where they go and what they do. They been out a long time. If they go into the assay office, stick close and see if you can hear something."

Hank Morse had come to El Paso with two friends to get into the gold business and thought the best way was to see who brought gold to the assay office, kill or rob them, and wait for the next one. Tom Sweet also knew gold, studied geology some, and wanted his own mine. He thought working with Hank might get him there, not understanding how Morse worked.

Sweet was young and naive, and after watching a prosector lose his gold, his mine, and eventually his life, he was planning his departure from the gang.

He wasn't smart enough to just walk away, though.

The third man was Pedro O'Malley, a mean spirited killer recently out of Huntsville. He and Sweet did not see eye to eye on one single subject and Irish Pedro had threatened to kill Sweet more than once.

I gotta get away from these people. Damn, I was so sure they knew what they were talking about and all they want to do is kill and rob some poor slob that mined the gold. Sweet had worked for a mining outfit in Colorado and thought he learned enough to go prospecting. *I'm gonna find myself dead or in prison is I stay with them much longer.* He never asked himself why he didn't just walk off.

Morse was sitting on the bench outside Clausen's when the boys, with help from Ed Twombley's crew of security guards, arrived with large, heavy bags filled with gold. Cletus Kilpatrick was inside when they arrived. "See the feller on the bench?" Snake asked. "He was most interested in our pack train when we rode in yesterday."

"Bet he approaches us when we're through here," Dog-man chuckled. "I'll follow your lead wherever it takes us."

Cletus introduced them to Leroy Clausen and he led them and their sacks into the back room. "This won't take too long. Go have a nice breakfast and when you come back I'll have an offer for you." He saw the questioning looks on their faces.

"There's never been a loss, gentlemen. Your gold is safe with Clausen's. Without men like you and George Dawson bringing us gold, we'd have nothing to sell."

"Thank you," Dog-man said. "Had a time gettin'

it here, ain't the time to lose it," he chuckled.

"Just look at all this stuff," Snake said. They were in the inner-workings of the assay office. "Must take a heap of learnin' to work this stuff. Me and old Dog here, we just look at the rock and think we see gold."

"We get inside the rock and prove you found gold," Leroy Clausen chortled.

When they left the office to cross the street to the El Dorado Cantina, Snake noticed a second man sitting with the first. "Now we got two sets of eyes on us, Dog." Snake nodded to the two men, smiled, and led the way to breakfast.

"How much you figure we got comin'? I don't even want to think about it. You scared me suggesting we're gonna be rich." Dog-man wasn't smiling as they took seats by a window that looked out on an open plaza in the center of El Paso. "Gonna hold me back if I have to worry about money."

"Ain't gonna worry none about mine. Just gonna spend it." Snake laughed. "Starting with a platter of eggs and beans mixed with chilies. Then a big old steak to sop up the egg yolks." He looked at the thin man standing waiting for their orders. "Make it for both of us," he said, and the man left. Snake poured their coffee.

"I figure we'll probably have three, maybe four thousand dollars, Dog. We could make Kansas in style, you know. Take the train."

"That's too much money, Snake. Wouldn't know what to do with it. I do need a new hat," he laughed. "Kansas, eh? All I know about Kansas is, it's north of where we are. You ever been to California? Heard some good tales."

"Heard it's kinda gentrified, big cities and all. I like the open plains. Got stuck one time, movin' a herd, when a herd of buffalo come through. They come through for two days, Dog. We had a time keepin' them walkin' beef steaks from joining the herd. We could catch a herd goin' north."

"Something to chew on, Snake. Seen a lot of buff up in the Dakotas. Let's think on that."

***

"I say when they get their pay-out from the assayer, we jump 'em," Irish Pedro said. "Take their money, make 'em sell us their mine. We done it before, Hank."

"I know we have, Pedro," Hank Morse smiled. "We sold that one mine three times." He was laughing, looking at young Tom Sweet who was frowning. "What's the matter, Sweet? You wanted a mine, eh?"

"Killin' ain't my game, Hank. It's time for me to leave this party of yours. I'm a minin' man, not a killer, not a thief. Don't worry, I ain't gonna be tellin' nobody about your plans."

"You sure won't be," Irish Pedro said. He had an old Colt Walker cap and ball pointed at Sweet's mid-section.

"No, Pedro." Hank Morse said it quietly, meaning, don't do it here where the whole town knows you done it. "Let's talk about this, Sweet, over a cup of whiskey." He got up and walked around the assay building to where they had their horses. Morse dug around in the saddlebags on his horse, searching for the bottle and Sweet and Irish Pedro walked toward a cottonwood tree to sit down.

Without breaking stride, Pedro O'Malley drove his long Bowie knife deep into Sweet's back, twisting it a couple of times, and let the man fall to the dirt. He quickly dragged the body into some brush and came back to the horses. "It's always better when there's no sound, eh, Pedro?" Hank Morse handed him the bottle. "Good job. Now, let's get back and watch for those two minin' men," he chuckled.

***

Cletus and Ed Twombley joined Snake and Dogman at the table. "Chillies are good this year," Twombley said. "Just right."

"That long valley north of Las Cruces grows some fine chillies," Cletus said. "What do you think, Dog-man?"

"I ain't never had this much beer for breakfast. I got no feelin' in my mouth. None a'tall, I tell you." He drank half a glass of beer and called for more to the group's delight. "Don't know how you boys can just right out eat those things."

"Northerners," Snake jibed. "All the same. They grow sweet peppers up north, Cletus. Did you know that? Did you boys drive that wagon full of gold all the way down from Santa Fe? Long ride."

"No, we're coming in from Las Cruces. The gold is brought in from Socorro, and points west. Lots of mining in that country. Silver and gold. Dawson guarantees delivery to Clausen's for the operators."

The fun was interrupted when Clausen came in to join them. "You boys must have struck a good one," he said. "I'm guessing you're gonna end the day with more than ten thousand dollars. The work's almost done. Come on by later and I'll have a bank receipt for you."

"Bank receipt's okay for town folk, Mr. Clausen, but we're gonna be movin' around the country some."

"I'll have some cash for you, too, boys," he smiled. "But I think Mr. Twombley will back me up, you can go into any federal bank with this receipt book, and draw out cash anytime you need more. Sure safer than walking around with the kind of money you'll be getting."

Twombley nodded, so did Cletus Kilpatrick, and Snake just shook his head, slowly, not really sure. "I guess you boys know more about money than me and Dog. Hell, I ain't never even thought about what you just said we might get. There's enough there for you to get that new hat, after all." Dog-man scowled at the jibe then laughed at the thought of ten thousand dollars.

Clausen finished his coffee, told the boys to come by in a couple of hours for their cash and receipt book, and headed back to his office. Kilpatrick and Twombley followed to finish their business with the assayer as well, and Snake stared at his empty coffee cup. "Ten thousand dollars? Dog-man, we're in trouble."

Dog-man chuckled softly, nodded his head, and called for another beer. "Better get for both of us," he told the barman. "New shirt and new hat, Snake. Hundreds of them." They stared down at the table-top for a few moments, then looked into each others' eyes. "Gonna take some gettin' used to, I do believe."

"Don't be obvious, Dog, but I think we're about to get some company. Two of those men sitting on the bench are giving us the big eye. Might get interesting in the next few minutes. Follow along now and don't look at them." Dog-man nodded and thanked the waiter when he put two full glasses of beer on the table.

Before the men at the bench could move, there was a ruckus of some kind. People were running around the side of the Clausen building, and some of them wore badges on their coats. "Looks like an excitement of some kind, Dog. Let's wander over and check it out."

The crowd was gathered around an old cottonwood tree and two deputy sheriffs were bent over what looked like a seriously wounded man. "He ain't dead, but with that wound, I don't know why," one deputy said to the other. "Let's get him to the doc's. Here, now, a couple of you boys help get this man to Doctor Montgomery's. Hurry now."

"That's one of the fellers was sitting on the bench when we came out of the assay office, Snake. Must have been a shake-up amongst the troops, eh?"

"What was that? Tell me what you just said," the deputy who seemed to be in charge asked. "I'm El Paso Deputy City Marshal Wilson."

"Well," Snake started off in his best Texas drawl, "me and my partner here come out of the assay office a while back and that man was sitting on the bench outside, he was with another man, and they give us the big eye. You know, like they wanted to know what we was doin' in that office, there."

"What did that other man look like? You know either of them?"

"No, ain't never see'd them before," Snake said. He looked at Dog-man for verification and Dog agreed. "Wait, now, if y'awl look at the corner of the building to your left, the other man is talking to a heavy-set Mexican right now."

Wilson spun around and spotted Hank Morse and Pedro O'Malley, and started toward them. Morse turned and sprinted to his horse but Irish Pedro drew his weapon, firing two quick shots at the approaching deputy, hitting him once, in the leg. Wilson, on the ground, had his Colt out and fired three times at the retreating O'Malley, knocking him to the ground with a bullet in his lower back.

O'Malley tried to crawl toward his horse, but only got a foot or two before on-lookers stopped him. Morse was racing out of town, toward Ciudad Juarez, on the other side of the border, as fast as his horse would go. "You got him, Wilson," Snake said, kneeling down next to the deputy. "Here, let me get you to your feet. Gotta get you to the doc's."

Wilson was on his feet but bleeding bad from the wound and Deputy Marshal Jose Castillo rushed over to help. "Get help and get that man I shot. These men will get me to Doctor Montgomery. Hurry, now." Snake was busy tying the wound off with his neckerchief.

"Better hurry, Dog. He's bleeding bad. Come on, Marshal," he said. Wilson had an arm around the boys' shoulders and they half carried, half ran with him to Montgomery's office, less than a block down the street. Others carried the Mexican. Montgomery already had the seriously injured Tom Sweet laid out on a surgical table. The grizzled old doctor was shaking his head looking at the horrible wound.

Amidst all that chaos, a tall, heavy, and angry man stormed into the offices, shoving people out of the way. "What the hell happened, Wilson? What's all the damned gunfire? Who's responsible for this?"

"Shut up!" Doctor Montgomery had had enough. "This is a doctor's office not a saloon. These men are in serious trouble, Marshal, so shut your bully mouth."

"This man's name is Snake, Marshal. He'll tell you everything while the doc fixes my leg. I'm not thinking straight right now," Wilson said. The blood was still running freely and Doc Montgomery pushed everyone aside and got Wilson on the table.

"Marshal, you can talk to anyone you like as long as it's outside. Got it? Don't make me say it again."

"Yeah, yeah, big man, big talk. All right, you two, outside." He started to grab Snake by the shoulder and Montgomery stepped between the two. "Get rough with outlaws, Altman, but not with people that bring wounded men into my office. Now, get out." James Montgomery, MD, came to his position through a back door. He was a young man, Massive shoulders and arms, laying track for the railroad, no education, but dreams. A gentleman's daughter was accosted by ruffians, Montgomery stopped the assault, and the gentleman in turn sent him to medical school. He has maintained his physical condition through the many years and Altman knew it.

El Paso City Marshal Jeb Altman was nearing fifty, and had been a bully his entire life. He was big in every department, hands, feet, belly, and the size he thought his head was. He towered over most and took up two spaces at the bar, which is where he was found most of the time. Many stories were told about how he continued to win election to the post of City Marshal, and some of them were probably true.

The one story that's whispered every election was that Altman had been a Texas Ranger and been drummed out of that highly respected organization. It's never discussed openly, but Deputy City Marshal Nelson Wilson had indicated that he'd seen the paperwork. Accidentally, of course.

Once outside, Altman shouted at the gathered crowd to move on and found some shade under a nearby tree. "Snake, eh? Damn strange name. What's yours?" He asked Dog-man.

"Called Dog-man," he answered, not sure of just what might happen next. He and Snake had been run out of Deadwood by a sheriff with a sense of humor, had been in a major confrontation with a criminal Deputy U.S. Marshal near Santa Fe, or was it Las Cruces. Hard to remember when so much goes on.

"Snake and Dog-man. Yeah, right. Tell me what happened, and don't be lyin'."

"I don't lie to nobody," Snake snarled back at the rude marshal. "You got an attitude, Marshal that's got me riled, some. You got a deputy in there shot up bad, you got a man that's been knifed, probably by the big Mexican that's trying to die in there, too. You get your attitude straightened out and I'll talk to you all day."

Dog-man always thought Snake had a temper but he'd never seen it in action. He calls me the mean one and just listen. This was something to see, this long skinny Texan giving the burly town marshal hell on toast. "Man's got a point, Marshal." Dog-man wasn't gonna let Snake get all the pokes and jabs. "We was helpin' the deputy and we could be helpin' you."

"Two smart Alex drifters not worth a dime ain't gonna be tellin' me what to do," Altman thundered just as Ed Twombley and Cletus Kilpatrick walked up to the doctor's.

"Easy, Marshal Altman," Twombley said. Twombley was as heavy as Altman but his weight was muscle and bone. "These men are in town on business. Farthest thing from broke saddle drifters. You talk tough with them, you're talking tough with me."

"Men have been shot up and knifed and I want the story," Altman almost shouted. He kicked some dirt, growled out some profane language, and glared at everyone.

"Then ask for it," Snake said. He was almost quiet, talking in a hushed tone. Dog-man expected him to say, please? He also thanked all the gods that he didn't. "Why don't we take a table at the El Dorado, have a cold beer, and me and Dog will be more than happy to have a nice conversation with you."

"Before you give Snake an answer you might want to know that you have a criminal loose, probably already in Mexico. Deputy Wilson told you about him and you've just sat on your thumb, talking big." Ed Twombley was angry and ready for a fight. "Wounded men trying to die in that doctor's office and you ain't done nothing but try to bully these two men. Wish we had a real lawman in this town. Wish we had the Rangers here."

Altman blew up but caught himself before he threw the first punch. He was shaking with anger and about to walk off when Jose Castillo came riding up fast and jumped from his running horse, panting. "Big man made it over the bridge. I followed but was way too far into Mexico to continue." He caught his breath, noticed that no one was paying him much attention. "Nelson okay?"

Altman glared at Twombley, Snake, and Dog-man, but didn't say a word. "Doc's working on him now, Jose. Did you notice which way that feller went? West or south? I'm not an officer of the law," Twombley said. "Just a citizen and I have my guards with me. We can ride across that river anytime and follow the outlaw. You're hindered by treaties but I'm not."

"You've got us with you, too," Dog-man said.

15.

"You gotta keep that Mexican alive, Doc. Him and the stabbed man are behind all of this." Wilson was weak from loss of blood but was still thinking like a deputy marshal. "Castillo is chasing another one, probably into Mexico, so we need these two alive."

"I'm doing my best, Nelson. I'd do better if I could be given just ten seconds and a scalpel, with your boss. No, easier to just shoot the bastard." Wilson was chuckling and laid his head down.

"I need to talk to that feller named Snake. Do you have someone you can send to find him?"

Doctor Montgomery called one of his nurses working on Irish Pedro. "Get that skinny Texan in here, Maria. Wilson needs him." He looked down at the deputy, grinned just a bit. "He'll be here short-ly but I ain't waiting, Nelson. This is gonna hurt a might," he said, and started probing around the bullet hole. Wilson tried to hold it in, not sound like all the others he could remember, and failed.

Those standing out by the tree saw nurse Maria running toward them and heard a howl of pain from inside the doc's. "Hope that's a good sign." Snake drawled it out with a short chuckle. "I've been known to sound off like that. A time or two."

"Pulling a splinter out of your behind is the one I remember," Dog-man laughed. Snake scowled. "You got drunk, slid off a bench and the bench got-cha," Dog-man laughed.

"Mr. Snake," Maria called out. "Doctor wants you."

"Mr. is it? Well, now," Dog-man said. He, Twombley, Snake, and Castillo all headed for the doctor's office, leaving City Marshal Altman at the cottonwood tree.

***

"All I can do is suggest you not go after this Hank Morse, Mr. Twombley," Deputy City Marshal Nel-son Wilson said. He had a twinkle in his eye saying that. "I sure hope you don't put much thought to what I said. Altman will have a fit and I can't let Castillo ride with you since he is a lawman. We have our treaties and they must be respected."

"Sure would be better if we had someone who spoke good Spanish riding with us, Wilson. Despite the fact I have four security guards with me, they have to guard what we will be bringing back to Las

Cruces. They can't go." Twombley wanted Castillo
along but knew he couldn't make a good case for
it. "Me, Snake, and Dog-man will chase him down.
Let's go boys."

"Wait." Jose Castillo opened his coat and pulled
off his badge, laying it on the bed next to Nelson
Wilson. "I didn't much care for this job, anyway,
Wilson." He winked at Twombley. "Hablo Español,
Señor," he said, winking at Twombley. "We're wast-
ing time if we want to catch that fool. Morse turned
to follow the river back toward New Mexico Territory and has more than an hour's lead on us."

They rushed for the door and heard Doc Montgomery cussing up a storm on the way. "He'll get
over it," Twombley said. "Not sure about Marshal
Altman, though."

"Doc said the Mexican would live and it's doubt-
ful that Tom Sweet will." Dog-man was shaking his
head. "That's a shame cuz Sweet wasn't really a part
of Morse's organization. We'd a probably made a
deal with him."

It was stifling hot when they rode south across
the bridge into Ciudad Juarez and turned to follow
the Rio Grande, upstream, leading them west and
then north into New Mexico Territory. No one
paid much attention and Jose stopped a time or
two, asking if anyone had seen the gringo following along the river.

"He'll follow right along until the river turns
north," Twombley said, "leading him into New
Mexico Territory.

"We'll be crossing our old trail, Dog. Those are
the Portrillo Mountains."

"Now that would be something if Morse was running toward Georgia's. I'm not sure I want to think about that."

Snake was laughing, slouched back in the saddle. "No, not Georgia's. That's the new trail. The old trail is when we left Las Cruces. You gotta remember these things, Dog. He'll follow the river right into Las Cruces. I got a cartwheel that says so."

"I ain't betting against you," Dog-man laughed. "I'm not really sure where the border is. I haven't had any idea where we are or where we been for so long, it don't matter."

"Once the river turns north, the border continues west but it ain't very well marked. Ranchers on the north side raid ranches on the south, and the other way around," Jose Castillo said. "Texans bring Mexican horses north and Mexicans bring Texas cattle south. Lawmen drink beer and talk about it." Dog-man thought that Castillo was the Mexican version of Snake, not allowing too much to interfere with a pleasant day.

"Our mine's about ten days that way," Snake pointed.

"Well, I won't tell anyone if you won't," Jose Castillo laughed. "Ten days that way is in Mexico about a hundred miles. Our man is definitely headed for Las Cruces. We can follow or go back and send a wire to Sheriff Baxter. Sending a wire would be faster."

"It would," Twombley said. "Let's do that. Will you get your job back?"

"Sure. Without me, Wilson is alone working with Altman," Castillo laughed.

"I wanted to chase that fool down a get in a fight with him," Dog-man said.

"That's coz you're the mean one," Snake laughed.

***

"There you are, gentlemen," Clausen said, and offered the bank receipt to Snake and one thousand dollars to Dog-man. "Each time you make a withdrawal it will be noted in the book so you will always know how much is left. Right now, that total reads, twelve thousand, four hundred fifty dollars. It's been a real pleasure working with you. I sincerely hope that mine of yours keeps producing."

Snake looked at Dog-man who was looking at him, neither one willing to reach out and take what was offered. "I ain't never seen that much money in my life," Snake said. Dog-man finally took the offered cash, folded it and shoved it in his shirt pocket. It took serious will for Snake to take hold of the bank book and slipped it into his shirt pocket. Both men stood for seconds, sheepish grins on their faces.

Dog-man and Snake shook hands with the gold dealer and walked out into bright sunshine. "A cold beer and a long talk," Snake said. He folded the five hundred dollars Dog-man handed him but wasn't smiling. They headed for the El Dorado and Snake stopped. "No, Dog-man, let's go to that little shack we stopped at coming in. I ain't comfortable thinking that I'm a rich man. Now, there's many a man with more money than I have, but none with as fine a partner."

"You should have been a poet, Snake." Dog-man was smiling but before they could change course and head for the little shack of a cantina, they saw two men giving them the eye.

The two men had walked out of the assay office behind them. "That was quite a sum Clausen said. Like to talk to those boys. Let's follow."

Dog-man picked up on the men following. "Remember what we were talking about, not heading back to the mine but letting it pay us one more time?"

Snake got a quick smile and kept right on walking. "El Dorado it is, after all. Let me know when they're close enough to hear." He was almost chuckling, and slowed his pace down just a bit. He stopped, reached down as if to pull a pant leg from a boot top. It took less than four strides, Dog-man seemed to trip, and Snake started talking, a bit louder than normal. Loud enough to be heard by Richard Solo and Tom Strickland, just a few feet behind him.

"Dog-gone it, partner, I really wish I could continue to work this operation with you, but, oh, man, I gots to get back to Saint Loo before my mother dies. Oh, God, Dog-man, I love her so much. Oh, this is just horrible." Snake pulled his neckerchief off and blew his nose, wiped his eyes, and hid his chuckle in its folds.

"I'm so sorry about that news from your mother, Snake. I can't work that mine by myself. I'd never find a partner again like you. What am I gonna do?" Dog-man had almost stopped, the two were in the middle of the dusty street. "Let's have a beer and see what we can work out. "You're the best partner a man could have. I'd never trust anyone like I trust you."

Snake caught a good look at the two men following and, used the crying act again, almost sobbing. They led the two across the street and into the El Dorado Cantina, and took a table a bit away from the gambling tables. They called for beer while Solo and Strickland watched from near the bar.

Richard Solo was tall and thin, had greased, slicked back black hair, wore a pencil mustache, and was dressed as a city dandy. Tom Strickland on the other hand was heavy, strong, with blondish hair, no facial hair, and blue eyes. They were opposites except for their business: Acquiring mines any way possible. At a nod they walked to where the boys were sitting.

"Pardon, gents," Solo said, a friendly smile on his face. Snake saw the little handgun tucked under the man's frock coat. "My name's Solo, Richard Solo, and this is my partner, Tom Strickland." Without asking, the two pulled chairs over and joined the table. "Didn't catch your names.

"Didn't give 'em," Snake said. He gave the impression that the men were interfering, but left the door open, too. "I'm Snake, this here's my partner, Dog-man."

"Couldn't help overhearing parts of your conversation coming over from the assay office. Sounded a lot like a partnership about to bust up." He turned and motioned to the barman to send a bottle and four glasses over.

"Well," Snake drawled out long and slow like,

"Yer gettin' kinda personal there, Solo. No offense meant, but kinda personal." Dog-man sat quiet, letting Snake do what Snake did best.

"No offense taken," Solo smiled. The barman brought the bottle and four glasses and Solo poured a round. "Here's to good claims and fine gold."

"Me and Dog-man here, made a good strike but my mother's dyin', even as we speak," Snake said. It was a halting comment and Snake hung his head a bit. Sniffled. "We're gonna have to give up our claim, I'm afraid. He can't work it alone and I got to get back up to Saint Loo. Oh," he cried out, "poor old ma ain't gonna be with us no more."

Snake grabbed the glass of whiskey and drained it before he ruined things by laughing. Dog-man was right along with him, making their chuckles seem more like sobs.

"Maybe Mr. Strickland and I can help you. We like to buy up working claims. It's easier than having to do all the work to get 'em up and producing," he laughed. Snake and Dog-man had to laugh along with him and gave little nods to each other.

"You boys turned in a heap of gold and that means there should be heaps more," Solo said, almost rubbing his greasy hands together.

"Yeah, there should be," Snake said. He was shaking his head, thinking about how much there might be, and wondering whether Georgia would let them pass by her joint. He held back a smile. "We planned on buying some heavy equipment and heading back to the claim when I got the wire about poor old ma. I don't want to run out on my partner, but I can't let my own ma die all alone, neither."

"I can't run that claim by myself and I don't want

a new partner either. I sure can't ask

Snake to ignore his ma when she's so sick and dyin'." Dog-man said.

"Why, that would be almost evil," Solo said. He picked up the bottle and poured whiskey all around. "Maybe we could work out something that would benefit both of us, you know, buy the rights to work your mine for a percentage," and he let the sentence just dangle some. He'd done that so many times it was becoming second nature to him.

He and Strickland would make a deal to work a mine for a percentage from the owner, then sell their working rights half a dozen times for a lucrative return. The owner would be burdened by half a dozen people claiming they have the rights to the workings.

"That might work for some," Dog-man said. "Don't think so in this matter. Snake's gotta get up to Saint Loo, and I don't know what I'm gonna do."

"It's horrible," Snake said. "Just horrible." He picked up his glass and drank it down.

"If I do anything, I think I'll just sell the claim outright. I've always had a hankering to get into ranching. Don't need a partner for that."

"That might be best, Dog-man," Snake said. "Sell the claim, split our money and head our separate ways. I gotta get back to Saint Loo just as soon as possible. She's so sick, that wire said."

Solo looked at Strickland, then at Dog-man. "Why don't we meet for supper and talk about that. You just might have something. Your mine is all put together and operating, all we have to do is start digging," Solo laughed.

"I don't think we need to wait until supper, Dick,"

Tom Strickland said, right on cue. "I'm willing to offer these boys five thousand for that claim right now."

"That's a good number," Solo said. He was already figuring out how many times he would be able to sell the claim. He would need an honest bill of sale and good map that he could reproduce at will. "For that kind of money we could work that claim and come out like these boys did."

"I think you heard some of the conversation at the assay office," Dog-man said. "Five thousand wouldn't buy that claim. No, sir. I might think of twelve or fifteen, but not five. What do you think, Snake."

"Couldn't make five sound right to me, Dog. You know the two leads we were following are high grade. No, won't give it away for five."

Solo looked at Strickland like they had a secret language, and Solo drummed the table. Dog-man counted Solo's fingers hitting the table-top ten times and held back a smile. He caught Snake doing the same. "You got a lot of expenses comin' up, Snake, with your ma dyin' and all. And, well, I don't want to push you boys, but five just won't work."

Solo looked back and forth at Dog-man and Snake and poured drinks around again. "The most that Mr. Strickland and I could offer would be ten thousand, gentlemen. Not a dime more."

"If that's in good old American cash, we'll take it," Dog-man said. "We only got to work that claim a couple of months this year and you know what we brought down."

At Solo's urging, they walked to the El Paso bank and he drew out ten thousand dollars. Dog-man accepted the money and Snake turned over a bill of sale and the detailed map they drew to the mine. Everyone shook hands and the boys watched Solo and Strickland walk away. The map showed the intersection where Georgia's place was but did not mention the little bar and outlaw hideout.

"You ever thought of taking up acting?" Dog-man was laughing as they made their way to the barn behind Clausen's Assay offices.

"Ain't going north." Snake said. He looked at the string of animals they had. "We don't need this many animals, Dog-man. Ain't going into the freight business."

"Nope, not going north, and yup, we don't. Kansas?"

"Kansas is north."

"Ever been to California?"

"Let's do that," Snake said. "We can take that road west out of Las Cruces and that would give us a chance to say goodbye to George Dawson. Cletus said that Dawson was spending the next six months at his Las Cruces offices. I like that old man."

"Think Solo and Strickland will get past Georgia's? I'm bettin' not."

"Those two are horse thieves, Dog. They ain't gonna work that mine. They'll have it sold in two days for twice what they paid for it. probably sell it two or three times before the winter's over. Georgia might have a whole new crop of customers come spring." Laughter rang through the old barn's rafters as the two packed two mules, saddled their horses, rode out for Las Cruces.

"Cletus said he'd sell the rest of our string and meet us down the road. Sure glad we got run out of Deadwood."

16

"It'll be good to see old George Dawson again. I liked that man. He'll try to put us to work, you know. He's got a way about him." Dog-man and Snake were looking for a good place to camp on the road to Las Cruces. "Cletus said he's been with the man for more than ten years."

"Ain't lookin' for a job," Snake said. "If I wanted a job I'd ride north and hire out with old Chet Hamilton and you could flirt with that spoiled daughter of his. Ha! That'd be fun to watch."

Dog-man didn't answer, just rode off the road toward a stand of rock with a few scraggly and thorny bushes nearby. "You gather wood, I'll build a fire pit. Think we'll run into that outlaw Marshal Eastwood?"

"Talked to Twombley about him." Snake stepped down and took the leads from all the animals. "With Three Fingers doin' a lot of talking, Eastwood was forced to resign as a Deputy U.S. Marshal. He ain't even in town, Twombley said. That Sheriff Baxter's a strange character, though. Sheriff told him poor old Jimmie Butters is dead, so we ain't gonna be ridin' into some kind of mess."

"Ain't like us," Dog-man chuckled. "I hope that sheriff followed up on the wire Wilson sent him about Hank Morse. It was gonna be us next. He wanted our mine, our money, and our lives."

"Tom Sweet didn't make it, Dog. Twombley said that the Mexican was gonna live and then, after they got him well and all, they'd hang him. Morse's got a lot to answer for."

They were on the road early the next morning and about mid-day Cletus Kilpatrick and Ed Twombley caught up with them, with their big wagon and six-up moving at a strong trot. Twombley had two out-rider guards out in front and two bringing up the rear.

"You're ridin' like you're expecting some kind of trouble," Dog-man said. "I thought you delivered your gold to Clausen."

"Delivered raw ore, like yours," Cletus said. "Bringing back cash and coin for the banks. Where you boys headed?"

"Wanted to say goodbye to Mr. Dawson then maybe off to California. Do some ranchin', maybe. They say the grass is so rich the cows get fat just walkin' through it." Snake had his Texas full on and it brought laughter from everyone.

"Dawson has an express contract from Las Cruces to Tucson. Runs once a month. You boys would be perfect for that run. One express wagon, one freight wagon, and generally two to six passengers on the express wagon. It's a mail contract, so good pay."

"You boys just don't let go, do you?" Dog-man

chuckled. "I betcha Snake and I will listen to what the old man says, though. Mighty rough country I'm thinkin'."

It was late in the day when they arrived in Las Cruces. "I could eat a buffalo," Dog-man said. "As long as you didn't cover it with those chilies you like so much." Snake laughed as the two got their pack mules unloaded and had a camp made up near the Dawson corrals. "George wants to see us first thing in the morning." Dog-man had been thinking about that mail run from Las Cruces to Tucson.

"I don't really want to work for someone, Snake, but it sure would get us more than half way to California and pay us to boot. We'll talk about it over that buffalo," he chuckled.

"That part about gettin' paid kinda strikes a chord," Snake said. "We used to ride a poke about half or less filled, and worked to get it filled. Now, here we are, poke overflowin', mules carrying enough to keep us alive and well for weeks, and talkin' about gettin' a job that pays. This thing about havin' a full poke ain't gonna be that much fun."

Dog-man had to think on that, not quite understanding the logic of having a full poke and that not being fun. "We'll talk about that over a roasted buffalo, Snake," he chuckled.

***

"I'm sure glad to see you boys," George Dawson said. "Old Clete tells me you did good with your minin' adventure, too. Glad for you. I've built my company on the good people I hire." He sat back in his little wooden chair in the outer office and lit a cigar. His set-up in Las Cruces was board-for-board duplicate of the one in Socorro.

"My competitors tell me I pay my people too much, but I say, to get and keep good people, you got to keep 'em happy. You've met many, so you know I'm right."

Earlier, Dog-man and Snake were in the middle of breakfast when Ed Twombley came into the little cantina to tell them that George Dawson wanted to see them right away. "He's in a twit about something and sent me out to bring you in quick."

They hustled across the broad open central plaza and into Dawson headquarters. Neither one could forget that first morning with Three-fingers giving them hell followed by the outlaw, Marshal Eastwood.

"The men we've met, Mr. Dawson, all say nothing but good things about you and your company." Dog-man wondered just where this conversation would lead. Dawson usually came right to the point, but was going in circles this time. "Twombley said it was urgent."

"Yes, well," Dawson said. "Important more than urgent, I guess. Cletus tell you about our run to Tucson?" The boys nodded, and gave knowing looks to each other. "I've had a hard time keeping people on for that run. Apaches are tearing up that country, Mexican banditos are getting more than adventurous, and good old American outlaws are active, too. It's the most dangerous run we have." He sat back and re-lit his cigar, giving each man a full look eye to eye.

"I've got drivers and guards for both rigs, the express wagon and the freight wagon, but the last two times, they've been hit by large groups of marauding outlaws. These are freight, mail, and passenger runs, so there is reason for the outlaws to attack. The first seventy five miles or so is right along the border which is ill defined at best.

"In places it's not defined at all. No one knows where it is. The Apache don't care about borders, nor do the Mexican banditos, or American outlaw gangs. I'd like to put your heavy guns out there, boys."

"What about the army? Don't they protect the roads?" Dog-man looked back and forth between Dawson and Twombley.

"The army is fair at protecting the little communities and ranching but they can't protect the highways." Dawson said. "This is mountain country with great areas of open desert. It's wild and dangerous with little water and few communities. We can't have stops every twenty miles or so because of the Indian threat. They eat more horses than we have, sometimes," he chuckled.

"We get chased off water, water is poisoned, roads are blocked by man-made landslides. Boys, this is one miserable run and only the best will do it. That's why I'm asking you to take the job. Make the run to Tucson and back at least twice for me. I know how much money you made in your mining adventure, so I won't even discuss money."

"I've never had as much money as I've got right now, Mr. Dawson, but I've also never had someone treat me as good as you have." Snake lost his typical Texas bluster and just let it all hang out. "I'll ride for your brand anytime, sir."

"Me too," Dog-man said, quietly, without any kind of gesture. "Me too."

***

"These look more like army combat maps than an express route map," Snake laughed, sitting in front of their campfire. "Just look at this." Dawson wanted them to stay at a hotel but the boys said their little camp near the Dawson corrals was just fine.

"You boys have no idea of what that money could mean for you," Dawson laughed. "A hotel bed with satin sheets and room service with a beautiful woman." He looked up at the ceiling, scratched his head and smiled. "I think you've made the right choice, though."

Snake was holding a map that showed the route through a mountainous section, with small marks to show where each attack on a run had been made.

"This says there have been five attacks over the last few months in this little ten-mile section of road. Dawson included a report on each attack for us. One gang is run by a feller named Orson Whitlock, another by a group of Apaches led by, hell, Dog, I can't even pronounce how he's got it spelled."

"Nice of him to offer the reports," Dog-man laughed. "You got your will wrote out?"

"Ain't even funny," Snake growled. "I bought a Winchester today and a revolver that fits better than my old one. Remember when we talked with old Chet Hamilton about taking care of his herds, not hiring on as gunmen? Have we made a mistake, Dog?"

"I remember how we promised we would never

be outlaws, Snake. We ain't, we haven't been, and we won't be. We're protecting, just like with old Chet and that selfish but gorgeous daughter of his. Protecting pilgrims trying to get somewhere, freight that needs to be somewhere, and mail that someone is expecting."

"Now who's the poet?" Snake laughed. "Bought a bottle, too," he said, opening it and taking a long swallow, pretending not to pass it over. "Dawson says the wagons will be fitted out at dawn and we should be ready." He handed the bottle to Dog-man.

"Each wagon has a driver and guard and we are supposed to be outriders?" Snake shook his head. "Something somewhere ain't right."

***

Ed Twombley shook Dog-man awake well before sunrise. "We got company, Dog-man, and a change of plans."

Dog-man was awake and on his feet in seconds, trying to get his gun belt fastened. Snake was alongside him and Twombley was stoking their fire. There was a fourth man, Las Cruces Sheriff Warren Baxter.

"Damned early for a visit, ain't it?" Snake asked. "Change of plans? Only plan I saw was me and Dog gettin' killed. I think Dawson's going about this backwards like. He called that outlaw by name, and some of his gang. There's where he should start. Take out the outlaw gang, not welcome it to the party."

Snake was starting to get riled and Twombley tried to settle him down. "Why don't you put that together as a plan and talk to George about it later."

"I don't give a damn about any of this nonsense," Sheriff Baxter growled. "I want to talk to you two about this feller Morse. I got a wire from Altman down in El Paso says to hold the fool, but don't say why or nothing. He's sittin' in my jail right now screaming his head off and I'm about to let him go."

"Good old Altman," Dog-man said. "Get a wire off to Nelson Wilson, Altman's chief deputy. He'll bring you up to date. Morse was working to steal money from Snake and me, had a partner called Irish Pedro who knifed a man named Tom Sweet. Sweet was also Morse's partner. Pedro shot Wilson and Snake shot Pedro. You and Wilson are lawmen and you need to talk to each other."

"You come over before sunrise to ask about this?" Snake was still riled some. "That coffee better start boilin' if it knows what's best."

"You boys come rambling through my territory and people die," Baxter said. "I don't much care for that. Jimmie Butters is dead. He said you killed the outlaw Clint Ayres. Why is it Butters would know that?" Baxter had his chin stuck out and was as riled as Snake.

"Good question, Sheriff." Dog-man needed to separate the two. "Don't remember someone named Ayers. Last time I saw Butters he was tryin' to sell us a map he had. Something about a gold claim. Hell, Sheriff, everybody sells gold claim maps, don't they?"

That got through to Snake and he relaxed and chuckled, remembering what the sheriff up north had said. "If you're fast enough, Sheriff, you could chase down a couple of men in El Paso would be glad to sell you a map, too."

"I want to know more about this Ayres," Baxter snarled. "Butters said that you killed Ayres and then you chased Butters off after tying him to his saddle."

"Like Dog said, don't know the man. If Jimmie Butters told you about him, you need to talk to Butters. I don't know anyone named Ayres. Butters is a thief, Sheriff, but I ain't seen him in a long time and ain't never seen anyone named Ayres."

"Bah," Baxter bawled and walked out of the little camp, yelling back at them. "I ain't done with you two. Somebody's gonna hang if Ayres is dead, and I'm bettin' it's you two." He all but marched out of the little camp as the sun came up.

"Yes, you are done," Snake whispered through soft laughter. "Coffee done?"

"We got to get out of this country, Snake. We can't take Dawson's job offer, or spend one more hour in Las Cruces either. We gotta pack up and ride out now. Jimmie Butters, dead or alive, is workin' to get us hung. Wish we'd never walked into that cantina, never met that man."

"I think you're right," Ed Twombley said. "I'll settle things with Mr. Dawson, but Baxter will hound you day and night if you stay or go to work for Dawson. He's got it set that you two are outlaws and he's gonna get you hung."

"Don't like goodbyes, Twombley," Snake said." He was pacing around the little campsite, kicked a rock or two and finally just sat down on a rock. "Ain't goin'," he said.

"What do you mean, ain't goin'? We gotta go," Dog-man said. "You heard Baxter, and what

Twombley just said. We gotta go, Snake."

"Nope, ain't goin'. We said it loud and clear when we got throwed out of Deadwood. We ain't outlaws and I ain't gonna be treated like one. We damn well cleaned out that bunch of no-goods in El Paso, worked real hard with old Nelson Wilson and made a friend out of Jose Castillo. No, sir, Warren Baxter ain't gonna make me into no outlaw."

Snake sat straight up on that rock, held his cup out for Dog-man to pour him another cup of coffee, and smiled like a ten-year-old with a new sugar stick. "Jimmie Butters, now, he was an outlaw. Hank Morse tried to steal our gold mine. Erwin Eastwood wanted us dead, and Three-fingers was gonna help him. Just look what we've been through, Dog. Damn me if I'm gonna let that Baxter make me into an outlaw. Was that feller that tried to kill us at our mine this Ayres fool?"

"Hadn't thought about that. Maybe. I'm thinking we need to have a long talk with old George Dawson," Dog-man said. "My first thought was get out of town and fast, but listening to you, Snake, I gotta go with what your thinkin'. Baxter's just a bull-headed old bastard who can't think past the end of his nose. Let's go talk to Dawson."

17

Dawson sat at his big desk in the office he did not like being in and faced Ed Twombley, Snake, and Dog-man, spread around the other side of the desk. "Warren Baxter's a cow dog that ain't never been trained, boys. He knows he's supposed to do something but doesn't know what or how, so just bulls his way in, wants to hang whoever's near, and blusters loud and long."

"That's about the way I see it," Snake said. "Problem is, it's us he wants to hang and we ain't guilty of no murder." Snake considered the death of the man they now believe was Clint Ayres fully justified and had no intentions of talking about it to anyone. "I ain't gonna be shoved off and made to feel guilty by no damned sheriff what can't think."

"I still think your best bet is to get out of town," Ed Twombley said. Dawson didn't say anything, just shook his head.

"Lawmen come in various shades of good and bad," the express company boss chuckled. "In this section of our vast country, we've got a lot of the bad or ornery types. Baxter ain't really bad, just bull-headed dumb." He sat back in his chair and looked up at the molded tin ceiling. "I'm gonna send a wire to Nelson Wilson in El Paso and ask him to come up and work with us on this. He's got the reputation of a fine lawman. Baxter himself has said so."

"I like him," Snake said. "Texian, you know. Family was in Texas before Sam Houston or Mr. Austin."

"On our Tucson run there is only one actual station, about twenty miles west of here. The rest of the stops are camp sites near water. One is in an Indian village," he laughed. "No fresh horses, no fixed food. Ride out to Mr. Penny's station, boys, and see what you can find out about a man named Orson Whitlock. He's one of the outlaw leaders that's causing me the most problems. Baxter won't bother you out there and it will give Wilson a chance to get him off your case.

"Mr. Twombley will give you a letter of introduction to Will Penny. He runs a fair station for the company, and you'll be protected."

"Sounds fine with me," Dog-man said. "We'll make up a camp near the station, Snake, and check out the countryside." Snake was quick to agree to the idea. It would get them out of town but they wouldn't be running away from that damn sheriff.

***

"I like this country, Dog." Snake was slouched back in the saddle as the two rode northwest out of Las Cruces. "Big mountains in front of us. Feels good to be on the road again. We don't get along very well in towns, do we?" The chuckle held about a ton of irony and Dog-man had to laugh right out. "Our ride down to Santa Fe was a good one, and on to Socorro. It was in the towns that things turn sour."

"Dawson wants us to help take out that outlaw gang, Snake. Wonder if maybe we should just ride on through to California." Dog-man was sitting straight in the saddle, a mean look on his face. "I'm kinda mixed up on where we are. We weren't wrong in killing Clint Ayres. Not in my mind."

"We weren't," Snake said. "No we weren't. We can't ride off, though. Don't know about the outlaws. Guess we'll do what we obliged ourselves to do, but when the Baxter thing is over, we gotta ride for California as fast as these old sway-backs will go."

"Dawson said this Whitlock fool seems to know exactly which runs to hit. Has four killers that ride with him."

"Odds are even, anyway," Snake laughed. "That must be Penny's Station back in those trees, Dog. Let's just play it easy and see what happens."

***

Penny's Station was a typical stage stop with a main house, large barn, and several corrals filled with horses and mules. There were three other outbuildings, and a well for fresh water. Inside the main house was a large open room that doubled as a kitchen and dining room, with three rooms off to either side. One was occupied full time by Will Penny and his wife, Claudia, a short, heavy woman about fifty or so. Penny was a string-bean, standing six feet tall and skinny. Snake figured he was in his sixties at the least.

Dog-man handed Penny the letter of introduction from Dawson when the boys walked into the station. "Read it to me," Penny said. "Don't have my glasses handy." He had a voice corrupted by years of heavy drinking and little eating, and Snake figured the man probably had never learned to read, glasses or not.

Claudia was upset when the reading was over. "Ain't never heard of such a thing, imposing on us like that. I'm supposed to clean up after you, wash your clothes, cook your meals? That old fool George Dawson has gone too far this time. I suppose you'll take the room we have for express passengers?"

She was a bundle of excited nerves, pacing around the generous main room of the station, shaking her fist in Dog-man's face, glaring at her husband. "Ain't gonna have it," she finally said and plopped down in a chair at the dining table.

"Ain't imposing, woman," Snake growled. "Don't want your filthy bed nor your sickly food. Here to do a job, like it or not." He turned to Will Penny who hadn't moved a muscle once his wife got started. "Dawson said you'd provide us with corrals and grain for our animals, Penny. We'll take care of ourselves."

Snake turned to Dog-man, fully riled now and ready to do battle. "Let's go make up our camp, get these animals unpacked and in a corral, and finish that bottle." He turned to Claudia Penny, sniffed, and walked out the door. Dog-man nodded to Will Penny, shook his head so the long hair blew about, and followed Snake.

"Nice show," Dog-man said. "I always like a warm welcome when we come to help someone, don't you? Maybe strip her down, tie her to a tree, and burn the wickedness from her evil soul?"

That almost brought Snake to his knees he was laughing so hard. "Thank you, Dog. You are a fine partner," he finally was able to say. "They got a lot of horses and mules in those corrals, Dog. Must be more here than that skinny old man in there. Can't see him changing out teams when the wagons come rolling through."

"Nothing was said, but you gotta be right. I don't like that woman. The less we have to do with her the better." Dog-man pointed to a stand of cotton-wood trees off and up a side hill about half a mile. "Let's see what we can do with that little piece of paradise."

They were unpacked and the animals taken care of and working on a semi-permanent lean-to when two riders approached. "Maybe what you were thinking, Snake?" Dog-man said. Snake nodded and slipped his rifle from its scabbard as the two pulled up in a cloud of hot dust.

"This is private property. Get your skinny butts off now," the squat, bearded one said. The other had his hand on his sidearm looking hard at Dog-man. "Got no use for trespassers. Move it now."

"Well, now, boys, ain't this just about the best welcome we've had today," Snake drawled out. "Glad to make your acquaintance. Name's Snake, this here's the Dog-man, and we're security guards what work for Dawson Express Company, so put your little pea-shooter away before I blow your fool heads off." The rifle had slowly come to bear on the one trying to get hold of his revolver. In that instant Dog-man had his Colt out and cocked, aimed at the middle of the mouthy squat one.

"Step down slow and easy boys," Dog-man said. "My partner there gets himself all riled and just starts shootin' sometimes, so let's be nice and slow." The two men looked a long time at Snake before they slowly stepped off their horses.

"Good boys," Snake said. "Ease them weapons to the ground and step back some," and he let off a round from his rifle, spraying sand and dirt on the squat one's boots. He jacked another round in, chuckled, looked at Dog-man. "Oops. Got away from me, Dog. Riled some, I am."

"Best sit down, boys, and tell us all about this private property nonsense. This is Penny's Stage Station, isn't it? Wouldn't want to think we come to the wrong place." Dog-man waved his Colt at a fallen log and the two almost ran to it and sat down. Snake picked up their weapons.

"Fat man," Snake said, pointing the rifle, "Start talking." The squat man was about five eight and two hundred pounds. He had a broad chest and narrow hips, a nose that had been worked over many times, and was bald under his broad sombrero. His beard was coal black.

"I'm Sam Decker," he said in a gruff voice. "We work for Will Penny. He don't want strangers moving onto his land. He won't like this."

"We don't much care for him," Dog-man chuckled. "Don't think this is Penny's land, Decker. I do believe it belongs to the Dawson Express Company." He turned to the other man. "How about you?"

He said, letting the Colt cover the other man.

"John Perkins," he said. "What did you mean when you said you're Dawson Express security men. I ain't never seen you before. What are you doing here?" Perkins was about average size, wore the clothes of a man that worked hard around stables and animals while Decker gave the impression he'd be at home in a rowdy saloon.

"We're here waiting for the next Tucson run, Mr. Perkins. What's your job?" Snake had cooled off just a bit, maybe regretting that Decker hadn't challenged him.

"Me and Decker take care of the animals, change out the teams, keep the leather up."

"Just out for a little ride this afternoon, were you?" Snake asked. Dog-man settled down near the fire ring with a cup of coffee, watching the show.

"Yeah, looking for game. Claudia likes deer and antelope."

"Don't look like you're very good at huntin', Mr. Perkins. You two come ridin' into our camp all blustery like this again and I'll shoot way before I start talkin'." Snake motioned with his rifle for the two to mount up and ride off.

"Need my gun," Decker snarled.

"I'll bring it down to Will Penny a little later," Dog-man said. He had a big smile on his face, poured another cup of coffee and motioned for the two to be off. "The extra mules in your corral is ours. Take good care of 'em." He watched them mount up and ride off fast.

"They weren't huntin', Dog," Snake said. He joined him at the fire and poured a cup. "Betcha a cartwheel one of 'em rides off sometime in the next hour."

"Nope, I'd lose that bet. Betcha a dollar we be followin'."

"Nope, either," Snake chuckled. "We're a couple of devious bastards aren't we? Why didn't Dawson or Twombley mention that Penny had two men working for him? Surely they would know. Somebody's payin' 'em."

"Somebody named Whitlock?" Dog-man chuckled. "That Decker's an outlaw if I ever saw one. Perkins is kinda sneaky, too. According to those maps Dawson gave us, Whitlock likes to hit the wagons when they go through that pass about ten miles west of here. Probably has a camp somewhere nearby."

"Seems strange to me that our friend, Warren Baxter, hasn't chased these outlaws. Did you talk to Ed Twombley about that?" Snake walked into the unfinished lean-to and brought a bottle out. "Inspiration," he chuckled.

"I think George Dawson is too easy going with the people he hires." Dog-man poured a healthy dose of whiskey in his coffee. "Good. Twombley is good at what he does but doesn't have any desire to do more than what he's asked to do. Baxter likes to bluster but isn't about to chase a real outlaw out across this desert and these mountains."

"And then we come along," Snake laughed. "We got a real talent for this kind of stuff, Dog. A real talent."

"If those two gentlemen don't do anything radical today, let's ride out to that pass tomorrow and have a look around," Dog-man said. "See if we can shake something out of the bushes. Those are goodly mountains out there."

***

Decker and Perkins put their animals up and headed for the main house. "What are we gonna say?" Perkins was walking a step or two in front of Decker when Decker asked.

"Ain't gonna say nothin'. Nothin'. You hear me? Those two bastards out there are gonna die tonight and we're gonna drag their bodies toward the Apache camps and mutilate them like the Injuns do." Perkins gave Decker a hard look before they walked into the main room.

"Howdy, Will. Looks like old man Dawson has sent some help to get rid of those outlaws, eh?" Perkins sat down at the table and motioned Penny to bring the coffee pot over. "Think they'll do any good?"

"About as good as Twombley's done. Somebody better start doing some good or Dawson will lose the mail contract. Next Tucson run is day after to-morrow, Perkins. There will be an express wagon and a coach on the run. Those two are supposed to ride with them for two more stops then come back here. Make sure they're outfitted."

Perkins finished his coffee and motioned for Decker to follow and walked out. They stayed in a bunkhouse behind the corrals. "Let's go have a drink and figure this out, Decker."

18

"Neither one rode out, Dog. I would have bet a lot of money on them goin'. What do you make of it? You're the mean one, remember."

"Bein' mean, like I am, Snake, I'd wait until late tonight and attack us. We be drinkin' whiskey and all, it would be easy to take us out. Drag us off and let the coyotes have a good supper."

"Bein' nice like, I wouldn't have thought of that," Snake drawled out, laughing some. "Well, then, Dog, let's get ready for the party."

They had their bedrolls made up to look like they were in them, grabbed their rifles and hid back in the shadows, letting the fire outside the lean-to slowly burn out. "Which one do you want?" Dog-man asked.

"Heavy one's stupid, I do believe, so I'll take him. T'other is smart and mean. Just right for you, Dog." He chuckled and pointed out toward the station complex. "Now, see?" He pointed at two men with their horses in the early dusk. "Just proves what a mean man you are, Dog. I'd a liked it better if no one showed up for this party, though. Seems like people just want to be mean to us." Dog-man didn't say anything but Snake could feel him nodding in agreement.

Two riders were walking their horses out of the corrals. "Ain't quite pitch dark and here they come." The riders stopped a hundred yards or so from camp and tied off their horses. That's when Dog-man noted that they had trailed two mules along. The dark night, trees, and heavy brush hid the movements of the two and Snake and Dog-man tensed for the attack.

It took the two station hands several minutes to work their way to the lean-to, and it was the squat one, Decker, who led the attack. He had an ax handle and drove it hard onto the two bedrolls, over and over while his partner, Perkins, stood back with a cocked rifle.

"That should do it, Decker. Let's get them loaded onto the mules." Perkins turned and walked into the shadows to bring the mules up when Dog-man stepped out and yelled, "Stop right there."

Perkins turned and fired, and ran hard for the horses. Dog-man fell to the ground, grabbing his side. Snake stepped out as Decker pulled his side-arm. Snake shot him in the middle of his large belly, and watched him pitch forward, dropping his weapon.

"Dog," Snake yelled, running to his side.

"I'm not hit hard, Snake. Go get him, Follow Perkins. Go!"

Snake ran hard for where the two outlaws had their animals tied, found one horse and two mules and grabbed the horse, hearing hoof beats off in the desert brush. He had the horse in a full run in half a second, and spotted the shadowy Perkins not too far in front of him. "I'm gonna follow you and kill you hard, Mr. Perkins," he growled. "You shot my partner and I'm gonna shoot you bad."

***

Dog-man crawled over to the almost dead fire and managed to get it burning bright. He pulled his coat and shirt off and found that the bullet had simply gone through thin skin on his right side, not penetrating the body itself. He got the bleeding stopped, cleaned it with hot water, and got a make-shift bandage wrapped around. It was a terrible fight but he managed to get somewhat of a bandage tied in place with his shirt.

"Interesting that we've fired off several shots and there's not a lamp lit down at the station," he muttered. "We ain't that far away that they didn't hear them shots." He found Decker, gut-shot, but still alive and dragged him to the fire. He managed to get his weapons safely out of the way and took a good look at the wound.

"You probably ain't gonna make it, Mr. Decker. Damn fool. Bled all over the bedrolls. Sorry to have to tell anyone this, but that bullet probably opened up every part of you in there. Want to tell me why you two were making this fool attack? You work for Whitlock, do you?"

Decker didn't say anything and Dog-man figured maybe he couldn't. "Use your eyes or your head. Can you hear me?"

Decker nodded and looked right at Dog-man. He could see the hate and the pain in those cruel eyes. "So, do you work for Whitlock?" Decker shook his head this time, but looked away and Dog-man got his answer. "Thank you." He got up slowly, feeling his wound still bleeding some, and added wood to the fire.

I better get a pot of coffee goin'. Old Snake's chasing Perkins, Decker's gonna die, and still there ain't no lamps lit down at the station. Is Will Perkins working with Whitlock, too? Decker all but told me he was. Decker's gonna have a hard death here shortly and I don't have a horse. We shoulda kept our horses up here.

Dog-man was bleeding more than he thought, and when he stood up to get the coffee going, he almost passed out. He crawled to the fire, untied his shirt and let the bandage fall away. "Damn it," he muttered. He pressed the bloody bandage hard on the wound, and held it there for several minutes until he felt comfortable enough to get his shirt tied back around. "Best if I just sit here next to the fire," he chuckled. "Course I couldn't move anyways."

***

The stars were bright enough that Snake could see Perkins about a hundred yards in front of him. After the initial run from the camp, Perkins had slowed his horse to a comfortable lope, never looking behind him, never knowing Snake was there. Perkins had ridden north at first and then turned west, snaking through washes, around great outcrops of rock, and now turned more southwest.

"He's heading for the main road," Snake whispered, looking hard at the stars. "Dog said he thought Whitlock had a camp somewhere near that pass where most of the robberies have taken place. Perkins is leading me right to their camp."

He tightened up thinking about that and knew he was riding into big danger. "Better keep these eyes wide open."

I could ride him down and kill him dead right now, and that's what I should do, him shootin' Dog and all, but I want to know where he's goin'. I'm stickin' with you, Perkins, so lead me into this outlaw's lair of yours.

Perkins stayed on the main road west across what Snake was calling outlaw pass, and after another mile, turned north into steep mountains covered in thin stands of scrubby pine and brush. Snake noticed they were on an actual trail, and stayed as far back from Perkins as he dared. "Don't want to lose sight of the fool."

The trail wound around the sides of hills, down into draws, across washes, some with water, and climbed higher with every turn. They went across a ridge and dropped into a long wide valley. Perkins came to an outcrop and stopped. "Resting that nag you're riding or what?" Snake murmured. Snake pulled his horse up near a stand of pine and watched.

Perkins waved his arms wide and high, twice, and then continued slowly walking his horse forward. Snake saw two men step out from behind a large rock outcrop. Snake got off his horse, moved off the trail and tied it off, getting back where he could see Perkins. Although there wasn't any moon, the stars were more than bright enough for him to pick out the men.

***

"You ain't supposed to be here, Perkins. What the hell you doin' here?" Gary Johnson asked. He and

Fingers O'Neil were standing behind the rocks as Perkins rode up. "Whitlock ain't gonna like this."

"He's not gonna like what I got to tell him, either. Dawson sent some guns to protect this new run coming through."

"All right, Perkins. Go on in. You go with him, O'Neil. I'll stick around, make sure he wasn't followed. You hear something, you come racing back." Gary Johnson was a thin, tall, half Apache killer. O'Neil was straight out of Huntsville. The two found Whitlock in a little Mexican town fifty miles or so south of the border, in jail with an Apache named Tommy Three Feathers, and they have all ridden together since.

It was after teaming up with Perkins and Decker that they were making real money off the stage and express runs on the southern rode to Tucson. It was Whitlock who thought of the two working for Will Penny that made it pay off. In order to do their job at the station, they had to be informed of schedules and merchandise.

Snake watched O'Neil and Perkins slowly walk their horses around the outcrop, leaving Johnson, who melded back into the shadows. Snake crept through the trees and scrub brush and found Johnson sitting on a rock. He had the makings for a smoke out, concentrating on getting one put together. Damn fool. Should know I'm here. Gonna be your last smoke, buster.

When Johnson reached in his shirt pocket is when Snake bashed his head in with a rock, the only sound being broken skull and falling body. Snake picked up the smoke, thought about it, and dropped it, chuckling softly. "Bad medicine, these smokes." He had a smile reaching for a cigar.

He worked his way through the rocks and brush, staying well off the trail, and saw a camp fire with several people standing around. They seemed to be arguing and Snake turned around, making for his horse as quickly and quietly as he could. That was a fine looking camp. Damn permanent if you ask me. Whitlock's planning on staying for a while.

It took him longer than he wanted to get back to the highway, but he made it and put his horse in a hard, fast trot for the station. "Old Dog-man better be alive when I get there. I'll be riled if he ain't."

Snake was within yards of the dark Penny's Stage Stop when he heard horse hooves drumming well behind him. He quickly put the horse into a hard run off the trail and toward their camp, stopping when he was in a stand of scrawny pines. He watched Perkins ride fast into the station yard and jump from his horse.

He was surprised to see the man run for the main house not the bunkhouse. "Now, ain't that interesting," he muttered. There were no lamps lit in the station, and slowly, two or three were fired up. "Sure wish I could hear what"s being said in there right now." He rode quickly up to the campsite.

19

"About time you got back, me bleeding all over, and Decker there, trying to die. Where you been?"

"Stopped off at Whitlock's camp to say howdy. He's got three other fellers working for him, plus of course, Perkins and Decker. Perkins is down at the station now, and I do believe Will Penny and that slob of a wife are working with the gang. I'm not sure we can take 'em on, Dog. I don't mind two to one, but this might be more than that. Might need some help with this one."

"We're twenty miles from Las Cruces, old man. Could be there before dawn. Get Dawson to send out some of those security people he has. Ride Whitlock down and be on our way to California."

"You ain't in no condition for a twenty mile ride. You work your way down to the station, see if you can learn anything and I'll ride out, bring Ed Twombley and some boys back. Don't be gettin' in trouble," he laughed. He was mounted and on his way, still laughing.

Dog-man took the time to re-dress his wound,

found the bleeding had stopped, and made his way out of the stand of trees for the station. He could feel the effects of the wound, but shook off the weakness. He was careful to skirt the corrals to keep the horses and mules from kicking up a fuss, and got as close to a window lit by a lamp as he could. That's Claudia doing the talking, not Will. She's giving Perkins the devil, wanting to know where Decker is.

"I told you to kill those two. All you had to do was walk up to their camp and shoot 'em dead. Where's Decker?"

"They shot him. Probably dead by now," he said. She stiffened at the comment and he continued. "I told Whitlock and he's bringing the gang down here. Gonna wait right here for the next Dawson shipment and then move on. He promised not to harm you or Will, so Dawson will never know that you helped us."

"I was gonna ride off with Decker, you damn fool." She was screaming right into his face. "I was gonna leave that drunken Will Penny and ride with Sam Decker. You've ruined my life, John Perkins," she screamed. Claudia Penny probably outweighed Perkins by fifty pounds or more and rushed at him, knocking the two of them to the floor. She had her short, fat fingers trying to wrap around Perkins' scrawny neck, but he was scrambling away.

He got to his feet, was about to kick her in the head when she lunged forward, wrapping her arms around his legs. They were on the floor again, he thrashing out with arms, fists, and feet, her desperately trying to hold on to him. She wanted to get on top, crush the man, strangle the life from him.

"You ruined my life," she screamed again and again, swinging wildly at the man. Perkins was able to get back on his feet when the shotgun went off. Will Penny had been awakened from his drunken slumber and fired one barrel of his long goose gun into the ceiling.

"What the hell's going on here," he demanded, leveling the gun at Perkins. "Claudia, what are you doing? What's the meaning of this, Perkins?" He drank himself to sleep every night and he was still about two-thirds drunk, and unable to grasp what was happening, holding onto a chair for balance with one hand, and the shotgun with the other.

Claudia scrambled to her feet, her face full of rage, and rushed at Will Penny, knocking the shotgun from his hands, pushing him to the floor, and kicking him in the head. "You drunken bastard," she screamed. Before Perkins knew what was happening, she grabbed up the shotgun and blew Will Penny's head into a shredded mess.

Claudia whirled on Perkins and tried to pull the trigger but both barrels had been emptied and Perkins leaped forward and knocked Claudia Penny on to the floor. He ripped the shotgun from her and tossed it aside, pulled his sidearm and pointed it at her head. "Don't make me kill you, Claudia. Whitlock will be here sometime after sunrise and we can get this all straightened out to your benefit."

He stepped back and watched her get to her feet, never taking the gun off target. She was bawling, screaming, and raging angry as she moved slowly around the large main room of the station, wild eyes searching for a way to get a weapon. "Get out of my home, Perkins. Get out now and if I ever see you, I'll kill you. Get out," she screamed.

Perkins slowly backed toward the main doors of the building, never lowering his weapon, never turning his back on the mean woman. He had his hand behind his back, letting his fingers feel for the latch, found it, and slowly backed out the door, closing it quickly, and turned to run for his horse.

Instead, he faced a cocked Colt held by Dog-man who gave Perkins a big smile. "Killed the lady's boyfriend, did you? Shame, shame, Mr. Perkins. Hand me your gun or die." Dog-man took the gun and motioned Perkins off the veranda and into the darkness of the night. "Just walk right up to our fine diggin's, Perkins. You have a little job to do when we get there and I have to figure out what to do with you before Whitlock gets here."

They found Decker dead when they arrived and Dog-man had Perkins drag the big man's body well off from the campsite. He got the fire up and hot, never taking the gun off the outlaw. He made Perkins get some coffee going, and turned to him, gun leveled at his mid-section. "What to do with you," he murmured. "Snake would tell me to just shoot you, you know that, right? That's probably the right answer, too," he chuckled.

"Turn around and face those trees, Perkins." He did and Dog-man rapped him hard with the butt of his Colt and went ahead and tied him tight to a tree. "That makes more sense than shootin' you, Mr. Perkins. You can thank me later." He poured some coffee and sat down on a rock. "We got, no, that ain't right. I got a problem. Perkins told Claudia that Whitlock would leave his camp to come here about sunrise. That ain't far off. About the time Snake is due in Las Cruces.

"Well, come on, Whitlock. I'll be as ready for you as I can get."

***

Snake made good time riding on a good, well-marked road, and slipped into Las Cruces well before sunrise. He rode up to the large barn and corrals behind the Dawson Express building and stepped down from his horse. The town was still mostly dark and he hadn't seen anyone.

"Make one move and you're a dead outlaw," Warren Baxter growled. "I thought that was you sneakin' around town. Drop your guns, Mr. Snake or die." Baxter must have spotted Snake riding toward the Dawson complex and followed. He had a nasty grin on his face when Snake turned to him.

"Ain't no outlaw, Sheriff. Here to tell Mr. Dawson about some outlaws, though. Me and Dog found the Whitlock outlaw gang's camp and they're gonna hit Penny's Stage Stop tomorrow. He's gotta know, Sheriff."

"You can't buffalo me, Snake. Drop your guns and I mean now." Baxter made a big mistake and waved his rifle in Snake's face. Snake grabbed it, it went off, and Snake ripped it from the sheriff's hands.

"I should just whip this across your big dumb head, Sheriff but I won't. Now, let's you and me walk into that big barn and wake some of those Dawson boys up."

They didn't have to, The rifle shot woke them up and it was Ed Twombley first out the barn doors. "What the hell?"

"Just me and the sheriff doing a little dance," Snake said. "We need to get with Mr. Dawson, Twombey. There's big trouble at the Penny Stage Stop. The two wranglers work for Whitlock and the gang is about to ride down on the station."

"Damn," Twombley said. "Why're you fightin' with Baxter?"

"Man can't think past his nose. Wouldn't listen to what I rode in to tell you. We gotta hurry, Twombley."

Baxter was fuming, and reached for his sidearm. Twombley stepped between the sheriff and Snake, facing the sheriff. "Calm down, Baxter, damn it. Have you heard one word that's been said? Knock it off right now."

"He's under arrest, Twombley. He attacked me, assaulted me. You're under arrest, Snake," he snarled, pointing a finger.

Twombley pushed Baxter back toward one of his security men. "Take him in the barn and get some sense in him. Let's go Snake, and find Dawson." Snake handed Baxter's rifle to the man and walked toward the Dawson building, now lit up with the fracas going on outside. Dawson met them at the door.

"Snake, Twombley. What's going on?"

Snake spilled it out as fast as his Texas would let him and Dawson nodded to Twombley. "We ride in ten, Ed. Leave two here and everyone else rides."

Twombley raced for the barn to get everyone saddled and on the trail. "You said Dog-man was wounded? How bad, Snake?"

"He took one through some side meat, Mr. Dawson. He'll be fine after he gets a few minutes of sympathy. Perkins was in the main house and all the lamps got lit. The Penny's must be involved."

"Will Penny isn't, Snake. The man hasn't drawn a sober breath in five years. It wouldn't surprise me, though, if Claudia was. She thought she was gettin' a free ride with Will running the station. Didn't occur to her there might be work involved."

Tim Rocha, one of Twombley's men, had Baxter calmed down enough that he could at least hold a conversation. Dawson told him what was going on and asked, since he was sheriff of the district, would he like to lead the posse.

"I won't ride with an outlaw," he snarled, pointing a finger at Snake.

"Neither will I, Sheriff," Snake said. "So long." He put the spurs to his horse and Twombley motioned for the seven mounted men to follow. They rode at a fast trot, only slowing to let the horses catch their breath once on the ride to the Penny Station.

"I sure do draw 'em in, eh, Mr. Dawson? Old Jeb Altman, a dismissed Texas Ranger serving as El Paso City Marshal and Warren Baxter, Sheriff of Las Cruces. Only lawman I've met that made any sense was Seth Bullock up in Deadwood."

"Sometimes men get themselves in situations they aren't capable of handling, Snake. You've done a fine job of finding two of them on this trip." There was general laughter over that. They were making good time and Dawson knew it was time to get primed for a fight.

"We don't know if Whitlock is there yet, boys, so let's slow it down and ride at a walk toward where Snake and Dog-man have their camp." Dawson led them off the main road when they were more than a mile from the station and well out of sight. "Let's try to keep the dust down, boys."

20

Orson Whitlock had his two remaining men saddled and on the trail as the sun blossomed on an already warm late fall morning. Whitlock was a mean man who scowled more often than not, carried a grudge to, and sometimes beyond, its endpoint, and thrived on hurting people, even if they worked for him. As they rode out of their concealed hideout, they found the body of Gary Johnson.

"What happened here, Fingers? You led Perkins in. What's this all about?"

Fingers O'Neil was off his horse running to Johnson's body. "He was alive when I left him. Perkins must have been followed." He took one look at Johnson's bashed in skull and remounted. "Perkins said Dawson had security people at Penny Station. One or more of them must have followed him here."

"That means they're waitin' for us," Whitlock muttered. "Perkins also said that Decker is dead. All right, then. Let's not ride directly to the station, boys. Let's come in from the north, across that one ridge and into the wash that leads through that stand of trees, north of the station. Don't plan on gettin' any help from Perkins or that fat woman Decker's been doing."

They didn't bother to bury the dead Johnson and rode hard on the main highway, turned north well before the station, riding cross country before turning back east for several miles. It was rough high desert country, rocky, steep in places, with deep ravines, cuts, washes, and granite cliffs slowing them down. Every bush was designed to hurt horse and rider.

"When we cross this ridge, the station will be in front of us about three or four miles out. Try to make as little dust as possible and we'll ride into the wash. Keep your eyes open and be quiet," he said, more as a snarl than a comment. "I'm about as angry as I want to be, with Decker and Johnson gettin' killed, and Dawson sending guns after us. I don't need any more stupid from anyone."

The three riders, in single file, crossed the ridge and dropped into the wash, riding at a slow walk. Dog-man was sitting on a rock near the fire tending his wound, which was trying to be infected. He had a pan of boiling water on a hot rock, dipping a clean rag. He was fully involved in cleaning the wound, muttering, groaning from time to time from the pain. He stopped once and poured a cup of coffee. "What was that?" He muttered, slowly getting to his feet.

Three men with rifles trained on him walked out of the trees. "One wrong move and you die," Orson Whitlock said. Dog-man's gun rig and shirt were next to the rock he had been sitting on and he simply stood still.

"If you boys are looking for the stage stop, it's on down the hill there," Dog-man said.

"We know where it is, lawman." Whitlock looked around the meager camp. "Take a look around, Fingers."

Fingers O'Neil walked to the lean-to and started going through what was piled about. Dog-man was looking at Whitlock, then Three Feathers, then his gun and knew he would be dead well before he could grab it. It's about time for Snake to come ridin' to my rescue, he almost chuckled.

"Look what I found." Tommy Three Feathers led John Perkins into the camp. "Decker's body is back in those rocks. Perkins says this guy's a Dawson security guard. His partner rode to Las Cruces to bring the law." Three Feathers walked up to Dog-man and slashed him across the side of the head with his rifle.

"That's for Decker," he said. He stomped his boot into Dog-man's ribs. "And that's for Johnson."

"That's enough, Three Feathers. We might need him for protection. Tie him tight but don't kill him." Whitlock motioned for Fingers to continue searching and sat down near the fire. "Bad timing," he muttered. He poured a cup of coffee and stirred the fire. "Find anything?" He yelled at Fingers O'Neil.

"Just normal camp stuff and some paperwork, which I can't read. Doesn't look important." Dog-man was conscious enough to understand and cringed when Fingers said 'paperwork'. That would be their bank receipts and booklet. They also had more than a thousand dollars cash hidden in their stash that Fingers must have missed.

Tommy Three Feathers had Dog-man lashed tight, laid out in the dirt near the fire, and Dog-man was trying to roll so he could sit up. Three Feathers kicked him in the ribs again. Dog-man was sure at least two of them were broken. His bullet wound was bleeding again, and his head had a deep cut across his brow, bleeding freely.

"Drag that ugly bastard off, Three Feathers. Can't stand watching a man bleed and not wanting to kill him," Whitlock said. "We need to have a long talk. What we had planned just went to hell, on us. Don't want to lose that money tomorrow, but Dawson's sending men out here changes things."

Three Feathers just grabbed the rope tied around Dog-man's feet and dragged him across the rocks to the trees and left him. Dog-man waited just moments before starting to work on his ropes. They were tight and well tied, he knew, but knew that he had a knife in his left boot if he could get to it.

"That express wagon, tomorrow, is supposed to be a big shipment, Whitlock," Fingers said. "Lots of gold coin and cash money is what Claudia said. Sure don't want to ride off on that."

"No, I don't either," Whitlock said. "If Dawson sent men out here for protection, and now one of them has reported what he found, then that shipment has already been cancelled. We're not riding off from it, Fingers. It ain't gonna be there. What we gotta do is silence Claudia and Will Penny and get out of this country. They know too much."

"Penny's already dead, Whitlock," Perkins said. "She blew his head into a hundred pieces with that shotgun." Whitlock laughed right out and poured some coffee in Dog-man's cup.

"Now, see?" Whitlock was still laughing. "She didn't need him anymore, so kill the bastard. Good for her, but she's gotta join him. We'll kill her, burn the station, and high-tail it for better huntin' country. Understand there might be easy pickin's around those mines west of us."

"What about Dawson's man? Just leave him or shoot him first." Three Feathers didn't care which. "That fat woman had a thing for old Decker. He said she was the worst he could remember," he laughed. "Think I'll pass. How about you, Fingers?"

"You get any of that, Perkins? Maybe I'll try," Fingers said, chuckling, giving Three Feathers a thumb's up.

"That wildcat is all yours," Perkins said. "You think about her. I'm gonna shoot the Dawson man. Make up for the gash in my head. Bastard."

"No, leave him be. Dawson'll have half a dozen riders coming down on us at any time, so let's get down to the station and take care of business. Bring him with us. He might be worth something to old Dawson. We can always leave him in the station when we light it up," he laughed.

**

"Riders," Snake hollered, pointing toward Penny Station. They were about half way to the campsite, riding single file through the open desert. "Three horses, no, four horses, but one holds what looks like a body. Damn, that better not be Dog-man."

"Let's ride, boys," Dawson yelled out, sinking spurs in his big horse. They spread out through the stunted brush, leaped small washes and brush in the way, and rode hard for the station. "They see us," Dawson yelled. "If that body slumped across that one horse is Dog-man, let's not make it worse. Shoot to kill, boys."

"Whitlock, look!" Three Feathers was pointing at the line of riders coming across the open plain, men holding weapons, and riding hard. "It's the Dawson posse. Make for the station."

They were a few hundred yards shy of the main building and raced for its protection. When they were getting close they came under fire from the big house. The three men pulled their horses up fast and dove for whatever shelter they could find. Whitlock was jammed between a rock and a fence post, neither one big enough to hide his large frame.

"Who the hell's shooting at us?" Whitlock yelled, crawling like a snake to a better hiding place. A rifle cracked and he felt the bullet blast its way into his leg. It went in just above his knee and exploded out at his groin. Whitlock howled in pain, saw a pulsing stream of blood arc into the morning air. He thrashed, tried to crawl, cried out in pain, and finally slumped in the filth of the stage stop dirt.

He tried to rise, grabbed at his groin, screaming, and another rifle shot ended his pain as it blew through his chest. "Decker taught the fat lady how to shoot," Three Feathers chuckled. "It's your fight if you want it, Fingers." Three Feathers wormed his way into the corrals, out of sight of the main house, and found a horse he could mount bareback. He had a rope through the horse's mouth, leaped aboard, and left the corral in a high six rail jump, screaming the Apache way.

Fingers O'Neil saw Perkins slowly working his

way toward the back door of the main house, put two quick shots into the front of the house and made his way through brush and rocks to join him. Perkins pointed at a window to the side of the back door. "If she saw you sneaking this way, watch that window. She's a dead shot, can take the head right off a chicken at fifty yards." He crouched behind a rain barrel, looked at Fingers for back-up, and sprinted to the door.

Fingers O'Neil didn't wait and fired three fast shots, one through the window and two through the door, and followed Perkins. Perkins crashed through the door and rolled across the large kitchen, gun in hand. Fingers was right behind him.

Claudia's rifle barked twice and Fingers moaned as one bullet drove through his shoulder as he hit the floor. The second bullet went through the top of his boot, breaking numerous bones before coming out the sole. The shock of the two shots was enough to knock Fingers out.

Perkins rushed for the wall and pressed himself to it. Claudia couldn't be more than ten feet on the other side and there was just the one door. He realized his mistake too late. Should have run with Three Feathers or just stayed outside and fought off the posse.

John Perkins was stuck. Claudia on the other side of the wall and a posse riding down hard on the station. He knew she would never just let him give himself up. She already tried to kill him several times. His only hope was to surrender to the posse before she got to him. The kitchen was large and there was just the one door leading out to the corrals. Between Perkins and the door were two long tables with benches, and a massive cast iron cook stove. To get to that door, he would have to do the same as when he came in.

He came into the kitchen at a run, through a busted up door, and dove over one of the tables. The heavy tables and benches stood in his way and he knew he was trapped.

21

"I'll get him," Snake yelled when Three Feathers made his break. "Find Dog-man." He spurred the horse into a wild full-out cross-country gallop, sitting firmly balanced this time. Three Feathers was on the main road, his long frame stretched out along the horse's neck. Snake several hundred yards behind, both horses racing at break-neck speed. The difference being, Snake's horse was worn-out tired, Three Feathers' was morning fresh. Snake watched the distance between them increase rapidly and knew he would never catch up.

Snake was not the kind of man who gave up easily and brought his horse to a comfortable trot for the long haul and kept close eye on the hoof prints left behind by the Apache killer. "Might be out for a while, pard," he said, as much to himself as to his horse. "That bastard can ride a horse." At the trot, his horse was able to catch his breath and get some strength back.

Three Feathers rode hard for several miles and brought his horse back to a walk, not knowing that he had someone following. They knew where our hideout was but even Whitlock doesn't know about the caves north of the pass. Three Feathers found the caves following one of the stage robberies and had a stash hidden there, which included some dried food, gold coins, blankets, and extra guns.

He rode across what Snake had come to call outlaw pass and turned north toward the high mountains. Snake saw where the half Apache killer left the road and followed, now at a walk. He's taking us to Whitlock's camp. The tracks were easy to follow and climbed rapidly through jumbled rock formations and stands of scrub timber.

It was when they came across a saddleback that Three Feathers moved off the trail to the outlaw camp. He followed the killer across the pass and down into a broad plain split by a massive rock wall. It was about two miles distant and Three Feathers was riding straight for it.

He saw Three Feathers less than a mile in front of him. "Whoa up, big boy," he said, moving into a small stand of pine trees. "Let's just watch for a minute or two."

Three Feathers rode straight up to that rock wall and seemed to disappear. "Now there's something you don't see every day," Snake muttered. He rode out from the trees and toward where he last saw the outlaw. "Well now," he muttered. There was a cleft in the wall and a narrow pathway that led in. "Oh, damn. Gotta do it," he finally said in a whisper.

Snake stepped off the tired horse and tied him to a rock outcrop. The pathway into the cleft was only about four feet wide and deep shadows filled the void. "That bastard could be waiting for me at any step I take," he muttered. He kept as close to one side as he could and slowly edged into the shadows. He was several hundred feet in when the cleft widened to twenty feet or more and even the sun managed to get in a bit. The rock walls were almost polished and Snake tried to imagine what the water crashing through would be like in a thunderstorm.

He stopped before walking into the opening and gave the area a good looking over. He saw where rushing water had carved its path and then caught a quick glimpse of Three Feathers moving into deep shadows on the east wall. "Another pathway through these walls? I'm gonna get you, mister. Real soon, too."

He followed along the wall of the deep cleft around to where Three Feathers had been and almost walked into a water carved cave. He fell to the ground and tried to peer around the edge. It was mid-day and the sunlight was intense. "Can't see into that dark hole, but I know you're in there," Snake whispered. He heard something. Was it someone moving around? No, it was someone or something scraping or digging into the sand.

"I gotta see," Snake grumbled and crawled slowly around the edge of the cave and into the shadows. The cave was only about ten feet high and twenty feet wide. It seemed to go deep into the rock, with the ceiling sloping down quickly. It took a couple of minutes for Snake's eyes to become accustomed to the dark. He could hear the scraping continue and slowly was able to spot the Apache killer.

Three Feathers was along the far wall, deep in the cavern, pushing sand around. "He's looking for something," Snake whispered. He watched for another couple of minutes, working on what to do next.

"Can't just wait around no longer," he muttered. He stood up, rifle in hand, and stepped toward Three Feathers. "Lose somethin', didja?" He already had the hammer back on the rifle and when the Apache outlaw spun, desperately grasping for his sidearm, Snake shot, jacked a round in, and shot again.

Three Feathers rolled away from the first shot which buried itself in the sand, but the second shot grazed his arm before hitting the rock wall. It ricocheted four or five times around that cave before falling to the sand. Both men were flat in the sand as the bullet whined near them.

"Give it up, killer. There's more than just me comin' for you." Snake was deep in the sandy cave floor.

Three Feathers was on his back, his arm bleeding some but not in serious pain He rolled, tried to get his weapon out, and Snake yelled out again. "Quit. You're done for. Time to die." Snake crawled forward a few feet and leveled his rifle. "Give it up." Three Fingers rolled hard through the sand, pulling his weapon, and fired twice, the bullets dancing all over the cave.

Snake buried himself and when the singing stopped, raised the rifle and killed the Indian with one shot. "Damn fool. Coulda killed me," he shouted. He walked over and kicked Three Feathers in the ribs. He looked around the cave, saw where Three Feathers had been digging. "What have we got here, another Whitlock hideout?"

He was on his knees pushing sand around where Three Feathers had been pushing dirt around and found a metal money box half buried. "Ain't the gang's hideout, is it, Mr. Dead Man. Whitlock know you were pilfering his loot? I'd bet not. Must weigh damn near fifty pounds."

He opened the box and found a considerable stash including cash, gold coins, watches, and jewelry. "Yeah, old Whitlock ain't gonna like to hear you been stealin' from the outlaw boss," Snake chuckled. "He just might want to shoot you, too." He looked over and knew that Three Feathers was dead. "I'm just gonna leave you right here, killer man, and go find my partner."

He had a hard time dragging the heavy money box back to where Three Feathers' horse was and couldn't get it up on the horse's bare back. "Well, just damn me," he muttered. He had to drag the money box and walk the outlaw's horse back to where his own horse was tied.

"This might be different," he said. He fought hard to get the money box up and on to the back of the saddle of his horse. It took considerable time and effort to get it secured. "Damn thing ain't worth the effort," he said more than once. Snake mounted the outlaw's horse, bareback for the ride back to Penny Station. "Ain't rode bareback since I was just a tadpole. Sure ain't the most comfortable way to ride but that money box weighs about three tons, I think. You dumb horse, you better be glad I'm thinking about your welfare."

***

Dawson led the rest of the group toward the station and motioned to dismount as rifle fire echoed from the back of the main house. Ed Twombley had his men spread out and surrounded the building and he ran hard for the corrals. He worked through the frightened horses and mules and saw the smashed and open back door, got through the fence rails and ran for the building.

Dawson and one man were right behind him. "Will and Claudia are in there," Dawson said. "Let's be careful now." He stuck his head around the busted up doorway and a bullet blasted its way just inches from him. "Damn," he said, backing up fast.

"Don't be doin' that again, boss," Twombley said. He got down on his belly and tried to look inside the kitchen. He saw Fingers O'Neil sprawled on the floor, bleeding but breathing, and Perkins standing, almost hugging the wall near a doorway. It was the rifle barrel sticking out from the doorway that held his attention.

"One of the Penny's has one outlaw down and bleeding and another ready to soil his pants," Twombley chuckled. "Chastain, run around to the front of the station and call off the Penny's. We'll take the outlaws from this end."

"No, wait," Dawson hollered. "No. Remember what Snake said. They might be involved with Whitlock. Go on around, Chastain, but don't expect to be welcomed. They could be part of the outlaw gang."

Chastain ran back through the corrals and approached the front of the station building. He jumped the rail onto the veranda porch and rushed to the big doors, which were slightly ajar. He couldn't see anyone at first glimpse, then spotted Claudia standing near the doorway at the back of the big room.

"Claudia, we're Dawson's people. Here to help.

Where's Will?"

Claudia Penny whirled and fired her rifle at the door, jacked another round in, and fired again. Chastain flattened himself on the wooden deck when she turned to fire, pulled his Colt, and shot her twice. She staggered but didn't fall, blood pouring from her chest wounds. She fired at the doorway again, jacked a round, and fell to the floor before she could pull the trigger.

Chastain ran to her and kicked the rifle away, and turning toward the kitchen saw Perkins step through, his pistol aimed at his head. "Damn you," Chastain howled, spun around and fell to the floor, firing a round off. Perkins shot too, and both men missed. Chastain rolled behind a large sofa in front of the fireplace and Perkins made a dash for the front door, firing a shot toward the sofa.

Chastain yelped when the bullet creased his buttocks and fired quickly at the running killer, knocking him to the ground, a bullet through his hip. Perkins fell onto the veranda deck and was trying to crawl off when Dawson kicked him in the head. Dawson grabbed the outlaw's gun and motioned for Chastain to come on out.

"Can't, Boss. Bleeding. Got me in the butt."

"Stay there, I'll have help for you as soon as we know it's clear."

Twombley, hearing the gunfire from out front, rushed into the kitchen and grabbed the gun from the wounded Fingers O'Neil and got him on his feet. That's when he saw the mangled body of Will Penny. "You bastards," he muttered.

"The fat woman did that," O'Neil whimpered.

They moved into the great room and Twombley

had O'Neil laid out on the couch. "You shot bad, Chastain?"

"In my butt," he laughed. Twombley got him out from behind the couch and took a quick look.

"Just a scratch," he laughed. "You were lying on some broken glass. You're fine." Chastain stood up, flexed his legs a bit, got a sheepish grin, and walked out into the sunlight.

***

Dawson had everyone gathered outside the station. "Somewhere between here and that stand of trees in the draw up there is Dog-man. Find him." He motioned for Twombley. "After we find Dog-man, it's time to start burying the dead and then start the search for Snake. It would be the most horrible thing if we lost both those men."

It took less than fifteen minutes to find the horse that Dog-man was tied to and get him free. He was conscious but hurt bad. His side and head were bleeding heavily and he had at least three broken ribs. Dog-man was carried into the main station and laid out on one of the large sofas in front of the fireplace. "We gotta get that bleeding stopped," Dawson said. "Ain't gonna lose this man. Chastain, ride like the wind for Las Cruces and bring the doctor. If Warren Baxter gives you any crap, shoot him." There weren't any chuckles and Chastain ran for his horse.

22

"I ain't rode a horse this way since I was just a boy," Snake remembered. "Pa laughed when I said I wanted a saddle. Laughed harder when I fell off." He was sitting straight up, bareback and only the lead rope used by Three Feathers in his hand. The lead was long and Three Feathers had it looped around and through the horse's jaw. He had the two ends of the rope for reins.

"Damn finely trained horse," he muttered. "A little knee pressure here and he turns, and a little on the other side and he turns. Acts more like a cow pony than something in a stage stop corral. Gonna be a long slow ride back to Penny Station, though, so I might as well enjoy this."

The mountain trail meandered around hillsides, across dry washes that would be raging torrents in a thunderstorm, through stands of stunted pine and desert brush. He kicked up a rabbit or two and that was the sum total of visitors on a hot fall afternoon. "I wish I'd paid attention to how far we ran. Ain't gonna make the station before sundown at this rate."

He was running out of daylight and many miles from the station. Snake had been awake and busy since before daybreak and was ready for a camp. He found a small stand of trees, a mud hole of a spring, and tied off the horses. There was grass and water, and he had a small fire going as soon as the horses were taken care of. Supper consisted of hard biscuits and coffee, and he made sure the fire was fully out before crawling into his bedroll. Didn't want any tell-tale smoke pointing out where he was.

"If it ain't angry and stupid marshals and sheriffs gettin' in our craw it's angry and stupid outlaws," he muttered. "Oh, Dog, you gotta be hurt bad and I ain't there for you. Damn, damn, damn." He was cussing softly as he drifted off to sleep.

It was black dark when he was awakened by what he was sure were footsteps. No moon and no stars. The sky was covered in heavy clouds, the wind was blowing, and there were flashes of lightening off in the distance. Rolling thunder was miles away, but echoed across the face of the mountains.

Even so, he was sure he heard footsteps. He had his rifle in one hand and revolver in the other, slipped into the stand of trees, and fought off the last of his sleep. Snake was flat on the ground behind some brush and watched two figures slowly move out of the night and advance on his bedroll.

Were there only the two? Why would they know he was there? The fire. He remembered almost too late that he was in Apache country. They had seen it or smelled it, and waited for the right time to attack. Outlaws, Apaches, and lunatic lawmen, he thought with just the hint of a chuckle, just right for me and Dog-man. One of the Indians swung a club onto the bedroll at the same time that Snake pulled the trigger of his rifle.

The second Indian just as quickly melded into the darkness and Snake could hear him running hard. Snake moved slowly back into his camp, checked to make sure the one was dead, and tried to hear where the second one might be. The camp site was on a small hill top, a broad ridge, with the main road at the bottom of one side and a dry wash at the other.

"There he goes," Snake murmured, hearing two horses clattering through the wash. "Time to move on." It was still pitch dark as he broke camp. "No fire, no food, just bad people tryin' to kill me and my partner." He had the one horse saddled, the strong box firmly tied in place, and jumped onto Three Feathers' horse. "Ain't even trying to be light," he growled, easing the horses down onto the main road. "We should be less than ten miles from the station, but with Apaches looking for me I do wish I had a saddle to ride in."

He had the horses at a comfortable lope, rode down the middle of the two-track roadway, and spent considerable time looking behind him. The thunder and lightning were blasting the heavens and it wasn't ten minutes and he felt heavy drops of cold rain falling. "That'll wipe out my trail," Snake chuckled.

It wasn't long before he had to pull up. The road dropped into a broad gulch that was running high. "Cain't get across there and it's too dark to look for a decent ford. Who am I kidding. With this rain, there won't be a decent ford. He found some trees and walked the horse in. He hunched down under a poncho to wait out the storm.

***

Chastain made it back to the station, Doctor Brett Canyon in tow, late in the afternoon. Sheriff Warren Baxter and one deputy, Otis Coppersmith, were also with him. Baxter swaggered up to George Dawson, Coppersmith right alongside. "Did those two outlaws cause all this, Dawson?"

"The outlaws you see spread out here are all dead, Baxter. At one time they were Orson Whitlock's gang. You can take your swagger someplace else or you can help get these outlaws buried." Dawson was furious and directed Doctor Canyon inside where Dog-man was. "Chastain, I told you to shoot this bastard."

Chastain tried to hold in the chuckles as he led the doctor inside and Twombley got a crew digging graves. "One member of the gang is still barely alive, Baxter. Whitlock and Perkins are dead. Will and Claudia Penny are dead." Dawson was an angry man and wasn't in any mood to take any crap from this fool of a sheriff. "Tommy Three Feathers ran off and Snake is chasing him right now. Only Fingers O'Neil is alive. This is my place, Baxter, so I won't put up with your stupidity. Help or leave out."

Dawson looked around at what was left of his stage station. Doors and windows busted up, bullet holes in walls and doors, and the couple who were supposed to run the place dead. He was glaring at Baxter and finally just stomped off.

"Coppersmith, help them out with those graves.

Deputy Marshal Wilson sent me a detailed wire on what took place in El Paso, Dawson," he yelled out. "Not sure I believe it all, but I ain't looking to hang those two. I ain't sure I want them around Las Cruces, though."

Dawson spun around, almost ready to go for his sidearm. "You're a hard-headed idiot, Sheriff. I can't tell you how much money those two have saved me in the last few months. I'm about to lead some men out to track down Snake. He's on Three Feathers' trail and that outlaw Apache is a killer. You're welcome to ride with us since this is your jurisdiction, but only if you come to your senses."

"I don't much care for you talking that way, Dawson. You might have a lot of money and a lot of people you can boss around, but I ain't one of them. I'm the sheriff in this jurisdiction and you'd be doing yourself a favor to remember that."

"The only thing I remember is you demanding a hanging for two young men that haven't broken a single law. If you're only here to work your jaw, then have at it. We're riding to help Snake. If you were any kind of a sheriff you would have been the one to break up this outlaw gang, not my people. Get out of my way," he growled, pushing his way past Baxter.

It was getting late and Dawson noticed the clouds building to the north. "Gonna be a gully-washer for sure. We'll take it nice and slow, watch the trail closely. We don't know where Three Feathers was riding to, so we gotta ride cautious like."

Chastain had a mule packed with enough food for two days and Dawson led a group out of Penny Station. Dawson, Chastain, and Twombley rode at a solid trot up the main highway toward Outlaw Pass. It took Warren Baxter less than a minute to realize he really did need to be in that posse. It was late coming, but he knew he should be leading the group and rode fast to catch up.

"The only thing we know is Snake followed the Indian out of the station. Keep a close eye to the sides of the road in case they veered off. Twombley, you're the best tracker. You lead."

"If Snake goes after Three Feathers the way he went after those outlaws north of Santa Fe, Three Feathers is already dead," Twombley said.

"Hope you're right," Dawson muttered.

It was hot, no wind, and the ride was just that, a ride across the desert, through country Mother Nature seemed to not much care for. They were almost six miles out when Twombley pulled up sharply. He was twenty yards or so in front of the group and Dawson rode up fast. "What?" He hollered.

"Too dark, Dawson. Let's make camp and hit it early in the morning. Gonna rain on us hard, too."

Nobody argued and camp was put together quickly, off the road near a great tumble of rocks. It was thunder late that night that got the group moving. The rain and wind weren't too far behind, and Dawson called the men together. "This is gonna wipe out any tracks that might have been left. We gotta keep going, though. Keep your eyes wide open, boys."

The main east-west trail was a sloppy mud hole in most places as they moved west. They were climbing out of a muddy draw when Twombley waved at Dawson.

"Shots, Mr. Dawson. Not too far in front of us."
Dawson and Twombley sat quiet and then another
series of shots echoed out of the late morning air.

"Let's pick it up, boys, Snake might be in trouble."

***

Snake had only made about three miles along the
edge of the flooded gully when he spotted movement on the trail behind him. He got back into a
steep and rocky area off to the north. He got the
animals tied to rocks and slopped his way up the
hillside into a small grotto where he could look
down on the flats below. The rain was incessant.
The rocks gave him protection and he had clouded
vision across the side of the hill. It was just minutes
and five Indians came riding fast up through the
rocks, right on his trail. They spotted Snake's trail
and immediately and started moving through the
scrub and rocks toward him.

"Now, see," he murmured. "If Dog-man were
here, the odds would be in our favor. Well, damn,
he ain't, and I gotta do all the fightin' alone. I'm
gonna have a talk with that boy." He made sure his
rifle and sidearm were fully loaded and that he had
more ammunition at hand. The Apaches moved
silently up the hillside using hand signals to give
directions. It didn't take long for them to find the
horses and start following Snake's trail through the
mud.

"Hope they don't mess with my stuff. Damn, that
strong box is right out in plain sight. Well if they
see it, maybe they'll quit looking for me." He had to
chuckle knowing that wouldn't happen. "Apaches

get on a good blood trail they don't get side-tracked by something as simple as gold or jewels."

One man stood out as the leader of the band and he was moving the others so as to give a broad front, making it difficult for Snake to see all of them at the same time. When they moved it was as a group and as they ducked and dove behind brush and rocks, Snake lost track of individuals.

"I ain't gonna let 'em get too close, by damn," he muttered. The five were spread across a thirty or forty yard front and moved slowly up through the brush and rocks toward his position. He brought his sights to bear on the large, squat, man who was giving all the commands. The Indian didn't make a sound when the bullet crashed through his chest, and the four remaining men didn't hesitate half a step, either.

"Only one thing on these boy's minds and that's my scalp," Snake chuckled. He fired at a second man and missed by inches. The four were on the ground, crawling toward him, one piece of brush or rock at a time. At a signal, all four fired into the rocks, bullets bouncing off and flying in every direction. None hit Snake but he couldn't tell you why.

"That's something I've sure as hell seen before," he murmured. "The way those bullets bounced off these rocks, each shot was like three or four." His time in the cave with Three Feathers danced in his mind and he knew he had to get out of that rock cavern.

He quickly abandoned his little grotto as being unsafe, and moved up the hill, using rocks and scrub pine for cover. He found two rocks close together allowing him good vision between them or on either side, and took a long aim at one of the Indians as he tried to move up the hill fast.

The shot dropped the attacker, but it wasn't a killing hit. "That won't do, Snake," he said. "A wounded one is just as dangerous still." The Apache was hit in the hip and was able to crawl under some brush. He quickly fired back at where he thought the shot had come from. All the other men did too, spraying the area but not coming close to Snake.

"I got it down to three and a half to one, Dog-man," he murmured. He looked out across the area, trying to locate each of the attackers and saw what looked like men on horses about a mile out. "More? Damn, damn, damn." He saw the wounded man working to stem the blood from his wound and took a long aim. "That's better," he whispered. He watched the man crumple into a dead heap at the shot. "Now, it's three plus however many are in that massive column stormin' after my hide."

One of the Apache attackers spotted the riders too, and signaled the others. They changed from being the attackers to being the defenders, and Snake smiled for the first time that day. "So, these newcomers ain't friends, eh? Oh, Dog-man, you should be here to see this." He saw one of the Indians trying to scramble behind some scrub brush and put a bullet deep in his back. The man wasn't dead, and Snake watched him writhe in pain.

"That ain't right," he muttered, and put the finishing shot in him. "You're welcome." The remaining two were running through the rocks and brush toward their horses and Snake was moving down the hill after them. "Dog-man, you'd like these odds."

***

"Up the side of the hill, there," Twombley howled back at the posse. "Looks like a bunch of Apache have someone trapped in those rocks." He was pointing up the side of the rock strewn hill when more shots were fired.

"Let's ride, boys," Dawson shouted, putting the spurs to his horse. Baxter and his deputy were trailing with Dawson and Twombley leading. They weren't able to get to the Apaches before the Indians got to their horses. "Hold 'em up," Dawson yelled. "Let's find whoever they were shooting at."

Snake recognized Dawson and Twombley immediately and stepped out, waving his rifle in the air. "Come on down," Dawson howled. "You hurt?"

"Only my pride," Snake chuckled. He climbed down through the rocks, found his horses, and walked them out. "There's a couple shot over that way," he pointed. "Don't know for sure if they're dead so don't just walk up on 'em. Apache. Met one earlier this morning, too."

"Think we should chase 'em, Mr. Dawson?" Ed Twombley asked.

"You'd never catch those wily bastards," Dawson said. "They know every inch of this country." He turned to Snake. "Catch that half-breed?"

"Yup, and found this." He untied the strong box and set it on the ground. "Filled with loot from some of the robberies, I think. How's Dog-man? Sure could have used him a couple of minutes ago."

"He's hurt but Doctor Canyon is with him. Says he'll be fine. You were right about the Penny's working with Whitlock, but not the real reason." Dawson explained how Claudia had fallen for one of the outlaws and planned on joining the gang.

Twombley saw Baxter, and Coppersmith casually ride up to them. "You just out for a Sunday ride, Sheriff? Those Apache devils were trying to kill Snake." Baxter ignored him and watched Dawson and Chastain as they were going through the contents of the strong box.

"You tryin' to say this is all that gang had?" Baxter was out of the saddle, pointing down at the loot and glaring at Snake. "What'd you do with the rest of it, Snake? Where did you hide the rest of the loot? I knew you couldn't be trusted." He was shaking his fist at Snake and Dawson was sure he was going to pull his weapon.

"You're a serious fool, Sheriff." Snake wasn't smiling and held his hand close to his sidearm. "But if you ask nice, I can lead you to Whitlock's hideout." He couldn't hold it back and chuckled. Snake looked at Twombley as if asking why Baxter was there. Twombley just shrugged.

"Three Feathers had a hideout of his own in a set of caves some west of here. There might be more. This is what he was digging up when I shot him." Snake walked over to Baxter. Got right up in his face and snarled. "Seems like you owe me and Dog-man an apology, Sheriff. We done your work." He turned to the deputy. "And yours. Only decent lawman I've met since me and Dog-man left Deadwood is Nelson Wilson down in El Paso." He shoved his chin out at Baxter, daring him to take a swing and turned to Dawson.

"You want to ride with me to Whitlock's hide

out? Then I got to get back to Dog-man. We got to get out of this country. People are crazy around here."

George Dawson was laughing and said he would be glad to ride with him. "Twombley, you and the men cover those bodies and join us."

"Why is it that Snake knows where Whitlock's hide out is? Why is it he knew where to find Three Feathers? Why is it he only brought part of the loot back?" Baxter was making a case and wasn't going to let up. Snake could see it in his eyes. Baxter had a great desire to kill him, and a crazed attitude in his bearing.

"Did it ever occur to you, Dawson, that this man might be the real leader of the Whitlock gang? That maybe he would be leading you into a trap, not into Whitlock's hide out? Snake needs to be hung, not praised." He turned to his deputy.

"Coppersmith, put irons on this man and escort him back to Las Cruces. You're gonna hang, Snake, right next to your partner, Dog-man."

Snake's rifle came up, fully cocked before Coppersmith could take half a step. Snake couldn't see it, but Twombley, Dawson, and Chastain all had their weapons in hand, too. "If there's gonna be a death, Sheriff, it ain't gonna be mine." Snake turned to say something to Dawson and stopped, surprised at all the guns aimed at Baxter.

What have I done? I've pulled a gun on a sheriff and now I've forced the good Mr. Dawson to do the same thing. They're gonna call me an outlaw and maybe even hang me, but damn it, I know I'm right. Poor Mr. Dawson. They'll run him right out of business. I ain't wrong in this.

"Gonna be hard to explain this, Mr. Dawson. You've opened a big door." Snake was glad for the back-up but knew what the actions might bring to Dawson and his company. "Me and Dog were gonna ride out, but I ain't gonna let you face this alone. I done the deed, but it's gonna be harder on you."

"I know, Snake," Dawson said. His voice was strong, his eyes narrowed for a fight. "Baxter, you're unfit to be sheriff, and I'm the one to tell the people of Las Cruces. Unbuckle your gun belt and step back. Coppersmith, you're in an awkward position right now. Where do you stand?"

"I don't think the sheriff is right, Mr. Dawson, but I am a deputy sheriff of Las Cruces. I wish there was another way …" and his voice trailed off.

"Whitlock's hide out is going to have to wait, I'm afraid," Dawson said. "We'll ride straight for Las Cruces. The county officials need to know what's been going on. I'm depending on you to do the right thing, Deputy Coppersmith."

Coppersmith stood on one foot and then the other for just a moment or two. "I won't stand in your way, Mr. Dawson. I understand what your doing and why, I think." He took a long look at Baxter who was furious.

"It's the end of your job, Otis Coppersmith. You're fired. And you, Dawson, I'll see to it that you hang for this. How dare you pull a gun on me. You'll hang right alongside these other outlaws. So help me, Dawson, you'll hang." He was almost screaming in his anger.

"We'll see, Baxter. We'll see," Dawson said. "Let's ride for the station."

"I gotta see Dog-man," Snake said.

"We'll pick him up at Penny Station, Snake. He can ride back in one of the wagons. Doctor Canyon is with him and will ride in with him."

23

"Well now," Snake said. He walked into Penny Station and found Dog-man sleeping under a warm blanket near the fire. "Ain't you all cozy and warm. Doc here says you got yourself all banged up pretty good. Busted ribs. Well they ain't much use anyway. Busted head. Don't use it that much, do you?" He was laughing and Dog-man was trying not to, those ribs hurting with every word Snake said.

"You get that big Indian? He's the one bashed my head and dragged my puny little body through the rocks."

"I got him, but it's something worse gonna happen." Snake took the next several minutes to tell Dog-man what had happened with Warren Baxter. "Old Mr. Dawson's gonna hang for this, Dog, and it was me that pulled the rifle on the sheriff."

"Dawson's pretty clever, Snake. I think he has a lot more to say about what goes on along his express routes than you think. I'd put my money on Dawson, not Baxter."

"Speaking of money," Snake said. His brow was

all furrowed and he got right serious. "All our money and that receipt book were in our kit. Did those bandits get it all?"

"Nary a penny, Snake. They went through all our stuff and missed it." He laughed, then howled in pain, grabbing his ribs. "Don't do that again," he said.

"We're gonna get you back to Las Cruces, and me and Dawson in jail, right away, Dog-man." He got up and walked out of the Penny Station to find the express company boss. They were fitting out the wagon for the ride back.

"I ain't gonna let you get in trouble just because of me," Snake said. "I'll lay my story out to a judge or whatever, but you ain't goin' down because of me."

"You're right, Snake, I'm not. And neither are you." Dawson was shaking his head and smiling as he motioned to bring a team up for the wagon. "Warren Baxter has been riding a narrow path for some time, Snake. I'll have a long talk with Judge Peters when we get back to Las Cruces."

Dawson turned to walk toward the main house, stopped, and turned back. "You're probably the bravest man I've even known, Snake. You have a set of standards that would be hard to live under, and I'm proud to know you." Snake had never been spoken to like that, ever. He just stood stock still, not knowing what to say or do.

Two Dawson men brought Dog-man out, one on each side, and got him loaded in a wagon, nestled in a bed of blankets for the twenty mile ride to Las Cruces. Coppersmith was in an awkward situation. He was a deputy sheriff, sworn and pinned, who had watched his sheriff taken down by members of the public. Many would think he should immediately put Dawson and Snake under arrest, but he was more sympathetic to what they were doing.

Dawson had a long chat with the young man and it was determined best if he were to be driving the wagon. It might not be seen by others as if Coppersmith were in cahoots with Dawson. "I know I'm gonna lose my job, Mr. Dawson, but I also know that what you and that Mr. Snake did was wrong on the one hand, but needed to be done on the other. I don't want you to go to jail, I don't want to either."

"Don't think either one of us will, Coppersmith. You did the right thing. You just drive the wagon and I'll do my best to keep us out of jail." There was no chuckle, but there was the slightest smile on Dawson's face as he turned away. "Let's get this show on the road boys, it's a long ride to town."

Snake was on his horse, in a saddle, riding alongside George Dawson. "I'm the one pulled down on Baxter, not you. You gotta protect that wonderful business of yours."

"I know, Snake," Dawson said. They were at a walk, strung out along the road. "It's those kinds of actions that make you and Dog-man special with me. Right from the first moments Clete Kilpatrick told me about how you broke up that robbery I knew what kind of man you were, knew I would like you, knew I would stand with you. Baxter has been wrong from the start."

"Who do you plan to bring all this to? Where will Coppersmith stand? He was willing to put the cuffs on me. I surely didn't want to shoot the man. Baxter? That might be a different story," he chuckled. It was a forced chuckle, Snake would have told anyone after seeing Baxter actually give every indication of being ready to shoot him.

"First stop will be the courthouse and a talk with the judge and then the county people. There have always been questions about his position, his elections. You stay with Dog-man at the compound. Wish we were back in Santa Fe."

"With Deputy U.S. Marshal Eastwood and Three Fingers?" Snake was laughing and Dawson finally had to as well. "We're going the right way."

Snake dropped back to ride alongside the wagon. "Well, gettin' yourself all beat up sure did put me in a bad spot, Dog. Hope you're proud of yourself."

"Worked hard at it, Snake. Spent some time gettin' it all planned out. How are you gonna get us out of this mess you've created this time?" Snake could see his partner cringe every time the wagon hit a rock or he got bumped. "Pullin' a gun on the sheriff and his deputy ain't something most people would do."

"What we're gonna do, Mister Dog-man, is keep George Dawson from goin' to prison and then we're gonna high-tail it for Tucson. Shoulda when we first talked about it. That Penny woman was something. Blew Will Penny's head to smithereens."

"What scared me, Snake, was when they were goin' through our stuff. Found our bank receipt book but didn't know what it was. I thought for sure they were gonna burn it. Had me trussed up like a hog waitin' for the boilin' pot."

"I see you got your new hat weathered up good. New shirt all ripped and tore. You're a mess, Dog. Them boys what went after you are more of a mess, though."

Dog-man took a long breath, cringing from the broken ribs. "What about that other feller, the one called Fingers? I thought he was alive? Would come back with us."

"He was shot-up worse than they thought and bled out. Whole gang is dead, Dog. That's why we said, right at the first, we ain't gonna be outlaws."

***

George Dawson and Ed Twombley led an angry Sheriff Warren Baxter into Judge Isaak Peters' office in the Las Cruces courthouse. The building was Spanish Colonial with a formal plaza in the center, tile roof, and tile floors, making every foot-step echo through the broad and high halls. Windows were deep set, surrounded by wrought iron, and most often, open. Deputy Otis Coppersmith trailed by a few steps, his head hung, not looking at anyone or anything.

"What's this all about, Dawson?" Las Cruces Municipal Judge Isaak Peters was a tall, elegant man. His mother's family dated back to the original Spanish invaders while his father's family were among the first Americans to invade the territory. "Most unusual, I must say." Dawson had insisted that Snake and Dog-man remain at the express company barns.

Dawson and Twombley spent the next hour discussing what had happened right up to but not including Snake pulling his rifle to bear on Baxter. Dawson left that out, but did explain that he and Twombley pulled their weapons to keep Baxter from shooting Snake. "In my opinion, Judge, Baxter is unfit for the position he holds."

"I'm not the least in favor of citizens taking the law into their own hands, Mr. Dawson. On the other hand I'm not sure there would have been an alternative." He turned to Baxter.

"I'm also not in favor of a lawman taking it upon himself to declare someone guilty and following up with an execution. This is most unusual. These are not the days of the Alcalde, Sheriff Baxter. An accused person is not a guilty criminal." He thumped the desk with a big fist, glaring first at Baxter, then Dawson.

He went over the notes from Dawson's discussion. "If George Dawson were to tell me that a man had saved him thousands of dollars and then someone told me that same man tried to steal a hundred," and the judge looked Baxter right in the eye, "I'd believe Dawson. Why do you bring this kind of stupidity to your office, Sheriff?"

He sat back in his chair, a thoughtful look in his face, and glared at Dawson and Baxter. "I think you're both wrong, but, in your defense, George, you did keep the sheriff from shooting a man. We'll hold a hearing on this matter day after tomorrow at ten in the morning. Baxter, you're temporarily removed from office until we clear this up." He looked at Dawson and Baxter. "You two stay away from each other." He waved them off and Dawson and company walked out of his office.

Baxter held back and glared as the express company head and his men walked out. "Those men are guilty as sin, Judge. They are all guilty and need to hang. I'll write the governor if you let them go. I'll see to it that you hang, too." He was screaming at the judge and Peters looked over to Otis Coppersmith who was standing next to the sheriff.

"This is not the behavior of a normal or sane man, Deputy. I want you to take him into custody and lock him up until we can have a hearing on his sanity. How long has this been going on?"

"For some time, I'm afraid," Coppersmith said. "The least little thing will set him off and he's threatened many with hanging. Most just walk away from him, but he did go for his gun on Mr. Snake and Mr. Dawson."

"Get him out of here and make sure the cell doors are locked," Peters said.

***

"Went a little easier than I thought," Twombley said. "Peters is angry, more so at Baxter than you, though."

Dawson had to chuckle. "I'm not really sure of that. It's going to be hard keeping Snake and Dogman from leaving, Ed. I'm afraid they'll have to be at that hearing. I just wish we had something tangible that we could offer the judge. The best I can do is bring Cletus Kilpatrick in to testify on their honesty."

"You have the strongbox Snake brought back and the fact that he came back. There was no justification for Baxter to try to pull down on Snake."

24

"We need to just pack up and get out," Snake said, easing Dog-man out of the wagon. They made it into the barn and Dog-man was laid out on his bed-roll. "Just ride for Tucson, look the country over, and head for California."

"Big difference between what we should do and what we can do. I ain't ridin' nowhere with these ribs. Besides, Dawson might just need us."

"That bothers me more than anything," Snake was stalking back and forth around the bed. He kicked a post, swatted at a fly, and finally sat down on the edge of the bed. "Well, then, Dog, get yourself well and we'll ride out."

It was later in the day when Nelson Wilson and Jose Castillo walked into the barn. Castillo had a lovely girl with him. She was probably close to twenty, had long black hair, bright brown eyes, and a smile that lit the barn.

"Got some dust blowing around, eh boys?" Wilson laughed, whacked Snake across the shoulders and nodded to Dog-man. "When I got the wire

from Baxter wanting all the dirt on you boys, I figured you might use some help up here."

"Could at that," Dog-man said. "Snake pulled a
gun on the sheriff."

"He was gonna shoot me," Snake yelled.

"Well, that's beside the point. And then Dawson
and his people pulled guns on the sheriff, too. What
do you mean the sheriff wanted all the dirt on us?
Ain't no dirt on us. We ain't outlaws, damn it." Dog-
man was getting riled, which tickled Snake.

"Watch out when Dog-man gets riled," he chuckled.

"Who's this lovely lady you've brought to doctor
my broken bones?" Dog-man smiled at the girl and
got one back.

"This my niece, Mercedez Lopez Castillo Cas-
tro."

"Mercedez, eh? As beautiful as you, my dear,"
Dog-man said. "Can you mend my broken bones?"

"Tio Jose said to be wise and careful around you,
Señor Perro," she giggled. Her eyes were dancing
with humor and Dog-man just huffed a time or
two, to everyone's enjoyment.

"Where's Mr. Dawson? I need to talk with him."
Wilson said.

"You'll probably find him at the courthouse
talking to the judge." Snake said. "He and Twombley took the sheriff to Judge Peters."

Wilson, Castillo, and Mercedez made their way
across the plaza to the elegant colonial building
and found Dawson just inside the big doors. "Need
to have a word with you, Mr. Dawson," Wilson said.
It took less than five minutes and Dawson led the
two El Paso lawmen right back into Judge Peters'

office.

"What now?" Peters bellowed. "This better be good, Dawson."

"Better than good, Judge. These men are Deputy City Marshals Wilson and Castillo from El Paso." He nodded to the two. "Wilson has something important to tell you."

"It's something you need to read," Wilson said. He handed the wire that Baxter sent him. "Sheriff Baxter sent me this wire several days ago."

Judge Peters scanned the paper, then sat back in his chair and read it word for word again. "What is the matter with that man," he murmured. "Damn fool." He handed the wire to Dawson who read it. "Well? Are those charges real?"

"Not a one, Judge. Just the opposite. Snake and Dog-man broke up a stage robbery and broke up a gang out to steal their mining claim or the money from it."

The judge looked at Wilson. "That so?" Wilson just nodded. "All right, then. We can forget the hearing. Baxter made a fool of himself here just moments ago and I had his deputy put him under arrest. I'll take all this up with the county officials. Deputy Marshal Wilson, please prepare a statement I can take along with this wire.

"You say those two men stopped a robbery in progress near Santa Fe, broke up a gang that murdered and stole mining claims, and Baxter pins them as the outlaws?" He looked at Dawson, then Wilson and Castillo. All nodded. "Baxter stepped over the line this time."

⁂

Chastain was overseeing half a beef being turned on the spit over a wonderful bed of coals, and the entire Dawson Express Company staff was on hand for the party. Over the past several weeks, Baxter was relieved of his position as sheriff and left town immediately, Dog-man's ribs healed but were still sore, and everyday Snake promised that they would leave town the next day, but the two never quite got out of town.

Mercedez rode out of town with her uncle despite Dog-man's saying how much his ribs hurt and that he was a dying man. Her tinkling giggle drove Snake nuts, brought scowls from Jose Castillo, and were fully enjoyed by Dog-man. "I like it when she calls me Señor Perro," he said.

"We're gonna miss you boys but I understand your desire for the open road." George Dawson poured himself, Snake, and Dog-man a glass of whiskey. "Here's a toast to California. Hope they're ready for you two."

It was a two-headed party, in celebration of Warren Baxter losing his job as sheriff and Snake and Dog-man heading out of town. George Dawson had one more little surprise for the boys.

"Wonder if I could talk you two into escorting this next shipment and stage to Tucson. Leaves out at sunrise tomorrow. Quick stop at Penny Station, the next stops, except one, are all camp stops to Tucson. Each wagon will have its own messenger, but you two will scout out any possible danger from Apache raiders to outlaws. It's worth another five hundred dollars to me," he said.

"Money does have a way of helping make decisions," Dog-man chuckled. "There isn't a chance in the world that we would say no, Mr. Dawson. We'll be protecting our poke, too."

"Marshal Altman in El Paso will be glad to know that you're traveling away from his territory," Nelson Wilson laughed. "You had him mighty riled there for a while."

"You need to take control down there, Wilson," Dog-man said. "We could be talked into staying, you know."

Wilson feigned horror and reached for the bottle, but Snake had hold of it first. "We be leavin' at sunrise, Wilson. Don't panic." Snake poured drinks around as Chastain hollered out that food was ready. A group of Mexicans working for Dawson had their guitars and trumpets, and the music was loud and lively. Even with hurt ribs Dog-man danced with every pretty girl in Las Cruces that night.

***

"We got a bad ride in front of us, Dog," Snake said. He and Dog-man were sitting in a cantina on the southwestern outskirts of Las Cruces. "Look at this map Dawson gave me. Two or more express companies have mail and other contracts using this road, but because of Indian and outlaw troubles, there's only two actual stage stops between here and Tucson. One at Penny Station and one at San Simon."

"What's in between?" Dog sloshed a beer down

after taking a whole jalapeño infused spoon full of beans. "Won't never get used to this."

Snake chuckled and gulped a spoon full with two chilies showing. "Ain't nothing but Indians and outlaws between the stations. One stop, about sixty miles out, is a Mimbres Indian encampment. The stops are water holes where we camp under the wagons. Mail, gold, and some dumb pilgrims are the load. We're looking at about 700 miles of no cities or towns."

"My kind of ride," Dog-man said. "Now you just stop and think about that for a minute. We've made up our minds to go to California and to do that, we gots to ride to Tucson. Mr. Dawson is gonna pay us to ride where we were gonna ride anyway. Ain't no problem here."

"Well it do sound better when you say it, Dog. Yup, it surely do. We're just out for a pleasant ride through Apache country looking out for desperate outlaws, protecting them that's going the same way."

"You are a poet, Snake." He sat back in his chair and a frown slowly came across his face. "There is one thing we haven't talked about and we need to."

"I know," Snake said. "Thought about it every night since that Mr. Clausen gave us that little receipt book. We have a lot of money, Dog. A lot of money, and it ain't all in that little book. We have more than a thousand dollars in cash between us and we don't even know how to spend a hundred." He was laughing and scared at the same time. "What are we gonna do about that?"

"My new hat was four dollars," Dog-man said.

"See? That's what I mean. We're ridin' out to

meet those wagons, but we ain't got no plan, Dog."

"Nope, you're wrong, Snake, my man. We got the same plan we had when we got run out of Deadwood. We were goin' south to the border to find gold, Remember?" Snake nodded and Dog-man smiled. "Well, we're ridin' west today to investigate the possibilities of California."

"Only one difference, Dog. Our poke's full to the top this time."

They were still laughing when they met the two wagons, one an express coach, the other carried merchandise. Each had a four-up hitch, a driver, and messenger or guard. Dog-man and Snake would be the outriders. "I think George Dawson knows us pretty well, Snake. Not a city, town, or village for seven hundred miles. So long, Las Cruces," he said, waving a battered up hat.

"I can almost smell the sweet green grass of California," Snake smiled.

A Look at Name's Corcoran, Terrence Corcoran (Terrence Corcoran Book I)

Terrence Corcoran carried a badge in Virginia City, Nevada until one day, in a drunken stupor, he shot the sheriff. Now he's returning to the Comstock looking to get his badge back and stumbles into a conspiracy that might put the sheriff, district attorney, and others in jail for a long time. A lovely working girl is brutally murdered, a Hungarian duke wants a Wells Fargo gold shipment, and the sheriff rehires him after first kicking him in a most tender spot. Corcoran was born on the ship bringing his family to this country, ran away to the frontier at an early age and brings his ideas of the old country and knowledge learned of the west to whatever mess he finds himself in. He's carried a badge, found himself in jail, and stands four-square for right, honor, and truth. You gotta love the guy.

AVAILABLE NOW ON AMAZON

ABOUT THE AUTHOR

Reno, Nevada novelist, Johnny Gunn, is retired from a long career in journalism. He has worked in print, broadcast, and Internet, including a stint as publisher and editor of the Virginia City Legend. These days, Gunn spends most of his time writing novel length fiction, concentrating on the western genre. Or, you can find him down by the Truckee River with a fly rod in hand.

Gunn and his wife, Patty, live on a small hobby farm about twenty miles north of Reno, sharing space with a couple of horses, some meat rabbits, a flock of chickens, and one crazy goat.

In Search of Abundance

Mountains of Cheese, Rivers of Wine,
and Other Gastronomic Utopias

Luisa Del Giudice

BORDIGHERA PRESS

Cover image: St Joseph's Day Altar and Table, co-curated by Luisa Del Giudice and Rosie Lee Hooks, and assembled by Watts Towers Arts Center artists, community, friends, and family. The altar was assembled in the Marian niche, left of the main altar, in St. Lawrence of Brindisi Church, Watts, on March 18–20, 2011 (Chapter 6).

This volume was produced in part thanks to Sharon K. Emanuelli, contributing copy editor.

Library of Congress Control Number: 2023940038

Published by
BORDIGHERA PRESS
John D. Calandra Italian American Institute
25 W. 43rd Street, 17th Floor
New York, NY 10036

Saggistica 41
ISBN 978-1-59954-185-3

Table of Contents

Introduction: My Search for Abundance   9
    The Immigrant Mantra   9
    The Diaspora–Food Nexus   11
    Food Memories   12
    Trauma and the Concept of Enough   14
    Problems in Paradise   17
    On Abundance, Sufficiency, and Food Justice   18
    This Volume   25

1. Mountains of Cheese and Rivers of Wine: *Paesi*   33
    di Cuccagna and other Gastronomic Utopias
    Gastronomic Utopias   34
    Cuccagna between Written and Oral Culture   38
    Iconography: Constructing Edible Paradises   43
    Cuccagna and Ritual: A Time for Feasting   46
    Naples as *Il Paese di Cuccagna*   49
    An Evolving Topos: Cuccagnesque Journeys and Immigration   55
    Cultural History and Personal Experience   60

2. Wine Makes Good Blood: Wine Culture   88
    among Toronto Italians
    Introduction   88
    Wine/Blood and Notions of Health   90
    Wine and Children   92
    Water and Wine   93
    Virile Wine   95
    Wine Cellars Old and New   96
    Between Tradition and Toronto   100
    His Wine Cellar, Her Food Pantry   103
    Conclusions   108

3. Rituals of Charity and Abundance: Sicilian St. Joseph's   115
    Tables and Feeding the Poor in Los Angeles
    Introduction   115
    Description of Los Angeles Tables   119
    History of the Cult of St. Joseph   123
    Geographic Distribution of St. Joseph Food Altars   130
        in Southern Italy
    Sicilian St. Joseph Tables in the Diaspora: 134
        New Orleans and Los Angeles
    Interpreting the Tradition: Table, Altar, Banquet   137
    Bread in Italian Culture   138

Dramatization of Migrant Journeys: Into Egypt   140
    and Out of Sicily
Private vs. Public Tables   145
Rituals of Abundance: Pre-Christian and New   147
    World Revisitations
Social Justice, "Sabbath Economics," and Feeding   149
    the Poor in Los Angeles

4. Ischian Cultural Sites on the San Pedro, California, Map   174

5. Pasta   193

History: Dough Versus Pasta   194
Terminology   194
Origins: East or West   195
Historical Landmark Versus Legend   196
Etruscan and Roman   197
Arab Sicilian Geographer   197
Genovese Barrel of *Maccheroni*   198
Gastronomic Utopias: *Cuccagna*   198
The Maccheronic Muse   199
Eighteenth-Century Naples as Pasta Capital   199
Immigrants and Pasta   200
Pasta as Emblem   201
Commercial Pasta: From Artisan Guilds to Multinationals   202
Wheat   203
Pasta Typology: Cutting the Linguistic Dough   204
A Raviolo by Other Names   204
Trends   206
Nutritional Value: Fat or Skinny?   206

6. Feeding the Poor—Welcoming the Stranger: The Watts   212
    Towers Common Ground Initiative and St. Joseph's
    Communal Tables in Watts

7. Treasure from Trees: Gold and Liquid Gold in the Oral   229
    and Archaeological Traditions around Horace's Sabine
    Villa in Licenza, Italy

Preliminaries   229
Background and Introduction   233
Folklore and Archaeology   234
Landscapes   235
Treasure as Metaphor   236
Archaeology and Oral Tradition   236
Treasure   237
Interpreting Narratives   239
Guardian of the Treasure   240

INDEX   249
ACKNOWLEDGMENTS   257
ABOUT THE AUTHOR   261

Introduction: My Search for Abundance[1]

THE IMMIGRANT MANTRA

I have heard the "*abbondanza*" mantra as far back as I can remember. During our earliest years in Toronto, Canada, as recently arrived immigrants from Italy, it figured foremost in our family life. Indeed, it was the singular idea that had propelled my parents forward, as it did so many other post-WWII economic refugees, fleeing war-torn and hungry Italy. The quest for abundance has been a perennial goal within immigrant families, from the first waves of migration—and not only for Italians, most assuredly. Millions left Italy behind because abundance (and even sufficiency) had come to be a decidedly elusive reality that could, at best, be simulated only during feast days. The incantatory *abbondanza* mantra, therefore, not only bubbled up from the very heart of Italian peasant culture and historic experience, it came to form a core value that continues to animate diasporic culture.

My family had suffered from hunger and want during, and even after, the Second World War. War-related food stories were abundant—my father risking death for stealing potatoes from under a guard's nose in a German Nazi concentration camp; my mother, in the prime of youth, turning to skin and bones as a *sfollata* (displaced person) in the mountains above Terracina; her father, malnourished but preferring to deny himself food in order to favor his daughter, and then, as the war was ending, dying from lack of sustenance. And our foundational migration story itself: in the post-war years, determined that his family would *not* live this way, my father *had* to find a way out, and he did.

---

1   The internal chronology of the essays in this volume has not been updated, for the most part, and reflects the dates and cited references of the original publication. This will cause a greater or lesser discrepancy, depending on each essay.

Emigration would offer that opportunity. The experience of food abundance started the moment he stepped aboard the transatlantic ship, where he could not believe the amounts of food on the mess deck. He especially remembers consuming as many hard-boiled eggs as he could. And he went on to enjoy such modest abundance during his first weeks and months in Toronto while lodged at his brother Pietro's home, waiting for the rest of his family to arrive. When my mother was finally reunited with him less than a year later, having followed on another ship, and then making the train journey from Halifax to Toronto with their three daughters, she did not recognize the man who had come to gather them at the Toronto train station—my father's face had so fattened up. Abundance was visible, manifested in changed bodies. Meanwhile, her transatlantic voyage was spent in sick bay, as they tried to nurse me to health, and scarcity trailed (me, at least) even on the train west, because my mother had run out of milk. Such a crisis was partially mitigated because another female passenger was kind enough to give her a bottle of milk for me. I often wonder how that traumatic experience imprinted itself on my psyche.

Who could blame immigrants for being so focused on, so obsessed by, food—with its accumulation, its processing, its consumption—vowing to never go hungry again? Small surprise that wine cellars, gardens, kitchens and basement kitchens, deep freezers and pantries, became the hubs of immigrant life. As did the activities of growing food, wine-making, foraging, fishing, and hunting. I remember our cantina stocked full of jars of cooking tomatoes, *gardiniera*, canned peaches and pears, hanging *prosciutti* and sausages, supplemented with store-bought supplies of pasta, canned goods, oil, and so forth, purchased in bulk whenever they were on sale. In fact, perusing grocers' sale flyers became a family pastime, as we surveyed where to strike next, in order to stock up the larder. (Chapter 2: "Wine Makes Good Blood: Wine Culture among Toronto Italians.") Attention to moderating diet, and dieting, was a foreign notion. Declining food was considered something of an insult. *Ma magna!* (Eat, for goodness' sake!), one would be admonished if one were too careful or, still worse, rudely mentioned dieting at the dinner table. Counting calories, as a modern concern, was simply incompatible with our family's peasant worldview and history.

THE DIASPORA–FOOD NEXUS

Food is perhaps one of the most well-developed aspects of immigrant culture, and the area of folklife that may be the most tenacious throughout the diaspora. Long after songs and tales and artisan skills were forgotten, the knowledge of making pasta, sausages, festive baking, or planting a garden, was not. This volume is about the food nexus in diaspora culture. It explores its mythic core as the gastronomic utopia, represented at its metaphorical heights in the *Paese di Cuccagna* (the Land of Cockaigne), which, in the immigrant's mind (and experience), came to be closely associated with America, the land where abundance (more and bigger) was law (Chapter 1: "Mountains of Cheese and Rivers of Wine: *Paesi di Cuccagna* and other Gastronomic Utopias"). These essays cover the myriad loci and means of the reproduction of abundance and its symbolic reenactments. Wine-spouting fountains in the mythic Cuccagna landscape came to be transformed into home wine-making and packed cellars. The verdant, hyper-productive *cuccagnesque* nature cycle evolved into gardens of plenty, double kitchens, whole animal carcasses neatly packed into freezers. The festive time of eating and drinking run amok, and thoughts of never having to work, evolved into the festivalization of the quotidian: fresh (festive) egg pasta-making and celebrations of all sorts [Figures 1–4], from grand Christmas and Easter celebrations, weddings, baptisms, communions, to full-blown patron-saint days, down to the Sunday *pranzo*. The many reenactments of Cuccagna, Land of Plenty, sometimes commemorated its opposite as well: the Sicilian St. Joseph's ritual pageant of the saints, for instance, seems often to have commemorated the immigrants' journey when, as strangers, they entered a new land, seeking hospitality, sustenance, and belonging. They created food altars or tables, even in the midst of Lent, to display gratitude, their traditions, and the ritual foods that fill body and soul: bread, the season's first fruits, as well as the many vegetables, fried foods, sweets, and fish in cornucopias of plenty, as a sort of "Sicilian Thanksgiving." All were invited to partake of the foods made sacred, because hospitality and feeding the poor are sacred. (Chapter 3: "Rituals of Charity and Abundance: Sicilian St. Joseph's Tables and Feeding the Poor in Los Angeles.")

FOOD MEMORIES

We all have our cultural, as well as our own individual, food memories, do we not? For me, the most poignant, magical, and entrenched memories relate to festivities, to the cantina, and to foraging for food. Festivities loomed large for us all. Christmas, for instance, meant days and even weeks of preparation: food shopping, aunts in the kitchen, cantinas and freezers filling up with special foods—persimmons, oranges and tangerines, whole nuts, *casatelle, ciambelle al vino, broccoletti* (broccoli rabe), fennel, ravioli and fettuccine, lots of fried seafood, torrone, and dried figs for *la Vigilia* (Christmas Eve). It was a veritable cornucopia of all good things. Eating was intermingled with other activities like playing cards (*tombola*) late into the night, and after midnight mass, a fresh batch of fried *zeppole*, raisin filled yeast dough sprinkled with sugar. We children especially loved these "sleepover holidays," when aunts and uncles and cousins would spend the night (even if we didn't live far from one another) in order to enjoy the full meal cycle of breakfast, lunch, dinner, and snacks all through the day and night, together.

Throughout Canada's few sunny months, there were even large family or clan picnics in the park, on a near-weekly basis. These were never casual affairs and no effort was spared. My aunts would prepare *lasagne*, bread cutlets, garden tomato salad, cookies, and more. Moka Express coffeemakers were placed on the BBQ for freshly made, hot espresso; watermelons were put in a cold stream or cooler; wine was often hidden in some innocuous coke bottle or other camouflage; and, in more recent times, special narrow *spiedini* grills are carted along for these events.

Weddings, of course, were the apex of over-the-top offerings. In the early Toronto days when one had all-day affairs, refreshments were served after the morning church ceremony, followed by a full lunch (for the smaller crowd); thereafter, one went home for a change of clothing, and returned to the reception hall for the evening extravaganza of dinner and dancing. The bad habit of *not* rsvp'ing (foreign to us), meant that one never knew how many would come and so, better a hit than a miss, one would provide an over-abundance of food. A non-communicated and conflicting wedding engagement meant that entire platters of cold-cut sandwiches (and much more) might be routinely thrown out, and it visibly pained my parents to remember such a sinful waste of good food.

I remember making wine in our Toronto basement, everyone helping, even the children. Wine seemed to be central to physical, emotional, and social health. Even children were expected to drink it at meals. As proverbs state, *"il vino fa buon sangue"* (wine makes good blood), and *"l'acqua fa male e lu vino fa cantà"* (water is bad for you [but] wine makes you sing). So important was the wine ideal to Italian peasants that when the masses emigrated they built wine cellars and made their own wine, some even for the first time. Thus, wine began to flow abundantly, just as it had in their beloved Cuccagna landscape (Chapter 2: "Wine Makes Good Blood: Wine Culture among Toronto Italians").

I remember the gardens of my youth. The tomato plants as one brushed up against them, with their dark, musky smell. Such a keen and specific smell, still brings me back to the first garden in the backyard of our shared Eversfield Road house in Toronto. There, a cousin and I would roam the tomato rows with salt shakers in hand, picking off plump fruit and eating it on the spot, sprinkled with salt—the tall plants hiding our own small bodies. Similarly, where a neighbor's cherry tree overhung our garage, we would climb up its branches, lie back on the garage roof, and lazily gorge on cherries by merely raising an arm. Ah, such sweet memories.

Foraging for wild foods, too, seems to reenact that land where food was free for the taking, and nature produced over-abundantly— where cows gave birth to multiple calves a day, roast chickens fell from the sky, a cauldron sat atop a mountain spewing forth pasta already covered in cheese, and so forth. I remember foraging in orchards, fields, lakes for a variety of foods: fruits at harvest time, fishing for smelts in the middle of the night, or collecting snails after the rains. (Only the men went hunting.) With bushel baskets in hand, we children would go to an orchard, pick fruit, and then eat cherries, plums, or peaches all the way home, stuffing ourselves in the back of my father's work truck, a tan-colored GMC, until we were sick. Fishing, too, recalls family outings and the patient search for food: smelt-fishing at night in Belleville, Ontario, as a child—the nets, the fire, the open grill—then huddling in the back of the GMC to warm up. As a child, I awaited the weekend, predawn wake-up call, to see if I wanted to go fishing with my father, and the long (sometimes too long) days fishing in his small motor boat. He never wanted to turn in and call it a day, always holding out for a larger, more abundant catch. For a once-commercial fisherman in Terracina, I suppose this might have been expected. "Let's just try casting over there..." I've experienced nature's wild abundance in so many ways, both then and now. More recently, it's taken the form of mushroom foraging in the forests of Oregon, of clams on its beaches, or of snails overlooking the Pacific in San Pedro, California.

TRAUMA AND THE CONCEPT OF ENOUGH

I inherited the mantra along with its way of life, and when I created a family of my own, continued food-centric practices and the abundance worldview for a long time. I, too, cultivated abundance, just as my immigrant family of origin had done. My parents had engaged in so many practices of shared abundance. For instance, relatives frequently dropped in and stayed for dinner, and I knew that what we had we would share in order to enjoy the spontaneous conviviality which we children (and adults) always loved—particularly if there were cousins involved. But, as for *Dio provvede* (God provides), despite the common currency of this phrase in our family, I also knew that my mother left nothing to chance (or god) when it came to food; in fact, a tacit motto, which I have assiduously practiced in my own life, runs something like this: "if it's enough, it's not enough." That is, one must to go well beyond any rational calculation of amounts needed to feed guests. Rather, one needed to prepare approximately twice as much as needed. I don't know whether this was a calculated energy-saving device: produce enough for leftovers so one wouldn't have to cook again (or start from scratch) the next day, or even that very same night—although my father tolerated few leftovers; or whether it may have been an aesthetic sense of abundant variety; or enacting a form of hospitality that was not seemingly minimal or miserly. I've more recently sought to curb this habit, paring down dinner offerings when I cook for guests, but do not always succeed.

I, too, sought to fill my life with joy, by cultivating that elusive sense of abundance through food, fortifying myself against a gnawing fear of emptiness, of want, of suffering, of "not-enoughness," and perhaps of generational trauma as well. At every dinner party, birthday and life-cycle celebration, I'd spend days in the kitchen. It seemed though that I could never provide enough, perhaps because I did not understand *enough*, and thus I felt *I* was never enough. And this sense of inadequacy may have extended to many other parts of my life, food perhaps being merely emblematic of a larger problem. Cooking and doing and creating too much can become an all-consuming approach to life, a life in perpetual motion and of endless accumulation—from dishes to menus, from publications to CVs, or from clothes (albeit thrift-shopped) and shoes in the closet! It has taken decades (and periodic therapy) to understand the problem, even as the tendency has waned with time. But, it has been only with the COVID-19 pandemic and its shift toward minimalization and essentialization, that the spell has been finally and definitively broken (I think). And yet, it is also true that, during these pandemic times, food, family, and convivial meals saw us through and literally brought home the vital importance of the dinner table, of family, particularly during such trying times. Yet, we learned that we *already* had abundance in spades, and that it just wasn't the sort of empty and ephemeral promise of *food* abundance. Rather, it was the intangible abundance of love that became so evident. We were reassured that this sense of fullness, well-being, and abundance didn't require food excess at all, just adequate amounts. And wellness, psycho-physical health, was especially strong when basic, good, homemade food, was present. In a return to basics, I, like so many others, finally learned to bake bread and to make pizza dough. And we returned to our gardens, to planting and watching food grow—just as our ancestors had done—the very natural roots of our peasant way of life. In our Southern California case, in Los Angeles, our garden treasures included oranges, kumquats, lemons, pomegranates, greens, tomatoes, zucchini flowers, and whatever else we were experimenting with from one year to the next [Figures 5–7]. To forage or to grow food, to gather food treasure, turning it into delicious meals for one's family and friends, were some of the most primal and atavistic food experiences, reactivated during these crisis times.

As was a focus on the hearth, where the home fires burn, overseen by one's home deities, or *lares*. It is where the warmth of a cooking source converges with the warmth of *radunanza*, of conviviality. I have known and loved the hearth meal—cooking and eating around the fire with family and friends. It is a primal experience and convivial pleasure I especially came to appreciate during multiple stays in Gressoney (Val d'Aosta) in the Italian Alps with its large, walk-in fireplaces; and even around a simple, handheld grill with feet, placed over raked coals in *l'abbendata* [Figure 8] in Terracina with family and *compaesani*, eating, singing, and carrying on. We have attempted to replicate such convivial hearth fireplaces in our Sierran mountain home.

These memories endure and encourage replication. I have created my own family rituals around food pilgrimages, such as those to San Pedro (Los Angeles's port city, with a large Italian population). I return to San Pedro whenever I need to relive my childhood market recollections, particularly marketing on early Toronto Saturdays. I relive such memories at the A-1 Imported Groceries and Deli on Eighth Street, which are often paired with a wild food hunt. Gathering snails in the proximity of the scent of sea air and sweet fennel, overlooking the Pacific [Figures 9–10], is among the more poignant (Chapter 4: "Ischian Cultural Sites on the San Pedro, California Map.").[2] Such forays represent an approximation of combined Toronto and Terracina experiences for me and my own daughters, and enjoyed by the larger family, and even friends, when they visit from Italy and Canada. These provisioning expeditions became existentially necessary. It was there I returned when

2   As an ethnographer and as a founding member of Slow Food L.A., I was immediately drawn to San Pedro's A-1 and to Marabella Vineyard Company. It was the market's and vintner's role in the preservation of traditional foodways, and the fact that they provided a "glue" for the community, which especially interested me, prompting me to create a Slow Food program around these sites in 2001. Foraging for snails also seemed an especially appropriate activity, given the association's emblem: the snail! See www.slowfood.it.

my father, a fisherman in his pre-immigration days, came to visit from Toronto. He'd buy fish straight from the fishermen and commune with them at the docks in his own closely-related dialect, reliving some of his happiest Terracina experiences. As we looked for meaningful and familiar signs of Italian life on the Southern California landscape, we also found the A-1 experience in San Pedro, an old-school market with a butcher counter, fresh bread and produce, and staples: pastas of all sorts, oils and canned goods, and so forth [Figures 11–13]. During the Christmas season it provides all the traditional essentials, and more. We'd purchase cold cuts and panini from the market, followed by snail gathering and a lunch at tables overlooking the Pacific. On our breathtaking coastal drive home, we stopped at Wayfarer's Chapel, and then Malaga Cove for espresso and to glimpse the replica Giambologna fountain. These are among my primal food experiences in Southern California, inextricably entwined with multigenerational family [Figures 14–17].

What would I consider my *most* primal food, my essential meal, my *soul food*? Pasta. (Chapter 5: "Pasta.") Especially fresh, homemade egg fettuccine [Figure 18]. I don't think it is coincidental that the iconic Cuccagna features at its very center, at its heights, the cheese mountain with a *maccheroni* cauldron on top! It strikes true. When going through a rough patch that requires comfort, I turn to fettuccine (handmade or from a box) in a simple tomato and basil sauce. It is the elemental dish. (When asked to help create an Italian cultural activity for my eldest daughter's fifth-grade class at Willows Community School, I decided that it had to be fresh pasta-making, with five or six pasta machines going simultaneously.)

PROBLEMS IN PARADISE

Where there is insecurity, one can at least enjoy conviviality around a table, creating an island of familiarity, joy, and abundance—simply through food consumption with others [Figure 19]. But *searching* for abundance, on the other hand, may be healthier than actually finding it. Our specific, longed-for Cuccagna—a meat- and fat-ladened gastronomic utopia—came to create health problems for many immigrants, as they learned (much to their surprise), that a cantina full of cured pork products might not make for such a healthy lifestyle. Moderation was indeed called for.

But festive time is never about moderation. It is about consumption run amok. Indeed, some of my food memories are neither so pleasant nor magical as Cuccagna would have it. I recall nauseating food memories, the boredom of abundance, the aversion we developed toward some foods—such as the mortadella. In this case, we could finally eat no more, because my father had finally *overdone* it, purchasing an entire mortadella (but no thin-slicing device!), and we had it coming out of our ears, until the remainder had to be thrown out. The same fate awaited the canned peaches and other preserves my mother laboriously made and stored in the cantina. It seemed that abundance achieved was not as pleasant as the seeking after it (*ce l'hanno fatto stomacà* [they made it nauseating to us]), as special foods became normalized and common. As the festivalization of the quotidian practically removed the *festa* category from our lives, few foods survived this process of excessive familiarity. Special foods became demoted on a non-ritual consumption basis. What were some of the once-special foods that suffered this fate? Sausages, persimmons, *broccoletti,* even prosciutto—which now came generally within reach of most immigrants (*alla portata di tutti*).

ON ABUNDANCE, SUFFICIENCY, AND FOOD JUSTICE

In recent years, I have been interrogating the immigrant's basic understanding and experience of abundance. What is abundance? Cultural, literary, and religious references to food abundance abound. Examples are found in the miracle of the fishes (John 21:1–14), the wedding at Cana (John 2:1–12), or in folk tradition, as the bottomless sack of food (Calvino: *Jump into my Sack*), the endlessly producing pasta pot (De Paola: *Strega Non[n]a*), the magic tablecloth. Are all these narratives actually cautionary tales about scarcity and abundance?

All of these tales seem to focus instead on the need to be generous, even when you are poor, because something miraculous can happen as a result. You may think there is not enough but the paradox of life is that if you give it away, you will get more in return. The childhood ditty or parable of the "Magic Penny" states that if it is given away, it will not only return to you, it will magically grow. Its refrain follows:

> It's just like a magic penny,
> Hold it tight and you won't have any.
> Lend it, spend it, and you'll have so many
> They'll roll all over the floor.
> (Reynolds 1955)

Which is nothing more than a parable of love.

Abundance is not necessarily a tangible good but a spiritual one. As for the tangible sort, the message seems to reaffirm that there is indeed enough if we remember to share whatever we have. Abundance is a communal good that can be achieved communally, and *not* through individual hoarding and consumption. In the folk tradition, we find these repeating dreams of never-ending food to quiet a hungry stomach—or perhaps, a disquieted mind. Knowing what is sufficient, however, is something else altogether. In the tale of *Jump into my Sack,* it is the man who contains himself, uses just what he needs and nothing more, who is able to handle the sack's power. The greedy man will abuse it. Indeed, the wise man in that tale eventually destroys the sack and the magic stick so that they cannot be selfishly over-used or abused.

And so too, has my preoccupation and engagement with food evolved, just as my understanding and experience of abundance is no longer what it once was. It is not about a stacked larder, freezer, or pantry. Indeed, I think an overload of stores may actually be an encumbrance to a sense of abundance. In my evolving understanding of concepts of abundance, I have kept my ears and eyes open while gathering intelligence on the topic of abundance from myriad different sources. Inevitably, some of these sources were religiously based: "manna from heaven" (Psalms 78:24), the multiplication of the loaves and fishes, the mythic land of milk and honey, not living by bread alone, the bread of heaven, and so on. A particularly memorable sermon on the feeding of the 5,000 by the Reverend Michael Fincher, St. Alban's Episcopal Church, Westwood, on Sunday, August 3, 2008, offered some needed clarification for me. He spoke of how living from a perspective of scarcity cancels the experience of abundance; and, on the reverse side, of how a theology of scarcity can be converted to a theology of abundance, by the understanding "that they had enough combined resources to feed everyone present and still have plenty left over." The clue is to be found in sharing within a community: "the very experience of community is itself an experience of abundance." Such a conversion requires various steps: 1. Building community. 2. Taking stock of resources and what each can contribute (that is, look at what you already have). 3. Expressing gratitude for what we have. 4. Offering these gifts and resources to those who need them (in our community and beyond). The goal is to "shatter the illusion of scarcity and share in the creation of abundance by living as if abundance is a reality" (Palmer 1990, 124–7).

It seems that everywhere we turn these days, we are faced with news of scarcity or impending scarcity: of petroleum (dwindling resources, war), scarcity of food (from flooding in the Midwest, from war); scarcity of water (due to drought, to climate change), and so on. And yet, stories such as the feeding of the 5,000 seem to focus on the idea that even in the midst of some very real experiences of scarcity, we still need to see abundance (of resources, of love). There is more at stake than satiating physical hunger, for the hunger is also spiritual and compassion for others is the remedy. Palmer affirms that we are called to break the "scarcity habit" and set aside our fears. By doing this, we actually *create* community. It's all about community.

> There is a powerful correlation between the assumption
> of scarcity and the decline of community, a correlation
> that runs both ways. If we allow the scarcity assumption
> to dominate our thinking, we will act in individualistic,
> competitive ways that destroy community. If we destroy
> community, where creating and sharing with others
> generates abundance, the scarcity assumption will
> become [even] more valid (Palmer, 127).

How can we feel richer with less and with simpler things? And there is a broader reason why we must consume less and yet feel abundance, nonetheless. I now consciously try to serve less at meals, to rid the cupboards and freezer and fridge of excess food, even though these entrenched habits die hard. Why? Partly to travel lighter and to live more simply. It is also absolutely necessary to return to a more natural rhythm of fast and feast and to avoid excess not merely on the personal level. This rebalancing in one's life contributes to addressing global inequities, world nutrition, and better management of resources. The global economy demands a more responsible use of the earth's bounty. It is healthy for our bodies, souls, and our planet. Win, win, win. This more expansive worldview points toward issues of food justice, to economic justice and cultural equity, to evening out playing fields so all can have the basics, what every human requires to live a decent life.

This broader sense of a communal good returns me to reflecting on my family's early Toronto days. None of us was rich, and the community was fairly egalitarian. We worked hard, and although we never really had many luxuries, we felt we were living well, and never considered ourselves poor or lacking. Ironically, it was only after experiencing luxuries, travel, and material abundance that I began to understand how this contributed to a fear of poverty. It seemed to indicate that the very act of rising in the social and economic order came to produce a concomitant fear of never having enough, the psychological need to surround oneself with stuff, to keep it, not give it away—or, at best, only symbolic acts of charity. But the persistent call of conscience has always been to feed the hungry, clothe the naked, shelter the homeless, comfort the sick, with sharing as the very cornerstone of so many faith traditions. Certainly, it is canonized in biblical texts. Abundance became a lot less tangible and more spiritual for me, just as generosity became more tangible. Give the food away because we all have more than enough. When I took the concept of *enough* truly to heart, the spectacle of food abundance (and waste) verged for me on the edge of revulsion toward the food fetish.

Food, in fact, and the right to it, requires social advocacy. If we are to truly see that our brothers and sisters are adequately fed, a form of "Sabbath economics" (Meyers 2002) or periodic redistribution of wealth, is demanded. We may remember all the ways traditional cultures have accomplished this feat, in the form of alms for the poor, food *sagre* or harvest festivals (where the first fruits are shared with all), St. Joseph's Tables/Altars where all are invited to partake, or even, from earliest times, allowing peasants to glean the fields after harvest. But *periodic* justice is not a complete solution. We must engage what Wayne Muller calls the "the theology of enough." The practices of abundant consumption must be checked. The peasant dream of abundance (as well as the middle class achievement of enough) must give way to a theology and *practice* of enough, even if capitalism banks on *never enough*, and on endless consumption and waste.

And yet, what is the reality of America today? More abundance and less generosity. Widening gaps between rich and poor. The last time I checked, 1 in 6 Americans went hungry. Imagine what the ratio might be for the rest of the world. In 2010, I was invited to teach at Addis Ababa University, in Ethiopia, and it was there that I realized that I had never actually come face to face with real hunger and abject poverty, that I had only heard of it. But here, hunger was everywhere visible on the streets. It broke my heart to see a mother, begging on the side of the road with her children. The magnitude of the problem seemed daunting. But we all know there is always *something* we can do, however small it might appear, to alleviate suffering. So, I made a habit of taking bread from my lunch and dinner table in the hotel and giving it to her every time I passed by. I also realized that I had never experienced this most elemental form of charity before: bread for the poor. An Italian could certainly understand this fundamental act, for bread was the elemental food, often the only food (and not a food accompaniment), for Italians over the centuries. The Siemens Hotel restaurant in Addis Ababa, where I lodged and ate most meals, was a fairly normal one by Western standards, but was impossibly lavish by local norms. And here were separate enclaves, the haves and have-nots, sharing the same piece of street, yet miles apart. Right next door to the hotel was the Istituto Italiano di Cultura (the Italian Cultural Institute), where an impromptu market was selling Italian vegetables (zucchini flowers, artichokes, and so forth) in plastic bags to parents picking up their children from the IIC school. What juxtapositions!

On the wider end of my own food justice spectrum, were programs I devised and curated, that moved outside the Italian cultural perimeter to embrace diverse communities—a St. Joseph's Table in Watts, as part of the Watts Towers Common Ground Initiative, for example (Chapter 6: "Feeding the Poor—Welcoming the Stranger: The Watts Towers Common Ground Initiative and St. Joseph's Communal Tables in Watts"). Our open table sought, not only to share food abundance, but to welcome the stranger. My attraction to the St. Joseph's Table tradition is undoubtedly because it comprises *all* the themes most dear to my Italian immigrant understanding of the hardships faced by migrants and by others on society's margins: the life of penury, the trauma of hunger, the necessity of wandering, the desire for hospitality and belonging (Chapter 3: "Rituals of Charity and Abundance: Sicilian St. Joseph's Tables and Feeding the Poor in Los Angeles").

Food and politics, of course, go hand in hand on a societal level. In my professional life, food has served a variety of cultural and political goals as well. I have been a longtime practitioner of dinner diplomacy and cultural advocacy. At such intimate home events, live Italian folk music was frequently performed as a way of introducing it to those who might never be otherwise exposed to it, inviting them to listen and, hopefully, to appreciate it in its more natural convivial contexts, thereby perhaps expanding guests' horizons, perhaps eventually opening more opportunities for it in more formal settings. I, myself, advocated for Italian folk culture in those more formal settings of exhibitions, concerts, and other public programs in museums, universities, and civic settings. We gathered touring Italian bands into our home, as well as locally based musicians and performers. We invited academic and community friends, as well as those on all sides of the Italian/diaspora spectrum—including Italian officialdom—to participate. More pointedly, when contemplating the Watts Towers Common Ground Initiative as a means of linking diverse communities around this Los Angeles landmark, it was around our dining room table that we came to a deeper partnership, and to forge a way forward. (Chapter 6: "Feeding the Poor—Welcoming the Stranger: The Watts Towers Common Ground Initiative and St. Joseph's Communal Tables in Watts.")

Food is scattered throughout my curriculum vitae, as this collection of essays demonstrates. But beyond my food writings, were other sorts of food-related activities, organizations, and events, often under the aegis of the Italian Oral History Institute which I founded and directed for about a decade, in partnership with a wide range of entities: for example, international organic wine expositions (Los Angeles 2001, New York 2002); participation in the founding of the Los Angeles Slow Food convivium, and decades later as a founding member of the Los Angeles delegation of *Accademia Italiana della Cucina* (AIC), Los Angeles (eventually becoming its *delegata* for a couple of years). I participated in the AIC until I became conflicted about this more elite sort of dinner club, and its allure of *mondanità* (worldliness),[3] and ultimately, the economic viability of local, high-end Italian restaurants. I was not interested in some of the goals and values of the organization. I did not believe in food "purity" or the absolute value of "authentic" Italian cuisine, and thus in vouching for such alleged "authenticity" in the global AIC guide to Italian restaurants. The first dinner I co-organized aimed to reduce costs and democratize the event, held at then recently opened Osteria Mamma. The cost was roughly half and the food quantity double the AIC norm. We had a huge turn out, and almost had to turn away guests, if it hadn't been for the wonderfully accommodating staff at the restaurant and "Mamma" Loredana Cecchinato herself beckoning everyone inside. The food was delicious. But we received this *critique* from at least one guest: it was like a wedding! That is, there was too much food. The Accademia and I were clearly mismatched; I eventually concluded that I could not sustain the concept (nor the cost) of indulging in lavish dinners, however delicious or appropriately priced they were (from a restaurateur's perspective).

---

3   During my tenure as delegate, I tried to introduce more educational programming, even lectures, and a greater interest in food traditions, home cooking, rather than high-end ingredients and wines typical of AIC restaurant dinners. Perhaps the most memorable events of my term as delegate—at least to me—because it combined food and food talk, was a home-based lecture on the history of Befana (given by my folklore colleague, Sabina Magliocco), and sharing home-baked items from AIC members' own traditions relating to this Christmas/Befana festive cycle.

THIS VOLUME

This volume reviews three decades of research, writing, and programming around the Italian immigrant food nexus. It does not offer a complete menu, but rather a tasting of food publications, departing from the core myth of the *Paese di Cuccagna* (the Land of Cockaigne), and evolving toward issues of food justice and sustainability. At its heart, however, is Cuccagna, deeply ingrained in my DNA, molded by my ancestors' experiences and deprivations, as well as Italian oral culture and history. Consider it the effect of accumulated trauma in our bones: "*la fame dent'all'osso s'è incarnita*" (hunger in our bones was made flesh). Hunger and its opposite, the dream of plenty, go hand in hand.

This collection also includes essays on: wine culture and the cantina among Toronto Italians; an Italian market in San Pedro, California; a study of a high-value food product, olive oil (Chapter 7: "Treasure from Trees: Gold and Liquid Gold in the Oral and Archaeological Traditions around Horace's Sabine Villa in Licenza, Italy"); the St. Joseph's Table tradition among Sicilians in Southern California, as well as my use of this tradition for Italian folk culture advocacy, as well as for more political goals of advocating on behalf of food justice programs in Watts (and for the Watts Towers themselves). The writing is alternatively scholarly and personal. It treats a fundamental preoccupation with food in the multigenerational practices of an ethnic group, while reflecting on my personal participation in such practices as they have evolved into the present. The volume also offers more traditional essays in cultural-historical scholarship, however—on the history of pasta and gastronomic utopias, as well as my ethnographic writing on belief and material culture based on fieldwork studies, in the instances of the *cantina*, St. Joseph's Tables, and markets.

WORKS CITED

Palmer, Parker J. 1990. *The Active Life: A Spirituality of Work, Creativity, and Caring*. San Francisco: Jossey-Bass.

Calvino, Italo, ed. [1956] 1981. "Jump in My Sack!" ("*Salta nel mio sacco*"). In *Italian Folktales*, New York: Pantheon: 1981. English translation of *Fiabe italiane*, edited by Italo Calvino, translated by George Martin. Torino: Einaudi.

De Paolo, Tomie. 1975. *Strega Nona*. Hoboken: NJ: Prentice Hall.

Muller, Wayne. 2000. *Sabbath: Finding Rest, Renewal, and Delight in Our Busy Lives*. New York: Random House.

Myers, Ched. 2002. *The Biblical Vision of Sabbath Economics*. Washington: Tell the Word.

Reynolds, Malvina. 1955. "Love is something if you give it away." https://people.wku.edu/charles.smith/MALVINA/mr101. htm (accessed April 19, 2022).

Figure 1: *Carciofi alla romana* (Roman-style artichokes with wild mint, *mentuccia*).

Figure 2: *Ceccamariti* or *ceccamarini* (*struffoli* in other traditions).

Figure 3: *Casatella* (a coffee, marsala, and ricotta pie).

Figure 4: *Ciambelle al vino, cannella e anice* (hard donut cookie with wine, cinnamon and anis seed).

Figures 1–4: Foods that have remained "special" foods, partly because I choose not to prepare them at most any other time than for the holidays.

Figure 5

Figure 6

Figure 7

Figures 5–7: Examples of my home-grown and homemade foods: kumquats and kumquat jam, olives to be cured in brine from our own trees in the Sierran foothills.

Figure 8: Otello Poldi, my nephew, repeating a much-loved Terracina tradition of *l'abbendata* (<*abbendare* [<Latin *VENTU*, wind], to fan the fire), inherited from his father, Giuseppe Poldi.

Figure 9   Figure 10

Figures 9–10: Foraged snails from San Pedro, California, prepared in the Roman style, with *mentuccia* (wild mint), rosemary, garlic, and tomatoes. They are individually scooped out with a safety pin or tooth pick, making sure to leave the digestive end of the body behind. The sauce is soaked up with bread.

Figure 11

Figure 12

Figure 13

Figures 11–13: Some of the foods I purchase at San Pedro's A-1 Italian Market: Neapolitan *sfogliatelle* (which I buy frozen to bake in my oven), olive oils, pasta, handmade sausages, and (once a year for my Christmas Eve seafood salad) octopus.

Figures 14–17: Food continues to engage our family's next generation, but my daughters, Elena and Giulia, have taken Christmas baking to an artistic level. Examples include: *bûche de Noël* in mossy California oak [Figures 14–15], another tree variety with holly and meringue mushrooms [Figure 16], as well as elaborately decorated sugar cookies [Figure 17].

Figure 14

Figure 15

Figure 16

Figure 17

Figure 18: My "soul food" consists of egg *fettuccine* with either a plain fresh tomato and basil sauce or a rich and slow-cooked *sugo* (ragù) with pork and beef.

Figure 19: A collegial dinner *al fresco* in our backyard, one of many gatherings typical in our pre-COVID home.

1. Mountains of Cheese and Rivers of Wine: *Paesi di Cuccagna* and Other Gastronomic Utopias

If you travel for seven months—four by sea and three by land—you will arrive at a gate.[1] There is a guard at that gate, and only if you promise to obey the law of the land, will he let you pass through. Here are what the laws command: you must promise never to speak of work, only of eating, drinking, sleeping, playing, and dancing. You must never mention the words *war, tilling, weaving*, or *sewing*. If you look carefully, over the gate, you will read this inscription: *chi più dorme più guadagna* (he who sleeps most earns most).

1   This essay was first published in *Imagined States: Nationalism, Utopia, and Longing in Oral Cultures*, edited by Luisa Del Giudice and Gerald Porter (Logan: Utah State University Press, 2001). Translations and photography, if not otherwise noted, are mine.

Variations of this paper have been read at the following meetings: Kommission für Volksdichtung (S.I.E.F.), Faroe Islands, 1993; American Folklore Society, Milwaukee, 1994; Museo ItaloAmericano, San Francisco, 1994; University of Hawaii at Manoa, 1995; UCLA, Los Angeles, 1995; Istituto Italiano di Cultura, Los Angeles, 2000.

For their various critical readings of this paper, I wish to thank Riccardo Grazioli, Bruno Pianta, Gerald Porter, Steve Siporin, and Edward Tuttle. I thank the following for offering references which were useful to my research: Pier Marco Bertinetto, Tom Cheesman, Catherine Detto, Reimund Kvideland, Massimo Montanari, Marcia Reed, Victoria Simmons, and Rudolph Vecoli. I wish to acknowledge and gratefully thank the following institutions for their permission to reproduce images which illustrate this essay: Civica Raccolta delle Stampe Achille Bertarelli, Milano; the Disney Publishing Group; Getty Research Library; Elemond SpA, Milano; Museo Nazionale delle Arti e Tradizioni Popolari (MNATP), Rome.

Once you have entered, and as you walk the streets, you will see some curious sights: rivers flow with wine, houses have walls of sausage and cheese, roast chickens fall from the sky, fish jump out of the pond and into your arms. From the trees hang shoes, stockings, hats. There are caves of gold coins and you can gather all you want. If you insist on speaking of work, the guards will immediately seize you and take you to prison, which, by the way, is made of cheese. There is a large palace of pleasure with beautiful women and perfumed beds. And right in the center of this land is a huge mountain of cheese. A cauldron sits on top and *maccheroni* and *tortellini* spew forth all day long, roll down the Parmesan mountain, and land in a pool of rich capon broth. Every fruit you can imagine grows in this place in all seasons. Hens lay 200 eggs a day, sheep eliminate ricotta cheese, ovens continually produce bread, cakes, and pizza, and you can find marzipan trees and cookies of every kind. There is no sickness or poverty, everyone has the title of baron or duke, and there are no tariffs. Therefore, if you are hungry and tired, my friend, forget your salads and vegetables, and come with me to *il Paese di Cuccagna* (the Land of Cockaigne).

So reads a Neapolitan broadside, here selectively paraphrased, entitled *La piacevole historia di Cvccagna* (The delightful story of Cockaigne), dated 1715, sung by a street performer, Giovanni il Tranese, but itself only one of the many reworkings of earlier broadsides on this theme (Zenatti 1884; Scherillo 1884) [Figure 1.1].

GASTRONOMIC UTOPIAS

The Paese di Cuccagna, Cockaigne/Lubberland (England), Schlaraffenland (Germany), Cocagne/Panigons (France), or Oleana (Norway) is a mythic land of plenty where rivers run with "milk and honey" (or wine, beer, coffee, or rum), food falls like manna from heaven, work is banished, and no one ever grows old. It represents one of the most persistent desires for a return to a terrestrial Paradise Lost.[2] The archetypal pattern of humankind's harmony with the divine and nature, followed by transgression and fall from grace, recurs widely in religious narratives (cf. Cocchiara 1956; Graf 1925; Cioranescu 1971; Costa 1972). That the myth of Cuccagna became, in the European folk worldview, a strictly sensual paradise and, in Italy, an essentially gastronomic utopia, confirms, through the inversion principle of utopian thought, that it was a "collective dream of the hungry masses" (Camporesi 1978). The Land of *Plenty* inversely reflects the Land of *Hunger*. In other words, utopian visions hold up a mirror reflecting that which the utopianist's society lacks and desires.[3]

Food, of course, is essential to most Edenic (and many Infernal)[4] representations, where nature gives forth its riches abundantly and without toil. In the Paese di Cuccagna however, nature becomes surrealistically hyperactive and magical: cows give birth to four calves a day, hens lay two hundred eggs, donkeys excrete gold coins. And while Adam was condemned to till the earth to feed himself, here poltroonery becomes the law. Further, unlike social utopias à la Thomas More, this poor man's paradise projects from the stomach rather than the mind, and satisfies basic needs: food, shelter, sex.[5]

---

2   *Paradise* apparently derives from the Persian *parādaijah* (walled garden), an otherworldly prize for the Muslim warrior, wherein lies a luxurious garden with fruit trees and plentiful beasts to be hunted. If these such edible paradises indeed are the heavenly goal, Vidari speculates, "*la religione esprime forse il ricordo di fami terribili*" ("religion perhaps records the memory of terrible famines" [1981, 40]). Richter sees in Cockaigne a flowing together of literary and mystical Judeo-Christian and Islamic sources (Richter 1989). On Schlaraffenland, see Ackermann 1994, and Richter 1989; on Cocagne, Delpech 1979 and Delumeau 1976.

3   For example, a crime-ridden society might crave an orderly, harmonious, and peaceable kingdom, whereas a developing society might project cuccagnesque visions such as the one here described.

4   In the literature and iconography (and hence in the popular imagination) of Christian Europe, Hell, too, was frequently depicted as a kitchen in which evil souls were roasted, fried, fricasseed, or eaten raw by a voracious, cannibalistic Satan.

5   This is not to say, however, that dietary concerns do not form part of literary utopian writings as well (see, for example, Chiarotto 1982 on More, Campanella, Bacon, etc.), although the perspective is markedly different and may concern systems of food production and distribution, for example. Indeed, the differences between these two utopic models and their value systems are rather marked:

In Italy, references to Cuccagna recur with the greatest frequency from the sixteenth to the seventeenth centuries and begin to wane during the eighteenth century (Camporesi 1978; Cocchiara 1956; Zenatti 1884) [Figures 1.2–1.7]. They were found in street literature (including games) [Figure 1.8],[6] in oral tradition (such as song and tales), and in high literature alike. Yet, that the largest number of attestations, and the most detailed, were destined for the public piazza, suggests in and of itself, that it had the widest currency among a popular audience. Indeed, Cuccagna was sustained largely in the popular imagination through vernacular genres such as street performances of song, broadside prints, and oral narratives. Further, the persistence of Cuccagna in Italian oral and popular tradition seems to document a condition of basic deprivation among the lower classes, which remained a constant in Italy well into the twentieth century (see Teti 1976 and 1984; Del Giudice 1993 and 2001). It is my contention that Cuccagna survives and animates Italian immigrant culture still.

Cuccagna may be considered an archetypic "imagined state." Its geographic ubiquity and historic longevity may be attributable to its expression of basic corporeal aspirations. It will survive at least as long as hunger and other deprivations continue. Cuccagna, as a powerful metaphor for abundance, has found myriad representations as it metamorphosed and evolved in surprising, unexpected ways, and has variously functioned in a range of societies throughout its long history. But beyond expressing a basic aspiration for adequate nourishment, the power of Cuccagna as symbol rests firmly in its ability to imagine, and thereby construct, an alternative social order. That is, while Cuccagna largely described this imagined state as an

---

indulgence vs. sobriety; the individual vs. the public good; a full belly and idleness vs. industriousness (cf. Richter 1989).

6   See the many food-related games found in the prints of Mitelli (in Bertarelli 1940): *Gioco della Cucagna* (The Cuccagna game, 131) [see Figure 1.8]; *Il gioco importantissimo del fornaro, banco, che mai falisce, chi hà robba da mangiar sempre hà moneta* (The most important game of the baker, the counter which never fails, where one who has food to eat never loses and always has money, 133); *Gioco della Signora Gola* (The game of Lady Gullet, 137); *Gioco Nuovo di tutte l'osterie che sono in Bologna* (The new game of all the taverns of Bologna, 138). See also Camporesi 1975.

edible paradise, it also abolished social ills and constraints while it celebrated values that were both anti-Christian and in tune with the social margins. As such, it remained a persistent symbol of possible and alternative worlds. Although this imagined state was largely a projection of bodily cravings, articulated through edible and spatial metaphors as a dream of social change and escape, it nonetheless animated Italian popular consciousness for centuries and sustained a craving for the imagined land of plenty, subsequently realized in actual journeys such as Italian mass migrations to America.

This essay then, concerns itself primarily with the Italian street variants of the myth as expressed through popular print and in oral tradition. It examines the sociohistoric and ethnographic foundations of this folk utopia as it reflected the tension between social classes in the Old World, as well as the role this driving myth behind mass emigration to America (otherwise known as Cuccagna) has played in Italian immigrant foodways and worldview.

Gastronomic utopias reflect culturally determined tastes and shared cravings. Northern European variants, for instance, differ widely from the Italian in the matter of diet and hence utopian foods. Scandinavian Oleanas may feature rivers of sour cream and mountains of porridge,[7] while the French land of Panigons has trees of butter, rocks of melted cheese, and pigs stuffed with chestnuts, and the Mexican variant presents tortilla hills, fountains of olive oil, and *sopaipilla* (fritter) trees (see, for example, Robb 1980, 337–38). The American hobo's vision of "hog heaven"—alternatively known as Ditty Wah Ditty, Oleana, or simply Nowhere—is expressed in the song "The Big Rock Candy Mountain," which projects the American taste for sugar and whiskey (cf. Rammel 1990);[8] whereas in Brer Rabbit's "Garden of Eatin'," at

---

7   On this motif in Scandinavian tradition, see Blegen and Ruud ca. 1936, 187–91; Amundsen and Kvideland 1975; Wright and Wright 1983, 221–23. See also two sound recordings of "Oleana": Harvey 1986, side 2, track 6; Glazer 1991, side 1, track 6.

8   Even though, according to Rosella Mamoli Zorzi (1989), in the Anglo-American world, asceticism and puritanism prevented the American utopia from focusing on food and pleasure, and therefore it became more symbolic, or figurative (Eldorado, Golden Land). However, "The Big Rock Candy Mountain," written by Harry K. McClintock in the early twentieth century, does seem to be

least in a Disney version (presumably adapting the African American tradition), we find hams, a chicken gravy river, hotcake plants, and a forbidden pork chop tree (Disney Enterprises 1992) [Figures 1.9–1.10]. Italy's Paese di Cuccagna instead frequently displays a cheese mountain with a cauldron on top bubbling over with tortellini, ravioli, or maccheroni (which historically were gnocchi),[9] rivers running with fine wines (such as Malvasia), and meats in great abundance. The high frequency of cheese and meat make protein and animal fats the most prevalent feature of Cuccagna. Rarely are vegetables mentioned. The centuries-old dietary norms of the lower classes—a diet based primarily on grains, legumes, and vegetables (the now fashionable Mediterranean diet)—is thereby inverted.

CUCCAGNA BETWEEN WRITTEN AND ORAL CULTURE

Although the first written attestations of Cuccagna appear in the literature of the late Middle Ages (for a thirteenth century French fabliau of this name, see Väänänen 1947), it should be assumed that this utopia was "*un atteggiamento mentale prima ancora che una prassi della scrittura*," that is, "a mental *attitude* before it became [fixed] in the written word" (Zaganelli 1989, 146; cf. Cocchiara 1956, 160–61).

While many Italian literary authors have, in varying degrees, written of Cuccagna (cf. Camporesi 1978), often referring to it with an ironic, satiric, or moralistic twist (for example, Calandrino, the fool in Boccaccio, *Decameron* VIII, 3), the "penny" press variety appears more indulgent (and less severe) with its willing audiences. Here instead lavish and detailed descriptions prevail. *Description*, in fact, is often featured in the titles themselves of the continual reworkings of this

---

an exception, since it features the hobo's vision of streams of whiskey, stew, and candy—as well as no work or police, and bulldogs with rubber teeth.

9   Note that maccheroni in the Middle Ages referred to gnocchi, "dumplings" of fresh flour (not of potatoes, obviously, since they were a later, New World addition to the European diet). Note too that the parmigiano cheese onto which they were rolled was their prime condiment since tomatoes too were added after the "discoveries" (Montanari 1987, 12; cf. Messedaglia 1942).

popular motif: for example, *Descrittione del Paese di Cuccagna vicino a S. Daniel, città del Friuli, stato della Repubblica Veneta* (Description of the Land of Cockaigne, near San Daniele, city of Friuli, state of the Venetian Republic; anonymous, Correr Museum, Venice); or *Discritione del Paese di Chvcagna dove chi manco lavora piv gvadagna* (Description of the Land of Cockaigne where he who works least earns most; Remondini di Bassano, seventeenth century, in Bertarelli ca. 1929, 51).

Cuccagna's widening appeal, in fact, coincided with the High Renaissance, just as real problems of poverty became more acute, with an ever greater proportion of the population excluded from the natural resources of forest and pasture (Montanari 1987, 12; 1993, 118–21). Note that in Cuccagna, nature's bounty is free to *all*. Against the images of wealth, patronage and self-celebration in the Renaissance, we can envision, at the margins of the grand tableaux, the beggars and vagabonds who now became endemic. Prisons and hospices for the poor grew, as did concerns over ways of feeding their vast numbers. Social historian Camporesi best describes this underworld of the poor and the *culture* of hunger in *Il paese della fame* (The land of hunger)—Cuccagna's mirror image (Camporesi 1978). It was precisely among the lower classes that the imagined land of Cuccagna gained enormous popularity. Of course, the humorous, ironic, and perhaps seditious aspects of this myth (in the worldview of vagrants) may have served to seduce the collective imagination toward an irregular life of leisure, indulgence, and freedom from the established social order.[10]

Famines in the mid-fifteenth century became especially acute as the search for new foods to stave off large-scale starvation (such as corn and potatoes from the New World) came to fill treatises on agronomy. Meat consumption decreased all over Europe, and bread made from the lower quality grains became the mainstay of the poor. Monotony and poverty of diet for the lower classes became the norm in Italy during the seventeenth century and remained so well into the

---

10   Pianta 1989 and personal communication. Other occupational (and anti-occupational) groups, sharing a similar worldview, such as Norwegian navvies (cf. Kvideland and Porter 2001) and American hoboes (cf. Rammel 1990), may have been attracted to such motifs for similar reasons.

twentieth century. Monotony of diet and reliance on a single staple were to cause real catastrophes all over Europe, since one bad harvest could mean death (as in Ireland) or else chronic vitamin deficiency and lingering disease (for example, pellagra for northern Italians).

Camporesi (1980) describes in nauseating detail the adulterated breads and the health hazards accompanying the use of lower quality grains (some actually hallucinogenic), as he does the many forms of aberrant social behavior spawned by hunger, from cannibalism to collective deliriums. (See, for example, the chapter headings in Camporesi 1980: "Vertigini collettive" [Collective Vertigo]; "Sogni iperbolici" [Hyperbolic Dreams]; "Paradisi artificiali" [Artificial Paradises]; "Il pane papaverino" [Poppy Bread].) Unwittingly, therefore, many Italians may have participated in the delirious visions other cultures attained through the intentional, sometimes ritual, use of known hallucinogens. One may conclude that a delirious and somnolent people could dream of such far off places literally with eyes wide open, and that the sort of relief Cuccagna song texts might have provided was akin to an addictive drug. This delirium could manifest itself in a variety of ways: from imposing food visions on the landscape (such as cheese mountains, wine rivers, money trees)[11] or the constructed environment (ships, houses), to projecting foods on celestial bodies (such as Menocchio, the Friulian miller and heretic who imagined the earth as a fermenting, wormy cheese; see Ginzburg 1976) or human physiognomy (such as Arcimboldo's food "portraits"). Such flights of food fantasy suggest a constant play between reality, illusion, and wish fulfillment. Yet food mirages were not merely figments of imagination: they actually reflected facts of social hierarchy.

The images of richly draped lords and merchants and splendid tables set with every imaginable delicacy are common enough in the history, literature, and iconography of the Renaissance, and they frequently found their way into the popular imagination via other genres as well (as in the marriage banquets that close many a folktale). The codification of social rank became important in every aspect of life, from the clothes one wore to the foods one ate, all carefully

---

11   On the other hand, food often does appear on the landscape in the form of toponomastics (see Desinan 1982).

monitored through sumptuary laws. One should eat, for example, "according to one's social status" (*mangiare secondo la qualità della persona*; Montanari 1993, 105). In other words, proper to a peasant's physiology were roots, coarse breads, and salt pork, while the noble's physique required fresh meats, fish, fruit, white bread, and strong wine. To subvert this "natural" hierarchic dietary order was to subvert the social order. Cuccagna instead abounds anarchically with the finest wines, white breads, cakes, and noble fowl.

Yet nobles were not to be deterred from ostentation and display. Ingenious architectural food fantasies and other sumptuous dishes were frequently paraded around the public piazza before the gaze of the common folk, then consumed by the few (Montanari 1993, 115–18).[12] How could the Renaissance banquet not emerge as a never-never land of glut and satiety? Were the mountains of cheese or the edible palaces so fantastical if we consider that princely guests were often regaled with actual edible landscapes in the form of sculpted marzipan castles or fountains of wine or with fowl cooked and dressed in its own feathers?[13] Such culinary tours de force find their way into the iconography of Cuccagna dreamscapes.

Is it any wonder then that mere lists of food, the insistence on vast quantities and on variety, might have entranced the street audiences in a mirage-like Paese di Cuccagna? Indeed, many of the texts meant for popular "consumption"—such as those of the street performer G. C. Croce (cf. Del Giudice 1998)—provided vicarious and surrogate gustatory pleasures, filling *mental* larders, creating *virtual* food,[14] through descriptions of foods which would never be

---

12   Indeed, Montanari contends, hunger can only be understood through the binary opposition of hunger and abundance, hence the title of his work, L'abbondanza e la fame (1993, 120).

13   The recipe "Per far pavoni vestiti con tutte le sue penne" (How to make peacocks dressed with all their own feathers) is reproduced in Guerrini (1879) 1969, 293–94. For other recipes on such culinary feats, see Giovann[i] de Rosselli's cookbook: *Opera nova chiamata Epulario, la quale tracta il modo de cucinare ogni carne, ucelli, pesci, de ognisorte, et fare sapori, torte, pastelli, al modo de tutte le provincie, [et] molte altre ge[n]tilezze, co[m]posta p[er] maestro Giova[n]n[i] de Roselli, Fra[n]cese* ([1574] 1974, 6, reprint).

14   This is not to say that this exercise was not also somewhat sado-masochistic,

actually tasted, but were only imagined. Broadside texts cataloging long lists of delicacies must indeed have had a hypnotic effect on the famished audience. And all this "bounty" for mere pennies, with the purchase of a broadside. Street performers' very livelihoods, of course, depended on providing what the audience wanted, since the sale of the broadside was the prime objective of any performer. The large number of surviving Cuccagna broadsides gives de facto evidence of the theme's popularity through time.

Can words be eaten? Contemporary readers of cookbooks may ask themselves a similar question, as might anyone who has ever participated in other virtual food experiences, such as discussing menus or recounting memorable repasts. And which ethnic group has cultivated the food narrative more than Italians? They, for example, readily engage in food-related discourse, often while in the very act of consuming food, compounding gustatory pleasures both virtual and real. In that gustatory space, what complex sensory response to food may be simulated? This curious mind/body phenomenon seems to engage both psychological and physiological responses (as captured in the phrase and experience: "it makes my mouth water"). Cuccagna song and prose narratives may find their modern-day counterparts in restaurant reviews and other professional food writings, while today's equivalent of lavishly depicted cuccagnesque prints may well be found in the (quasi-pornographic)[15] art of food photography— which has the late-twentieth-century virtue of satisfying without adding calories. Nonetheless, "faux foods" are a modern-day marvel: titillating to the senses but noncaloric.

---

for merely filling one's ears was little consolation for not filling one's stomach. An Old Irish *Vision* recounts the tale of a bound Cathal forced to listen to long lists of food without being fed: "Though grievous to Cathal was the pain of being two days and a night without food, much greater was the agony of listening to the enumeration before him of the many various pleasant viands, and none of them for him!" (*The Vision of MacConglinne* 1936, vision 573). I thank Victoria Simmons for this reference.

15   It has been stated somewhere that the modern illustrated cookbook is "pornography for women." I thank Gerald Porter for this note.

ICONOGRAPHY:
CONSTRUCTING EDIBLE PARADISES

The myriad iconographies of Cuccagna may be more powerful even than the broadside song texts they frequently accompany (cf. Pezzini 1989, who cautions us not to view them as subordinate). Some narrate via vignette and caption in a decentered, comic strip manner [Figure 1.11 for *Il Mondo alla Riversa*], while others stand on their own as elaborate and detailed illustrative popular prints, yet all favor detailed captions to orient the viewer. Such depictions of Cuccagna landscapes are among the most enduring remnants of a collective popular print tradition, together with illustrated proverbs, the Roverso Mondo (Topsy Turvy World), the Ship of Fools, *mestieri ambulanti* (itinerant occupations), and others.

The artist/architect's ingenuity here comes into play as he gives marvelous shape to popular food fantasies. He constructs these fantastical ships, palaces, pyramids, cities, islands, mountains, with wondrous edible building materials (just as Arcimboldo constructed thematic portraits out of food, flora, books, and so forth). Besides wine rivers and cheese mountains, these materials included ricotta and cheese walls, cobblestones of cheese, cooked capon stairs, roofs of *cialde inzuccarate* (sugared biscuits). Edible ships might feature a rudder of salami (*soppressata*), nails of fennel stalks, planks of mixed innards (*frittaglie*), rigging of pork intestines (cf. Rossi 1888, 406–7). Textual utopias were sometimes even accompanied by actual maps, helping the "pilgrim" negotiate the way. Indeed, each Cuccagna text seems to be generated by "its own more or less explicit geography" (*una propria geografia più o meno esplicita*; Pezzini 1989, 279).

Cuccagna plays with the whimsical through iconographic and linguistic acrobatics: for example Pierre de la Maison Neufve's *Familière description du très vinoporratimalvoisé & très envitaillegoulementé Royaume Panigonnois, mystiquement interprété l'Isle de Crevepance* (Firsthand description of the very vinoporragimalvoisied and very envictualigullemented Panigonnois Kingdom, mystically interpreted as the Isle of Bustbelly; Armand Hammer Museum 1994, 400, and plate 9). The Italian iconographic tradition,[16] beginning as early as the sixteenth century, seems as well to revel in the playful and the pleasurable (and at least once, in the pornographic—see the nineteenth century (*L'albero della Cuccagna* [Figure 1.12]) and refrains from the visual moralizations found in some northern European variants (such as Brueghel's *Land of Cockaigne* or the "women's Cuccagna" represented in the figure just mentioned), just as its textual street variety typically differs in tone from literary texts.

What role did the street performer specifically play in the construction of Cuccagna as an imagined state? Street performers, it is well to remember, shared the social stigmatization of itinerants of all kinds. They were often perceived as vagrants themselves, living on the social margins, and hence suspected of sharing and promoting counter- or sub-cultural values.[17] They may indeed have had a vested interest, therefore, in promoting imagined and alternative "states," both existential and social. Did Pied-Piper bards of Cuccagna not seek, after all, to lure their audiences, however light heartedly, to follow them on journeys, and to abandon the status quo (as did, for example, Giovanni il Tranese, mentioned above)? The ongoing battle the Church and civil authorities waged against street performers had its own political significance, corroborating that the performers were perceived to be dangerous and capable of destabilizing the social order. Certainly, the repertoires of street performers have often featured, beyond pure entertainment, social commentary and have voiced sociopolitical views in tune with their socially oppressed audiences (cf. the journal *Il Cantastorie* [Street Singer] 1981–). Their compositions

---

16   Significant Italian iconographic representations may be found in Angeleri 1953, 122, n.159, and 131–32, n.184; Bertarelli 1940, n.605; Bertarelli 1974, fig. 13 and n.553, fig. 14; Camporesi 1978, 228–32; di Mauro 1981, 97, n.169, and 120, n.239; Morelli 1969, 139; Segarizzi 1913, 236, n.258; Toschi 1964, fig. 105; Vidari 1981. Many related depictions from other traditions as well as the Italian may be found in Harms 1983; Harms and Kemp 1987; Fortunati and Zucchini 1989; Rammel 1990; Disney 1992, 9–10.

17   Until recently, for instance, they were closely associated with markets and fairs and hence, as itinerants, shared in their negative social status (Leydi 1978). On the Pavese street performer, see Callegari's account of his father shaming his farming family by becoming a street singer (Centro di Studi 1978, 310–12).

were not only subject to constant surveillance, as *con licenza dei superiori* ([published] with the permission of authorities) attests, but the street performers' freedom of movement and performance as well was carefully monitored and often curtailed, until very recently (Ghidoli 1985). The constraints placed on their freedom of expression probably resulted in a preponderance of performances in a comic or satiric vein, such as those of G. C. Croce (Del Giudice 1998). In the case of Cuccagna texts, we might ask, were street performers merely inducing a deceitful and compliant somnolence in their audiences in order to sell them their wares, or were they instead helping to keep an impossible dream—partly their own—alive?

An imagined state, which proposed complete idleness (and perhaps imprisonment) for the industrious worker, represented a profound subversion of social, as well as theological, values. The Cuccagna tradition in fact found its place in various social movements relating to, for example, labor and immigration. In its Scandinavian (and Anglo-American) traditions, which highlighted monetary wealth and the laborless utopia, Cuccagna became part of labor and occupational cultures of the nineteenth century (cf. Blegen and Ruud ca. 1936, 187–91; cf. Kvideland and Porter 2001). According to Pianta (1989), in Italy it was the image of the "triumphing" of the socially marginal in Cuccagna that provided a backdrop for the Communist anthem, "Bandiera rossa" (Red flag). Cuccagna indeed promotes counter-Christian ideals inasmuch as it does not support the virtues of resignation, self-sacrifice, and mortification of the flesh but rather celebrates the sins of gluttony, licentiousness, and idleness.

It has been widely affirmed that Cuccagna presents a static and conservative worldview and does not aspire toward social reform,[18]

---

18   It has also been noted that it was precisely during times of severe strictures and social repression that topoi such as Cockaigne, Feast of Fools, and Carnival—that is, *temporary* safety valves—became most necessary and efficacious, for example, during the times of Rabelais, Cyrano, and Marivaux (cf. Trousson 1989, 35). The evolution of Cuccagna, for instance, during the seventeenth century was, in part, due to the increasing rigidity of economic conditions, the reaffirmation of social class and privilege, and the culture of the Counter Reformation, intent on quashing all expressions of presumed immorality and licentiousness (cf. Montanari 1987, 12).

that it does not attack the social hierarchy or institutional injustice head on. In Cuccagna instead, the peasant merely wishes to live as the lord is perceived to live: idle and well fed. Rather than abolish the aristocracy, here instead everyone has the title of duke or count. Yet lest we are lulled into thinking that Cuccagna's long life is merely a series of tired and repetitive representations, basically unchanged throughout, let us recall, as Kunzle (1978) has shown for its sister *topos* "The World Upside Down," that the broadside press, by its very nature, was primarily concerned with the flux of history, suggesting it had an urban audience which observed and participated in the process of history. Within the "formulaic" *contrasti*, vignettes, and so forth, there was room for innovation, nuance, and satire. "'Pure' formal fantasy and subversive desire, far from being mutually exclusive, are two sides of the same coin" (Kunzle 1978, 89).

Although the Cuccagna motif may have found itself assisting sociopolitical goals, it did not generally itself engage in overt political discourse. Cuccagna as an imagined state represented primarily a gastronomic utopia and therefore was content to revel in the carnivalesque—an abundant and meat-based diet, conventional expressions of social inversion, and the joke—only to return to social order once the escape valve had been turned off and the performer moved on to another piazza. Cuccagna, indeed, came to be closely associated with Carnival and, through this association, came itself to co-opt aspects of social criticism always implicit in carnivalesque "reversible worlds" (cf. Babcock 1978). As Bakhtin has amply shown, though, laughter forms such an integral part of folk culture that the culture of fools is an important ingredient of festival generally, Carnival specifically, and represents ultimately a means of compromising authority through social inversion (Bahktin 1968).

CUCCAGNA AND RITUAL: A TIME FOR FEASTING

Between Carnival and Cuccagna is much semantic overlapping (or "reciprocal contamination," according to Pianta 1989, 31). At times,

Cuccagna broadsides make this connubium explicit (see *Il trionfo de Carnavale nel paese de Cucagna* [The triumph of Carnival in the Land of Cockaigne] in Bertarelli ca. 1929, 25; Toschi 1964, table 55; *Trionfo dei Poltroni* [Triumph of the poltroons] in Zenatti 1884). Carnival revelers even find their place in the iconography of Cockaigne (cf. Pianta 1989). Cuccagna celebrates a perpetual Carnival of abundance and indulgence, while meatless Lent, as stated in at least one northern European Cockaigne variant, occurs but once every twenty years. Cuccagna represents festive time run amok. Like Carnival—at least in its latter in*carn*ations—Cuccagna features pigs,[19] sausages, and other pork products (in other words a winter diet) and a fat king "triumphing" in a procession of cooks and scullions [Figure 1.13, and smaller vignettes, as in Figures 1.2–1.4], but unlike King Carnival, Cuccagna has no calendrical restrictions, and hence never dies.[20]

Carnival, as folk drama and as elite spectacle, ranged from "grotesque eating performances"[21] to *commedia dell'arte,* and was accompanied by rich oral and literary traditions. Primary among the carnivalesque literary and oral traditional genres, however, were the many *contrasti* (or mock battles) between Carnival and Lent (cf. Lozinski 1933; Grinberg and Kinser 1983), battles between a *carn*ivorous and rotund boyish Carnival and a mean, piscivorous, and haggard Lenten crone. But the relentless alternation of feasting and fasting, of abundance and hunger, in the liturgical calendar, never adequately balanced in the actual lives of peasants, which instead tilted heavily toward the latter states.[22] The battle of the proteins (meat versus fish) impinged

---

19   In northern European versions, in fact, Carnival's emblematic animal, the pig, is frequently depicted running about with a knife in its back, ready for carving.

20   For King Cockaigne in the German tradition, see the illustrations in Harms 1983, n.28, and Harms and Kemp 1987, n.41, which are likely derivative of the Italian *Il trionfo di Carnevale nel paese di Cucagna*, 1565.

21   On "gluttony artists" and "performing omnivores," compare Cheesman 1992, 1993, and 1996. Cheesman contends that they actually document large-scale social trauma (Cheesman 1992, 51–52), just as the ongoing preoccupation with food in immigrant cultures seems to do, I might add.

22   Sanga sees in the worldview of marginals, hobos (and peasants and immigrants as well), the reflection of these "paleolithic [biological] rhythms," and a worldview therefore dominated by the philosophy of the *crapula*; that is, to glut whenever

little on their diets alas, since fish was seen on their tables almost as rarely as meat. Italians had long been "vegetarian by necessity and not by choice" (Pellegrino 1952, 24).

Cuccagna's ritual dimensions are clear, and even in common parlance Cuccagna has remained a term for abundance and celebration. Linguistic remnants of Cuccagna in many Italian dialects reduce the once richly articulated place to simply *festa* (feast or good time), as in *che Cuccagna!* expressed as *che pacchia!* (what a great time!). To Italians, this altered state of feasting, the much craved "time out of time," continued to be obsessively and endlessly replayed in immigrant life until the festa itself became redundant and practically obsolete (Teti 1984; Del Giudice 2001, ch. 2 this volume). Indeed, ritual abundance, and hence Cuccagna, is reenacted with every life- or nature-cycle celebration (such as a baptism or wedding), weekly and seasonal markets or fairs (for example, St. Martin's as it is celebrated in Santarcangelo in Romagna [Sobrero 1994]), harvest festivals and saint's days (on *sagre*, see Vidari 1981, 44; on food altars, for example, see Del Giudice 2010, ch. 3 this volume), and even Sunday dinners. All replicate, celebrate, and give thanks for the miracle of prodigious nature and divine goodness. The altar of Christianity is a dinner table. The last act of God on Earth was to break bread together with disciples in the Last Supper. God himself *is* food (in the Eucharist). As Gandhi once noted, food is the only form in which God dare appear to the poor.

But while the cuccagnesque is implicitly part of any festivity, rituals making *explicit* reference to Cuccagna are rarer. A significant example may be found in the greased Cuccagna pole (*l'albero di/della Cuccagna*) [Figures 1.14–1.15] which is still featured at many public festivities in Italy (see Maggini 1977, 9–11; Coltro 1982, 152–59; Ciceri 1983, 172) and among immigrants (see Noyes 1989; 1995, 449–52),[23] and provides yet another spatial metaphor of distance and

---

the opportunity arises (cf. Sanga 1994, 39–40).

23 This *albero* may originally have been a Maypole, a phallic symbol (cf. *L'albero della Cuccagna* in Fortunati and Zucchini 1989, fig. 25), decorated with flowers (cf. Barletta 1981). On the "planting of the tree" (the ritual pole) in traditional contexts, see Scafoglio 1994b, "Le radici dell'albero." For print depictions of the *Cuccagna* pole see Toschi 1964, 147, figs. 24–27, and in the Getty Collections (Vol. 1: Amboise-Ferrara), two variants of "*alber[i] della Cuccagna*," dated 1735 and signed G.A. Belmondo.

unattainability. Typically, hanging high atop a greased pole or *albero* ("mast" or "tree," perhaps either recalling the Ship of Fools or the magical trees of the Cuccagna landscape) are prizes—the symbolic remnants of those vast territories of yore: salami, sausage, or prosciutto (that is, pork products recalling the Carnival pig), wine (as in former cuccagnesgne rivers and fountains), a bag of money (recalling caves of gold coin and gold-excreting donkeys), pasta (for the giant Cuccagna cauldron), cheese (for a mountain), and so forth. But in at least one recent instance, in the Verona area, the Cuccagna pole yielded coupons for free gasoline, rather than food (Parks 1993, 210)!

Cuccagna may not be a *u*-topia so much as it is a *poli*-topia. It is nowhere and everywhere. It is a movable feast. For Goethe it seems to have been Italy; for the Lithuanians it was Hungary; to immigrants it was America. How do these realignments occur? Let us consider one very significant case for its Italian contexts.

NAPLES AS IL PAESE DI CUCCAGNA

In seventeenth-century Italy, it was Naples that became explicitly associated with the Paese di Cuccagna and with Carnival. Indeed, Naples' magnificent and irreverent Carnivals were famous all over Europe during this time. There are several reasons for imagining Naples as a Paese di Cuccagna. As it was then, it has remained a "Land of Plenty" for the few and the "Land of Misery" for the many. The axis upon which the world of Cuccagna turns is that of social inequality. Yet, where there is misery, there too is the hope of abundance. The topography of Cuccagna required peaks and abysses. These peaks were frequently rendered in architectural constructions stressing vertical height (cf. Barletta 1981). More specifically, however, the Mountain of Cheese spewing forth maccheroni seems to be none other than Vesuvius, a (gastronomic) emblem of Naples, by then the maccheroni-eating capital of Italy. There are other gastronomic Vesuvii one may cite, such as a volcano-like *Plumpodingo alla napolitana* (Neapolitan plum pudding), presumably served hot, since it is depicted as emitting a plume of smoke from its crater (Vidari 1981, 40) [Figures 1.16–1.17].

During the earlier part of the seventeenth century, Neapolitans themselves *literally* replicated this landscape in popular Carnivals in the form of the Cuccagna "mountain," *"il monte di Cuccagna"* or *"coccagna"* (Mayer [1840] 1948, 234–235). Like a Vesuvius, it emitted maccheroni, sausages, *focacce* (flat breads), and other foods which slid down its sides and were gathered—fought over—by the common people. These mountains were movable *carri* (floats) which made their way through the city (Mancini 1963). Unlike the ideal of endless bounty however, in practice the competition for limited goods was a typical feature of this ritual, as it continued to be in the subsequent contests to scale greased Cuccagna poles.

It was the Spanish (and then Austrian) regimes of the latter Settecento in Naples, which best capitalized on the Cuccagna concept however. Intuiting the importance of this theme for the populace, these regimes actually staged periodic Cuccagna festivals in the public piazza before the Royal Palace. These were no longer given by the people, by members of their own class, but rather *for* the people *by* the ruling class (Scafoglio 1994). This politically astute use of Cuccagna, which wove together traditional motifs and celebrations—but bending them to official objectives—began to take hold under what were, arguably, the most oppressive regimes Neapolitans have ever known. The evolution of the festivity began with the suppression of the movable *carri*, traditionally offered to the populace by the various *arti* and *mestieri*, that is, artisans and guilds (especially the food-related ones: millers, bakers, butchers). During the first decades of the 1700s, these floats were converted into a single, fixed architectural structure, strategically placed in front of the Royal Palace (Scafoglio 1994a, 12) [Figures 1.18–1.27]. Contrary to official rhetoric, they were not bestowed from above but rather continued to be financed by the corporations. At this time, however, it was the royalty who commanded full attention at the expense of the corporations, thereby denying the latter a direct rapport with the people. The king himself became the festivity's focal point: *Cocagne c'est moi*, he might have said [cf. Figure 1.23, with a royal portrait displayed at the apex of the structure]. The once egalitarian spirit of the popular Neapolitan Cuccagna festivities (such as the itinerant floats) now confirmed and heightened the social hierarchy. This case merely provides another example of how the absolutist regime in Naples elaborated in numerous variations the "fiction of sovereign generosity and abundance" (Feldman [2006] 2007) in theater (*opera seria*), on the piazza, and elsewhere.[24] Grand *apparati* called *macchine della Cuccagna* (Cuccagna machines) were assembled as ephemeral, edible structures, encrusted with various foods and consumed by the hungry crowd on each of the four Sundays of the Carnival season. As seen in one contemporary oil painting (from *Settecento Napoletano* 1994) [Figure 1.27], the king and the aristocracy could view the frenzied, famished struggle to dismantle the Rococo marvel of food from the balconies of the Royal Palace, while the official guards controlled the crowd below. The king's guard gave the signal of attack and in five to eight minutes the structure was completely demolished and picked apart by the hoards of *lazzari* (beggars) who sometimes knifed each other in the process—all under the entertained gaze of the royal court (Scafoglio 1994a, 35). The structure was patched and reassembled, and the sack was repeated on the three successive Sundays of Carnival. This ritual spectacle created for the people became a spectator sport for the bestowers who, one is sometimes reminded in the literature, either enjoyed it as hidden voyeurs, or could snicker at the spectacle of barbarism and uncouthness in full view from the royal balconies and could thereby publically reaffirm their social superiority.[25]

---

24   This was the age of ingenious *apparati* and mechanisms, capricious and inventive techniques that enhanced, indeed made, theater and spectacle—on the public piazza as well as in the theater proper. Any occasion (baptisms, funerals, births, marriages) provided a pretext for erecting them, and major architects and artists, with a solid artisan tradition at their disposal, were set to work on the design and construction of these often "*creazioni capriciosissime,*" (most capricious creations [Mancini 1964, 3]). The art of *scenografia* (stage sets) was born from such an Italian milieu, and its identity merges with architecture during the Baroque period (cf. Mancini 1964, introduction; see also Mancini 1968).

25   Similar spectacular feedings of the poor at the public trough could have been witnessed in many parts of Italy. The traditional dispensing of dowries, for instance, was often followed by a public banquet; for example a print entitled *Banchetto dato ai Giardini Pubblici a duecento sposi* (A banquet given in the Public Gardens for 200 newlyweds), shows couples seated on *palchi*, raised planks built for the occasion on the public square (Bertarelli and Monti 1927, 218). Under

Such Cuccagna monuments were erected on other occasions of royal commemoration, such as weddings, birthdays, and so forth (see banners on prints in *Settecento Napoletano* 1994 and in the Collection of Festival Prints, Getty Research Library) [Figures 1.18–1.27]. They frequently took on the form of temples, mountains, or ships, interweaving mythological motifs, and invariably emphasizing *verticality*. The mythological recollections of a golden age, as noted by Barletta (1981) and Feldman ([2006] 2007), were intended to cast the king in the role of bestower of all riches and social harmony.

Of what foods did this feasting consist? While the quality of the foods (primarily meat and bread) may not have been high, the quantities needed to be vast (Barletta 1981, 33–34). Some of the animal carcasses were quartered and pinned to the structure while other live animals were hunted down. The violence, cruelty, and barbarism of this Neapolitan festivity were inevitably noted by tourists on "the grand tour." De Sade, for one, in search of strong festivals, described one Neapolitan Cuccagna in great detail: the intentional collapse of the *macchina*, with the subsequent death of many, the pinning of live animals to the monument, the general waste of animal (and human) life, and the transgressive aspects of the festivity. He concluded that the very essence of this festival was cruelty and its enjoyment (in Scafoglio 1994a, 37–38).

Coinciding as it did with the great famine, the 1764 festivities marked the turning point for Neapolitan Cuccagna as it resulted in tragedy—and insurrection (Scafoglio 1994a, 57–87). During that Cuccagna season, some of the bolder participants did not wait for a royal signal but, under the eyes of the king, impudently attacked the structure itself. The violence that resulted from such a desperate situation was quickly snuffed out, but did not resolve itself in any institutional change from above. Rather, in a collective ritual expiation of guilt, the people both prayed for forgiveness and pleaded for a miracle—not to the king, but to San Gennaro, Naples's patron saint. This penitential resolution was well liked by Church and Court alike. Cuccagna, thereafter moved quietly and progressively farther away from

the gaze of refined citizens, perhaps, the inelegant and uncouth country brides and grooms must have once again provided good fun!

the Royal Palace, and by the end of the following decade (1779), was substituted with the traditional (and safer) distribution of dowries to poor girls (i.e., *maritaggi*).

Such rituals explicitly linking the city of Naples (and the king himself) to the imagined state of Cuccagna created and sustained a fiction, a *mask* of royal magnanimity, while ignoring the ongoing plight of its poverty-stricken citizenry. Carnival was the traditional time for donning masks, after all! It is well to remember that while Charles VI played King Carnival, the people's traditional (i.e., commedia dell'arte) mask—in perfect opposition to the rotund reveler—remained Pulcinella. Unlike the fat king, Pulcinella was the perennially starved and scurrilous maccheroni-eater, and has remained an emblem of the city to this day. During the seventeenth century in Naples, as part of a general crackdown on the more pagan aspects of festivities all over Europe, this campaign also translated into the Church's attempt to banish Pulcinella (Scafoglio 1994a, 42–45).

Even into the nineteenth century, though, when the Cuccagna machines had been put aside for over a century, Naples was still associated with Cuccagna by at least one novelist. In her 1891 novel, *Il Paese di Cuccagna*,[26] the Neapolitan writer Matilde Serao insightfully used Cuccagna as a metaphor for the widespread lottery mania that was devastating the rich and poor of that city. Serao here continued a time-honored *literary* tradition of moralizing on the Cuccagna theme and focusing on its darker and dangerous side. The desire for a material paradise on earth varied according to class. By playing the lottery, a nobleman wished to restore his family fortunes, a merchant to open a pastry shop in a more fashionable quarter of Naples, but to Antonietta, of the urban poor, to win the lottery would mean to eat maccheroni and meat morning and night, every day! A rather modest dream, one might say, and yet one which eluded Italians until the post-WWII era. Serao here describes the psychology of Cuccagna as a preying Lotto agent reflects:

---

26 Published in 1891, and during the previous year as installments in *Il mattino*, Naples. A more recent edition, edited by Mario Pomilio was published in Florence by Vallecchi in 1971 (Serao [1891] 1971). On Naples and Cuccagna, see also Serao (excerpted from her *Il ventre di Napoli*) in Carabba 1976.

> He saw again [in his mind] the weeks of Christmas, of
> Easter, when the game became frenzied, fierce, so great
> was the desire of the people to enter into the long-
> dreamed-for Land of Cockaigne, and he saw himself
> again, always happy over those delusions which ended in
> painful disappointment; happy that the mirage blinded
> the weak, the foolish, the sick, the poor, the hopeful—all
> those who longed for the Land of Cockaigne, happy that
> of all those who had been infected by the disease, none
> would be saved; delighted that during major feast days, the
> rage increased, and gaming increased, as did his percentage
> [of the sales].[27]

Such delirious dreams have comforted the poor and overworked,
and always will. The sharp rise in American gambling, from bingo
and state lotteries to full-fledged casinos, painfully corroborate that
such dreams of instant wealth are thriving yet. Early immigrants to
this country, and others (Bernardi 1994, 122–23, 133), had similar
dreams. The flight to Cuccagna, the Land of Plenty, in fact, became
the propelling myth behind Italian mass emigration, a mass exodus
at its height precisely as these pages of Serao's were being written in
the 1890s. Many purchased steerage class tickets to paradise, boarded
ship at the port of Naples itself, and headed for the "new world"—to
America, where the streets were said to be paved with gold,[28] and where
they believed they would never go hungry again. But, as one wit has
it: they quickly learned that not only were the streets *not* paved with

27   "[R]ivide le settimane di Natale, di Pasqua, in cui il giuoco diventa furioso,
feroce, tanto è il desiderio del popolo di entrare nel sempre sognato Paese di
Cuccagna e si rivide sempre lui, contento di quelle illusioni che finivano in una
dolorosa delusione, contento che quel miraggio acciecasse i deboli, gli sciocchi,
gli ammalati, i poveri, gli speranzosi, tutti quelli che desideravano il Paese di
Cuccagna, contento che tutti, tutti quanti fossero attaccati da tale lebbra, che
niuno se ne salvasse: contentissimo, quando, nelle grandi feste, cresceva l'ardore,
e cresceva il giuoco, e cresceva il suo tanto per cento" ("Don Crescenzio's via
crucis," Serao [1891] 1971, 535–36).

28   Of course, the Gold Rush itself did much to reactivate that part of the
myth, as many Europeans (not necessarily of the lower classes this time) made
the transatlantic journey as gold seekers. And wealth has remained the substance
of the American Dream, one might add.

gold, they were not paved at all, and furthermore, the immigrants themselves would have to pave them (cf. *Italians in America* 1998)!

The theme of hunger was widely present in the literature of the nineteenth century since it was, after all, a painful reality of Italian streets from north to south. But hunger had been a staple of oral traditions long before (on narrative, see Beduschi 1983; Bottigheimer 1986; Tatar 1992; on lullabies, Del Giudice 1988, 276–77). How many classic tales spoke of great famines whereby a hero/ine would venture out into the world to find their way; or the horrific—but all too common—cases of attempted cannibalism at the hands of ogres and witches, mirage-like gingerbread houses, or lavish wedding feasts ending many a happy-ever-after tale? Traditional narratives are especially important sources for understanding ethnographic food systems. In the Italian tradition, many are the magic tablecloths, sacks, or pots which produce food whenever asked to do so (Cusatelli 1982; Luciani 1994; Milillo 1994). Numerous Italian tales begin with the scattering of large families due to famine; children (often brothers) are sent into the world to seek their fortune (Calvino 1956, introduction and "Jump in My Sack," tale 200). For Italians, a people with a long history of emigration, these tale types take on curiously ethnographic undertones, and may indeed be considered emblematic tales of migration. Not surprisingly, they have endured among immigrants themselves both as tales (see Agonito 1967, 52–64) and as oral histories—corroborating Calvino's maxim that *le fiabe sono vere* (folktales are true). Not only were these tales "true," but so were the fantastical fictions of Cuccagna and Upside-Down Worlds (partly) materialized through the immigrant experience.

AN EVOLVING TOPOS:
CUCCAGNESQUE JOURNEYS
AND IMMIGRATION

Cuccagna has proven surprisingly resilient: It has come to assimilate a wide range of motifs and genres in literature and oral tradition, as well as intersected ethnographic and historic realities. Cuccagna indeed is a cauldron into which new ingredients have been continuously added over the centuries (Cocchiara 1956). Therein can be found the Ship of Fools (Barca dei Rovinati, Galea di Cuccagna), Topsy Turvy Land (Il Roverso Mondo),[29] and especially Carnival, not to mention myriad minor oral-expressive and literary genres. Cuccagna's most recent metamorphoses, however, may be found in Italian immigrant culture, and in children's literature (see Del Giudice 1997; 1998). It is on its place in immigrant culture that the remainder of this paper will focus.

Cuccagna tales circulated in oral narrative, illustrated street songs, and kept an imagined state alive, but certainly did not coincide with any on the Italian political map. Progressively, they helped shift its geographical configuration from the *old* world to the *new*. Italians came to associate Cuccagna with America as it was *imagined* and as immigrant propaganda—and immigrant narrative itself—came to depict it: the land of plenty, the land of opportunity, and the land of equality.

Oddly, it may be Cuccagna's intersection with the travel tale, so prevalent during the Renaissance, an "age of discoveries," that may have provided a distant source for future journeys. In that earlier narrative genre, which characteristically merged truth and fantasy in marvelous tales of discovery, new and surprising worlds (largely "imagined states" of their own) came to present themselves as possible alternative worlds. Some depicted abundant, verdant landscapes, laden with all manner of fruits and edible wildlife. Others spoke of clement and benign nature where natives lived in a state of innocent bliss and in social harmony. These narratives reflect the growing body of utopian literature.

Whereas fantastic voyages had been, as we have seen, a staple of oral and literary traditions, masses of Italians, from the nineteenth to the mid-twentieth century, found themselves aboard *real* ships bound for North and South America, as well as the farther reaches of the world (such as Australia). The banner on one Cuccagna print in particular, might well be describing an immigrant ship sailing to the Americas were it not for the fact that it was published centuries earlier: "The ship of the bestower which departs for Trebisbonda, where all the failed, the ruined and consumed, and those who cannot show their faces on

---

29   On this motif, see Cocchiara 1963; Kunzle 1978; and Lafond and Redondo 1979. On the general topic of inversion, see Babcock 1978.

account of bad debts, are invited."[30] Might echoes of this Ship of Fools have stirred somewhere in the subconscious of immigrants boarding transatlantic freighters to the New World, ships on which literally millions of Italians sought passage to a new Cuccagna?

Somewhere between folly, desperation, and wish fulfillment lies the existential state of Cuccagna. In truth, even the street variety had always pointed to the fact that Cuccagna was an elaborate lie, a tall tale, a fiction not to be taken too seriously. Had it not frequently been given facetious place names such as Nowhereland and *dietro le Alpi che non si trovano mai* (behind the Alps which are never found), and hadn't its various authors borne fictitious names such as Messer Bugia (Mr. Lie), Bugiardello (Little Lier), or Signor Valcercha (Mr. What-have-you)? These expedients did not make the people dream of such marvelous places with any lesser fervor. The dream for a better life and a better state—in the political as well as existential sense—fueled the mass emigrations from Italy. This was a dream of profound renewal, fully embodied in the imagined land of Cuccagna, but only partly found in the new land of America.

How do such patently fictional and fantastical dreams come to be believed by a people? How do such lies actually prompt to action? Consider this analogy: The legend of the "flying African" in African American folk culture did much to fuel a belief in the possibility of breaking the chains of slavery and escape. The belief in the ability of early-arrived Africans to take wing and fly back to their homeland—but in reality (and only later) on the Underground Railway to the North—had real and positive consequences. "The story of 'flying Africans' was so important to slaves because it provided them with the magical powers needed to escape brutal reality, and the legend's metaphorical use provided the ability for psychic survival. It taught that escape was possible. And many slaves did escape." Metting goes on to claim: "Oral traditions . . . protect and empower readers through lessons on survival, identity, and health" (1994/1995, 285–86). The belief in Cuccagna did as much for Italians escaping to the New

---

30 "La barca de' rovinati che parte per Trebisonda, dove s'invitano tutti i falliti, consumati e male andati, e tutti quelli che non possono comparire al mondo per li gran debiti" (Croce 1946, 287).

World—emigrating, despite official resistance to the mass exodus, despite the many accounts of danger they would encounter.[31] From the discovery of America onward, a desire for *renovatio* (renewal), and the marvelous descriptions of a *nuovo mondo* (new world) circulated among the peoples of Europe, and when mass migrations were finally possible, brought millions of the destitute to the New World (Honour 1975; Chiappelli, Allen, and Benson 1976; Franzina 1995). Immigrant narratives are full of such aspirations. Conversely, and on a more sinister note, it was precisely the fiction of Cuccagna, narrated in all its appealing detail, that helped Europeans lure and enslave many Africans during the age of slavery (Minton 1991).

Myriad representations of America as a mythic land of plenty may be found in immigrant personal narratives and correspondence, but also in propaganda literature, in tour books, in immigrant agents' brochures, in nationalistic political writings, and in the popular literature of the nineteenth century. For Italians, America was alternatively known as *Il Nuovo Mondo* (the New World) and *La Terra Promessa* (the Promised Land)—and one should not discount the literal sense of this term, for peasants-turned-immigrants sought land, cultivatable land (Del Giudice 1993, 55), and *Cuccagna* (Vecoli 1988; Franzina 1992).

A basic aspiration, however, and one abundantly elaborated in the landscape of Cuccagna, was the desire to feed a hungry body. As Teti (1984, 9) succinctly summarizes the immigrant's relationship to food (in this case, speaking of Toronto Italians): "They carry with them the traditional culture and values of the peasant world, but especially bodies marked and undernourished, an ancient hunger, the aspiration toward a better world, toward a world of abundance that in the old country could not be achieved."[32] The most dramatic change

---

31   On Italian songs of emigration, see Savona and Straniero 1976. One song in particular, "Mamma, mamma, mamma, dammi cento lire" (Del Giudice 1989, tape 1, side B, 9), popular among immigrants, warns against the journey and ends in shipwreck.

32   "Si portano dietro la cultura e i valori tradizionali del mondo contadino, ma soprattutto i corpi segnati e denutriti, una fame antica, la tensione a un mondo migliore, a un mondo dell'abbondanza, che in patria non avevano potuto realizzare" (Teti 1984, 9). I was delighted by Teti's writings, found after the substance of this paper was already completed, for they corroborated many of my own intuitions and findings on Toronto Italian immigrants.

that occurred in the life of every immigrant to the New World, in fact, regarded diet—a most immediate and tangible gauge of success and literal fulfillment. Writing in an immediate post-WWII milieu, Pellegrino looks back on his own family's migration in the 1930s, and personally recalls "an experience in which millions of immigrants to America have shared" (1952, 33): "I found, first of all, the meaning, the consumable, edible meaning, of a simple word, lost in the dictionary among thousands of others—the meaning of the word *abundance*" (Pellegrino 1952, 27). Pellegrino recounts some of the (tall) tales told about America/Cuccagna which he later experienced to be true: tree trunks so large several couples could dance around them, wheat fields so vast no train could cross them in a single day, meats, sweets, fine clothes for *everyone* (so that one could not distinguish the rich from the poor—a recurrent cross-cultural theme in immigrant narratives), and incredible waste. Literally, therefore, one could find not gold but food in the streets. Furthermore, nature may have given up many of its riches freely in the new land, but not without toil. Pellegrino and his family, residing on the edge of a forest in Washington State, lived off the fat of the land, collecting edibles (nuts, mushrooms, wild game, berries, etc.) and firewood at their pleasure.

Immigrants and food are indeed firmly linked in American consciousness. Culinary metaphors for ethnic immigrants themselves abound. In the great cauldron of immigrant America, itself a "melting pot," a homogeneous stew sits bubbling, while, nonetheless, food continues to set social boundaries and contribute to ethnic stereotyping. Folklorists recognize the truism "you are what you eat" as a means of marking a group by its most basic (or its oddest) food. In America, where ethnically mixed communities are common, this is an especially marked tendency. The dominant culture has labeled the French *Frogs*, the Irish *Potatoes*, the Germans *Krauts*, and the Mexicans *Beaners*. Italians have continued to be gastronomically stereotyped as pasta-eaters or *Spaghetti-Benders*. On the other hand, Anglo-Canadians are known as *Mangiacakes* ("Cake-eaters")—or simply as "Cakes" to Toronto Italians.

Italian (and other) immigrants came to this land, in part, to escape hunger. Those who emigrated during the post-WWII wave could not have known that a decisive turning point for all Italians, even in Italy, was just around the corner. It came to be known as *il boom economico* (the economic boom) or *il miracolo italiano* (the Italian miracle) of the 1960s. During these miracle years, Italy suddenly became a Cuccagna of its own (cf. Parks 1993, 60, 82–84, 210). Only then did the eating habits of common Italians profoundly change, and the long-held desire for meat finally become appeased. Meat became a daily staple (Somogyi 1973; Montanari 1992) as vegetables, legumes, and even pasta diminished somewhat in importance. As a negative outcome, of course, national health surveys marked an increase in coronary disease.

CULTURAL HISTORY AND PERSONAL EXPERIENCE

A look at Italian immigrant foodways, narrative, and worldview, immediately makes evident that food became the primary focus of their lives as immigrants (cf. Teti 1984; Chairetakis 1993; Del Giudice 1993; 2000; 2001; 2010, ch. 3 this volume). Italian immigrants' obsession with food seems indeed to document and embody centuries-old mass traumas. I am coming to the conclusion, however, that the legacy has farther-reaching effects than imagined. That is, not only can we readily find its imprint on those peasants-turned-immigrants themselves, who personally experienced hunger, but in their third and fourth generation progeny. These latter-day, peasant-derived diaspora Italians have creatively metamorphosed this basic preoccupation with food in far more "evolved" ways. They may no longer tend vegetable gardens, make their own wine, cure their own olives or prosciutti, or stock cantinas, but they still display this attachment to food through occupations as high-end restaurateurs, vintners, food distributors, food critics, writers of cookbooks, and so forth. On a personal note, I too found myself progressively on this trajectory, as I came to understand for instance, *how* and *why* the immigrant experience moved this present research and involvement in food organizations such as the International Slow Food Movement.[33] Ultimately, these combined

---

33 This represents an international movement to safeguard local foodways, products, and producers, while educating the public on global food economics and their impact on biodiversity and food traditions (see www.slowfood.com).

activities corroborate my thesis that Cuccagna animates immigrant consciousness still, mine included.

How many ways had I experienced firsthand, the central role of food in my family's life and worldview? While growing up in the 1960s and 1970s in the Toronto Italian community to which I had immigrated as an infant of five months, it seemed to me that an inordinate percentage of discourse revolved around food (favorable markets and costs), as did the amounts of time spent on food-related activities (making wine, bread, pasta, cheese; planting a garden; gathering wild foods, fishing, hunting). Most socialization occurred around a table (family dinners, picnics, and visits from *paesani* [fellow townspeople]). At the very center of all family and community ritual moments, both sacred and profane, there was food, from the obligatory, twice-yearly Catholic Eucharist at Christmas and Easter (followed by major feasting), to the lavish wedding banquets, baptismal parties, and even Sunday dinners. Around the dinner table itself, food discourse and food narratives were common: the pre-immigration, personal-experience narratives regarding my father's life as a peasant *and* a fisherman (both food-centered occupations); war stories on both sides of the front: stealing potatoes from under an official's nose while in a German prisoner of war camp, as told by my father, or the ongoing trauma of procuring food during the war years, and of watching her father fail and eventually die (essentially from starvation), as told by my mother. These bleak narratives occasionally alternated with the more wondrous, and truly cuccagnesque, tales of food literally falling from the sky (as fish were deposited on the beach during a hurricane), or gutters gushing with olive oil (from a carter whose load of oil jugs had crashed in the streets; Del Giudice 2001, ch. 2 this volume).

It was in response to these specific personal and communal immigrant experiences that the need to search for traces of a coherent peasant cultural past was awakened. Although it was in library and archive alike that I found the mythic land of plenty known as Cuccagna, it was through lived experience that I found it to be *true*. This dialogue between recent and remote past convinces me that cultural historical research of this sort is strictly relevant to the present, that it actually contributes to writing the history of a people in large measure without a written historical record. Furthermore, it confirms the importance of personal life experiences and field work for folk cultural research, as well as for conventional, historical inquiry. That is, folklore research combined with oral historical methodologies and archival research make a mutually sustaining and convincing partnership.

Cuccagna indeed, became a concise and eloquent emblem onto which could be hung many personal, but also common, experiences of peasant and immigrant life. I believe it makes a powerful symbol for Italian immigrants. How far had the songs which spoke of a mythic land of plenty—sung by street performers in the public squares of Italy over the centuries and told in folktales shared among family and community—taken a people! On many far-flung shores, Italians translated this *imagined* state, first into hovels, and ultimately into dream houses—a brick at a time (Del Giudice 1993). But unlike the laborless utopia, they learned to construct it with their own hands. It is no coincidence that Italians came to so dominate the food and construction industries in many lands, so eager were they to realize their imagined world (and so had their own strong artisan traditions given them the skills to accomplish this realization). On those new domestic landscapes food reigned supreme and Cuccagna was reenacted at every possible turn, for while hunger itself may have been vanquished, the fear of hunger and scarcity kept cuccagnesque practices alive (Del Giudice 1993; 2001, ch. 2 this volume). Little did they realize the paradox of *Cuccagna* however: in the very act of festivalizing the quotidian, they would exorcise, and thereby render, Cuccagna—never actually a place but the *desire* for place—obsolete. Through the literal embodiment of this imagined state into their own flesh and blood—by their overindulgence in cuccagnesque abundance—Cuccagna, they have discovered, may indeed be detrimental to personal and cultural health. Yet, should the search for mountains of cheese and rivers of wine be abandoned, might not the very center of Italian folk cultural practice and identity, so bound up in food—and in the search for its abundance—unravel?

WORKS CITED

Ackermann, Elfriede Marie. 1944. "*Das Schlaraffenland* in German Literature and Folksong: With an Inquiry into its History in European Literature." Ph.D. diss., University of Chicago.

Agonito, Rosemary. 1967. "Il Paisano—Italian Folktales of Central New York." *New York Folklore Quarterly* 23: 52–64.

Amundsen, Svein Schroeder, and Reimund Kvideland, eds. 1975. *Emigrantviser*. Oslo: Universitetsforlaget.

Angeleri, Carlo. 1953. *Bibliografia delle stampe popolari a carattere profano*. Florence: Sansoni.

Armand Hammer Museum of Art and Cultural Center. 1994. *The French Renaissance in Prints: From the Bibliothèque Nationale de France* (exhibition catalogue). Los Angeles: Grunwald Center for the Graphic Arts, UCLA.

Babcock, Barbara A., ed. 1978. *The Reversible World: Symbolic Inversion in Art and Society*. Ithaca: Cornell University Press.

Bakhtin, Mikhail M. 1968. *Rabelais and His World*. Translated by Helene Iswolsky. Cambridge, MA: M.I.T. Press.

Barletta, Laura. 1981. *Il carnevale del 1764 a Napoli: protesta e integrazione in uno spazio urbano*. Naples: Società Editrice Napoletana.

Beduschi, Lidia. 1983. *Leggende e racconti popolari della Lombardia*. Rome: Newton Compton.

Bernardi, Ulderico. 1994. *A catàr fortuna: storie venete d'Australia e del Brasile*. Vicenza: Neri Pozza.

Bertarelli, Achille. Ca. 1929. *L'imagerie populaire italienne*. Paris: Duchartre and Van Buggenhoudt.

Bertarelli, Achille. 1940. *Le incisioni di Giuseppe Maria Mitelli*. Milan: Comune di Milano.

Bertarelli, Achille. 1974. *Le stampe popolari italiane*. Milan: Biblioteca Universale Rizzoli.

Bertarelli, Achille, and Antonio Monti. 1927. *Tre secoli di vita Milanese nei documenti iconografici 1630–1875*. Milano: Hoepli.

Blegen, Theodore Christian, and Martin B. Rudd. Ca. 1936. *Norwegian Emigrant Songs and Ballads*. Minneapolis: University of Minnesota Press.

Bonanni, Luciano, and Giancarlo Ricci. 1982. *Cucina, cultura, società.* Brescia: Shakespeare and Co.

Bottigheimer, Ruth B., ed. 1986. *Fairy Tales and Society: Illusion, Allusion, and Paradigm*. Philadelphia: University of Pennsylvania Press.

Calvino, Italo. 1956. *Fiabe Italiane (raccolte dalla tradizione popolare durante gli ultimi cento anni e trascritte in lingua dai vari dialetti da Italo Calvino)*. Turin: Einaudi, 1956. Reprint, Milano: Mondadori, 1993. Printed in English as *Italian Folktales*. Translated by George Martin. New York: Harcourt, Brace Jovanovich, 1980.

Camporesi, Piero. 1975. "Carnevale, Cuccagna e giuochi di villa (Analisi e documenti)." *Studi e problemi di critica testuale* 10: 57–97.

Camporesi, Piero. 1978. "La scienza del ventre: declino e morte di Cuccagna." In *Il paese della fame*, 77–125. Bologna: Il Mulino.

Camporesi, Piero. 1980. *Il pane selvaggio*. Bologna: Il Mulino.

Carabba, Claudio, ed. 1976. *Napoli d'allora: testimonianze di Matilde Serao e Edoardo Scarfoglio*. Milan: Longanesi.

Centro di Studi. 1978. *Centro di Studi sul Teatro Medioevale e Rinascimentale: Il contributo dei giullari alla drammaturgia italiana delle origini*. Città di Castello: Bulzoni.

Chairetakis, Anna L. 1993. "Tears of Blood: The Calabrian *Villanella* and Immigrant Epiphanies." In *Studies in Italian American Folklore,* edited by Luisa Del Giudice, 11–51. Logan: Utah State University Press.

Cheesman, Tom. 1992. "Gluttony Artists: Carnival, Enlightenment and Consumerism in Germany on the Threshold of Modernity." *Deutsche Vierteljahrsschrift* 66: 641–66.

Cheesman, Tom. 1993. "Performing Omnivores in Germany circa 1700." In *Studies in the Commedia dell'arte*, edited by David J. George and Christopher J. Gossip, 49–68. Cardiff: University of Wales Press.

Cheesman, Tom. 1996. "Modernity/Monstrosity: Eating Freaks (Germany, c. 1700)." *Body & Society* 2, no 3: 1–31.

Chiappelli, Fredi, Michael J. B. Allen, and Robert L. Benson, eds. 1976. *First Images of America: the Impact of the New World on the Old.* Berkeley: University of California.

Chiarotto, Sergio. 1982. "L'alimentazione e le utopie rinascimentali." In *Cucina, cultura, società,* edited by Luciano Bonanni and Giancoarlo Ricci, 113–18. Brescia: Shakespeare and Co.

Ciceri, Andreina Nicoloso. 1983. *Tradizioni popolari in Friuli.* 2 vols. Udine: Chiandetti.

Cioranescu, Alexandre 1971. "Utopia: Land of Cocaigne and Golden Age." Translated by Sally Bradshaw. *Diogenes* 75: 85–121.

Cocchiara, Guiseppe. 1956. "Il paese di *Cuccagna*: l'evasione dalla realtà nella fantasia popolare." In *Il Paese di Cuccagna*, 159–87. Turin: Einaudi.

Cocchiara, Guiseppe. 1963. *Il mondo alla rovescia.* Turin: Boringhieri. 2nd ed., 1981.

Coltro, Dino. 1982. *Mondo contadino: società, lavoro, feste e riti agrari del lunario veneto.* Verona: Arsenale.

Costa, Gustavo. 1972. *La leggenda dei secoli d'oro nella letteratura italiana.* Bari: Laterza.

Croce, Benedetto. 1946. "Del 'Paese di Cuccagna' nelle storie popolari italiane e di un'epistola del Goethe." *Goethe* (Bari) 2: 283.

Cusatelli, Giorgio. 1982. "Cucina di fiaba e cucina da fiaba." In *Cucina, cultura, società,* edited by Luciano Bonanni and Giancarlo Ricci, 237–40. Brescia: Shakespeare and Co.

Del Giudice, Luisa. 1988. "Ninna-nanna-nonsense? Fears, dreams, and falling in the Italian lullaby." *Oral Tradition* 3: 270–86.

Printed in Italian as "Ninnananna-nonsense? Angoscia, sogno e caduta nella ninnananna italiana." In "Europa Zingara," edited by Leonardo Piasera, special issue, *La ricerca folklorica* 22: 105–14 (February 1991). Brescia: Grafo.

Del Giudice, Luisa. 1989. *Italian Traditional Song.* Los Angeles: Italian Heritage Culture Foundation and Istituto Italiano di Cultura. 2nd ed., Los Angeles: Istituto Italiano de Cultura, 1995. Book and sound recording.

Del Giudice, Luisa. 1993. "The 'Archvilla': An Italian Canadian Architectural Archetype." In *Studies in Italian American Folklore*, 53–105. Logan: Utah State University Press.

Del Giudice, Luisa. 1997. "Tomie de Paola and the Writing/Illustrating of Italian Folk Culture." *Italian Americana* 15, no.1: 22–30.

Del Giudice, Luisa. 1998. "Giulio Cesare Croce" and "Paese di Cuccagna." In *Encyclopedia of Folklore and Literature,* edited by Mary Ellen Brown and Bruce Rosenberg, 148–50, 487–89. Santa Barbara: ABC Clio.

Del Giudice, Luisa. 2000. "Italian American Folklore, Folklife" and "Italian American Food and Foodways." In *The Italian American Experience: An Encyclopedia,* edited by Salvatore J. LaGumina, Frank J. Cavaioli, Salvatore Primeggia, and Joseph A. Varacalli, 237–45, 245–48. New York: Garland.

Del Giudice, Luisa. 2001. "Wine Makes Good Blood: Wine Culture among Toronto Italians." Chapter 2 this volume. First published in *Enthologies* 23, no. 1: 1–27.

Del Giudice, Luisa. 2010. "Rituals of Charity and Abundance: Sicilian St. Joseph's Tables and Feeding the Poor in Los Angeles." Chapter 3 this volume. First published in *California Italian Studies* 1, no. 2. https://doi.org/10.5070/C312008894.

Delpech, François. 1979. "Aspects des Pays de Cocagne: Programme pour une Recherche." In *L'image du monde renversé et ses représentations littéraires et paralittéraires de la fin du XVIe siècle au milieu du XVIIe,* edited by Jean Lafond and Augustin Redondo, 35–48. Paris: Vrin.

Delumeau, J. 1976. "Pays de Cocagne et fête des fous." In *La mort des pays de Cocagne: comportements collectifs de la Renaissance à l'age classique*, 11–29. Paris: Panthéon, Université de Paris, Sorbonne, Centre de recherches d'histoire moderne.

Desinan, Cornelio C. 1982: "Toponomastica e alimentazione in Friuli." In *Cucina, cultura, società*, edited by Luciano Bonanni and Giancarlo Ricci, 43–49. Brescia: Shakespeare and Co.

di Mauro, Alberto. 1981. *Bibliografia delle stampe popolari profane dal fondo Capponi della Biblioteca Vaticana*. Florence: Olschki.

Disney Enterprises. 1992. *"Walt Disney Presents Uncle Remus and His Tales of Brer Rabbit."* Edited by Bob Foster and Cris Palomino, art by Dick Moores, coloring by Cris Palomino. *Walt Disney's Comics and Stories*, no. 576. In *Disney's Colossal Comics Collection*, J6C96 091. Disney.

Feldman, Martha (2006) 2007. "Abandonments in a 'Theater State': Opera, Festivity, and Famine in Naples, 1764," revised. Chapter 5 in *Opera and Sovereignty: Transforming Myths in Eighteenth Century Italy*. Chicago: University of Chicago Press. First published in *Italian Opera in Central Europe*, edited by Melania Bucciarelli, Reinhard Strohm, and Norbert Dubowy, 2006. *Volume 1: Institutions and Ceremonies*, 1–25. Berlin: Berliner Wisschenschafts.

Fortunati, Vita and Giampaolo Zucchini, eds. 1989. *Paesi di Cuccagna e mondi alla rovescia*. Florence: Alinea Editrice.

Franzina, Emilio. 1992. *L'immaginario degli emigranti: miti e raffigurazioni dell'esperienza italiana all'estero fra i due secoli*. Paese (Treviso): Pagus.

Franzina, Emilio. 1995. *Gli italiani al nuovo mondo: l'emigrazione italiana in America, 1492–1942*. Milan: Mondadori.

Ghidoli, Paola. 1985. "'Suonatori d'inconcludenti strumenti': Musicanti girovaghi e spettacoli di piazza a Milano nelle carte di polizia dell'Archivio di Stato 1815–1840." In *Milano e il suo territorio*, edited by Franco Della Peruta, Roberto Leydi, and Angelo Stello, 805–62. Mondo popolare in Lombardia series. Milano: Silvana.

Ginzburg, Carlo. 1976. *Il formaggio e i vermi: il cosmos di un mugnaio del 500.* Turin: Einaudi. Printed in English as *The Cheese and The Worms: The Cosmos of a Sixteenth-Century Miller.* New York: Penguin, 1982.

Glazer, Joe. 1991. *Welcome to America: Joe Glazer Sings Songs of the American Immigrants.* Silver Spring, MD: Collector Records. Sound recording.

Graf, Auturo. 1925. "Il mito del paradiso terrestre." In *Miti leggende e superstizioni del Medio Evo*, xi–175. Turin: Chiantore/Loescher.

Grinberg, Martine, and Sam Kinser. 1983. "Les combats de Carnaval et de Carême: Trajets d'une metaphore." *Annales ESC* 38: 65–98.

Guerrini, Olindo. (1879) 1969. *La vita e le opere di Guilio Cesare Groce.* Bologna: Bibliotheca Musica Bononiensis. Reprint, Bologna: Forni.

Harms, Wolfgang and Cornelia Kemp, eds. 1987. *Deutsche illustrierte Flugblätter des 16, und 17, Jahrhunderts: die Sammlungen der Hessischen Landes—und Hochschulbibliothek in Darmstadt. Kommentierte Ausgabe.* Tübingen: Niemeyer.

Harms, Wolfgang, John Roger Paas, Michael Schilling, and Andreas Wang. 1983. *Deutsche illustrierte Flugblätter des Barock. Eine Auswahl.* Tübingen: Niemeyer.

Harvey, Anne-Charlotte. 1986. *Memories of Snoose Boulevard,* Minneapolis: Skandisk. Sound recording.

Honour, Hugh. 1975. *The New Golden Land: European Images of America from the Discoveries to the Present Time.* London: Pantheon.

Il Cantastorie: Almanacco dello spettacolo popolare (The street singer: Popular entertainment almanac). 1981–. Giorgio Vezzani, journal editor. Reggio Emilia.

Italians in America. 1998. New York: A & E Home Video. The History Channel. Videocassette.

Kunzle, David. 1978. "World Upside Down: The Iconography of a European Broadsheet Type." In *The Reversible World: Symbolic Inversion in Art and Society*, edited by Barbara A. Babcock, 39–94. Ithaca: Cornell University Press.

Kvideland, Reimund, and Gerald Porter. 2001. "Working the Railways, Constructing Navvy Identity." In *Imagined States: Nationalism, Utopia, and Longing in Oral Cultures*, Logan: Utah State University Press, 80–97.

Lafond, Jean, and Augustin Redondo, eds. 1979. *L'image du monde renversé et ses représentations littéraires et para-littéraires de la fin du XVIe siècle au milieu du XVIIe*. Paris: Vrin.

Leydi, Roberto. 1978. "Spettacolo in piazza oggi: i cantastorie." In *Il contributo dei giullari alla drammaturgia italiana delle origini* (Centro di studi sul teatro medioevale e rinascimentale), 295–338. Roma: Bulzoni.

Lozinski, Grégoire, ed. 1933. *La Bataille de Caresme et de Charnage*. Paris: Champion.

Luciani, Tiziana. 1994. "Al 'Fornelletto d'oro': fiabe di cibo tra fame e abbondanza." In "Antropologia dell'alimentazione," edited by Mario Turci, special issue, *La ricerca folklorica* 30: 59–70 (October). Brescia: Grafo.

Maggini, Emilio. 1977. *La Cuccagna*. Viterbo: Gojaria Viterbese.

Mancini, Franco. 1963: "Le maschere e i carri di Carnevale nel periodo barocco," In *'Nferta napoletana*. Naples: Edizioni Scientifiche Italiane.

Mancini, Franco. 1964. *Scenografia napoletana dell'età barocca*. Naples: Edizioni Scientifiche Italiane.

Mancini, Franco. 1968. *Feste ed apparati civili e religiosi in Napoli dal Viceregno alla capitale*. Naples: Edizioni Scientifiche Italiane.

Mayer, C. A. (1840) 1948. *Vita popolare a Napoli nell'età romantica*. Translated from German by Lidia Croce. Bari: Laterza.

Messedaglia, Luigi. 1942. "Maccheroni non maccheroni." *Lingua nostra* 4 (1942): 97–99.

Metting, Fred. 1994/1995. "Exploring Oral Traditions through the Written Text." *Journal of Reading* 38 (Dec./Jan.): 282–89.

Milillo, Aurora. 1994. "Il sistema alimentare nelle fiabe popolari europee." In "Antropologia dell'alimentazione," edited by Mario Turci, special issue, *La ricerca folklorica* 30: 51–58 (October). Brescia: Grafo.

Minton, John. 1991. "Cockaigne to Diddy Wah Diddy: Fabulous Geographies and Geographic Fabulations." *Folklore* 102: 39–47.

Montanari, Massimo. 1987. "La strada da Bengodi a *Cuccagna.*" *La Gola* 7–8 (July/August): 11–12.

Montanari, Massimo. 1992. *Convivio oggi: storia e cultura dei piaceri della tavola nell'età contemporanea*. Bari: Laterza.

Montanari, Massimo. 1993. *La fame e l'abbondanza: storia dell'alimentazione in Europa*. Rome: Laterza.

Morelli, Giorgio. 1969. "Le stampe popolari della Biblioteca Vaticana," *Lares* 35: 137–46.

Noyes, Dorothy. 1989. *Uses of Tradition: Arts of Italian Americans in Philadelphia*. Philadelphia: Philadelphia Folklore Project.

Noyes, Dorothy. 1995. "Group." *Journal of American Folklore* 108 (430): 449–78.

Parks, Tim. 1993. *Italian Neighbours: An Englishman in Verona*. 2nd ed., London: Mandarin Paperbacks.

Pellegrino, Angelo M. 1952. *The Unprejudiced Palate*. New York: Macmillan.

Pezzini, Isabella. 1989. "L'utopia e la mappa: appunti per un problema." In *Paesi di Cuccagna e mondi alla rovescia,* edited by Vita Fortunati and Giampaolo Zucchini, 277–86. Florence: Alinea Editrice.

Pianta, Bruno. 1989. "Furfanti trionfanti." In "La piazza: ambulanti vagabondi malviventi fieranti," edited by Glauco Sanga, special issue, *La ricerca folklorica* 19: 27–32 (April). Brescia: Grafo.

Rammel, Hal. 1990. *Nowhere in America: The Big Rock Candy Mountain and Other Comic Utopias*. Urbana and Chicago: University of Illinois Press.

Richter, Dieter. 1989. "Il Paese di *Cuccagna* nella cultura popolare: una topografia storica." In *Paesi di Cuccagna e mondi alla rovescia*, edited by Vita Fortunati and Giampaolo Zucchini, 113–24. Florence: Alinea.

Robb, John Donald. 1980. *Hispanic Folk Music of New Mexico and the Southwest: A Self-Portrait of a People*. Norman: University of Oklahoma Press.

Roselli, Giovann[i] de. (1574) 1974. *Opera nova chiamata Epulario, la quale tracta il modo de cucinare ogni carne, ucelli, pesci, de ogni sorte, et fare sapori, torte, pastelli, al modo de tutte le provincie, [et] molte altre ge[n]tilezze, co[m]posta p[er] maestro Giova[n] n[i] de Roselli, Fra[n]cese.* Venice: V. Viani, 1574. Reprint, Rome: Riccio.

Rossi, Vittorio. 1888. "Il Paese di *Cuccagna* nella letteratura italiana" (Appendix II). In *Le lettere di Messer Andrea Calmo riprodotte sulle stampe migliori*, 398–410. Turin: Loescher.

Sanga, Glauco. 1994. "Il ritmo alimentare 'paleolitico' dei marginali." In "Antropologia dell'alimentazione," edited by Mario Turci, special issue, *La ricerca folklorica* 30; 39–40 (October). Brescia: Grafo.

Savona, Virgilio A., and Michele L. Straniero, eds. 1976. *Canti dell'emigrazione*. Milan: Garzanti.

Scafoglio, Domenico. 1994a. *La maschera della Cuccagna: Spreco, rivolta e sacrificio nel carnevale napoletano del 1764*. Naples: AGE.

Scafoglio, Domenico. 1994b. *Le radici dell'albero*. Salerno: Gentile.

Scherillo, Michele. 1884. "Storia di Cambriano contadino." In *Giambattista Basile: archivio di letteratura popolare* 2, no. 11: 83–84.

Segarizzi, Arnaldo, ed. 1913. *Bibliografia delle stampe popolari italiane della R. Biblioteca Nazionali di S. Marco di Venezia*. Vol. 1. Bergamo: Istituto Italiano d'Arti Grafiche.

Serao, Matilde. (1891) 1971. *Il Paese di Cuccagna*. Milan: Treves (previously published in 1890 in installments in the daily *Il mattino*, Naples). Reprint, Mario Pomilio, ed. Florence:

Vallechi. Printed in English as *The Land of Cockayne*. 2 vols. New York: Collier, ca. 1900.

Settecento Napoletano: Sulle ali dell'aquila imperiale 1707–1734. Naples: Electa. 1994.

Sobrero, Paola. 1994. "L'orgia e la beffa: la tradizione di San Martino in Romagna." In "Antropologia dell'alimentazione," edited by Mario Turci, special issue, *La ricerca folklorica* 30: 71–82 (October). Brescia: Grafo.

Somogyi, Stefano. 1973. "L'alimentazione nell'Italia unita." In *Storia d'Italia*. Vol. 5, *I documenti*, 839–87. Turin: Einaudi.

Tatar, Maria. 1992. "Table Matters: Cannibalism and Oral Greed." In *Off With Their Heads! Fairy Tales and the Culture of Childhood*, 190–211. Princeton: Princeton University Press.

Teti, Vito. 1964. *Stampe popolari italiane*. Milano: Electa.

Teti, Vito. 1976. *Il pane, la beffa e la festa: Cultura alimentare e ideologia dell'alimentazione nelle classi subalterne*. Florence: Guaraldi.

Teti, Vito. 1984. "Carnevale abolito dall'abbondanza." *La gola* (February): 9.

Toschi, Paolo. 1964. *Stampe popolare italiane*. Milano: Electa.

Tranese, Giovanni Il (Giouannino detto il Tranese). (1715) 1884. "La piacevole historia di Cuccagna" (Napoli: Monaco, 1715). In *Giambattista Basile: archivio di letteratura popolare* 2, no. 11: 84–85.

Trousson, Raymond. 1989. "I mondi alla rovescia: finalità e funzioni." In *Paesi di Cuccagna e mondi alla rovescia*, edited by Vita Fortunati and Giampaolo Zucchini, 17–36. Florence: Alinea.

Turci, Mario, ed. 1994. "Antropologia dell'alimentazione." Special issue, *La ricerca folklorica* 30 (October). Brescia: Grafo.

Väänänen, Veikko. 1947. "Le fabliau de Cocaigne." *Neuphilologische Mitteilungen* 48: 1–36.

Vecoli, Rudolph. 1988. "'Free Country': The American Republic Viewed by the Italian Left, 1880–1920." In *In the Shadow of the Statue of Liberty: Immigrants, Workers and Citizens in the American Republic*, edited by Marianno Deobuzy, 36–56. Saint Denis, France: Presses Universitaires de Vincennes.

Vidari, Pier Paride. 1981. "L'ambiente della bocca: il sistema del mangiare sul territorio / Landscape of the Mouth: Man's Alimentary Relationship with His Habitat." In "Progetto mangiare / Eating as Design," edited by Giorgio Origlia, 40–49. Special edition, *Album* 1. Milan: Electa.

The Vision of MacConglinne. 1936. In *Ancient Irish Tales,* edited by Tom Peete Cross and Clark Harris Slover. New York: Barnes and Noble.

Wright, Robert L., and Rochelle Wright. 1983. *Danish Emigrant Ballads and Songs*. Carbondale: Southern Illinois University Press.

Zaganelli, Gioia. 1989. "La *Cuccagna* francese del XIII secolo: un mondo sghembo." In *Paesi di Cuccagna e mondi alla rovescia*, edited by Vita Fortunati and Giampaolo Zucchini, 143–52. Florence: Alinea.

Zenatti, Albino, ed. 1884. *Storia di Campriano contadino.* Bologna: Romagnoli.

Zorzi, Rosella Mamoli. 1989. "Mondi alla rovescia: Paesi di Cuccagna e distopie nella cultura anglo-americana." In *Paesi di Cuccagna e mondi alla rovescia,* edited by Vita Fortunati and Giampaolo Zucchini, 183–94. Florence: Alinea.

Figure 1.1. First stanzas of *La piacevole historia di Cvccagna, Posta in luce per Giouannino detto il Tranese* (The delightful story of Cockaigne, brought to light by Little John, alias the man from Trani). Naples: Nicolò Monaco, 1715. (Reproduced from Tranese [1715] 1884, 84–85.)

Figure 1.2. *Discritione del paese di Chuvagna dove chi manco lavora piv gvadagna* (Description of the Land of Cockaigne where he who works least earns most). Bassano: Remondini, 1606. Civica Raccolta delle Stampe Achille Bertarelli, Milano. (Reproduced from Bertarelli 1929, 51.)

Figure 1.3. *La Cvccagna: descrittione del gran paese de Cvccagna dove chi piv dorme piv gvadagna* (Cockaigne: description of the great Land of Cockaigne where he who sleeps most earns most). Rome: Anonymous Italian, Rome, 17th century (rpt. 1799). Civica Raccolta delle Stampe Achille Bertarelli, Milano. (Reproduced from Bertarelli 1974, 62.)

Figure 1.4. Il paese di Cuchagnia dove chi manco lavora più guadagnia (The Land of Cockaigne where he who works least earns most). Two engravings joined for a ventola (fan). Bassano: Remondini, 1730. Civica Raccolta delle Stampe Achille Bertarelli, Milano. (Reproduced from Bertarelli 1974, 63.)

Figure 1.5. *La Cvcagna nvova, trovata nella Porcolandria l'anno 1703 da Seigoffo, qvale raconta, esservi tvtte le delitie, e chi dessidera andarvi, gli ariva prestissimo con il pensiere con tvtta facilità. E finalmente qvi chi sempre vive mai more* (The new Cockaigne, discovered in Porklandia in 1703 by Youreadolt, who recounts all its delights, and he who wishes to go there, may easily get there with his mind, and in no time at all. And finally here he who always lives never dies). G. Mitelli. Civica Raccolta delle Stampe Achille Bertarelli, Milano. (Reproduced from Bertarelli 1940, 111, fig. 553).

Figure 1.6. *Il trionfo di Carnavale nel paese de Cvcagna* (The triumph of Carnival in the Land of Cockaigne). Venice: Ferrante Bertelli, 1569. Civica Raccolta delle Stampe Achille Bertarelli, Milano. (Reproduced from Bertarelli 1929, 25.)

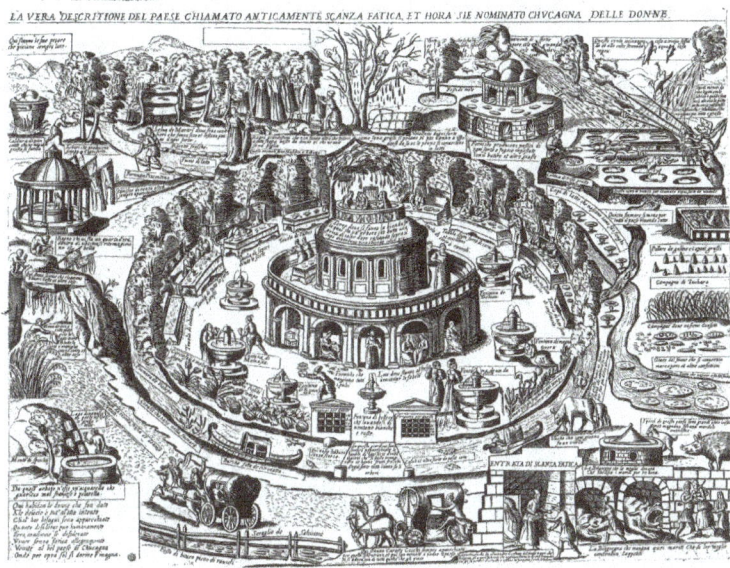

Figure 1.7 La *vera descritione del paese chiamato anticamente Scanza Fatica et hora sie nominato Chvcagna delle donne* (The true description of the land once called Shirk-Work, and now known as the Women's Cockaigne). Rome, circa 1650. Civica Raccolta delle Stampe Achille Bertarelli, Milano. (Reproduced from Bertarelli 1929, 50.)

Figure 1.8. *Gioco di Cvcagna che mai si perde, e sempre si gvadagna* (The game of Cockaigne where you never lose and you always gain), 1691. Civica Raccolta delle Stampe Achille Bertarelli, Milano. (Reproduced from Bertarelli 1940, 131.)

Figure 1.9

Figure 1.10

Figures 1.9–1.10. "Garden of Eatin," in *Walt Disney Presents Uncle Remus and His Tales of Brer Rabbit*, © Disney Enterprises Inc. (Reproduced from Disney 1992.)

Figure 1.11. *Il mondo alla riversa* (Upside-Down World). Rome: Anonymous Italian, c.1650. Civica Raccolta delle Stampe Achille Bertarelli, Milano. (Reproduced from Bertarelli 1974, 60, fig. 38.)

Figure 1.12. Anonymous Italian, *L'albero della Cuccagna* (Cockaigne pole), 19th century; oil painting, private collection. (Reproduced from Fortunati and Zucchini 1989 [fig. 17].) A satirical, pornographic, and mysogynistic version of the greased Cuccagna pole. It might easily have been entitled *Cuccagna delle donne* (women's Cockaigne) since it seems to be aimed at/against diabolical women and their insatiable sexual appetite. Traditional Cuccagna representations normally present palaces of pleasure in which males are sexually catered to. Yet another example of the *Roverso mondo* or the Upside-Down World.

Figure 1.13. *Il Triomfo del Carneval* (The triumph of Carnival). Venice: Ludovico Siletti. Museo Nazionale delle Arti e Tradizioni Popolari, Rome: IV, 7, d, number 01964. The fat King Carnival reigns in the Land of Cockaigne.

Figure 1.14. *Albero della Cuccagna* (Cockaigne pole). Museo Nazionale delle Arti e Tradizioni Popolari, Rome: IV, 7, a, number 250.

Figure 1.15. *Albero di Cuccagna*. An example of a Cuccagna pole in an Italian festival setting. (Reproduced from Toschi 1964.)

Figure 1.16. *Plumpodingo alla napolitana* (Neapolitan plum pudding). (Reproduced from Vidari 1981, 40, fig. 1, detail.)

Figure 1.17. In an example from Bologna, a festive Vesuvius, a mountain of delights, spews forth riches. Festival of the Porchetta (roast pork), was held on August 15–24. On the last day, St. Bartholomew's Day, a roast pig was thrown to the people to commemorate August 24, 1281, when the city was liberated from a bloody civil war. *Il Vesuvio delizioso in occasione dell'annua fiera, e festa Popolare della Porchetta fatto rappresentare nel primo anno [1665] della legatione dell'Em.mo Sig.r Cardinale Caraffa, sendo Confaloniere l'Illmo Sig.r Marchese Balì Ferdinando Cospi, dagli Ill.mi / ed Eccelsi Sig.ri Anziani, li Sig.ri Gio Battista Sanuti Pellicani Dottore, Comendator Carlo Banci, Co. Annibale Ranuzzi, Andrea Buoi / Zotto (?) Guidalotti, Ermete Bargellini, Odoardo Zanchini, e Co. Cesare Malvasia* (The delicious Vesuvius on the occasion of the annual fair, and public Roast Pork festival assembled during the first year [1665] of the legation of the most Eminent Cardinal Caraffa, being Gonfalone the most Illustrious Marquis Balì Ferdinando Cospi, by the most Illustrious and Eccellent Elders, Lord Gio[vanni] Battista Sanuti Pellicani, Doctor, Commendator Carlo Banci, Commendator Annibale Ranuzzi, Andrea Buoi / Zotto Guidalotti, Ermete Bargellini, Odoardo Zanchini, and Commendator Cesare Malvasia). M. Mitelli F. Civica Raccolta delle Stampe Achille Bertarelli, Milano. (Reproduced from Bertarelli 1940, 55, fig. 292, detail).

Figure 1.18

Figure 1.19

Figures 1.18–1.27. Prints and renderings of monumental, food-encrusted Cockaigne "machines" (*macchine della Cuccagna*) erected in Naples on the square before the Royal Palace to commemorate royal occasions: Figures 1.18 (1729), 1.19 (1730), 1.22 (1731), 1.24 (1732), 1.25 (1733) on November 4, name day of Charles III/ VI, king of Spain; Figures 1.20 (1730), 1.21 (1731), 1.23 (1732), 1.26 (1733) for Empress Elizabeth Christina's birthday, August 28; and Figure 1.27 for Bourbon King Charles's visit to Naples, May 16, 1734. Except for Figure 1.20 (Domenico Antonio Vaccaro, designer, and Francesco di Grado, sculptor [cf. Figure1.28]) and Figure 1.27 (by Nicola Tagliacozzi Canale and Bartolomeo de Grado), all monuments were designed by Cristoforo Rosso and sculpted by Neapolitan Francesco de Grado. Collection of Festival Prints, courtesy Getty Research Library P910002.

Figure 1.20

Figure 1.21

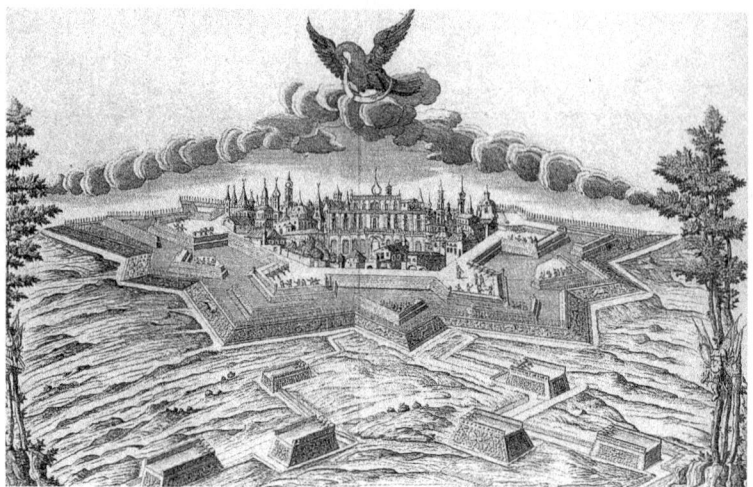

Figure 1.22

Figure 1.23

Figure 1.24

Figure 1.25

Figure 1.26

Figure 1.27

Figure 1.28. Filippo Falciatore, *Cuccagna al Largo di Palazzo* [cf. Figure 1.20], 18th century; oil painting. Electa Archive, Elewood SpA, Milano. (Reproduced from *Settecento Napoletano* 1994, 136.)

2. Wine Makes Good Blood: Wine Culture among Toronto Italians

For my father, Alberto Del Giudice
Terracina, February 7, 1923–Toronto, November 7, 2007

INTRODUCTION

Lu vinə fa bon sanguə (wine makes good blood)[1] and *l'acqua fa malə e lu vinə fa cantà* (water is bad for you [but] wine makes you sing).[2] These were two of the many wine-related idioms with common

The internal chronology of this essay has not been updated, for the most part, and reflects the dates and cited references of the original publication.

1   A Terracinese codicil to this proverb states: "... *e la fatiga fa ittà lu sanguə*" (... and work causes you to shed blood).

2   This essay was first published in *Ethnologies* 23, no. 1 (2001), 1–27. Unless otherwise noted, translations and photography are mine.

I thank those who contributed to this study by allowing me to interview them: Giulio and Amelia Belli (July 7, 1998), Antonio and Jolanda D'Angelo (April 13, 1998), Gianpaolo and Anna Del Bianco (April 12, 1998), Alberto and Liliana Del Giudice (April 13, 18, 1998), Carlo and Marisa Del Giudice (April 14, 1998), Egismondo and Esterina Del Giudice (April 13, 1998), Vincenzo and Ada Di Ninno (April 12, 1998), Franca and Sam Pantaleo, Rossana (Di Zio) Magnotta of Magnotta Winery Corp. (July 30, 1998), Nick Fasola of Cilento Wines, and Anthony Martelli (architect) of Greenpark homes. I thank others for acting as consultants and mediators: my sisters, Claudia Del Giudice Galletta, Franca Del Giudice Poldi, Irene Del Giudice D'Angelo, and brother-in-law, Domenico Galletta. The debt to my father, Alberto Del Giudice, a font of information, is vaster and abiding. Without his enthusiasm for life and for wine, I might never quite have experienced their full significance.

Collectively, the following Italian regions were represented in the fieldwork for this essay: Abruzzi, Calabria, Friuli, Lazio, Puglia. Since many interviews alternated between Italian and Italian dialects, I have simplified their citation in this essay, by translating and paraphrasing passages into English.

conversational currency in our Toronto Italian household. Both equate wine consumption with good health. Because Italian immigrants to Toronto largely emerged from regional peasant cultures, it is not surprising that wine continued to be central to health beliefs, foodways, expressive and material culture, and a food-centered cosmology, and that it ultimately embodied sacred truths.

Past research on Toronto Italians variously explored food's place in the domestic and mythic landscapes of immigrants: from the kitchen, garden, and wine cellar of home (Del Giudice 1993), to the mythic Paese di Cuccagna (Land of Cockaigne), a *gastronomic utopia*, still embedded in immigrant consciousness (see Del Giudice 1998; 2001a, ch. 1 this volume). While these previous writings touched only briefly on wine and wine cellars, the present paper elaborates the wine nexus and explores the meanings of wine—material and symbolic, historic and contemporary—in the culture of predominately first-generation Toronto Italians. The larger picture delineates how wine figures in several key binary oppositions in Italian folk culture that oppose wine to water; wine to bread (in gendered terms this is embodied in mythic Bacchus vs. Ceres); blood to body (in Christian terms); and the semantics of red vis-à-vis white wine. But here I focus on Italian life in Canada, and how Italian historic and symbolic contexts intersect the culture of Toronto Italians, through family history, through personal experience and anecdote, and to a lesser extent through direct historic sources. I intend thereby to provide snapshots of how cultural history and personal experience constantly intertwine in the praxis of folk culture.

As is true for many Toronto immigrants, viticulture formed an integral part of my own family history. My father's was a grape-producing peasant family in Terracina (southern Lazio), on his maternal and paternal sides.[3] My father's parents, Giovanni and Luisa (Palmacci) Del Giudice, owned approximately 10,000 square meters of vineyards.

---

3   Curiously, issues of gender equity have crept into my research. Just as wine research seems to balance a predominately female perspective in previous food writings, it also complements recent work on women healers and my female genealogy (Del Giudice 2001b), with something of a male counterpart through this essay's focus on my father's occupational genealogy.

They were primarily grape growers, not vintners, and whereas quality was a prime concern with regard to table grapes prepared for markets in Rome, only discards went into home winemaking. My father did not particularly like nor drink wine as a young man in Terracina. His own winemaking and consuming days largely began when he immigrated to Toronto in the mid-1950s.

Terracina vineyards were the locus of many family narratives (e.g., my grandmother's buried "liquid gold" treasure story; see Del Giudice 2022), of communal life (e.g., choral singing), as well as the source of many sad memories (e.g., family feuds over inheritance). The vine had been the blessing and the curse of their peasant life. My father developed a hatred for the land and from a young age vowed never to remain a *contadino* (peasant). Ironically, had they not sold off the vineyards (particularly in the now fashionable San Felice seaside area) to earn passage on transatlantic ships, they too might have enjoyed the payoffs from rampant post-WWII land development. The thought of what *might* have been haunts my father still. He had spent most of his childhood and adult life in Italy working the fields and although he has not practiced viticulture in over forty years, has retained a technical dialect lexicon which is impressive and still called forth with ease—so engrained had those movements, those judgments, their words, become. The vine was life. In Terracinese dialect, at least, they are one and the same: *la vita*. Wine therefore was indeed, "life's blood"—through genealogy (literally in the blood*line*), as much as providing the family's *live*lihood. Wine made good blood in more ways than one.

WINE/BLOOD AND NOTIONS OF HEALTH

The majority of Italian immigrants to Toronto came directly from the land, bypassing modernization and the industrialization of Italy's postwar boom in the 1960s altogether. Their attitudes remained deeply embedded in a hitherto unbroken continuum of peasant civilization. Wine was at the center of their cosmology, as well as their religious system. In the sacramental body and blood of the Eucharist, the wine/blood equation became firmly rooted in Christian cultures (Bernardi

1995, 8). Wine, indeed, was one of the contributions the southern Mediterranean made to Christianity and its rites, as were bread and olive oil (Montanari 1993, 24–30). Yet Christian culture here merely built upon pagan usage and pagan symbols already firmly in place, and endowed them with new meanings. Many rituals of Italian folk Catholicism continue to reenact the blood sacrifice quite literally (e.g., the *battenti* or flagellants of Basilicata), and blood-related miracles (e.g., the liquification of St. Gennaro's blood in Naples) continue to capture the popular imagination, even though they are no longer sanctioned by the Church. Blood and religiosity in Italian folk culture continue to be intimately linked. It may not require a large leap of faith, therefore, to extend the *spiritual* benefits of blood (wine) to notions of *physical* wellbeing. In other words, sacramental blood (wine), along with sacramental flesh (bread), make one spiritually *and* physically whole. The blood/wine binomial runs deep, permeates many areas of expressive culture, belief (official *and* unofficial), and notions of health, and is widely operative in folk medicinal practices. I might even speculate that it was the strong liturgical association of wine as blood that contributed to a widespread preference for *red* wine (besides its assimilability to notions of health, i.e., rosy cheeked, a "picture of health," vs. "white as a ghost," sickly).

The medicinal uses of wine are millennial and, in the Italian folk pharmacopoeia, feature prominently. Wine is taken internally, fortified with herbs, cooked into syrups, and as distilled spirit, used externally as liniment. But apart from such uses, from specific intestinal to muscular ailments, wine is seen as contributing to general wellbeing. Wine (along with bread) is largely considered a staple *food* of great nutritional value and as such is considered the best preventive medicine. Full-strength wine (as opposed to *vinello*; see infra), was traditionally reserved for the sick, the convalescent (e.g., postpartum women), and the aged (for whom it was considered the "milk of old age"), and was frequently set aside for periods of particularly strenuous labor, such as the harvest.[4] Wine gave energy, prevented illness, but played an

---

4 Various photographs capture this moment, but one in particular features a priest, prominently dispensing largesse as he pours wine for his workers (*L'alimentazione* 1998, 167); another shows a Bergamasque farmwife pouring

important role in social health too, marking convivial and celebratory gatherings of joy and grief.

WINE AND CHILDREN

No less than to the aged, wine was considered beneficial to children. When we children had colds, we were given wine cooked down to a delicious syrup (together with honey, lemon, and bay leaves), and several fortified wines were cheerfully given to us as tonics, such as *vino di China* ("*Ferro China*")—of which I was *not* fond, and *marsala all'uovo* (egg-fortified marsala, Sperone brand)—which was never given in large enough doses as far as we children were concerned. Marsala (or coffee) was added in limited amounts each morning to a *zabaione*—known to us simply as *ovə šbattutə* (beaten raw egg yolk with sugar)—to fortify us before we set off on the long walk to Duncan B. Hood Public School—often through snow and rain. Daily wine consumption was strongly encouraged in children as well, to make healthy and strong bodies: (red) wine makes good (red) blood. As an anemic child, I was given not only red meat (and also, then-loathed liver, cooked to resemble shoe leather), but red wine as well. In this equation of red wine with red blood can perhaps be seen a transaction of sympathetic magic (similar to the supposed effects of eating walnuts to improve brain power, given their loose resemblance).

Indeed, the acculturation of children to these wine values was valiantly practiced among first-generation Italian immigrants for whom the idea of a legal drinking age was foreign. We were served wine with dinner, even if it had to be made more palatable by mixing it with *gassosa* (carbonated white soda) or ginger ale. I recall watching the dark red wine trickle in plumes down into the effervescing glass, turning its contents a pleasant rosé, and feeling rather important about having partaken of some forbidden fruit. The game was for my father to pretend that he had slipped in more than he had intended, and that we had gotten away with it. But by the time we grew past the age of nine or ten, not even this fiction washed, for we shunned wine altogether.

---

wine for the men at the time of haying (Merisio 1983, n.24).

The issues of the correct use of alcohol and the *cultural* attitudes toward temperance[5] have often caused a direct, head-on collision (pardon the macabre pun) between traditional immigrant attitudes and the Anglo establishment in Canada. Some immigrants may even have used wine consumption, as Piedmontese American Joe Cappello apparently did, as a marker, stating: "I am not a member of mainstream Anglo Saxon-derived [American] culture" (Clements 1990, 22). Anglo-Canada has now been partly converted to wine culture, thanks perhaps to the great numbers of wine-drinking immigrants from many ethnic groups, who have shared their customs, their attitudes, and their homemade wine. But the victory may have proven pyrrhic, since the general conversion of second- and third-generation Italian immigrants from wine to carbonated drinks (and beer), and hence from ethnic to mainstream credo, has been vast.

WATER AND WINE

A significant binary opposition in Italian peasant culture was that of water vs. wine, an opposition that might be viewed in Levi-Straussian terms, as analogous to *le cru et le cuit,* that is the natural vs. the cultural, or in this instance, the natural vs. the cultured (fermented). While wine was considered healthful, water frequently was not. If wine was thought to produce good blood, conversely, many proverbs often expressed negative judgments of water, such as *l'acqua 'nfrascica i ponti* (water rots bridges; cf. Galanti 1981, 65, 68). Or, put more succinctly: *L'acqua fa male, e lu vinə fa cantà* (cf. supra). Carrying this belief to absurd lengths, my father still prides himself—transferring a centuries-old prejudice to the New World—that during most of his life he has never drunk water!

---

5   On the acculturation of Italian Americans to American drinking habits, see Lolli et al. 1958, esp. 98–101. On the importance of generational data on the acculturation of Italian American drinking behavior, see Simboli, 1985. Among interesting findings cited are that Italians (in Italy) disassociate drunkenness and alcoholism in their perception of problem drinking. Italians indeed, have a high rate of cirrhosis, while they have a low rate of social problems connected with drinking.

The custom of mixing water (later soda) with wine is ancient, but in most parts of peasant Italy, this blend seems to have been made by necessity, and remained in immigrant culture largely by force of habit, or also as a way of softening frequently poor-tasting homemade wines (cf. infra.). *Lu vinu havi ad essiri turcu* (wine should be "Turkish" [i.e., Muslim]—that is, "unbaptized" with water), tells one Sicilian proverb (cf. Alaimo 1974, no.1109)! Strong, unadulterated wine was the ideal. Weak, tempered, watery wine was the reality.

The wine/water (cf. *vino/vinello* or full-strength vs. watered wine) opposition marked the boundary between the festive and the quotidian. Festive days of gastronomic abundance alternated with the many days of want and privation, that is, the common daily lot of peasants over the centuries (cf. Ciceri 1983, 366; Del Giudice 2001a). *Vino/vinello* also functioned as social marker. In general, the best wines went to landowners, while the dregs or once-pressed grapes could be enjoyed by laborers. The practice of second-pressing (watered) grapes was common all over Italy, and was known most frequently as *vinello* or *vin piccolo*—a *small* wine (cf. small beer, beer of low alcohol content), the wine of daily consumption. The barrel containing this *vinaccia* might be watered frequently—as long as some color and flavor were present—but it resulted in wine that easily turned moldy and acidic. Water ran through the skins and stems again and again till spring, as the wine became ever lighter in color, and progressively lost any alcoholic content. Again, red (wine) and white (water) lay in stark opposition, setting up a common perception of wine/life and strength, against water/weakness and lifelessness, as peasants witnessed the progressive blanching, or loss of the fluid's vitality. There were many ways of prolonging the life of grape wine itself through a series of recyclings to the last drop of all possible juice, color, and flavor (e.g., *vinello*, or distilled as *grappa*). There were also many grape wine substitutes, made with plants, fruits, and berries (see *L'alimentazione* 1998, 168–72), known as *vini dei poveri* (poorman's wines)—the ingenious concoctions of largely mountain folk.

VIRILE WINE

Red wine, life's blood, was closely associated with manhood and virility. This virility was socially determined as well: the relative gradation of alcohol coincided with social hierarchies, so that *small* wine (*vin piccolo, vinello*), was the domain of peasants as *low* men on the totem pole. Further, wine figured at the center of a male cosmology, creating and cementing male bonds across generations (cf. Clements 1990), in a sort of brotherhood of the grape. Visual corroboration of the hypothesis that (red) wine functions as a symbol of virility may be found in a genre of photograph that poses conventionalized convivial (and largely male) settings. Here someone inevitably holds up a bottle or a glass of wine (as in a toast), or is captured in the act of pouring wine for the camera's benefit. Women were rarely photographed in the act of drinking wine. From a female perspective, the wine/virility nexus instead was often a source of conflict and dread. Wine may have been important for male bonding, bringing forth a song, a tale or two, but it also unleashed other, darker behaviors such as violent sexuality.

Drunkenness was considered foreign to Italian culture and generally abhorred. Excessive drinking was instead associated with northern Europeans (emblematically by Germans—"trinkers"—considered drunks from the Renaissance onward),[6] and in Toronto with the *Ingles* (a generic term for Anglo-Canadians and other northerners). Anglo drinking habits (including binge drinking, hard liquor, and drinking alone) have always been an object of criticism among Italian Canadians, whose traditional drinking behavior is characterized by drinking in moderation, at meals, and in convivial settings foremost. Indeed, Italians, for whom the prevailing notion of health called for equilibrium, considered drunkenness to put this balance (and hence general health) at risk and therefore avoided it (cf. Migliore 1996). Further, liquor laws created by Anglo-Canadians—in general, hostile to wine (cultures) in the earlier part of the century—made *private* wine

---

6   My father recalled that among his non-Italian neighbours was one in particular who would have "drowned himself" in wine ("he would have [even] drunk mud!"). This man would buy jug wine by the week. "They really drank when they drank," my father recounted, with evident disapproval.

consumption among immigrants the norm, and helped increase the importance of the domestic wine cellar as a haven against estranging cultural values.

WINE CELLARS OLD AND NEW

To the older, first-generation Toronto Italian immigrant (over sixty-five) with a direct experience of life in Italy, the *cantina* of memory varied widely, and was alternatively identified as a communal wine cellar; the village vintners' wine cooperative (cf. Fr. *cave*) where bulk table wine was made and sold; or a tavern,[7] traditionally marked with a *frasca* (branch, frond)—the universal Italian sign of the tavern since Roman times. In addition to these public uses, the term also referred to a privately owned (domestic) cellar, normally sparsely stocked; a corner of a barn; even a roughly finished back room or shallow, underground dugout, separate from, but close to, the farmhouse where wine, wine accoutrements (and, more rarely, food) could be stored. This *cantina* was designated by a variety of dialect terms[8]—variation that itself suggests the *cantina* had no single conventional form. It is likely this last type, a cross between a dugout and roughly finished room, that provided the closest equivalent to the later, fully evolved, Toronto wine cellar. The *cantina*, as it is presently known among Italian immigrants to Toronto, is an uninsulated (north-facing) basement room of varying

---

7   This use of *cantina* was also transferred to some New World public settings as well, as attested in Boston's North End, in Simboli 1985, 70. Much recent Italian scholarship has explored the place of the tavern in Italian folk culture. It was a bastion of male culture, with its own preferred games: cards, *passatella* (for rules, see Giggi Zanazzo in Rossetti 1979, 292–299), *scalino, morra, ruzzica* (in Rome). The osteria had its (often deadly) rituals and found its way into literature as a frequent locus for fights and tragic endings, of intrigue and conspiracies, etc. It was a favored meeting place for Rome's *bulli* (whence bully or thug in English), as it necessarily was for the carters who delivered wine from the surrounding provincial wine-producing areas (cf. "L'osteria, club dei bulli," "I giochi;" in Rossetti 1979, 194–210).

8   E.g., *solare* in Abruzzo, *cellare, ceddaru, solaru* in Calabria, *càneva* or *canevin* in the Veneto, *crota* in Piedmont, *rispensa* (*dispensa*) in Sicily, *slér* (cellar) in the Swiss Alps (cf. *Atlante* 1929–1940, vol. 7, 1342: s.v. *cantina*).

dimensions (from 5 feet x 5 feet to 20 feet x 22 feet, or beyond, in tune with the *archvilla* mentality).[9] It functions both as a repository for wine and pantry for foods. There is some debate as to whether foods and wine can or should coexist, but the fact is, in most *cantine,* they do. Wine cellars are now a regular feature of new homes, especially of those built by Italian-owned construction companies.

The *cantina* has become a well-defined area of the home, and there is surprising uniformity as to its contents. It typically contains wine in glass gallon jugs or demijohns (bottles and barrels more rarely) [Figure 2.1]; wine equipment (funnels, press, siphons, etc.);[10] mason jars of garden vegetables (especially tomatoes),[11] *giardiniera* (mixed pickled vegetables) or fruit; cured meats such as *prosciutto, soppressata,* and sausages; more rarely, cheese; but also store-bought canned foods, pasta, oil, and other items found *a spèce* (on special; bargain-hunting is more than a part-time pastime for many) [Figures 2.2–2.5]. The *cantina* can also contain wild foods such as mushrooms and snails, a greatly prized delicacy for many peasant Italians [Figure 2.6].[12] Frequently,

---

9   Anecdote has it that at least one cantina was so large, its owner (a young computer specialist) actually created a computerized inventory to keep track of it! The "archvilla" (Del Giudice 1993) is an Italian Canadian architectural expression, widespread in Toronto beginning in the 1970's, which prominently featured arches, and tended toward the aggrandizing of domestic spaces.

10   A very small number of these objects made the transatlantic voyage and are being progressively reincarnated into plastic, while the wine press (and barrels) are actually becoming obsolete, thanks to ready-bought juice. Immigrants did add one item, however: the glass gallon jug, the obvious unit in the Anglo-American system of liquid measurement, which in America gave the name "jug wine" to the bulk table wines immigrants generally produced.

11   A recent evolution in methods of preserving tomatoes, a staple of Italian diet among Italians in Toronto, is to freeze them whole, rather than can them, which apparently long maintains their fresh flavour and requires less work. When cooked into a light tomato and basil pasta sauce (*sugo finto,* faux sauce, as we call it, because it has no meat), they are indistinguishable from the fresh tomato variety. My aunt Marisa, who processes about three to four bushels of tomatoes a year, is now freezing about half and canning the rest.

12   G. Belli, recounting with evident joy the pleasure of collecting snails in the Humber Valley area, noted with an expert's eye how this variety—small, but tasty (and still black and white)—was actually preferable to the larger Italian variety (with more fat in the neck) as he remembers them from past experience in the

in the battles between wine and food for cellar space, the scales tip on the side of food. When such *cantina* divisions do occur, they tend to develop along gender lines: a wine cellar for him, a food pantry for her.

While a fair measure of Italian wine culture may have been lost, home winemaking itself, and the *cantina* specifically, not only survived in diaspora contexts, but may actually have increased in size and certainly in importance. So much so among first-generation Italians that one man might declare: "*Senza la cantina non c'è niente*" ("Without the cantina there is nothing"). How and why did the *cantina* acquire such significance? In Italy, many factors contributed to the relative *insignificance* of the domestic wine cellar. Pre-WWII peasant incomes were so meager that stockpiling of wine (and food) was impossible.[13] Because table wine was easily obtainable locally, in most parts of the Italian peninsula, home winemaking was not a necessity. For immigrants however, good table wine was not readily available at reasonable cost, so they had to make their own. Many, in fact, acquired direct winemaking experience only in Canada. Just as for many of the other staples in the traditional diet, only great personal or familial efforts, including kitchen gardens and home winemaking, could guarantee such items. Further, while frequent but *small* purchases (e.g., of food, of wine) characterize buying patterns in Italy, in Toronto peasant habits of thrift, long familiarity with the seasonal harvest, and increased income made large scale purchases (and hence the domestic wine cellar) ideal. Never had their *cantine* been better stocked, and during the long Canadian winter months, *all* summer food savings were a boon.

The mantra of *abbondanza* and its practice made the ever-larger wine cellar necessary. This abundance even spawned new customs, such as inviting family and friends to dinner, whereas "there [in Italy] you couldn't, [because you] didn't even have enough, even for yourself," as my father remembers. The *cantina* (and the freezer)

Lazio region. Although he does not go often, eating snails about two or three times a year made him content—a sentiment I share completely.

13   "[The *cantina*] is much more important here. We store everything in it. In Italy we bought food day by day; we didn't have money. Here I used to buy 200–500 pounds of meat and put it in the deep freezer! In Italy you wouldn't even have seen that much meat at the butcher's! Who ever saw that amount of meat?" (A. Del Giudice).

made a spontaneous, simple supper always possible. Indeed, the most frequently cited reason for making such vast quantities of wine even today is that it should be shared with family and friends when they come to visit. Wine could also acquire professional currency: in his early Toronto days as a self-employed painting contractor, my father would give gallons of his wine to clients and superintendents of apartment buildings, as potential employers. Around the holidays however, he would purchase cases of whiskey and ten to twenty turkeys as gifts to thank those who had helped him throughout the year. It is interesting to note that while homemade wine could be given informally, store-bought, and hence more special (certainly more mainstream) foods and drink seemed to be more appropriate gifts for the high holidays. Store-bought bottles of whiskey or Italian liqueurs also marked special gift-giving occasions among Italians.

I have suggested elsewhere that the *cantina* filled primarily a deep-seated *psychological* need (Del Giudice 1993, 62–63). To Antonio D'Angelo, for whom the *cantina* was fundamental ("without the *cantina* there is nothing"), and who had known hunger during the war years, I asked if he still feared hunger in this country. He answered: "Who can say it won't return? It can always return: war is war." Hunger may indeed be a thing of the past, but the *fear* of hunger is not easily vanquished.

Wine was but one of the items which came to fill the centuries-old desire for abundance. In fact, the *cantina* likely became a focal point of the home *because* of its association with the dream of *Cuccagna* (cf. Del Giudice 1993; 2001a)—and not merely among Italian Canadians but to diaspora Italians elsewhere.[14] The powerful and ever-surfacing mythic Land of Cockaigne, a largely gastronomic utopia, featured flowing rivers of wine as an important element in Italian *Cuccagna* iconography from the Middle Ages onward. Sometimes, though, real life events proved

---

14   For example, even among the poorest Veneto immigrants, who had emigrated to Brazil in search of the Land of Cockaigne, the praises of the *cantina* continued to be literally sung. In a poem entitled "Cantina" (by Pe. Joao Leonir Dall'Alba, *Stianni in Colónia*, Editora Lunardelli, cited in Bernardi 1994, 222–223) and in analogous poems on the harvest, foods, kitchen utensils, the kitchen, *polenta*, and so forth, the author gives a catalogue of all the riches ("*ben di Dio*," God's bounty) found in the wine cellar, and explains how it is used in times of feasting.

just as marvelous. My mother vividly remembers an incident which occurred in Terracina in her youth: A carter returning from an olive mill in the mountains was carrying a precious load of freshly-pressed olive oil in demijohns. The roads were rough, unasphalted, and the apparently unswathed glass containers hit up against each other—and broke. Oil gushed out, running along the stone gutters (*canaletti*) on this and that side of the road. Everyone came out to collect as much as they could. What a feast for them, but what a loss for the carter. A similar, real life Terracinese cuccagnesque tale tells of people coming to gather fish after a tornado at sea (*tromba marina*, sea "trumpet") dropped a great load of them on the beach—like manna from heaven!

BETWEEN TRADITION AND TORONTO

What happened when the time-honored wisdom about making and consuming wine, learned in the sunny villages of Italy, was transferred to frigid Toronto? Agrarian calendrical proverbs provided the peasant a sort of farmer's almanac. The problem with much traditional wisdom, of course, is that it is locally produced and therefore, often only locally applicable. As Rossana (Di Zio) Magnotta (cf. Nusca 1998), professionally acquainted with Italian home winemakers in Toronto, has observed: "Why is winemaking still largely an *October* event when the conditions and materials are available all year round?"[15]

Interestingly, both Cilento Wines [Figures 2.7–2.8] and Magnotta

---

15   Unlike California, where Italians have been well-represented in the wine industry, there are fewer Italian vintners in the province of Ontario—perhaps because it is a fairly new sector of the economy. Yet, because Italians are so abundant demographically, one might have expected their greater representation within the Wine Council of Ontario. There are exceptions: Rossana and Gabriel Magnotta (Magnotta Winery), Grace and Angelo Locilento (Cilento Wines), Ron and Nicole Speranzini (Willow Heights Estate Winery), Carlo Negri (Colio Estate Wines), Sal D'Angelo (D'Angelo Estate Winery), Giovanna and Rosanna Follegot (Vinoteca Premium Winery), Leonard Pennachetti and Angelo Pavan (Cave Spring Cellars), Gary Pillitteri (Pillitteri Estates Winery), Donald Ziraldo (Inniskillin), among approximately forty listed in the 1998 Wine Regions of Ontario *Calendar of Events* (see guide: *Wine Regions of Ontario* 7, Spring 1998, for some history and description of Ontario wineries).

Winery began as suppliers of must (Vin Bon and Festa Juice respectively) to home winemakers and evolved into wineries with their own line of bottled wines (and retail boutiques) in the 1990s. Magnotta produces wine, beer, and distilled spirits.

Why do Italians still insist on making and fermenting wine in the ill-suited *cantina* where the temperature is much too cold, and fluctuates greatly?[16] Further, the cleaning and preparation of barrels require more serious consideration than traditional methods provided. While Italian conditions were ideal and produced practically fool-proof wine, she noted, the conditions for home winemaking in Canada are markedly different: grapes are often not completely ripe when picked, they travel long distances, and they become contaminated or moldy. New environments create discrepancies for traditional ways which no longer apply, or require modification. "Unscientific" methods of determining the length of fermentation, according to Magnotta, simply produced disastrous effects in many instances.[17] I too have many memories of wine that tasted like vinegar,[18] and of my father, in constant denial, claiming, against any "objective" taste test, that the quality of the homemade was superior to store-bought wine, dismissing the latter as *pieno di medicina* (full of medicine, i.e., chemical additives). But peasants had a long history of drinking bad wine, of valuing quantity over quality, so why should they think any differently now? Quality, for Italian men and their homemade wine, I have come to conclude, is largely subjective anyway.

---

16   Actually, Toronto wine cellars become so cold at night that low temperatures arrest fermentation and often merely postpone it to the spring, when the wine is in bottles. Alternately, the fluctuating day/night temperatures cause constantly interrupted fermentation.

17   Many of these Italian wine beliefs, some aspects of traditional vinification, and the problem of their transferral to the Canadian environment, were discussed in an interview with Rossana Magnotta. I thank her for her generous and intelligent *disponibilità*, or openness.

18   In the Eversfield Road house, the first basement room adapted to *cantina* use was too close to the furnace and turned wine consistently to vinegar. But when my father and his brothers pooled their efforts to put in a proper *cantina* under the veranda (but not north-facing), I don't remember that the quality of the wine appreciably improved. The Dallas Road (Willowdale) *cantina* may have produced better wine.

Wine technologists have been engaged in a battle over traditional methods on this and the other side of the Atlantic. For instance, a strong bias against any sort of additive (natural or not) exists among peasants. In our family these were designated with the generic term *"medicina"* (medicine).[19] Foreign or unnatural additives still provoke suspicion and fear, for vinification had essentially been considered a *natural* process requiring *natural* (lunar),[20] and perhaps *supernatural* (i.e., saints') intervention, but *not* chemicals. Some immigrants fear ready-pressed must (juice) for similar reasons; that is, one cannot know what additives it might contain.[21] Yet the school of hard knocks has forced many home winemakers to finally add sulfite to barrels, to bring their wine in for analysis, and finally, to buy ready-pressed juice from companies such as Festa Juice or Vin Bon, thereby avoiding the mess and guess work. The trend toward purchasing juice (*mosto*) ready for vinification has made the wine press almost obsolete in Toronto, except for the diehards who refuse to give up old ways [Figure 2.9].

Several objective factors in the winemaking process could be problematic, of course, but folk belief also pointed to *cultural* hazards which might influence the quality of wine—e.g., women. It was (and partly, still is) commonly believed that menstruating women should not be involved in winemaking (or in the canning of tomatoes, for that matter—note the common color denominator). This belief was possibly due to a perceived conflict of lunar phases, for both winemaking and menses were determined by such lunar activity. Perhaps though, it was also perceived as a case of "bad blood" (menstrual), *contaminating*

---

19 Cf. Engl. "doctored wine" (treated with chemicals, adulterated).

20 According to tradition, the position and phases of the moon seemed to be especially important during the most delicate phases of racking (*travaso*) and bottling (cf. *Cultura Popolare* 1978, 60, caption to fig. 19). In folk culture, empirical observation of the moon's phases dictated many agricultural activities: harvesting of grain, cutting of trees, planting of seeds (Bernardi 1995, 10). A modern fringe of organic vintners seeks to revive such folklore under the label *Biodynamic*.

21 My father tells an Italian joke about the dishonest vintner calling his son to his death bed, and finally divulging a trade secret, since his son would be carrying on the business. He says: son, I want you to know that wine can be made with grapes too!

"good blood" (wine). Among the battles Rossana Magnotta has had to wage among Toronto Italians, by far the most challenging was indeed a gender battle. While one battle pitted scientific methods against traditional wine lore, the second involved her being a woman in a man's (wine) world. A supportive husband and partner, Gabriel Magnotta, who publicly deferred to her lab expertise whenever a customer asked for advice, her own Italian heritage and ability to speak Italian, as well as a strategically astute manual on home winemaking (Magnotta 1988)—allowing information to be transmitted through the neutral medium of print, requiring no face-to-face encounter—eventually brought her victory.[22] In fact, Magnotta Winery Corp., the company that went beyond Festa Juice, now sells a wide range of wines, is the third largest winery in Ontario, and is on the Toronto Stock Exchange. Yet, it has maintained a large and loyal home winemaking clientele.

HIS WINE CELLAR, HER FOOD PANTRY

While I pursued the gender question tangentially, it became clear during my research that gender distinction was woven into the wine culture. For example, gender determined patterns and types of wine consumption (e.g., women's wine vs. men's wine). The use of wine cellar space sometimes resulted in separate wine cellars altogether (e.g., his *cantina* / her *cantina*). The functions and uses of wine as they related to health and nutrition (e.g., women used wine for health remedies and for cooking) are opposed to wine used as a vehicle for male socialization, hence figuring largely in the contexts of male leisure and pleasure.

First, and at the most general level, the entire domain of winemaking and wine consumption has been a male one since Roman times (Ciceri 1983, 556, n.484). Further, there were effeminate wines (sweet dessert wines, light white wines), and manly ones (potent red wines). In

---

22 While the Italians were largely won over, due to the common strategy of convincing a few loyal clients who then spread the word among friends and family, the more intransigent Portuguese clientele was another story altogether. Her gender, apparently, has remained largely an insurmountable obstacle for this ethnic group.

our household, reds were for drinking, whites for cooking. Among immigrants, men make wine (with the help of women and children, normally in assisting roles—cleaning, fetching, and so forth), bestow wine as gifts, age it for special celebrations, boast about its alcoholic content, challenge each other over its quality and over quantities consumed. Wine has often served as a symbolic surrogate of, or a vehicle for, issues of virility, both individual and collective. Through such traditional drinking games as *passatella,* common experiences of social impotency and class struggle in the macrocosm of society could be transferred to the microcosm of the game, as one player asserted his dominance over the others, by playing boss (*padrone*). The quantities of wine consumed in this game (and the power to deny wine to others), directly reflected on one's manhood, power, and savvy—which is why the game so frequently ended in violence. A "dry" game (*restare "olmo"*) proved an affront to one's manly honor and required avenging.

Passatella soon lost its raison d'être among an immigrant society in Toronto that was relatively homogeneous in socioeconomic status. And because wine became widely affordable and hence abundant (no more *vinello*), it may no longer have been viewed as a limited good. But hierarchies played out through the medium of wine found other modes of expression, nonetheless. For instance, in our household, one of the ways the pecking order unfolded between my father and my brothers-in-law was through the never-ending debate regarding quality, relative alcohol content, and choice of whose wine to serve at special celebrations (and hence who would reap the ritual wine compliments). Denial of the superiority of my father's wine was/is viewed as a direct affront to him as patriarch, for in the "natural" hierarchy, the older man is due the respect of the younger men. Tensions with few other means of expression in a shared household can thus be diverted into (symbolic) wine talk.

Questions of virility and dominance were raised through male–female tensions as well. For instance, I sought to determine the extent of female vs. male use of the *cantina*. In Italy, the *cantina*, as wine cellar, was male space. In Toronto, it is largely shared, yet not without evidence of some contestation, for an ambiguous line demarks the food (female) / wine (male) *cantina* domains.[23] A few men protested the presence of food as contaminants to wine (as wine technologists concur, I might add). One *cantina* fanatic dismissed canned tomatoes as pertaining to his wife's *cantina*. When their children were asked to fetch up tomatoes, confused, they frequently asked from which *cantina*, Mom's or Dad's? Such completely discrete spaces however, are not common.

Red seems to be the *cantina*'s predominant color, and certainly varying hues of red account for the most important items stored there: red wine, canned tomatoes, *prosciutto,* sausages, and other cured meats. Indeed, red wines—deep, full-bodied, and potent—had a prestige among immigrants that the whites could not match (cf. Malpezzi and Clements 1992, 237). In our case, although Terracina was famous for its muscat grapes which produced a deep golden wine, the wine we made in Toronto was blood red (i.e., zinfandel, alicante, and later, cabernet). The fate of white wine, on the other hand (only a few gallons' worth made each year), was for women's work of cooking (chicken, fowl, sausage, snails, etc.) and baking (e.g., *ciambelle*), or, mixed with red to produce a rosé vinegar for salad. Only recently have white wines—perhaps markers of upward mobility—made a dent in this predilection.[24]

Immigrant culture sought to festivalize daily life and in so doing made several traditional celebrations obsolete (e.g., St. Martin's Day, Carnival). This cult of abundance required the multiplication of once special foods (e.g., cured meats, potent red wine), and hence intimately linked the *cantina* to the festivalization process.[25] In an attempt to

---

23   In my case, this competition has been transferred to the refrigerator: how much space wine (and other potables) should take (husband), as opposed to food (me)!

24   In at least one folk riddle, in fact, white wine is equated with urine: *vino vinello, / sincero e bello, / andrai in prigione e ci resterai tanto / finché da nero diventerai bianco* (wine, little wine, / pure and beautiful, / you will go to prison and will remain there a good while / until from red you will become white).

25   It was during one of the family gatherings to make *coppa* (or head cheese), in fact, that I first remember hearing the archaic, traditional songs from Terracina (particularly the pilgrimage song to Vallepietra), an experience which influenced later folklore career choices (Del Giudice 1994).

finally sate our appetite for cold cuts (*affettati*) as children, my father once brought home an entire *mortadella* (the large size!)—but no slicer—to hang in the *cantina*. We soon became disgusted with the thickly sliced slabs with which school lunches and after-school snacks were made, for what seemed to be unrelieved months on end. We children became responsible for its consumption. It took approximately fifteen years for any of us to want a *mortadella* sandwich again![26] My father's cult of (food) abundance had, in this instance (and in others, alas), gone too far. He summed up the experience of many Italians when he stated that:

> To me the *cantina* was truly important; it was the heart of the house, and provided *grascia per la famiglia* [abundance for the family]. We [immigrants] are attached to our families, we give them *abbondanza*, everything we can. We'll turn handstands [*salti mortali*]. I have never allowed my family to want for anything. It was ugly in the old days, [but with the *cantina*] you felt more protected. Everything is in the *cantina*.

It was generally understood that hunger and want were evil, but that abundance could be more so, for it induced a sort of satiety and apathy. And yet, as a *paesano* Vincenzo Saccoccia, whom we viewed as a wit and wise man, said, somewhat settling that account: "*La grascia è più brutta della carestia, ma io voglio stare in mezzo alla grascia.*" (Abundance is more terrible than famine, but I want to be in the midst of abundance.)[27] This is one of my father's favorite sayings.

---

26   Now I consider it comfort food, and nothing can quite recall a mood of innocent childhood, as can a fresh baked panino with *thinly* sliced *mortadella*. When in need of a dose of home (Toronto, family), I go to San Pedro (Los Angeles' port, with a sizeable Italian community) with my daughters, to pick Mediterranean snails on public land, overlooking the ocean; we also buy fresh bread and *mortadella* and enjoy them under the trees in a park (see ch. 4, this volume).

27   A published variant upon which Saccoccia's seems to elaborate comes from the same region: *la grascia stufa* (abundance becomes tiresome; Galanti 1981, 63). As an illustration of the negative side to abundance, my father tells of searching the entire vineyard over as a child, looking for that perfect bunch to eat, and never seeming to find it. One lesson to be learned from this anecdote: When there is too much of a good thing, one never seems to be satisfied.

The *cantina* indeed was especially memorable around the time of major festivities: Christmas, Easter, communions, or baptisms. At Christmas, for example, we could find there, reassuringly the same every year, *lasagne*, roasted chickens, Roman-style minted artichokes (*carciofi alla romana*), eggplant parmigiana, *broccoletti* (rapini), fennel, homemade sausage with coriander seed, *casatella* (a traditional Terracinese coffee, liqueur, and *ricotta* pie), *ciambelle* (in its Terracinese variant, something of a hard donut made with flour, oil, anise seeds, cinnamon, sugar, and wine), *torrone* (nougat), persimmons, tangerines, and assorted unshelled nuts. The wine cellar was a place of body-warming nourishment and joy, despite its bone-numbing cold in winter. I'm not certain which scenario was more exciting to us children: sneaking in to sample foods being prepared for the feast, or returning at leisure to the *cantina* afterward to finish up these specialties before those foods disappeared and we awaited the next cuccagnesque glut. It was not *visions* of sugarplums that danced in *our* heads!

That childhood memories should immediately come to my mind when the *cantina* is evoked does not seem coincidental. The *cantina* may be to foodways what the folktale is to oral expression—primal, symbolically packed, and linked to the early oral years. Childhood *cantina* narratives are plentiful and meaningful to immigrants and I can relate one or two of my own. I remember cleaning glass gallons and admiring them all gleaming and in a row on the wooden plank shelf in a somewhat cave-like *cantina* in our first Canadian house at 14 Eversfield Road; the exciting gush of juice rushing from the wine press as the grapes were crushed; and the pungent, acidic smell around the cellar. I would try my hand, applying all my strength, to the back and forth action of the wine press rod, hearing the clicking sound as the wooden blocks were pushed down. But I especially remember the delicious taste, slightly alcoholic and effervescent, of freshly squeezed juice. Another childhood gustatory recollection involves a night spent at my cousin Amelia's, with whom I had grown up in the old Rogers and Dufferin neighborhood, but who had by then moved to a newer suburban home in Downsview, as we had to Willowdale. We waited until parents had gone to sleep and all was quiet to sneak into the *cantina*. Our victim, a *prosciutto* (cured ham) which had just been "started," hung all moist and ruby red. We attacked with blunt knives and gouged out large chunks, took them back to bed, and slowly gnawed as we talked late into the night, savoring the salty pork—without fat, and without bread![28]

CONCLUSIONS

Current and changing health concerns have taken a toll on traditional foodways, some of which are now perceived to be quite unhealthy. Wine, cheese, and cured meat production/consumption has dramatically decreased, and, in some cases, has been abandoned altogether. At least one man is in denial, protesting that such foods should *not* be victimized. As a former shepherd, he took great pride in making his own cured meats and cheeses, but now, afflicted with diabetes, high cholesterol, and cancer, he can no longer indulge in these delicacies. Others insist that these health biases are culturally determined and state that, while an Italian doctor understands the health value of wine, the *magnacake* (or simply "Cake," "Cake-eater;" i.e., Anglo-Canadian) doctors did not.[29] "When we are gone, it [these foodways] will all be over," was a leitmotif running through much of my fieldwork. Of course, these statements often veiled a sense of mourning for the loss of fortitude,

---

28   Eating foods, especially prized foods, without bread accompaniment, was considered wanton and somewhat sinful (cf. *companatico*, in Italian, meaning everything that could accompany the main food—that is, bread; on bread in Italian folk culture, see Del Giudice 1997). We even have a term for it in our dialect: *cannarutizia*, and one so guilty is called a *cannarutə/a* (large-throated, big-gulleted). Of course, in those cholestrol-innocent days, we were expected to eat all the fat attached to whatever meat was being served, including the long strand of disconcertingly white fat that ran the length of a slice of *prosciutto*. *Hand*-sliced *prosciutto* could make the width of meat wonderfully thick, but that of fat disgustingly so.

29   Is wine good for you, I asked? "*Per dio se fa bene!* (By God it is!). You go to Italy and doctors will tell you that a glass of wine, not more, is great for you. It is *come lu furmaggio sop'ai maccaronə* (like cheese on pasta). . . . These *magnachecchi* (*magnacake* (It. dialect) / *mangiachecchi* (It. pl.) / *Mangiacake* (Italiese) or "*Cake*" > "*Cake-Eater*") doctors, don't understand anything, but now they are changing because they're beginning to understand from us."

virility, health, and one's own youth. Some room for optimism exists though, for as Magnotta has noted, a recent trend toward home wine (and beer) making will mean that the art will not be completely lost, even though it may no longer be linked to traditional methods. And the *cantina* continues to be filled with plenty of Italian foods, although not necessarily handmade, for thrift continues to be considered a virtue.[30]

In the old days wine flowed in our house, and the *cantina* was well-stocked with glass gallons, as well as musty old barrels and pressing equipment. Two bypass surgeries for my father have meant that only a demijohn or two of wine remain in his shared *cantina*. His wine-pressing equipment, no longer needed, remains a curious artifact of an earlier time. For decades, wine and winemaking had appeared to me shrouded in mystery. Only through fieldwork did the relative simplicity of winemaking reveal itself, although accompanied by a glimpse of a very rich and complex cultural system behind it, which I am only now beginning to decipher. I have also come to appreciate that many of my wine attitudes have largely been shaped by Italian traditional culture: that is, wine should be consumed with meals (not before); drunkenness is intolerable; wines should be honest and simple, and so forth. I have little patience with the fetishisms, high cost, and hoopla of wine connoisseurship—all a matter of silly excess. And I have come to appreciate why a now deceased brother-in-law, Giuseppe (Pep) Poldi (a quintessential Terracinese, to my mind; Del Giudice 2001b), didn't care if he drank wine that came from a *plastic* bottle, so long as it was intrinsically good (*genuino*), and could be put to good *convivial* effect. I now have Pep's well-worn and absolutely ordinary wine glasses, as a reminder of his love of wine and the many outdoor *(a)bbendate* (grilling parties) behind their hilltop house in Terracina, overlooking the sea and olive groves.

What caused me to venture into this foreign land? Perhaps wine culture acquired special significance for me only recently, as my father's health began to ebb. In April of 1998, he faced slight chances of surviving his second bypass surgery at the age of seventy-five. While

---

30　It may be a peasant heritage, or the home winemaker's eye to thrift, which inspired Magnotta's motto, Affordable Excellence. The economic factor is still a crucial one favoring the continuation of home winemaking. One man insisted that few would continue to make their own wine if wine stores sold reasonably priced wines. Making wine from juice or grapes varies in cost from $1.50 to $3.00 per bottle.

he lay on a hospital bed facing the grim future, I tried to bring forth happy and restorative memories through wine talk, allowing us intimacy without emotive effusions. These charged moments elicited deep memory. As he spoke into the microphone, I was painfully aware that these might be his last recorded words. I tried to understand how wine, life, death, and memory might be connected.

My father's wine press awaits shipping to my home in Los Angeles. I am honored and burdened by the responsibility of this gift. Beware the (family) gifts you accept, for eventually they exercise an irresistible pull and seem to call on you, perhaps against your will, to pay *them* homage.[31] But if wine *did* make good blood, it did so for me too, and on many fronts. The "bad blood" between my father and me, from those estranged adolescent years, has been replaced by the good. When I visit him in Toronto, I often joyfully share in his wine. We are reconciled, and through research such as this, I have come to more fully understand and appreciate him. Wine is healthful and life-giving, but so are wine memories. Is it ironic that sickness and fear of death brought many such memories urgently to the fore? In thrifty peasant fashion, in fact, together we seemed to be pressing all possible substance from the grape, to the last drop and beyond, so that even the fermented vapors themselves—the ethereal and evanescent wine memories—might sustain life still.

WORKS CITED

L'alimentazione nella tradizione vicentina. 1998, edited by Gruppo di Ricerca sulla Civiltà Rurale. Vicenza: Accademia Olimpica.

Atlante linguistico italo-svizzero: Sprach-und Sachatlas Italiens und der Südschweiz (Italian–Swiss Atlas). 1929–1940. Eight volumes, edited by Karl Jaberg and Jakob Jud. Zurich: Ringier.

Alaimo, Emma. 1974. *Proverbi siciliani.* Florence: Martello-Giunti.

---

31 For other such charged gifts—a rosary from my grandmother and an archaic written prayer from my great aunt, both of whom were healers—and the spiritual odyssey these entailed, see Del Giudice 2001b.

Bernardi, Ulderico. 1994. *A catàr fortuna: Storie venete d'Australia e del Brasile*. Vicenza: Neri Pozza.

Bernardi, Ulderico. 1995. *Creaturam vini: I riti del vino*. Milano: Camunia.

Ciceri, Andreina Nicoloso. 1983. *Tradizioni popolari in Friuli*, Vols. 1 and 2. Udine: Chiandetti.

Clements, William M. 1990. "Winemaking and Personal Cosmology: A Piedmontese-American Example." *New York Folklore* 16, no. 1–2 (January 1): 17–24.

Cultura popolare nell'Emilia Romagna: Espressioni sociali e luoghi d'incontro. 1978. Milan: Silvana.

Del Giudice, Luisa. 1993. "The 'Archvilla': An Italian Canadian Architectural Archetype." In *Studies in Italian American Folklore*, edited by Luisa Del Giudice, 53–105. Logan: Utah State University Press.

Del Giudice, Luisa. 1994. "Italian Traditional Song in Toronto: From Autobiography to Advocacy." *Journal of Canadian Studies*, 29 (Spring): 74–89.

Del Giudice, Luisa. 1997. "Tomie de Paola and the Writing/Illustrating of Italian Folk Culture." *Italian Americana*, Winter: 22–30.

Del Giudice, Luisa. 1998. "Paese di Cuccagna." In *Encyclopedia of Folklore and Literature*, edited by Mary Ellen Brown and Bruce Rosenberg, 487–489. Santa Barbara: ABC Clio.

Del Giudice, Luisa. 2001a. "Mountains of Cheese and Rivers of Wine: *Paesi di Cuccagna* and other Gastronomic Utopias." Chapter 1 this volume. First published in *Imagined States: Nationalism, Utopia, and Longing in Oral Cultures*, edited by Luisa Del Giudice and Gerald Porter. Logan: Utah State University Press.

Del Giudice, Luisa. 2001b. "Cursed Flesh: Faith Healers, Black Magic, and Death in a Central Italian Town." In *Italian American Review* (John Calandra Institute) 8, no. 2: 45–56. A revised version was published in 2011 in *Italian Folk: Vernacular*

Culture in Italian-American Lives, edited by Joseph Sciorra, 189–196. New York: Fordham University Press.

Galanti, Bianca Maria. 1981. *Proverbi laziali commentati*. Palermo: Edikronos.

Lolli, Giorgio, Emidio Serianni, Grace M. Golder, and Pierpaolo Luzzatto-Fegiz. 1958. *Alcohol in Italian Culture: Food and Wine in Relation to Sobriety among Italians and Italian Americans*. Yale Center of Alcohol Studies, Monograph 3. New Haven: Free Press.

Magnotta, Rossana. 1988. *Winemaking Made Simple: The Festa Way*. Toronto: Festa Juice. https://www.festajuice.com/Files/winemaker/FestaWay_EN.pdf.

Malpezzi, Frances M., and William M. Clements. 1992. *Italian-American Folklore*. Little Rock: August House.

Merisio, Pepi. 1983. *Mestieri d'una volta*. Milano: Silvana.

Migliore, Sam. 1996. "Wine, Health, and Sociability: An Italian Family Experience in Cape Breton." In *The Centre of the World at the Edge of a Continent: Cultural Studies of Cape Breton Island*, edited by Carol Corbin and Judith Rolls, 221–33. Sydney, Nova Scotia: University College of Cape Breton Press.

Montanari, Massimo. 1993. *La fame e l'abbondanza: Storia dell'alimentazione in Europa*. Roma: Laterza.

Nusca, Mark. 1998. "Grapes of Wrath." In *Eyetalian*, Summer: 24–27.

Rossetti, Barolomeo. 1979. *I bulli di Roma: Storie e avventure d'amore e di coltello da Jacaccio ar più de l'Urione: Quattro secoli di vita sociale e di costume*. Roma: Newton Compton.

Simboli, Ben James. 1985. "Acculturated Italian-American Drinking Behavior." In *The American Experience with Alcohol: Contrasting Cultural Perspectives*, edited by Linda A. Bennett and Genevieve M. Ames, 61–76. New York, London: Plenum.

Figure 2.1: Traditional demijohns protected with basketry and bushel baskets in the Di Ninno cantina. Note the potted bay tree weathering the cold winter there.

Figure 2.2: *Prosciutto* (ham) curing in the Di Ninno cantina.

Figure 2.3: The Del Bianco cantina with tomato jars, cured *soppressata*, and aging Friulano cheese.

Figure 2.4: The D'Angelo cantina, with homemade *soppressata* and *prosciutto* curing.

Figure 2.5: D'Angelo's homemade cheeses curing.

Figure 2.6: Freshly gathered snails in the Belli cantina.

Figure 2.7

Figure 2.8

Figures 2.7–2.8: Stylized hand-painted murals at Cilento Wines, Vaughan, "demonstrating the old world tradition of wine making."

Figure 2.9: Home winemaking supplies at Magnotta Winery, Vaughan.

3. Rituals of Charity and Abundance: Sicilian St. Joseph's Tables and Feeding the Poor in Los Angeles

In memory of Virginia Buscemi Carlson
Villafranca Sicula, Agrigento, Sicily, July 9, 1935–
Downey, California, January, 28, 2007

INTRODUCTION

This essay explores the mid-Lenten Tavola di San Giuseppe (St. Joseph's Table) in Los Angeles, situates this tradition within its historical and geographic cultural contexts, and seeks to interpret its various meanings.[1] The custom of preparing food altars or tables in honor of

---

The internal chronology of this essay has not been updated, for the most part, and reflects the dates and cited references of the original publication.

1   This essay was first published in *California Italian Studies* 1, no. 2 (2010), https://doi.org/10.5070/C312008894. Unless otherwise noted, translations and photographs are mine.

These conjoined phenomena have been researched and reported in various formats and settings: "St. Joseph's Tables and Feeding the Poor in Los Angeles" (American Folklore Society annual meeting in Lafayette, Louisiana, Oct. 1995; Culinary Historians of Southern California, Los Angeles Public Library, March 13, 2004; All Saints Church, Pasadena, Women's Council, March 5, 2005; Academy of Sciences, Ljubljana, Slovenia, April, 2004); "Joseph Among the Angels: St. Joseph's Tables and Feeding the Poor in Los Angeles" (Dept. of Cultural Affairs, *Living Roots '97* Conference, Los Angeles, April 12, 1997); "Italian Folklife in California: Continuity of Tradition" (Conference on *Italian Migration in the United States*, Los Angeles, Istituto Italiano di Cultura, February 7, 1998); "Food and Ritual Performance: St. Joseph's Day Tables and Feeding the Poor in Los Angeles" (annual meeting of the American Italian Historical Association, San Francisco,

St. Joseph is an expression of Southern Italian (conspicuously Sicilian) folk religion with various elements at its core. On the one hand, it represents a propitiatory sharing of abundance and the cultural exorcism of hunger. On the other—within its Italian Christian matrix—it is an affirmation of the patriarchal family, as well as an intertwining practice of hospitality and *caritas*. Finally, in its diaspora manifestations, it presents a symbolic representation of the migration narrative itself, transposed in the Josephine dramatization of the Holy Family's Flight into Egypt, along with an immigrant success story as codicil.

I will reconstruct the cartographies and stratified meanings of this food ritual in Los Angeles, largely employing the methodologies of oral historical and ethnographic research, but, as this narrative moves into the

November 11–13, 1999); "The Invisible Made Visible: St. Joseph's Day Tables and Applied Oral History in Los Angeles" (International Oral History Association meeting, Istanbul, June 2000); "Food and Ritual Performance in the Sicilian American St. Joseph's Feast" (Symposium on *Women and Food*, Women's Studies, The Huntington Library, November 23, 2002); "The Invisible Made Visible: Food and Ritual Performance in the Sicilian St. Joseph's Day Feast" (Series on *Art and Ritual*, UCLA Department of Art, March 3, 2005); "Sicilian St. Joseph's Tables and Feeding the Poor: Ritual Food Practices and Social Advocacy" (Istituto Italiano di Cultura, Addis Ababa, Ethiopia, Feb. 23, 2010).

I wish to thank for their assistance in documenting tables over the years: Virginia Buscemi Carlson, Kenneth Carlson, Doug De Luca, Jennifer Pendergrass, Kenneth Scambray, Raymond Skelton, Steve Weimeyer, and Erica Turley. My thanks to all those who have participated by being interviewed for this study (too many to mention), opening their parishes, their homes, and their hearts. I especially thank those who helped make possible the UCLA Hammer Museum's exhibition "St. Joseph's Table and Feeding the Poor:" my co-curator and friend (to whom this study is dedicated and who is no more), Virginia Buscemi Carlson, as well as Carmen Alongi, Matteo Alongi, Robert Barbera, Maria Battaglia, Charlie Campo, Kenneth Carlson, Vita Circo, Gaetano D'Aquino, Celestino Drago, the Federico Bakery, Stefano Finazzo, Maribel Gonzalez, Lucy Guastella, Concetta and Antonio Pellegrino, Sam Perricone, Carlo Piumetti, Mimmi Pizzati, Joseph També, Edward F. Tuttle, and Elena Tuttle. The table was blessed by the Reverend Father Vincenzo Buccheri while the chants were offered by members of the St. Joseph Society of Mary Star of the Sea Church, San Pedro. I also thank colleagues and friends who have read and commented on earlier versions of this essay: Elizabeth Bisbee Goldfarb, Edward F. Tuttle, Dorothy Noyes, Joseph També, Charlene Villaseñor Black, and the journal's reviewers.

twenty-first century, I will consider the Sicilian American tradition as it confronts further demographic shifts and diverse recontextualizations, and I will extend my analysis to encompass contemporary initiatives of interethnic understanding and social advocacy. While this essay builds on previous writings on concepts of abundance and gastronomic utopias, on food practices among Italian immigrants (Del Giudice 2000, 2001a, 2001b), and on the capital role played by food in Italian cultural identity, this study of food altars and communal rituals of charity also seeks to integrate an "ethnography of compassion" that I began explicitly embracing over three decades ago (Behar 1999, 1996; cf. Del Giudice 2009a; cf. González 2003), which bridges academic discourse and social engagement.

I first saw a St. Joseph's Table in 1989 while mapping the Italian community of Los Angeles for the City's Cultural Affairs Department's Folk and Traditional Arts Program. The department wanted to know *who* and *where* the Italians were in this sprawling city, for they appeared to be invisible, despite the fact that, according to the latest 2000 census, Los Angeles counts itself the fifth largest city in the US for population of Italian descent. While earlier Italians had been amply documented by California historian Gloria Ricci Lothrop,[2] the more recent presence of Italians had yet to be fully assessed. My ethnographically inclined *A Preliminary Survey of Italian Folklife in Los Angeles* (Del Giudice 1990), which metamorphosed in 2005 into www.ItalianLosAngeles. org,[3] helped continue the documentation effort. I especially looked at Italian social and ceremonial life, the community's associations,

---

2   For an extensive bibliography of Lothrop's writings, including her *Italians in Los Angeles*, 2003, see "Further Readings: Italians of Southern California," http://www.italianlosangeles.org/index.php?1&223&224. On the early Little Italy of Los Angeles, see Gatto 2009, *Los Angeles's Little Italy*.

3   The Web site www.ItalianLosAngeles.org was a project of the nonprofit Italian Oral History Institute (IOHI)—which I founded and directed from 2000 to 2007 (formerly known as the Italian Oral History Project, 1994–2000)—and was conducted in collaboration with UCLA students and community volunteers. For the genesis of the IOHI, an outgrowth of my Italian folklife courses at UCLA, and the evolution of this project, see "About Us," http://www.italianlosangeles. org/index.php?20. The IOHI, a unique institution which bridged academic and public sector, produced many innovative conference/festivals, and publications. It was dissolved in 2007.

foodways, markets, traditional arts, games, and so forth. Lothrop's research helped fuel the Italian community's effort to reclaim the Historic Italian Hall in the heart of the Pueblo de Los Angeles Historic Monument, beginning in 1990. The community's visibility or self-awareness has grown considerably since the early 1990s, thanks to many diverse efforts and initiatives, including the founding of the Italian American Museum of Los Angeles (IAMLA), housed in the Historic Italian Hall.[4]

Searching for Italian life and community in a city without a traditional "Little Italy"[5] was challenging. I discovered though that there were *many* Italian communities—diverse, of course, in their regional provenance, but even more so in socioeconomic status, in migration experience (including the most recent *transnationals—Italiani in fuga* [Italians in flight][6]), and in their ways of expressing ethnicity—in short, they represented all phases along the Italian–Italian American continuum. Yet, amidst all the variety, one community celebration most captured my attention: St. Joseph's feast and its tables, the evolution of which I have been observing and documenting for four decades (see Del Giudice 2014a).[7]

---

4 See "Italians in Los Angeles: Guide to a Diverse Community": http://www.italianlosangeles.org/index.php?1&221.

5 On the question of Los Angeles's "Little Italy," see Del Giudice 2007. Although resident Italians have now become rare in the area, the community in and around St. Peter's Italian Church, Casa Italiana (in present-day Chinatown) and across the Los Angeles River, in Lincoln Heights, are sometimes considered to have formed the city's historic Little Italies, while the very heart of the Pueblo de Los Angeles Historic Monument counted among its business owners and residents many Italians in the nineteenth century. Los Angeles Historic Italian Hall, http://www.italianhall.org/history.php; also see note 2.

6 Italy's "brain drain" (*cervelli in fuga*) is ongoing, representing a largescale exodus of mostly young, educated Italians, seeking abroad the opportunity to exercise the professions denied to them in Italy.

7 The collections of the IOHI are currently housed in the UCLA Ethnomusicology Archive. The finding aid for this collection can be accessed at http://content.cdlib.org/view?docId=kt7870289c&chunk.id=dsc-1.2.6&brand=oac. See IOHI Collections in Works Cited for a listing of field materials on St. Joseph's Tables. I continue to add to this collection.

DESCRIPTION OF LOS ANGELES TABLES

But what exactly is a St. Joseph's Table? Here follows a description of tables observed in the Los Angeles area from 1989 to 2009. St. Joseph's feast day is March 19 but often lasts from one to three days—sometimes causing a conflict of loyalties and social scheduling for Irish-Italian American households, since St. Patrick's Day falls on the seventeenth. St. Joseph's Tables include a devotional altar with a statue (or image) of Joseph holding the infant Jesus [Figures 3.1–3.3], either rising up from the table or separate from it. The table is always blessed by a priest before the foods are consumed [Figure 3.4]. Closest to (or on) the altar is the highest concentration of sacred objects and foods, where the large, traditional, ritual braided breads (often referred to as *cucciddati*), weighing from three to seven kilograms and dedicated to the Holy Family, are placed. These largest votive breads represent: a cross or crown for Christ, a palm frond for Mary, a staff (*vastuni*) for St. Joseph [Figure 3.5].[8] Implements of the Passion (ladder, tongs, and so forth) are sometimes present [Figure 3.6], as are *emblemata* of Joseph the Carpenter's trade (saw, nails, plane), for example, as is common in Salemi (in the province of Trapani). The table is laden with elaborate food displays and more randomly distributed smaller and fanciful zoomorphic, and phytomorphic breads, in such forms as birds, flowers, animals, fish, fruit, grapes, wheat. These smaller breads also hang among verdant festoons of foliage (in Sicily, laurel or myrtle, and here, citrus).[9] Because it falls within the meatless season of Lent

---

8   See "La Festa di San Giuseppe in Sicilia," http://www.sicilyland.it/festa_san_giuseppe_sicilia.htm, for greater detail on the breads, as they are found in Acate (Ragusa): e.g., *u vastuni do Patriarca, il pane di Maria* with a rose, as well as a palm frond; and finally, *il pane di Gesù, u Bamminieddu,* decorated with jasmine, birds, and symbols of his Passion. In Puglia instead, the votive breads for the altar are basically large and donut-shaped (known as *tòrtini* in Uggiano). On the breads themselves are imprinted the various symbols identifying each saint: three circles for the Christ child; a rosary for Mary, and a walking stick for Joseph (Arcano 2007).

9   E.g., in Salemi, entire chapels *"sono rivestite interamente di mirto, alloro e adorne di pani, arance e limoni"* (are entirely covered in myrtle, laurel, and decorated with breads, oranges, and lemons;" Giallombardo [1981] 1990, 24). Since March 19 coincides with the pruning season, these greens are fairly easy

and is something of a mid-Lenten festive reprieve during a period of deprivation and fasting (although in post-Vatican II times and in some parts of Sicily meat is prepared for St. Joseph's feast day), the tables feature vegetables (fried or stuffed cauliflower, artichokes, zucchini, eggplant, peppers, cardoons, fava bean, asparagus, peas, peppers) [Figures 3.7 and 3.9], *frittate* (omelets) of every sort, literally and symbolically prominent fish [Figure 3.10], fruit (the season's finest first fruits—*primizie*—in baskets or arrangements replicating cornucopias of plenty [Figures 3.11–3.12]), and sweets: *persiche* (cream-filled pastries made to look like peaches), *cassadini/cassadeddi* (sweet ricotta filled ravioli or *panzerotti*), *sfinci* (most frequently, cream-filled puffs with cheese, chocolate, and orange zest), *cannoli*, *cucciddati* (also referring to fig and nut-filled cookies; see Piccitto 1977), *cuddureddi* (*ciambelle* or donut-shaped cookies, but also referring to round breads with a hole in the middle, variant: *cucciddati*; see Varvaro and Sornicola 1986), and increasingly today, commercial baker's confections [Figure 3.13] and even store-bought *biscotti* or *panettone*—normally a Christmas specialty originating in Lombardy. To have traditional Sicilian sweets and breads for the diasporic table today, one relies largely on home bakers, women and men in the community who know their family traditions and contribute to the tables.[10]

Although the votive breads are the key ingredient on the table, breads are increasingly giving way to cakes and cookies. Do we attribute this to an acquired American taste for sugar? (See Del Giudice 2001a,

---

to come by. Our UCLA Hammer Museum exhibition featured greenery from orange trees and kumquat bushes from my own backyard.

10   In Los Angeles, the input of traditional Sicilian bakers is waning, as many have retired or passed away, so that it is difficult to find bakers who know how to make these artistic breads and cakes. Vincent Gambino was one such baker who was known for his elaborate cakes for Casa Italiana. His cakes apparently made the front page of the daily *Herald Examiner* and the *Los Angeles Times* (oral reports). He is remembered for once making a cake in the form of the Italian peninsula, one of Sicily, and of the leaning tower of Pisa in all its detail. His pastries are missed by the Sicilian community. Virginia recalls the huge personal energy invested in these activities on the part of the women involved. She herself worked for two months on her table, making all the breads for display and for distribution. She had three freezers set up for this purpose and gave away 150 kilos of bread and nearly "killed herself" in the effort.

ch. 1 this volume.) Actually, Sicilians themselves seem to have the sweetest tooth of all regional Italians and have a long tradition of artistic marzipan confections, ritual cakes, and cookies, and a particular genius for creating faux fruit (and fish: e.g., *pesce d'uova*; *pesci di funghi*),[11] along with candy figurines (*i pupi*) of lambs, human figures, horses; sweet bones (for *i Morti*) or eyes (for St. Lucy). Marzipan fruits in realistic shapes and colors trick the eye and beckon from pastry shops every Christmas and Easter.[12] This penchant for sweets may have been formed, in part, by the Arab presence on that island centuries ago. *Nota bene*: the word for *sugar* (*zucchero*) in Italian comes to us via Sicily, which received it from the Arabic *sùkkar* (Caracausi 1983, 407; Mintz 1987, on history of sugar).

The table tradition also features a pageant of the costumed Holy Family (*i santi*), with the addition of an angel or two, who process from door to door, are twice turned away, and then ultimately find shelter and food at the home of the family sponsoring the table. While private tables are normally given by one devotee and his or her family, friends, neighbors, business associates, and others may make donations of food or money to the host family. A devotee must "beg" for these donations. The public feast in such a multiethnic environment as Los Angeles also frequently becomes an expression of ethnicity (Italian or Sicilian), in what, in the jargon of folklorists, is called an "ethnic display event" (e.g., with flags, ethnic costumes, banners).

One of the most fully articulated celebrations occurs at Mary Star of the Sea Church in San Pedro. A procession with saint's niche is accompanied by women (and men) of the St. Joseph Society, with

---

11   Given the Sicilian genius for creating *trompe l'oeil* foods of one sort and another, it is interesting to note that bread and breadcrumbs, mixed with vegetables, frequently are modeled to imitate fish (another sacred symbol of the St. Joseph Table)—e.g., *pesci d'uova*; *pesci di funghi*—continuing in savory dishes the delight of sweet marzipan faux foods such as *frutta di Mortarana* (Field 1997, 395).

12   Uccello's 1976 seminal work on Sicilian breads and sweets includes many beautiful photographs of Martorana fruits, Easter and Christmas hearts, jellied candies, bones of the dead for All Souls day, eyes of St. Lucy, and many others for a variety of nature and life-cycle occasions. Another valuable and exhaustive study, including visual documentation of Easter ritual breads, can be found in Ruffino 1995, which features Easter wreaths concealing eggs in a variety of fanciful shapes: e.g., doves, pineapple, baskets, donkey, horse and cart, etc.

Vita Gracchiolo† or other members periodically rallying the devoted with the traditional cry of "*Viva Gesù, Maria, Giuseppe, evviva!*" and followed by children in ethnic costumes, a marching band, with guilds, societies, and confraternities behind their banners, and ending in a large banquet including *pasta e ceci* (a chickpea soup with small noodles) and seafood salad (or fried calamari), courtesy of the fishermen of this port city [Figures 3.13–3.17].[13] This was (and still is) the parish church of two Italian island fishing communities—the Sicilians and from farther north, off the coast of Naples, the Ischians—as well as of the Croat fishermen of San Pedro.[14] The church has its own St. Joseph Society, founded by Sicilian women [Figures 3.18], whose yearly task it is to organize the public charity event and feed hundreds from the church kitchen. In Sicily, confraternities played a large role in the public celebrations. In 1998, when we curated the UCLA Hammer Museum table (n.8 and infra), the society was celebrating its twenty-fifth anniversary and was present to sing novenas. Indeed, along with elaborate foodways, a significant number of Sicilian oral expressions (songs, orations) dedicated to St. Joseph have also been maintained among local Sicilian women.[15]

---

13 Among the obligatory dishes at a Pugliese table are instead fish and *lambascioni* (wild onions)—along with ritual breads in the shape of a large donut (Arcano 2007). In some areas of southern Puglia, there are nine obligatory dishes that the saints must eat, in this order: 1. *i lambascioni* (wild onions); 2. *i vermiceddhri* (*vermicelli*, a pasta dish); 3. *i bucatini al miele e con mollica di pane fritta* (pasta with honey and fried bread crumbs); 4. *i ceci bolliti in "pignata"* (chickpeas cooked in a terracotta pot); 5. *i cavoli lessi con olio d'oliva* (boiled cabbage dressed with olive oil); 6. *il pesce fritto* (fried fish); 7. *lo stoccafisso al sugo e cipolle* (cod with onion and tomato sauce); 8. *le pittole e i fritti al miele* (pittole and fried dough drizzled with honey); 9. *il finocchio* (fennel). The meal is accompanied by wine, of course. On Pugliese tables, see also "Tavole di San Giuseppe," n.d., and "Le tavole di San Giuseppe," n.d.

14 Since 2004, the Associazione Ischitani nel Mondo has published a journal on emigrant Ischian communities, including that of San Pedro, California: *Pe' terre assaje luntane: L'emigrazione ischitana verso le Americhe* (e.g., Del Giudice 2007, ch. 4 this volume).

15 A novena dedicated to St. Joseph hinges on "*Lu viaggiu di San Giuseppi*" (the voyage of St. Joseph) and was sung by blind *cantastorie* (street performers) in Sicily, with the accompaniment of organ and violin. "*A Trapani i mercuri sulenni furono istituiti con prediche e musica da Fra' Santo di San Domenico*" (In Trapani,

HISTORY OF THE CULT OF ST. JOSEPH

In placing the evolution of the cult of St. Joseph in its Eastern Mediterranean, Western European, and thence European diaspora contexts, one must necessarily consider certain key narratives with their accompanying iconographies and how these were used by the Catholic Church. With prominent Spanish leadership, Counter-Reformation theology carefully guided Josephine iconography and continued to shape folk religious traditions around the patron feast day of St. Joseph in Italy and on into New World Sicilian devotional life. This historic overview, therefore, may help us better understand the sources of the Sicilian custom under study.

The carefully crafted image of St. Joseph as the patriarchal *paterfamilias*—of the Holy Family and the Universal Church— promoted not only the veneration of fatherhood in Joseph, but of male authority within the Catholic Church, and it encouraged reverence

---

solemn Wednesdays were instituted, with sermons and music by a Holy Brother from San Domenico). For oral expressions recorded in Los Angeles, see materials in the IOHI Collections. A "St. Joseph Rosary and Song Book" assembled by Rosalia Manzella Orlando (and dedicated to her mother Paolina Manzella and to Giuseppa La Fata) for the St. Joseph Society of Mary Star of the Sea Church, San Pedro, lists eleven songs and prayers for St. Joseph and two for the Madonna. One of the St. Joseph's songs in Sicilian (7) is the "A Trapani, . . ."

Canzoncina a San Giuseppe

Dio vi salvi Giuseppi	Li santi pi vui l'amuri
Cu Cristu e cu Maria	L'affettu e lu piaciri
Sta bedda cumpagnia	Unn'aiu chi vi riri
A vui fu data (2 times)	Aiu vita e morti (2 times)
A vui fu cunsignata	Morti vurria la sorte
Maria la virginedda	D'avirivi l'assistenti
Tutta pura e tutta bedda	Gesù Maria e Giuseppi
A vui tuccau (2 times)	Eternamenti (2 times)
Di li santi fustivu elettu	Cantari vurria sempre
Di Diu fustivu amatu	Maria di l'auri santi
Fedeli miu avvocatu	St'armuzza mia si impigna
E prutitturi (2 times)	E si ni va cuntenti (2 times)

for paternal authority in the heart of all Catholic families in the most intimate foyer of domestic life. This patriarchal narrative was likely conceived as a counterbalance to the far more ancient and ingrained veneration of the feminine divine in the form of the Madonna. In *Creating the Cult of St. Joseph*, UCLA art historian Charlene Villaseñor Black masterfully demonstrates the theology and politics behind the cult of St. Joseph. At its most extreme, the image of Father and Son attempts to displace (literally to dethrone) the iconography upon which it was closely modeled, that of Madonna and Child. The visual instance of a deferential Mary actually on her knees at the feet of her husband and son (2006, 67) is particularly striking for its inversion. At its most benevolent, the image of Joseph as a "mothering father" (cradling, embracing, and teaching his son a trade) fostered new discourses around masculinity in Hispanic society, thereby encouraging new models of: 1) engaged fatherhood and 2) useful manual labor— neither of which prevailed at the time. Alongside Joseph's image as the nurturing[16] "foster father" of Jesus, were equally compelling images of the worker–saint (Joseph the Carpenter)[17] and the Holy Family's

---

16 How does the Sicilian St. Joseph tradition play with gender roles? Turner and Seriff (1987) give a feminist reading of the private tables observed in Texas, exploring how the "ideology of reproduction" at its center sacralizes "woman's work" of nurturing and caring—always the focus of the tables themselves. Women cook the foods, bake the breads; they literally feed the saints. Therefore, although St. Joseph is indeed the namesake of this feast, it celebrates *women's work*, for the altar is actually a "*woman's altar*." So too is an altar normally a response to a *woman's* vow; and it is the *women* who sing novenas to the saint. Men instead roughly function as helpmates and do the heavy lifting. In other words, according to the authors, the public event outwardly focuses on the male saint as a *paterfamilias*, while the private event (the actual preparation of the altar) focuses on woman's work. The tables observed in Los Angeles cannot be said to *strictly* adhere to this division of labor, for men cooked the pasta, stirred the sauce, and baked the bread (as professional bakers) alongside the women. And men were as much "givers" of tables (e.g., També, Perricone) as were women (e.g., Buscemi Carlson, Vaccaro). The *majority* of the cooking and baking, the singing of novenas, and especially the intimate knowledge of culinary traditions, were clearly in the women's domain, however. On Texan traditions, see also Texas Tavola, 2007. Circe Sturm gave a report on these elaborate Texas tables at the 2008 annual meeting of the American Italian Historical Association in New Haven.

17 But more accurately the "builder" < Greek *tèkton*, which the *Vulgate* translated as FABER.

Flight into Egypt (Joseph as Migrant)—all images amply repeated throughout the Catholic world, Old and New.[18]

Does this Hispanic cult have much to do with tradition in Southern Italy? It is well to remember the centuries-long presence of the Spanish hierarchy (largely through Aragonese Viceroys from 1409–1516; as direct rulers from 1516–1713; through Neapolitans until 1816), and its affiliated religious institutions in Sicily (and the Italian South).[19] Thanks in part to Spanish hegemony, Joseph became deeply rooted in Sicilian soil. Although the official cult may have been created to counter that of Mary, it was likely reappropriated and made popular among Sicilians.[20] Mary, however, resurfaces in the pageant that accompanies the Sicilian tables, reaffirming the Earthly Trinity. She is also hailed, along with Joseph and son, in the ritual calls of the devoted. We will return to this issue below. Here follows a brief summary of the cult's rise and evolution.

During the first centuries of Christianity, the private cult of Joseph appears to have arisen in the Eastern Church (e.g., among Egyptian Copts), while the public and liturgical cult was not codified till much later during the fourteenth and fifteenth centuries. St. Bonaventure

18   Despite concerted efforts to promote such gendered imagery in New Spain, colonials reverted to a more indigenous veneration of the Mexican Madonna, i.e., la Virgen de Guadalupe (Villaseñor Black 2006, 157 f.).

19   See "List of Viceroys of Sicily," http://en.wikipedia.org/wiki/List_of_ Spanish_Viceroys_of_Sicily. "Dynastically, the rulers of Aragon and then all Spain occasionally controlled not only Sicily but much of southern Italy (the Kingdom of Naples). Several, including the remarkable Charles V, were Hapsburgs who ruled not only Spain and her possessions but also Austria and various lands of central Europe. This period lasted for over two hundred years, until the War of the Spanish Succession and the brief reign (1713–1720) of Vittorio Amadeo of Savoy."

20   The Josephine cult indeed is considered to be largely the product of Spain: "Il tipo devozionale di Giuseppe, sempre più diffuso a partire dal secolo XVI ha origine in Spagna. Il culto di San Giuseppe ha un suo vertice nella cappella di San José in Toledo, dove si trovava inizialmente anche il quadro di *San Giuseppe* dipinto da El Greco." (The devotional genre of St. Joseph, evermore popular, beginning in the 16th C, had its origins in Spain. We see the height of the cult of St. Joseph in the San José Chapel of Toledo, where initially El Greco's painting of St. Joseph also was to be found. See: "*San Giuseppe: Padre putativo*"). For a detailed consideration of this cult, see especially Villaseñor Black 2006. See also Stramare 1993 for the contemporary cult.

(1212–1274) and St. Teresa of Avila (1515–1582) were counted among Joseph's most ardent promoters. Indeed, until the early Middle Ages, Saint Joseph is rarely depicted, and where he does appear, he is included in groupings with patriarchs and ancestors of Christ. One of the earliest depictions of the saint in his own right, holding the emblematic flowering branch, is in a fresco at Santa Croce, Florence, by Taddeo Gaddi (1332–1338).

Although the Gospels speak little about Joseph, the Evangelists' relative silence was embellished by theologians who created a rich narrative tapestry upon which iconography rested and with which it interplayed. We learn of a series of premonitory dreams in which Joseph was: a) reassured of pregnant Mary's purity and his decision to marry and protect her (and the future Messiah, of course); b) warned of Herod's murderous intent on the innocents of Bethlehem in order to prevent the reign of the Magi-announced Messiah, and c) warned that the family should flee into Egypt, coupled with the subsequent admonition to return to Nazareth from Egypt after Herod's death. We know that Joseph is of the royal lineage of David (see Luke's lengthy genealogy, ch. 3), although he exercised the humble profession of builder (carpenter), and that he died of natural causes with his son and wife by his side. St. Joseph is known simply as "a just man." Later he is persistently referred to as Jesus's "foster father" (*"il padre putativo"* in Italian; paraphrasing Luke, ch. 3.23). Many additional narratives however (e.g., the story of St. Joseph the Carpenter, widely diffused in the fourth century) largely derive from Eastern Apocrypha. From this Eastern cultural and religious milieu derives the image of Joseph as an old man (sometimes a widower; hence the predominance of early depictions of the saint with a long white beard, infra *"la varva* [<barba] *di S. Giuseppe"*). But in essence, Joseph was a silent saint. Indeed, the story of Joseph within the Church seems to be one of increasing presence and focus. Joseph comes in from the wings to center stage. To literalize this metaphor, we recall: *"è noto come la genesi del teatro religioso cristiano sia da cercare in ambienti appartenenti alla Chiesa orientale, prima attraverso la drammatizzazione della Passione, in seguito anche degli episodi legati alla Natività"* (It is well known that the origins of Christian religious drama are to be found in settings related to the

Eastern Church, first in its dramatizations of the Passion, and later also in the events relating to the Nativity. Giallombardo 1990 [1981], 9). According to this scholar, the Flight into Egypt pageantry present in Sicilian St. Joseph traditions directly relates to Eastern Byzantine tradition. It might do well to remember, however, that liturgical drama existed in all parts of the Catholic world. Nonetheless, among his iconographic attributes, Joseph is depicted with a flowering branch, a walking staff, carpenter's tools, and a lily (symbol of purity). By 1538, a St. Joseph's carpenters' guild was founded in Rome (San Giuseppe dei Falegnami), dedicating its St. Joseph Church in 1596.

In the West, the tradition develops from the eighth century forward, while the date of his feast fluctuates, for several centuries, between July 20 and March 20. Joseph is closely associated with Benedictine monastic settings, but by the end of the fourteenth century, most all the major orders, starting with the Franciscans (1399), adopt this patron feast day, although with alternating dates all over Europe. In 1479, the feast of March 19 enters the rite but was celebrated only in Rome, thereby contributing to an increasingly public and liturgical cult. In 1621, Gregory XV instituted March 19 as an obligatory feast day for the entire Church. A few decades later, thanks to the Carmelites in Italy and Spain, the new celebration (*Patrocinio di San Giuseppe*) was officially adopted by the Church. Many confraternities (especially carpenters) elected him as their patron saint. In 1714, Clement XI accorded to Joseph his own mass and special offices. In 1870, Pope Pius IX extended the patronage of St. Joseph to the Universal (i.e., worldwide Catholic) Church, celebrated on the third week after Easter. In 1955, this feast was abolished and was substituted by Pius XII with a celebration of Saint Joseph the Worker on May 1 (co-opting the Communist International Worker's Day). The celebration of Joseph's marriage to Mary was abolished in 1961 (Giallombardo 1990; "San Giuseppe: Padre putativo").

Giallombardo points to the heavy Byzantine influence on the Sicilian church, hence accounting, in part, both for the early presence of the *dramma sacro* in Sicily (thence on the genre's influence on Sicilian traditional cultural forms, such as the St. Joseph's pageant), and on the figure of Joseph himself as an older man (supra. *la varva di San Giuseppe*). Indeed, many of the prayers, songs, and novenas in honor of St. Joseph[21] insist on his old age. Joseph's great age became hotly contested, and the Western Catholic Church came to strongly oppose it since the advanced age (and implied impotence) of the holy husband appeared to devalue the virginity of Mary. The Western Josephine iconography came to insist instead on the saint's *younger* age and vitality before reevaluations of Joseph returned him to his older age in the fifteenth century.

In its Sicilian traditional adaptations, according to Giallombardo, the cult of St. Joseph seems to represent a confluence of earlier Eastern and later Western Church influence. The fact that Sicily for a long time came within the orbit of the Eastern Church also meant that it tended to accept non-Catholic versions of Church teachings. If we look at the entire panoply of Sicilian festivities, we indeed find the stratification of the two traditions. In Sicily, in fact, Josephine devotions go from January to September, with many and varied elements finding expression therein, from pre-Christian fertility rites (food abundance, bonfires, and ritual breads) to strictly Christian ritual dramatizations, iconography, and narrative.

The variant forms taken by Josephine celebrations may well result from syntheses of historically layered, anthropological, and ethnographic convergences. This semantic accumulation is present, if latent, in the various forms of his feast day in the communities that celebrate him. Joseph has been invoked by multiple categories of supplicants, a fact which points to his de facto versatility and the range of meanings his narrative embodies. His diverse attributes (e.g., Joseph the Worker, Joseph the Carpenter, A Just Man, Joseph the Patriarch, Joseph and

---

21 The IOHI Collections (2000–2007) include several recordings of such chants (e.g., "San Giuseppuzzu," frequently sung as a novena on successive nights leading up to March 19) by Sicilian women in the Los Angeles area. Vita Gracchiolo, a font of Sicilian religious oral traditions (e.g., songs, orations, sung rosaries, ritual calls), and other women, were recorded by me in San Pedro after the blessing of the private table given at the home of Maria and Agostino Vaccaro, on March 17, 1995. Chants sung in Upland, California, at the private table given by the "Arbresche" (= ethnic Albanian, from Piana degli Albanesi) Mistretta family in March 1998, were recorded by Kenneth Scambray. There are several St. Joseph songs in Sicilian that are still sung, e.g., the novena.

the Good Death) have earned him a great number of confraternities, professions, social groups, and even nations that have adopted him as their patron saint. He is the patron saint of workers, carpenters, economists, solicitors, fathers (= Italian Father's Day), the dying, the poor and marginalized, of lost causes.[22] The list continues:

> Innumerevoli sono le categorie che lo considerano loro speciale patrono: viene invocato per l'infanzia, gli orfani, i vergini, la gioventù, le vocazioni sacerdotali, le famiglie cristiane, i profughi, gli esiliati. É speciale patrono degli operai in genere e segnatamente dei falegnami e degli artigiani. Si ricorre a lui inoltre per le malattie agli occhi, per gli ammalati gravi ed in particolare per i moribondi.

> (Innumerable groups consider him their special patron; he is invoked for childhood, orphans, virgins, youth, the priestly vocations, Christian families, refugees, and exiles. He is the special patron of workers in general, and specifically of carpenters and artisans. He is also called upon for diseases of the eyes, for those gravely ill, and especially for the dying; Giallombardo 1990).

As an old and slightly comical figure, he was even considered the patron saint of drunks, and so too the patron of cuckolds (especially in medieval times). As a saint always accompanied by his (flowering) walking staff, and as the journeying saint, I would posit that he might make an ideal patron saint of migrants (see infra). St. Joseph indeed seems to do overtime as an all-purpose worker–saint. Attesting to the popularity of the saint in Italy is the ubiquity of the name *Giuseppe* throughout the Italian peninsula from Trento to Palermo. *Giuseppe* is the most popular name given males (paired with *Maria* for women), judging by 1982 telephone directories studied by Emidio De Felice (1,718,000 such). In Palermo, for example, *Giuseppe* numbered 14,303, *Salvatore* 9,408, and *Pietro* only 3,570 (1982, 91 and 332 ff).

---

22   A popular legend has Joseph arguing with God over freeing a thief (sometimes Mastrilli, a brigand of Terracina) from hell, threatening to leave Paradise and taking his wife, her dowry of saints and angels with him—suggesting perhaps, Joseph's sense of equity and his defense of social outcasts.

Sermons, both historic (see Villaseñor Black 2006) and contemporary (e.g., in conjunction with St. Joseph Tables in Los Angeles; see IOHI Collections), give us a good indication of how Joseph is to be "officially" interpreted even today. These tend to focus on Joseph's special and intimate relationship with his son, since he raised, guided, provided for, and taught the future savior of humanity, making Joseph critical to the Salvation and Redemption narrative. Joseph is always a faithful and obedient servant of God, accepting his role as good husband to Mary and as father to Jesus—an ideal family man, in other words. As a "virgin" father, he provides the ideal complement to the "virgin" mother Mary. In Sicily, in fact, the costumed threesome of the St. Joseph day pageant are alternatively referred to as *i santi* or as *i virgineddi* (even when they were *not* played by children). Further, in early iconography, this Earthly Trinity (i.e., the Holy Family) was considered to be something of a mirror image of the Heavenly Trinity and as such frequently depicted as the human incarnation of the divine family constellation (Villaseñor Black 2006). In Italy, indeed, "*s'impone la tipologia della Sacra Famiglia che nel Barocco è vista anche come Trinità Terrestre*" (the typology of the Holy Family asserts itself, which in the Baroque period is viewed as the Earthly Trinity; Giallombardo 1990). With these historic accounts as background, it is time to tackle the cartographies of St. Joseph's Tables and, more importantly, the actual substance (pardon the pun) of Sicilian devotional food practices—the focus of this essay.

GEOGRAPHIC DISTRIBUTION OF ST. JOSEPH FOOD ALTARS IN SOUTHERN ITALY

In mapping the Italian community of Los Angeles, it became apparent that many aspects of Italian folklife seemed to be especially well preserved among Sicilians. Primary among their traditions is the St. Joseph's Table. In tracing the provenance of the Los Angeles-based table tradition, I soon discovered that the altar/table tradition was widely diffused throughout Sicily. In the account of the preeminent nineteenth-century Sicilian folklorist, Giuseppe Pitrè ([1900] 1969), tables were ubiquitous. For example, in S. Croce Camerina (Province of Ragusa), at the turn of the last century, "*Non vi è quasi famiglia . . . che per devozione non imbandisca una mensa per ricevere, in onore di S. Giuseppe, della Madonna e di Gesù, tre poveri, che sceglie tra le persone più bisognose del paese*" (There is hardly a family . . . that for devotion does not make a table to receive, in honor of St. Joseph, the Madonna, and Jesus, three poor people, chosen from the town's most needy; *Feste patronali in Sicilia* 1900, as cited in Uccello 1976, 75). Although the tradition is widespread in Sicily, it appears to be strongest in the West, especially in the provinces of Palermo, Trapani, Salemi, Enna, and Agrigento. But it is also found in Ragusa, Catania, Siracusa, and the Egadi Islands. Sicilian sites with strong St. Joseph traditions—not all focusing exclusively on tables, but some on *i vampi* (bonfires; see Piciotto 1977) or other associated aspects of the richly stratified festa—include: Alimena, Caccamo, Ganci, Monreale, Roccapalumba (Palermo); Campobello di Mazara, Gibellina, Vita (Trapani); Pietraperzia, Scicli, Valguarnera (Enna); Favara, Ribera (Agrigento); Rosolini (Siracusa); Marettimo (Isole Egadi); Acate, Santa Croce Camarina (Ragusa); Mazzarrone, Mirabella Imbaccari, Palazzo Adriano (Catania). (See "La Festa di San Giuseppe in Sicilia" n.d.)

The tables reported in the Los Angeles area for this study are represented by immigrants from Trappeto, Terrasini, Piana degli Albanesi (Palermo), Favignana (Trapani), Villafranca Sicula (Agrigento), Valguarnera Caropepe (Enna).

Nonetheless, regional variants on the table tradition can be found throughout the Italian South, although, for the most part, not as elaborately articulated (e.g., Abruzzo/Molise,[23] Lucania, and notably

---

23   Although, Giuseppe Colitti notes that, during a recent visit to the Museo da Migração in Sao Paolo, Brazil on June 21, 1998, he transcribed the elaborate list of dishes for the St. Joseph's table to be thirteen (sometimes nineteen) in the tradition of the Molise region, and that besides the Holy Family and angel, twelve guests were normally invited to play the role of the Apostles—all taking precisely assigned places at the table, and that after the recitation of prayers, the woman of the house served them in stocking feet, beginning with St. Joseph (personal communication). See www.giuseppecolitti.it and the website of the research center he directs: www.centrostudivallodidiano.it.

in the Salento, the southernmost tip of Puglia). In the area of Taranto, for instance, it is known as *la mattarèddə* (<*mattrə* <Gr. *maktira,* wooden bread trough). In other Salentine provinces of Puglia, the towns closely associated with the tables are Giurdignano, Poggiardo, Uggiano la Chiesa, Cocumola, Minervino di Lecce, Casamassella, Otranto, Lizzano, San Marzano di San Giuseppe, San Donaci.[24]

Although emigrants from all these regions may be found in the United States and are well represented in Los Angeles, St. Joseph Tables have been almost exclusively associated with Sicilian Americans. And when unable to prepare them in their New World environments, some families (e.g., the Delia and Riesi families, Sicilians of Patterson, NJ, as reported by Uccello 1976, 75) instead sent contributions back to Sicily in order to *"fare la cena al Patriarca"* (make a dinner for the Patriarch). Sicilians, I found in my Los Angeles-based research, seemed especially committed to preserving their cultural heritage. Could this be due to the increased dose of prejudice (contributing to increased insularity) felt by the earliest immigrants? Or to a presumed cultural conservatism even pre-emigration? It is unclear. As Sicilian American Virginia Buscemi Carlson (1935–2007)[25] passionately

---

24 The Salentine tables, judging from available images, seem to be distinctive in the even, replicability of the plates laid out. They are all the same (although in odd numbers and ready to be served to the saints). In Uggiano, at least, the tables do not appear to be rich and varied cornucopias of plenty but rather give the impression of a cafeteria line. Here, it is the head of the household, as St. Joseph, with his *bastone*, who signals the beginning of the meal, and strikes the ground with his staff at the successive eating rounds until the ritual meal, shared with his other saint guests, is over. As with Sicilian tables, here too the tables can be viewed by pilgrims on the eve of March 19 and throughout the next day. Frequently, a small table is set at the entrance of the home where the *"pacino"* (small bread), *lambascioni* (wild onion), and fried dough sweets can be taken away by visiting pilgrims. On March 19 instead, St. Joseph and the other saints (a minimum of three and a maximum of thirteen—again always an odd number) eat precisely the same things.

On other forms of traditional Salentine culture, notably music (including the music of the Griko minority of the Grecìa Salentina), see *Alan Lomax in Salento*; Del Giudice and Van Deusen 2005; sound recordings: *Italian Treasury: Puglia*; *Canto d'amore: Canti, suoni, voci della Grecìa salentina*; and *Bonasera a quista casa*.

25 Let me give a sense of the psychological dynamics at play in the Virginia and Sam partnership by exploring the worldview and personality of Virginia

affirmed: "Without our traditions, there would be nothing left: we would be just like everyone else" [Figure 3.19]. In 1998, it was with Virginia and the Sicilian community in Los Angeles that I had the privilege of co-curating a St. Joseph's Table [Figures 3.20–3.22] at UCLA's Armand Hammer Museum, right next to the visiting exhibition *The Invisible Made Visible: Angels from the Vatican*. The juxtaposition

---

Buscemi Carlson†. She loved all traditions, especially Sicilian and Greek; engaged in folkdances of all sorts; enjoyed Rock & Roll, Country and Western, as well as Italian and specifically Sicilian music; and ate all types of ethnic food. She assiduously watched National Geographic documentaries in her enthusiasm for learning about other cultures. Most importantly, within the context of this study, she constantly saw links across cultures (e.g., within foodways: semolina for Norwegians and Sicilians, the method of killing chickens for kosher Jews and Sicilians). She stated: "I have learned by mingling with other races that things, in the end, are very much alike." Virginia's life was living proof of the concept expressed by Juan Gutierrez (National Roundtable on Folk Arts in the Classroom) decades ago: "When you have a passion for your own traditions, you are sensitive to the traditions of others."

Virginia was proudly and even fiercely Sicilian. She served a term as president of Arba Sicula and was a local authority on all things Sicilian (which is one of the reasons Sam Perricone engaged her to make a St. Joseph's Table at St. Joseph Church). Born in Villafranca Sicula (Prov. of Agrigento), she came to New York (where her mother was born before returning to Sicily) when she was 11 years old. She moved to California only as an adult, after divorcing her first (Italian) husband. She returned to Italy in 1971 for the first time and maintained an active link with Sicilian friends and relatives. Her house was a monument to *Sicilianità* and Ken, her Swedish Norwegian husband, cheerfully supported her ethnicity. Yet Virginia was no die-hard "in-grouper," threatened and defensive. She believed that it was important to be "modern" while still valuing one's own traditions and dialect, and dismissed out of hand the snobbery of modern-day Sicilians (and Italians) who felt it was a step up the social ladder to have shed traditions and all traces of Sicilian dialect. She held up her own father (91 in 1989) as her cultural hero. He was educated, learned his Italian grammar beautifully, read novels to pass the time and enrich his command of the national language, but also freely spoke Sicilian. Indeed, it seemed to her that he was far ahead of others for knowing not one but two languages. (She regretted not having taught her children to speak Italian but attributed this reluctance to the complication of having to translate for her husband—although Ken insists he would have simply learned it.) Virginia believed Sicilians to be more strongly attached to their island's traditions than other Italians to theirs. Indeed, I too came to discover that Sicilians still danced their tarantella, knew and sang dialect songs informally, practiced their religious rituals, and widely maintained their culinary traditions.

of an abundant food altar of local folk tradition next to the imposing paintings and sculptures from Rome was curiously moving. In more ways than one, the local community (and not just the Vatican angels) was being made *visible*.

SICILIAN ST. JOSEPH TABLES
IN THE DIASPORA:
NEW ORLEANS AND LOS ANGELES

Anecdotal evidence suggests that tables are to be found all over North America, as well as in other places to which Sicilians emigrated.[26] For example, a Campanian colleague, Giuseppe Colitti, reports (via email communication) that in the late 1990s he had found a long list of the *pietanze rituali* (ritual dishes) prepared for the feast of St. Joseph at the Museo dell'Emigrante in São Paolo, Brazil. In Los Angeles, as I have noted, the custom of preparing St. Joseph's Tables is widespread and may be considered one of the major folk celebrations of the Italian community today—thanks, in part, to the efforts of the Italian Catholic Federation (ICF).[27] Not long ago, someone estimated that as many as

---

26 And they are likely present elsewhere, despite the lack of formal documentation. Anna Maria Chupa (n.d.), in her "St. Joseph's Day Altars" ("Louisiana Project: Land, Environment, Culture," Houston Institute for Culture: http://www.houstonculture.org/laproject/stjo.html), also reports researching the tables in Gretna, Louisiana, and Starkville, Mississippi. Tables have been reported in Texas as well (see Turner and Seriff 1987) and continue to be researched by Circe Sturm, who reported on these tables at the 2008 American Italian Historical Association meeting in New Haven, CT. See the film *Texas Tavola: A Taste of Sicily in the Lone Star State*, 2007, 34 min., directed by Circe Sturm and Randolph Lewis.

27 The primary sites for viewing St. Joseph's Tables in Los Angeles are Casa Italiana, the social hall adjacent to St. Peter's Italian Church (the only national parish in the Southland); Mary Star of the Sea Church (the home parish of the original fishing communities, Sicilian and Ischian, in San Pedro, Los Angeles's port community); and some years at Villa Scalabrini (the Scalabrinian retirement home in Sun Valley). Today, they are largely affiliated with churches within the Italian Catholic Federation (ICF).

It was Father Andrew Pisano (of Pugliese provenance), himself a devotee of St. Joseph, who was instrumental in diffusing the *public* table tradition via the ICF throughout Southern California. According to Pisano, the first

one hundred private and public tables were given each year.

Further, besides crossing Italian regional lines, the custom has even crossed ethnic boundaries. In New Orleans, for example, many African American Spiritualist churches where Voodoo (<Haitian *Vodou*) is practiced, have long been preparing St. Joseph's Tables. The syncretistic nature of Vodou allows for a stratification of deities where indigenous and Christian saints share identities (see Cosentino 1995). I here recall the sage words of Ralph Rinzler, cofounder of the Smithsonian Folklife Festival: "There are two ways to preserve folk culture. You can pickle it and put in on the shelf or you can share the seed" (in Bowman and Zeitlin 1993, 2). Sicilians in the diaspora have been sharing for decades.

The St. Joseph's Table in New Orleans is not an insignificant custom, given the city's high percentage of Italians from the mid-nineteenth century onward, many of whom were Sicilians. It is not surprising then that the St. Joseph tradition in New Orleans has continued to be strong.[28] Consequently, there would have been ample opportunities

---

table given publicly in a church was at Mary Star of the Sea Church in San Pedro in 1958. Previously, tables had been prepared exclusively in private homes (see Speroni 1940, for early tables in southern California). Pisano's personal view of folk tradition was rather enlightened, given the sometimes hostile attitude of clergy toward such folk cultural expressions. He stated that he felt strongly about these traditions, that they are in fact good for the faith, and that while the Bible is primary, traditions form an important corollary, as a "source of truth." Traditions are, in his view, a living *proof* of faith, and in fact, in those for whom faith is weak, folklore seems to reinforce religious observance through devotional practice. Pisano considered the tables a beautiful tradition that should be diffused throughout Los Angeles parishes. He conceded, however, that no group prepares the tables with more devotion or splendor than the Sicilians. He too recognized the danger in the loss of traditional culture and noted that the next generation does not feel these traditions as strongly and they ought to be encouraged to preserve and transmit them. At Mary Star of the Sea Church, in San Pedro, one can safely say that the tradition is deeply rooted and will not easily pass away. (See Fr. Pisano's Los Angeles Times obituary [2005] at https://www.legacy.com/us/obituaries/latimes/name/andrew-pisano-obituary?id=26538436.)

28 The "Virtual St. Joseph's Altar" provides much useful information regarding altars in Louisiana, http://www.thankevann.com/stjoseph/. It reports that the 2008 altar (its tenth) had 4,000 visitors and over 224 offerings. Members of The Greater New Orleans Italian Cultural Society (GNOICS) built their first *public*

for all ethnic groups to experience them. African Americans not only have given St. Joseph's Tables of their own, but have assimilated St. Joseph into their own pantheon of deities. Anna Maria Chupa (n.d.) reports that in her New Orleans research on Damballah, this African spirit came to be associated with St. Patrick and with Moses, and she also saw frequent references to St. Joseph. Spiritualist churches that honored Black Hawk as a patron spirit of social justice simultaneously honored St. Joseph and Moses in prominent positions on their altars.

It is clear that the St. Joseph's Table seed had fallen on fertile ground among Louisiana African Americans who themselves largely grew up in a Catholic tradition of altars, sculpted figures, and saintly iconographies. Edward Saxon (1945) notes that the attraction among Louisiana African Americans is toward the figure of St. Joseph the Worker and is invoked especially for his assistance in finding work or shelter. We may speculate that the tradition may also have appealed for a variety of other reasons: the spectacular food displays, the pageantry of costumed dramatizations, the focus on the poor and marginalized, and obviously, the symbolic value of St. Joseph himself and his defense of the humble, the hard working, and the defenseless.

The Mardi Gras spirit of Louisiana Creoles seems also to have had a profound effect on the tradition. In New Orleans, St. Joseph was married to the grand ball tradition and frequently the saint's day ended with dancing in many quarters of the city. In the past, such parties, not confined to Italians, nor even to Catholics, were ubiquitous. Apparently, African Americans frequently donned their Mardi Gras costumes on St. Joseph's night. The mid-Lenten reprieve represented by the St. Joseph calendrical occurrence might have warranted this quality of joyous festivity (see Del Giudice 2001a, ch. 1 this volume), although in its Sicilian origins, never had such abandon been observed. St. Joseph, despite the occasional merrymaking around bonfires, was more Lenten and less Carnivalesque in spirit.

---

altar in 1967 "on the front steps of the St. Joseph church on Tulane Avenue." In 1978, the altar location was moved to the Piazza D'Italia, due to inclement weather in previous years (Chupa n.d., 98). Private tables, however, had likely been given among Sicilians from their first years in Louisiana.

INTERPRETING THE TRADITION:
TABLE, ALTAR, BANQUET

Within the St. Joseph's Table tradition several convergences and morphologic syncretisms appear to have occurred over time (see Rituals of Abundance, infra.). Such layering may also be discerned in the variation in nomenclature: is it a table (*tavolata, tavola*) or an altar? That is, although the terms *altar* and *table* seem to be used almost interchangeably, they more likely represent a blurring of two historically superimposed worldviews, Antique/Classical and Christian, roughly corresponding to table and altar. Tables indeed range from the pared to the extravagant. The sacramental breads on the altar, of course, forming the minimal "table" are still the norm in private settings, where the food may instead be spread out in an altogether separate room (also likely due to constraints of physical space). Public tables seem to revel in visual gastronomic excess.

But what is the elemental relationship of the profane and sacred as it focuses on the "food altar" in honor of St. Joseph? Where precisely does the abundant, elaborate table end and the altar begin? Where is the ancient rite of spring to be discerned (if it is) as distinct from the more sober and parsimonious Christian votive items? The divide may be illusory and may point to a duality of thinking around issues of sacred and profane. Giallombardo reminds us that it is well known that many religious matrixes recognize the domestic hearth (with its *lares* [gods of the hearth]) *to be* the elemental altar (1990, 12). The altar and *mensa* tend to converge as one and the same (cf. MENSA `table, board' > dial. It. *mèsa* `madia' = 'bread trough, kneading board' DEI 2433; MISSA > It. *mèssa*), although here with a significant difference between the human and the divine: in the St. Joseph tradition, one does not *consume* the divine, as in the Christian Eucharist, but rather it is *those* portrayed as *doing* the consuming (*i santi*) who *are* divine (14).

While the focus of the St. Joseph tradition is on the saint himself and associated ritual breads, that is, on Christian *agape* in the form of a communal meal, clearly the table lends itself to displays of gastronomic abundance and excess (all the foods associated with the festivity, and the table too, are blessed by the priest before anyone partakes). But, in fact, the collective meal provided to the poor is a basic, simple meal; the foods taken away by visitors are minimal (bread roll, orange, fava bean); while the foods found on the table and served to the saints are varied, rich, special status foods. The latter are frequently destined for some special group: honored guests of friends and family, the priests of the congregation, the Holy Family itself—and no longer the poor. The nonperishable foods collected for the occasion (dry pasta, oil, packaged foods) are sometimes given to retirement homes and orphanages or distributed to the visiting needy.

In the Sicilian tradition and its diaspora reenactments, all forms ranging from minimal to maximal altars and tables are present. In Trapani, the most elementary form of altar is found—upon which are received offerings of food and drink, to be consumed by the saints. The altar presents a three-tiered step ladder to the divine, in an apparently archaic form found throughout the Eastern Mediterranean: "*La sua diffusione è attestabile in tutta l'area del Mediterraneo orientale, fin dalle epoche più antiche e nella forma a ripiani che appare dominante in Sicilia*" (Its diffusion is attested throughout the entire Eastern Mediterranean from the earliest times and in the tiered form which appears to predominate in Sicily; Giallombardo 1990, 15). The altar is often made to look like a shrine (an enclosed devotional niche), and then again may be an extension of the shrine, or it may be set up in a separate space altogether. It is not clear if those partaking perceive a subtle division between table and sacred altar. Giallombardo speculates that an influence of the Church may account for the disposition of objects: that is, it may not be a coincidence that on the steps of the altar are those items most readily associable with Christianity: bread, wine, oranges ("*I cibi dell'antica agape Cristiana*"), whereas *profane* foods are more distant from it.

BREAD IN ITALIAN CULTURE

As I have written elsewhere,[29] the primal role of bread in Italian culture (and in the Christian rite, of course) cannot be overstated and serves

---

29 E.g., Del Giudice 1997.

as an important point of reference for understanding not only the sacrament of the Eucharist, but the central place of bread on the Sicilian (and Pugliese) St. Joseph's Tables. Bread forms one of *the* sacramental foci of Christianity, along with wine—both southern Mediterranean legacies.[30] And Southern Italy's is a quintessentially Mediterranean food culture. Bread is the staff of life and for centuries was the stuff which barely kept the masses this side of starvation in the South (while *polenta* or cornmeal filled this function in the Italian north). Direst poverty was known as *"miseria di pane"* ("bread poverty")—when even the minimal meal was not possible. The most elemental form of charity, in fact, was giving bread to the poor.[31] It is *the* basic food and hence is sacred (like corn to the Hopi, rice to the Japanese). It is never wasted nor disrespected since it is conceived to be or to represent a divinity *embodied*—the body of Christ, for example. Consequently, there are many creative uses of old bread in *la cucina rustica* (or peasant cooking): it is recycled in soups and stews, grated as breadcrumbs, made into *bruschetta*, toasted, soaked, sautéed, etc. The primal activity of baking bread is also the symbol of hearth and home. It is a moral touchstone. How many dialects sum up the honest and generous as *buono come il pane* (as good as bread)? Close friends broke bread together as *compagni* (from companione < cum + panem; cf. *companatico* which suggests that bread is the mainstay for which other foods—cheese, olives, vegetables—formed only a

---

30   Especially after the arrival of Islam on the Mediterranean scene (post-seventh-century invasions), the Mediterranean itself became a dividing line in terms of foods: whereas wine and even bread had been sacred foods in Islam and Christianity, and were generally common to Mediterranean cultures, the Christian shift northward meant that wine and bread (along with pork, the foods of the New Europe) became predominant markers of Christianity, thereafter separating Medieval Christian Europe from the Islamic world (Montanari 2000, 191).

31   A traditional Italian anticlerical perspective may see in the official Church hierarchy's involvement in the tables as an example of the proverbial money-seeking Catholic priest. On a less cynical note, it may be remembered that this feast reinforces key concepts of Christian *caritas* and hospitality, that is, of feeding the poor, caring for orphans, and other weak and defenseless members of society (cf. traditionally, articulated as caring for widows, orphans, prisoners, and providing dowries for poor girls). The distribution of daily bread was a time-honored and visible form of charity for many churches throughout Italy.

collateral accompaniment). The preparation and consumption of bread is always an act of devotion,[32] a daily ritual, and in Sicily, the variety of ritual breads is truly vast. Charitable bread distribution in Sicilian tradition was not exclusive to the feast day of St. Joseph, but was also practiced on the feast of Saint Anthony (June 13), when breads were brought to church, blessed, and then distributed to the poor.[33] Buscemi Carlson recounted organizing such a distribution at her own parish of St. Raymond's in Downey (Interview, October 21, 1995).

DRAMATIZATION OF MIGRANT JOURNEYS: INTO EGYPT AND OUT OF SICILY

The dramatization of the Holy Family's migrant journey is alternatively known as *"Fuga in Egitto," "Parti di San Giuseppe,"* or *"Funzioni,"* (Giallombardo 1990, 9).[34] Indeed, one of Joseph's key attributes is the wayfarer's staff. Joseph himself is a seeker, a migrant, in search of food and shelter for his family. In the pageant, the saints or *"virgineddi"* ritually knock on three doors (known as the *"tupa tupa"* or "knock, knock") and ask to be let in; they are twice turned away and then given hospitality [Figure 3.23]. It was the three of the poorest of the village, including orphans, who were traditionally dressed as Mary (a young girl), Joseph (an old man), and Jesus (a small child). They were

---

32   Note the variety of sacred symbols which frequently were imprinted on bread or the many rituals of devotion which accompanied its preparation and consumption (kissing the loaf of bread, making the sign of the cross over it, the taboo against turning it upside down or dropping it on the floor, etc.). In part, this reverence also reflected the understanding that it *physically* represented the body of Christ and therefore should be handled with care and awe.

33   In Puglia, another way to fulfill one's vow to the saint is simply to prepare St. Joseph breads (or a special pasta dish, *vermiceddhri*) and to distribute these to the faithful as they exit church, or else to deliver them house to house. The recipient repays the favor by dedicating a prayer to the devotee.

34   I thank Steve Siporin for calling my attention to the appropriateness of Egypt in the Hebrew Bible as a synonym for food (especially bread), which brought the earlier Joseph and his brother to that land. Evidently, it became a recurrent pattern of the hungry in times of famine, albeit Sicilians were likely unaware of this notion.

then seated directly at the table and served a substantial meal (a taste of every item of blessed food or sometimes a ritual three).[35]

It is not exactly clear when or how the table tradition began in Sicily, but one might posit that it had a direct link to the promotion of Joseph by the Spanish establishment and roughly coincides with the Spanish presence in the South (even though the table tradition is strictly a Southern *Italian* folk custom without counterpart in Spain or its former colonies). It is the dramatization of the Holy Family's hospitality-seeking, which may be the link between the Sicilian Flight into Egypt pageant and the Mexican Nativity tradition of *Las Posadas*, which seems to so closely coincide with it.[36]

The saints in present-day public celebrations are normally comprised of a young couple and a young boy, who usually walks the procession hand-in-hand with his "parents." At least in one occasion, they *are* his parents, although this is not the norm. Playing one of the saints seems to have become something of an honorary role since it no longer tends to be enacted by the poor—and therefore has no stigma attached to it. They walk in procession and behind them follow the guilds and the general public. After the saints have eaten, and not before, all are invited to the communal banquet where typically a "poor man's meal"—either a bean soup (*pasta e ceci*) or a *Milanisa* (pasta with fresh sardines, fennel, pine nuts, and raisins, topped with sweetened and toasted breadcrumbs, to replicate sawdust from a carpenter's workshop), or even Trapanese couscous, all depending on Sicilian provenance, together with bread and fruit—is served. No one is turned away. In Sicily, often an olive branch or palm frond over the door signaled that a family had opened its home to the community [Figure 3.24]. After supper, guests are given blessed foods, a bread roll, perhaps an orange

---

35 In Otranto (and other areas of Puglia), the "saints" vary from a minimum of three (Mary, Jesus, Joseph), to five (with the addition of St. Ann and St. Joachim); to seven (with St. Elizabeth and St. John), nine (St. Zachariah and St. Mary Magdelene), eleven (St. Catherine and St. Thomas), and finally thirteen (St. Peter and St. Agnes)—in increments of male/female paired saints ("Le tavole di San Giuseppe" n.d.).

36 Sicilian tradition is rich in various genres of folk theatre (e.g., *L'Opera dei Pupi* or marionette theatre based on the *gesta* of Charlemagne and the Paladins) and extends to religious pageants (*sacre rappresentazioni*).

or lemon (recall that Sicily is Italy's citrus grower), and a fava bean to take home [Figure 3.25]. The special foods from the table are given as gifts or sometimes auctioned off. Bits of the blessed bread have historically been used as talismans, to keep away storms or hunger. In the African community of New Orleans, fava beans (also known as "lucky beans") were also used as good luck charms. The statue of St. Joseph itself is supposed to assist sellers in selling (if buried upside down in the yard) or buyers in finding a home.[37]

It appears to me that St. Joseph has been particularly attractive to Italian Americans, in part, because of his close association with the paradigm of Joseph as *Migrant* or Wanderer (beyond Joseph the Worker and Joseph the Patriarch).[38] It does not take a long stretch of the imagination to see a strong identification of immigrants with Joseph—himself an *emigrant*—fleeing into Egypt, a stranger in a strange land, at the mercy of a foreign and historically hostile people who had enslaved the Jews. Some parts of the analogy closely align, while others less so. Many Italian immigrants were forced to flee their village homes as economic refugees and were equally at the mercy of their foreign (and frequently hostile) hosts. The welcome was not always warm, as Sicilians in particular were subjected to some of the harshest forms of prejudice and hatred by their host nationals *and* by other regional Italians—at times, just as foreign to them.

---

37   A recent *Los Angeles Times* article ("3 BR, 2 BA, plastic saint buried in yard," April 19, 2009) reports on the marked increase in the practice of burying the statue upside down to sell property (and removing it when the sale is made) during the current recession as homeowners are desperate to make sales in a sagging market. You can even buy a kit to help you accomplish this task. Philip Cates, a Modesto, CA-based mortgage banker and owner of www.StJosephStatue.com, has sold more than a quarter million do-it-yourself kits since he launched the mail-order company in 1990. And it is not only Italian Catholics who are buying them. See: "Devotion to St. Joseph to Sell your house," http://www.thankevann. com/stjoseph/sellhome.html. You can also go on a St. Joseph shopping spree and buy, among other artifacts, T-shirts, prayer cards, and tote bags, at http://www. cafepress.com/thankevann. (On the Virtual St. Joseph Web site, this practice is attributed to St. Teresa of Avila who was apparently assisted in the opening of Carmelite Convents throughout Europe with her traveling statue of St. Joseph!)

38   Indeed this was the narrative followed by Fr. Pisano (see n.26) in his sermon at the Mistretta altar in 1998 and by Fr. Provenzano at Mary Star of the Sea Church, in San Pedro, in 2009.

For wayfaring peoples with a long history of migrations behind them, Mediterranean peoples understood the ideal (and absolute necessity) of practicing hospitality. Lodging the traveler and feeding the stranger were key cultural values throughout the Mediterranean world, from ancient times to modern. In the Christian era, indeed, numerous hagiographic tales illustrate how in assisting the stranger one may actually be welcoming into one's midst the divine presence disguised in human form (e.g., St. Christopher, St. Martin). And in pre-Christian times too, the motif of "entertaining angels unawares" was known (e.g., the story of Abraham just before the destruction of Sodom and Gomorrah; many Elijah the Prophet tales). Hospitality is a sacred duty.

Emigration from Italy, for the most part, was not a matter of choice but of necessity. Poverty, underdevelopment, and natural catastrophes caused millions to flee during the nineteenth and twentieth centuries in a mass migration that had had no equal. One of the most commonly shared foundation legends as the basis of the St. Joseph's Table tradition is found almost exclusively in diasporic written and oral sources. It involves variations of the following:

> The tradition of building the altar to St. Joseph began as far back as the Middle Ages [sic] in gratitude to St. Joseph for answering prayers for deliverance from famine. The families of farmers and fishermen built altars in their homes to share their good fortune with others in need.[39]

This narrative follows a fairly standard sequence of communal crisis (famine, plagues, etc.)–prayer–divine intercession.[40] As far as I can tell,

---

39 E.g., Virtual St. Joseph Altar. These are especially evident in local publications, many of them apparently relying on an oral tradition. They provide a good indication of the narrative as it widely circulates. There are a plethora of such "how to" guides for creating St. Joseph's Tables. I cite merely one example: Sisters of St. Joseph 1985, *Viva San Giuseppe: A guide for Saint Joseph Altars*, St. Joseph Guild, New Orleans, LA.

40 For the wide range of crises—personal, communal, national—upon which St. Joseph's intercession has been said to have had positive effect, see especially Villaseñor Black, who lists them in detail as they occurred in Spanish and Mexican settings.

there is little trace of this narrative in homeland Italian literature. Still, it bears a resemblance to other tales in the Italian oral tradition that also appear to be linked to migration. As I have written elsewhere:

> Numerous Italian tales begin with the scattering of large families due to famine, as children (often brothers) are sent into the world to seek their fortune. For Italians, a people with a long history of emigration, these tale types take on curiously ethnographic undertones, and may indeed be considered emblematic tales of [im]migration. Not surprisingly, they have endured among immigrants themselves both as tales . . . and as oral histories—corroborating Calvino's maxim that *le fiabe sono vere* (folktales are true). Not only were these tales "true," but so were the fantastical fictions of *Cuccagna* and Upside-down Worlds (partly) materialized through the immigrant experience. (Calvino 1956; Del Giudice 2001a, 48, and ch. 1 this volume.)

In other words, the options open to the starving peasant, fisherman, or shepherd, it seems, was either to pray to saints for a miracle (cf. the tradition's foundation legend), to emigrate, or to resort to crime (cf. the well-known saying *"o migranti, o briganti"*). Millions departed in search of *basic* material sustenance. And many found it in abundance. The custom of the St. Joseph's Table seems to focus on these pivotal themes of famine, migration, and found abundance.

If this "happy ending" seems somewhat implicit in the St. Joseph's Table tradition, here is a way it *might* be "read." While the tables do in fact symbolically focus on the poor, this *festa* also discretely: a) dramatizes the story of immigrant success, b) celebrates the work ethic, and c) affirms the patriarchal family—pillars of the Italian immigrant ethos. In fact, opulent tables are possible *as a result of* material success and depend on many generous donors. Tables, therefore, may also be a form of tribute to family businesses (often food-related), which heavily sponsor them. As such, the tables can inadvertently become monuments to immigrant triumph. Food—its production and distribution—has indeed sustained numerous Italian immigrants in America. Therefore, what better way to enshrine the source of many an immigrant fortune than in food for the table?[41] Hundreds of kilos of cheese and pasta, gallons of oil, and cases of wine are donated to the tables each year, to be consumed, sold, or distributed. Both wealth and its redistribution therefore, are often twin items on the St. Joseph's Tables.

PRIVATE VS. PUBLIC TABLES

This oblique narrative may be especially operative in public displays. But what motivates private tables? Where ought we draw a separation between the private and the public spheres of the celebration? In traditional Italian village settings, we are told, such a separation was not as clearly demarcated: in Sicily, any "private" table was to be open to anyone who chose to participate. In earlier Los Angeles neighborhoods too, more ethnically homogeneous and compact, this lack of strict demarcation appeared to obtain (Speroni 1940). For example, in these smaller immigrant neighborhoods, streets continued to function as extensions of "private" space.[42] It is attested that in Sicily, in fact, the more archaic tradition was to place the altar/table *outside* the home (e.g., in the courtyard or outside one's front door), while today instead it is prepared in larger *inside* locations (e.g., a grocer's warehouse). Indeed: "*In tutta l'area del Mediterraneo antico e classico, comprese le culture italiche, è documentato infatti il passaggio dei culti alle divinità dall'esterno all'interno*" (In the entire Ancient and Classical Mediterranean, including Italic cultures, the sacred cults' passage from exterior to interior has been documented; Giallombardo 1990, 16). But ancient practices aside, this shift may more likely here be attributable to modern and urban uses of private/public space.

---

41 Writing in the early 1980's, Giallombardo noted the tendency toward conspicuous consumption, even in an ostensibly charitable tradition such as the St. Joseph table: "*Oggi . . . si può leggere il senso di una fruizione legata a istanze fortemente avvertite di esibizione individualistica del proprio benessere socioeconomico . . . costosi antipasti, dolci più elaborati ordinati al pasticciere, frutta pregiata . . .*" (Today . . . one can discern a strong tendency toward individualistic ostentation of one's socio-economic wellbeing . . . costly dishes, elaborate sweets ordered from the baker's, special fruits . . . ; Giallombardo 1990, 28).

42 Cf. Sciorra's research on yard shrines (1993) and *presepi* (2001) in New York.

When I began to document tables in Los Angeles in the early 1990s, a full range of celebrations along the private/public axis existed. At the private end of the spectrum were more modest tables meant primarily for the enjoyment of family and friends (e.g., Vaccaro, Buscemi, També, Grammatico Frka, Russo, Mistretta tables). Tables were sometimes presented in semipublic spaces such as restaurants (e.g., the early tables of Perricone) or in a social club; yet increasingly they have become public charitable events, sponsored by corporate groups (the ICF, a saint's society or church guild) and are connected to specific parishes or cultural centers (e.g., Casa Italiana, Mary Star of the Sea, or even at the Istituto Italiano di Cultura in Westwood, but made by the Patrons of Italian Culture in the mid-2000s). Father Pisano seems to have played a key role in this shift of focus toward public tables (see n.26).

Many, though, continue to be *private* devotional tables prepared as an *ex voto,* to the saint to secure his favor or in response to a petition which has been granted (*per grazia ricevuta*), to celebrate one's name sake, as a devotion to one's favorite saint, or as a general "Sicilian Thanksgiving." In the literature and in oral narration, one finds a variety of stories of sick children cured, sons returning from war unharmed, husbands saved from a serious accident, and so forth. [43] But tables are not always given as an act of devotion and prayer; they may also be given for the simple pleasure of inviting guests to a celebration (or

---

43   E.g., the Vaccaro's have given a table for over 25 years, beginning a few years after the birth of their daughter, who was born with congenital health problems. Maria Vaccaro tells of how she had actually forgotten her promise to the saint but was reminded of this vow one year by fava beans growing in her garden, which jogged her memory and prompted her to begin preparing her yearly tables. Virginia Buscemi gave a table for her brother who was scheduled to have heart surgery in 1987. Although it had been scheduled twice before, each time the doctor had been called out of town. The 3rd scheduling fell on the morning of March 19 (St. Joseph's Day), and so it seemed to Virginia to be a propitious coincidence. Joseph També's family in NY gave tables in the 1940's so that the saint might protect his two older brothers who had gone to war (one returned, the other did not). Other private tables have been given by Josephine Grammatico Frka and by Virginia and Jack Russo of San Pedro—apparently inheriting this family practice from mothers who had passed away. Private tables, of course, tend toward the keeping of a vow, whereas the public tables are geared toward public charities—in part to feed the poor, and also to support charitable organizations and parishes themselves.

as an act of heritage preservation). In any case, although a table may represent the outcome of a personal vow (normally expressed by a woman), the execution and production of the actual altar includes a devotee's spouse, family, *comari/compari,* and *paesani* (godmothers/godfathers and one's own townsfolk) for no *one* person could possibly accomplish such a culinary tour de force. St. Joseph's Tables therefore are always something of a cooperative, communal event.

RITUALS OF ABUNDANCE: PRE-CHRISTIAN AND NEW WORLD REVISITATIONS

The tendency to see pre-Christian fertility rites in diverse ritual behavior has been a long-standing one among scholars of traditional cultures in the Mediterranean. It is especially evident among Italianists as well as in the general literature on Italian traditional culture—where antiquity seems generally to confer cultural status. And it may be especially strong in the case of Sicily, where the ancient world is everywhere evident on the landscape itself and induces one to make such links. *Proving* such continuity in actual cultural practices, however, is more challenging. Are St. Joseph's Tables indeed an expression of pre-Christian spring fertility rites? As my colleague Dorothy Noyes, warns: "After all, the seasons, scarcity, anxiety about harvest . . . don't go away with Christianity, and modern Sicilians on their desertified land probably faced much harsher anxieties about scarcity than antique Sicilians living in the breadbasket of the Empire (personal communication)." She suggests that *non-Christian,* rather than *pre-Christian,* might be a more accurate term.

Nonetheless, food altars such as this *do* seem to replicate rituals of abundance at the heart of key calendrical occurrences in agrarian societies—anticipating the harvest in spring, celebrating the harvest in spring and fall. Sicily remains a predominantly agrarian economy. Several specific features in the contemporary St. Joseph tradition may comfort the desire to identify aspects of such rites in the "tables of plenty." For example, the tables feature the season's first fruits, including ripe shafts of wheat (or pasta), as well as freshly germinated wheat buds (the so-called *giardini di Adone* [Gardens of Adonis] for the feast of Aphrodite and Adonis in ancient Greek culture)[Figure 3.26]. It may be relevant to recall that in pre-Christian times the cult of Demeter, the goddess of grain, was particularly strong in the Sicilian interior and that a major ritual celebration in her honor occurred mid-March (St. Joseph's feast day is March 19). The pagan cult of Ceres (>cereal or grain) centered on Enna where in Roman times a sanctuary to the goddess became the focus of agrarian fertility rites. Even today, the overall effect of a beautiful table is to represent Earth's bounty in an endless variety of dishes—an *"orgia elementare"* as Giallombardo puts it—and to collectively celebrate and share that abundance in the form of a communal banquet. This scholar, too, identifies beneath the veneer of Christian culture and the birth-death-rebirth cycle *"un consistente sostrato di origine precristiana: per quanto il culto ufficiale lo abbia via via espunto, tale nucleo originario continua ancora oggi a costitutire il senso profondo della diffusissima venerazione popolare"* (a substantial pre-Christian substratum: despite its exclusion from the official cult, the original nucleus continues to this day, and comes to constitute the profound sense of this widely felt folk veneration.")[44]

The naturalistic shape of the breads (birds, flowers, animals, fruits), the presence of fava beans, the building of bonfires, are also identified as recalling practices linked to the world of the Ancients. Although bonfires are normally associated with the summer solstice (mid-June, St. John the Baptist feast day, June 24), they are here also present at the spring equinox (mid-March or St. Joseph, March 19). Further, in all of Italy, the sweets most closely associated with Joseph are not bread, but fritters of all sorts, the empty and filled variants. *San Giuseppe frittellaro* (St. Joseph the Fryer) is responsible for *frittelle* in Latium, for Neapolitan *zeppole,* or Sicilian *sfinci* (filled cream puffs)—apparently both of Arabic derivation: *zalabiyah* and *sfang,* both designating forms of fried pastry. In ancient Roman times, such sweets were prepared

---

44 She goes on to affirm: "La valenza vitalistica legata al cibo si rivela in modo conclamato nella dimensione orgiastica delle tavole in cui si ostentano l'abbondanza e la varietà ricchissima delle pietanze preparate in onore di san Giuseppe." (The food's vitalistic valence is specifically represented in the orgiastic dimension of the tables, in the ostentatious way abundance and the rich variety of dishes are prepared in honor of St. Joseph; Giallombardo 1990, 10.)

for *Liberalia*, a festival held on March 17 in honor of Bacchus and Silenus in proximity of their temples (Field 1997, 399)

But elsewhere in the Christian ritual calendar (e.g., Easter, Christmas), the non-Christian and Christian ideologies live as a fairly balanced *connubium*. And so it would appear also for St. Joseph's Tables. In any case, there seems to be little awareness of any ideological conflict, and likely there is no conflict in the minds of participants (see Noyes's comment above). At times, altars and tables cohabitate, and at others, they are spatially discrete. The profusion of dishes that dominates public spectacle produces a visual cornucopia that overwhelms and delights. It appears that the Cuccagna festive paradigm is a constant (if sometimes latent) one, even here in the context of the most solemn Christian occasions of fasting and self-denial (see Del Giudice 2001a, ch. 1 this volume), for it appears here during Lent itself as a mid-Lenten reprieve from such deprivations.[45]

SOCIAL JUSTICE, "SABBATH ECONOMICS," AND FEEDING THE POOR IN LOS ANGELES

But the Christian narrative, particularly in diaspora contexts, seems to be equally strong in this ritual of abundance and *hospitality*. In the St. Joseph tradition, one welcomes the Holy Family and thereafter *all pilgrims* into one's home, sheltering and feeding them. It is important to remember that the *questua*, or begging ritual, is a key component of giving a table (and of course is reenacted within the pageant by the saints themselves). This ritual begging of food, the humbling of oneself before friends, family, business associates, and even strangers, is in fact a necessary aspect of giving a table and cannot be delegated. (It was originally performed barefoot, *scalzi*, or at least in stocking feet, as a

---

45   The battle between meat and fish—Carnival and Lent—of course, has a long and codified tradition in Italian folk culture (and throughout Christian Europe), and many a formal *contrasto* or battle between a gluttonous Carnevale (depicted as a jolly and rotund man) and Quaresima, a haggard, stingy old woman, can be found in the broadside and chapbook press from the Middle Ages forward. The sausage, in particular, as a symbol of Carnival, was a featured item of Cuccagna too (cf. Del Giudice 2001a, ch. 1 this volume).

symbolic act of humility.) For anyone giving a table, it would appear, this created an *embodied* experience of poverty and fostered empathy for the actual poor.[46] In other words, until one has begged for food or lived on the streets, one cannot fully understand or care for those who must do this day after day. Indeed, it has become the daily reality of a growing number of people in Los Angeles today—for the unemployed poor, the homeless, and the migrant (often one and the same).

The focus of the tradition, of course, is always on the table and on feeding the community—whether that is a restricted circle of family and friends, a neighborhood, or a village; whether there are the truly needy among them or not. The pageant seems to have become secondary or sometimes eliminated altogether. (As repeated in the literature and as corroborated in my own field research, it is harder to find the "poor" who are willing to impersonate the saints, and therefore it is often relegated to children. The role may have more recently become honorary: as was noted in March 2009 in San Pedro, the actual family of *santi* had been on a waiting list for five years.) Variations occur in the logistics of the pageant (houses in the neighborhood? around one's own house or banquet hall?)[47] and in how the funds are gathered: food may be sold or auctioned, a donation may be requested for the meal or for viewing the table. Candles, figurines, prayer cards, and other artifacts may also be sold, or paper money pinned directly to the saint's

---

46   In Marettimo (Isole Egadi), bonfires (*vampi di San Giuseppe*) are lit for the saint (*"fare la Duminaria"*), one next to the other in honor of Jesus, Joseph, and Mary. *"Ciò accade alla vigilia del 19 marzo, secondo una tradizione popolare per il quale il santo rappresenta tutti i poveri che soffrono il freddo e la fame."* (This happens on the eve of March 19, according to one folk tradition, when the saint represents all the poor who suffer from cold and hunger. This clearly seems to be a post hoc, Christianoid explanation of the bonfires, which are a standard feature in non-Christian rites of spring.) Again, a communal dinner is shared and those who cannot participate are served in their homes. In Ribera (Agrigento) *la stragula*, carted by two oxen, represented abundance and *"la gloria del santo patriarca mediante alcuni elementi carichi di valore simbolico, quali il pane e i rami di alloro."*

47   Where the parish is predominantly non-Sicilian, the celebrations are on a smaller scale. The Irish parish of St. Raymond's in Downey (Virginia's parish), for instance, held a small procession around the parking lot, not around the block. A private celebration may have a pageant only around one's own house, or if neighbors are congenial and interested, involve other homes as well.

sashes [Figure 3.27; cf. Figure 3.1]. Formerly in Sicily, significant funds could be raised by auctioning off St. Joseph's beard and funds might be given directly to Jesus, Mary, and Joseph (that is, the poorest members of the village).[48] In Sicily, the table tradition historically represented a *direct* form of wealth redistribution at a time of year when food stores were low (i.e., by actually feeding the poor). Today, tables generally help raise funds for charities of various sorts (see n.30).

Through the tables, the community, in fact, feeds *itself* in the form of a communal meal for rich and poor, thereby leveling somewhat the division between charity givers and receivers, and mitigating the stigma attached to hunger. Those involved in charitable food programs frequently attest to how important it is to partake of a communal meal side by side *with* the poor as a respectful and even transformative gesture for the poor themselves and for those who are not poor. The shared banquet enshrines the value of hospitality as a social and religious rite. It also seems to remind the collectivity that at any given moment the one may become the other—as the wheel of fortune is constantly in motion. This is a profound lesson upon which we might all reflect. The recent recession in fact is raising the topsy-turvy world to our consciousness once again, making abundantly evident that those who had never previously been subjected to the *indignities* of bread lines or soup kitchens are now being forced into these unfamiliar venues.

A begging ritual allows us to experience, to some extent, the psychology and *physicality* of poverty itself. For immigrants, it may even commemorate family history and ritualize the immigrant experience per se. It cannot be denied that the wandering and "knocking on doors," the search for food, lodging, work,[49] may be a powerful reminder of

---

48   Cf. Uccello 1976, 74, fig. 51 "Varba di San Giuseppe," Valguarnera.

49   The regional histories of hospitality in the Mediterranean provide numerous examples of sites of hospitality on rural, maritime, and urban landscapes, which included monasteries, hostilaries, pondocheions, "accepting all comers." This "open door policy" led to pondocheions being associated with the low life of prostitution and thievery, seedy and insecure places by late Roman times. These, apparently, emerged in the Islamic world as Arabic *funduqs* (emerging in the eighth and ninth centuries) for pilgrims but came to fill an increasingly commercial role for world traders—so that they came to provide new charitable and mercantile roles in the Muslim world. In Italy, the *fondaco* emerged after merchants discovered the

early immigration as so many experienced it (see Del Giudice 2009b). Hospitality and the injunction to open one's doors to the stranger is a long-rooted ideal in Mediterranean culture, and in Italian culture is particularly engrained (see Herman Clapp 2009).

The fact is that the poor are no longer Sicilians (once so abundant), nor even Italians, and it is now *we* who must welcome the stranger, the migrant, the "other," and feed the poor in our midst. That *community* we serve may now be interethnic and interfaith. How does one reconcile cultural preservation of specific customs in a multiethnic society? What is lost and what is gained? Certainly some intragroup dichotomies and intergroup misunderstanding may necessarily result. One Sicilian, in tears over the beauty of the St. Joseph's custom, maintained that no one could truly understand what St. Joseph meant to a Sicilian. And even the most generous givers of tables (those truly heeding the call to "feed the poor") nonetheless experience some loss of meaning when the tradition is shared with an out-group that does not necessarily understand it (see Estes 1986–87), nor appreciate its special foods. How do groups develop strategies to deal with these questions of cultural

---

funduq in Egypt and North Africa, but here evolved into warehouses for goods rather than people, and became highly profitable to governments as they more closely monitored people and goods, and increased their taxation. Commonalities in the intercultural Mediterranean world between the second and sixth centuries apparently originated in a common Greek cultural ancestor, for in order for there to be travel throughout the region, there had to be places to rest along the route. This reality produced closely related forms of hospitality in a "family of institutions" which disappear in the early modern period. The longevity of such institutions up until the sixteenth century, suggested that "housing the stranger" be he wanderer, merchant, pilgrim, or student, created a point of shared—if varied—experience of hospitality throughout the Mediterranean. The worldly *pandocheions*, in Christian narrative, alternatively came to represent both a locus of temptation and a locus of charity. That is, early commentators, including Origen and Augustine, interpreted the inn in the story of the Good Samaritan, as a symbol for the Church itself. In one of his sermons, Chrysostom exhorted his listeners to open their doors to the stranger and to let their houses serve as "pandocheions for Christ"—linking this institution to Christian charity. And yet, in another sermon: "Do you not know that the present life is a journey? . . . You are a traveler, . . . a traveler and a wayfarer. These present things are a road." For this most illuminating history on the regional variations of "lodging of travelers" in Christian, Jewish, and Muslim contexts, from the first to the sixth centuries, see Constable 2003, introduction, from which this note derives.

alienation in a multicultural society? There are creative and generous ways to do this. One might cope with these opposite pulls by, for example, participating (or producing) two events in tandem, the one intimate and more "authentic" among family and friends, while the other an altruistic event serving a broader group of the needy, thereby answering the call to practice charity in the world.

Facing the dilemma over ethnicity versus the mandate to actually feed the poor in a communal meal, Sam Perricone† resolved the debate in favor of the latter [Figures 3.28–3.29]. In fact, to my mind, no one seems to have taken the "feeding of the poor" more literally,[50] or accomplished it with more grace, than Sam. In 1989 and 1990, when St. Joseph's Tables first caught my attention, Sam and his friend Virginia Buscemi Carlson were giving a table at St. Joseph's Church (a poor, largely Latino parish in East Los Angeles, at Twelfth and Los Angeles Street). It was a symbiotic relationship. Virginia (repository of many Sicilian traditions), along with many members of Arba Sicula (Sicilian Dawn, a cultural association) decided to "reclaim" the feast to ensure its "authenticity" and organized a table (largely using the resources of Sam).[51] During the two-day period, over 1,500 people were fed a lavish (*not* a poor man's) meal of pasta, grilled swordfish, fennel salad, fruit, traditional sweets, bread, and

---

50   Father Giovanni Bizzotto (a Scalabrinian), formerly at St. Peter's Italian Church on N. Broadway in Chinatown, is another example of this fervor for feeding the poor, as the Church under his direction became a focal point in the neighborhood for the feeding of the homeless and migrants from the Casa Italiana kitchen.

51   She was introduced to Arba Sicula in 1970 in New York. Her friends, the Lobellos, went to Italy in the 1970's, talked about starting a branch in Los Angeles, and joined with Madeline Vinci to begin a chapter. They announced the first meeting at Casa Italiana in *L'Italo-Americano* alone and had 400–500 people turn up. Many had to be turned away. The majority of Sicilians, she stated (as well as the Italians found in Sons of Italy, Unico, the Garibaldina Society) were 85–90 percent American-born. Although such clubs may include a few members from Italy, the latter do not seem to have a lasting interest in these clubs, since they perhaps tend not to feel their own ethnicity threatened. Virginia noted that it seemed ironic that it was the Italian *Americans* who seemed to know their traditions better than recently arrived Italians. Indeed, upon returning to Italy later in life, she was greatly disappointed to discover that she seemed to know more about Italian traditions than Italians did. Arba Sicula, she said, was trying to return Sicilians to their traditions.

even wine. ("Let them enjoy themselves," he generously insisted.) Sam provided only his finest and refused to cut corners (e.g., costly swordfish, extra virgin olive oil), despite Virginia's protestations. Although not all may have appreciated the swordfish or the fennel (for they may be acquired tastes), Sam nourished the community in the best way he could and did so in a spirit of joy rather than duty. In an event of this scale, it is well to note that the stigma of begging is avoided since the meal is shared by many—richer and poorer alike. Nonetheless, evidence of discarded swordfish was offensive to some Sicilians. Why and how did Sam and his family (including his 90-year-old mother) do this? Sam is in the produce business and so food has been the focus of his professional life (Sam Perricone Citrus, Inc.). Many business associates (a large number of them Jewish, in fact) have contributed over the years to his patron saint's celebration. Further (according to Virginia), although a second-generation Sicilian, he has never forgotten his roots nor his early poverty and especially remembers when he was a young married man holding down two jobs, working day and night. When he became prosperous and returned to Sicily during a St. Joseph celebration one year, he was inspired to make a table of his own—first in his restaurant, Salvatore (at Olympic and Soto), for many years, sending the proceeds to St. Joseph's Church, then at the church itself.

Opportunities for public education are always available and can partly smooth the way for intercultural understanding. One apologist, Sicilian actor Lou Cutrell, warmly insisted while addressing the largely Latino congregation of St. Joseph Church in 1990, that "you don't need to be Sicilian to have a table" (cf. "you needn't be Jewish to have a Mitzvah").[52] Both the St. Joseph Mass and the explanation of

---

52 In fact, in Los Angeles in the late 1990s/early 2000s, a Hollywood synagogue had initiated a citywide "Mitzvah Day" during which a wide range of charitable activities were organized, so that anyone who might want to participate could help the needy, accompany the elderly on field trips, paint club houses, plant a school garden, and so forth. Much to the chagrin of some Jews, resistance to this name (and the religious provenance of this tradition) apparently caused it to be renamed "Big Sunday." The philanthropic community service day was adopted by Mayor Villaraigosa of Los Angeles and promoted as a citywide effort in the

the legend and food altar custom preceding the communal banquet were translated into Spanish. At the banquet itself, gratitude came in many languages and forms. One Native American *danced* his "thank you" for those giving the table. Virginia's desire was that in planting this seed in the parish it might germinate and later thrive on its own. She was disappointed when, after she became ill and was no longer able to organize it herself, the table was discontinued. Without her direct involvement—and one would posit, without the personal and cultural resonances inherent in the custom for Sicilians themselves— the tradition did not take hold. It seemed clear that, in this instance, Sicilians remained at the core of the tradition, while others (primarily Italians) took on a satellite function. Absent such direct support, the custom sometimes wanes.[53]

The impulse to share traditions across ethnic and socioeconomic boundaries, as well as the call to engage in social action in a contemporary world, is not unique to this project. Folklorists (community and public sector) have variously devised ways of commenting on and impacting the communities in which they live. Within the Italian context, we may point to various examples: the attempt to bring real Turks to the Giglio celebration in Nola early in the new millennium, the placing of a baby from a foundered immigrant ship in the manger of a *presepio* on the Puglian coast. Closer to home, we may point to the activist *presepi* of Joseph Sciorra (2007). All these instances provide examples of *living folklore* offering political commentary and encouraging compassionate action as they address real-life and current issues of migration and racism, war, and global economic crisis, for example.

My own current thinking on ethnography as spiritual practice has redirected many of my ethnological efforts as well, many of them strongly influenced by notions of social equity: for instance, here in the case of St. Joseph's Tables with issues of food justice and poverty;

mid-2000s.

53 In 2004, I was invited to speak to the Women's Council of All Saints Pasadena (a prominent, activist Episcopal church), because they wanted to assemble a table for the homeless and for foster families. They did this in conjunction with Trader Joe's and Whole Foods. I suspect that the event was not repeated in subsequent years.

in the Watts Towers Common Ground Initiative with issues of art, migration, and development (Del Giudice 2014a, ch. 6 this volume; 2014b). If we were to return to a Christian ideological matrix (not at odds with leftist economic-based thinking, in this instance)—and here a language actually appropriate to the Christian Italian folk tradition of St. Joseph's Tables—such rituals of charity and redistribution may be considered a practice in "Sabbath Economics" (Myers 2002), which I am beginning to explore. Indeed, Sabbath Economics, in part, pertains to the periodic redistribution of wealth in society, the pardoning of debts, and the dismantling of patterns of hierarchy, wealth and power. Another current movement that seeks to enact some of these concepts is the "Simple Living" or Simplicity Movement, which teaches sufficiency (what is enough?) as well as global sustainability ("live simply so others may simply live").

The economic downturn has increased the numbers of the poor and homeless in Los Angeles (as it has all across the country and the globe), as the many new soup kitchens, food programs, and refugee missions, attest. Thus, this ethnically specific, food altar custom has gained renewed relevancy. As a ritual of food redistribution, St. Joseph's Tables are indeed a "feast for our times." This tradition with remote cultural roots addresses issues which are both contemporary and urgent, demonstrating once again how traditional cultures may enrich modern urban life and help tackle some of its most persistent problems.

But the impulse to engage in cultural preservation of such traditions (cf. "heritage" discourses) comforts not only "tribal" interests but global wellbeing also (cf. Del Giudice 2009a). And I am becoming evermore interested in how the two sides of my own activities (as they address ethnology and spiritual practice) may be put to best use. I have written elsewhere of how ethnologists may have a specific ability to recognize and address some of the imperatives of the United Nations's "Earth Charter"—in particular, "Recognize and preserve the traditional knowledge and spiritual wisdom in all cultures that contribute to environmental protection and human wellbeing" (II.8.b); "Recognize the ignored, protect the vulnerable, serve those who suffer, and enable them to develop their capacities and to pursue their aspirations"(II.9.c); "Protect and restore outstanding places of cultural and spiritual significance" (III.12.d); "Recognize the importance of moral and spiritual education for sustainable living" (IV.13.f). In some modest way, I see my own research on this food altar tradition, and the social activism it seeks to promote, as contributing to the ideals of this charter.

How do we, in practice, both affirm our own cultural practices and ethnicities while helping to solve critical global concerns—both globally *and* locally? How do we begin "sweeping at our own feet?"[54] And how can ethnographers specifically "listen globally" and "act locally?" What ethical obligations might motivate our work? And how can we academics overcome our seemingly constitutional aversion to utopian discourse and action (although we may be adept at analyzing them from a safe distance)? We can all, I believe, creatively imagine ways to harness our own best traditions and identify indigenous practices that work—the better to preserve and *share* them.[55] At times, the inherent humanity and beauty of a cultural tradition will make it infinitely adaptable and acceptable to others. Harnessing energies, goods, and historic practices within the community can have many

---

54 As I have recalled elsewhere, during the U.N. Status on the Commission of Women meeting in New York in 2008, I became acquainted with the Beijing Platform for Action, the Beijing Circles process, and the concept of "sweeping at your own feet." When a Western woman asked her African sisters what she could do to help alleviate suffering on that continent, the Tanzanian woman responded with a story: When she was a little girl and overwhelmed by the task her mother had set before her of cleaning the family's entire hut, the girl asked: "Where shall I begin?" Her mother answered: "Begin by sweeping at your feet." I take this to mean not only that we must begin working on behalf of the United Nations Millennium Development Goals (target date 2015), in *our own* backyards, but that we must begin in small, community-based ways. Together with the Reverend Joanne Leslie, in 2008, we have started the first Beijing Circle in Los Angeles, at St. Alban's Episcopal Church, to address just these goals. It is now in its second year.

55 By way of example (for there are many similarly minded organizations today), the innovative nonprofit Bread for the Journey seeks out community leaders who are already known and effective in their *own* communities and supports their work with micro-grants. There is no sense reinventing the wheel, nor *not* relying on indigenous knowledge and expertise. It is a best practice to engage in partnerships of this sort.

positive benefits *within* the group, as well as *without*. In our case, given their food genius and the cult of abundance, their heightened aesthetic sense in food practices, and the generous spirit with which hospitality is traditionally practiced, Italians stand to accomplish what mere food kitchen programs do not and cannot do.

WORKS CITED

Arcano, Beatrice. 2007. "Le Tavole di San Giuseppe a Uggiano La Chiesa" (St. Joseph's Tables in Uggiano La Chiesa). Accessed April 8, 2022, http://www.prolocosalento.it/docs/index. shtml?A=c_uggiano2.

Behar, Ruth. 1996. *The Vulnerable Observer: Anthropology That Breaks Your Heart.* Boston: Beacon Press.

Behar, Ruth. 1999. "Ethnography: Cherishing our Second-Fiddle Genre." *Journal of Contemporary Ethnography* 28, no. 5: 472–84.

Bonasera a quista casa: Antonio Aloisi, Antonio Bandello, "Gli Ucci"— Pizziche, stornelli, canti salentini (CD). 1999. Lecce: Edizioni Aramirè.

Bowman, Paddy, and Steve Zeitlin. 1993. *Folk Arts in the Classroom: Changing the Relationship between Schools and Communities,* a report from the National Roundtable on Folk Arts in the Classroom, Washington, D.C, May 3–4, 1993. Archived by Local Learning Network, https://locallearningnetwork.org/ resource/folk-arts-in-the-classroom-changing-the-relationship-between-schools-and-communities/.

Calvino, Italo. 1956. *Fiabe Italiane (raccolte dalla tradizione popolare durante gli ultimi cento anni e trascritte in lingua dai vari dialetti da Italo Calvino).* Turin: Einaudi. Reprinted, Milano: Mondadori, 1993. English translation by George Martin: *Italian Folktales,* New York: Harcourt, Brace Jovanovich, 1980 (and New York: Pantheon, 1980).

Canto d'amore: canti, suoni, voci nella Grecìa salentina (Love Song: Songs, Sounds, and Voices from the Griko-speaking Area of the Salento) (CD). 2000. Lecce: Edizioni Aramirè and UCLA Dept. of Ethnomusicology.

Caracausi, Girolamo. 1983. *Arabismi medievali di Sicilia* (Medieval Arabisms in Sicily). Palermo: Centro di Studi Filologici e Linguistici Siciliani. Supplementi al Bollettino 5.

Chupa, Anna Maria, n.d. "St. Joseph's Day Altars." *Louisiana Project: Land, Environment, Culture.* Houston Institute for Culture, http://www.houstonculture.org/laproject/stjo.html.

Constable, Olivia Remie. 2003. *Housing the Stranger in the Mediterranean World: Lodging, Trade, and Travel in Late Antiquity and the Middle Ages.* Cambridge, New York: Cambridge University Press.

Cosentino, Donald. 1995. "Imagine Heaven." In *Sacred Arts of Haitian Vodou,* edited by Donald Cosentino. Los Angeles: Fowler Museum of Cultural History, UCLA.

De Felice, Emidio. 1982. *I nomi degli italiani.* Venice: Marsilio.

DEI, *Dizionario Etimologico Italiano.* 1968. Carlo Battisti and Giovanni Alessio. Florence: Barbèra.

Del Giudice, Luisa. 1990. Preliminary Survey of Italian Folklife in Los Angeles, for the Folk and Traditional Arts Program, Department of Cultural Affairs, Los Angeles. https://www.worldcat.org/title/preliminary-survey-of-italian-folklife-in-los-angeles/oclc/1116060105&referer=brief_results.

Del Giudice, Luisa. 1997. "Tomie de Paola and the Writing/Illustrating of Italian Folk Culture," in *Italian Americana* 15, no.1: 22–30.

Del Giudice, Luisa. 2000. "Italian American Folklore, Folklife," 237–45, and "Italian American Food and Foodways," 245–48. In *The Italian American Experience: An Encyclopedia,* edited by Salvatore J. LaGumina, Frank J. Cavaioli, Salvatore Primeggia, and Joseph A. Varacalli. New York: Garland.

Del Giudice, Luisa. 2001a. "*Paesi di Cuccagna* and other Gastronomic Utopias." Chapter 1 this volume. First published in *Imagined States: National Identity, Utopia, and Longing in Oral Cultures*, edited by Luisa Del Giudice and Gerald Porter, 11–63. Logan: Utah State University Press.

Del Giudice, Luisa. 2001b. "'Wine Makes Good Blood': Wine Culture Among Toronto Italians." Chapter 2 this volume. First published in *Ethnologies*, 23, no. 1: 1–27.

Del Giudice, Luisa. 2005. Italian Los Angeles: The Italian Resource Guide to Greater Los Angeles. www.ItalianLosAngeles.org, accessed April 8, 2022.

Del Giudice, Luisa. 2007. "Ischian Cultural Sites on the San Pedro, California, Map" / "Siti culturali ischitani sulla mappa di San Pedro, California." Chapter 4 this volume. First published in *Pe' terre assaje luntane: L'emigrazione ischitana verso le Americhe / In Lands Far Away: Ischian Emigration to the Americas*, 18th edition. Dual-language publication. Ischia: Associazione Ischitani nel Mondo.

Del Giudice, Luisa. 2009a. "Ethnography and Spiritual Direction: Varieties of Listening." In *Rethinking the Sacred*, proceedings of the Ninth SIEF Conference in Derry, Londonderry, UK, June 16–20, 2008. Edited by Ulrika Wolf-Knuts, Department of Comparative Religion, 9–23. Turku: Åbo Akademi University, 2009 (series: Religionsvetenskapliga skrifter).

Del Giudice, Luisa. 2009b. "Speaking Memory: Oral History, Oral Culture and Italians in America." In *Oral History, Oral Culture and Italians in America*, selected papers from the 38th AIHA annual meeting, Los Angeles, 2005, edited by Luisa Del Giudice, 3–18. New York: Palgrave Macmillan.

Del Giudice 2014a. "Feeding the Poor—Welcoming the Stranger: The Watts Towers Common Ground Initiative and St. Joseph's Communal Tables in Watts." Chapter 6 this volume. First published in *Politische Mahlzeiten / Political Meals*, edited by Regina Bendix and Michaela Fenske, 53–65. Dual-language pubication. Berlin: Wissenschaftsforum Kulinaristik (Science Forum for Culinary Studies), Lit-Verlag.

Del Giudice, Luisa. 2014b. "Sabato Rodia in Watts and the Search for Common Ground," introduction. In *Sabato Rodia's Towers in Watts: Art, Migration, and Development*, edited by Luisa Del Giudice. New York: Fordham University Press.

Del Giudice, Luisa, and Nancy Van Deusen, eds. 2005. *Performing Ecstasies: Music, Dance, and Ritual in the Mediterranean.* Claremont Cultural Studies, Nancy Van Deusen, General Editor, Ottawa: Institute for Medieval Music, 2005.

Estes, David C. 1986–87. "St. Joseph's Day in New Orleans: Contemporary Urban Varieties of an Ethnic Festival." *Louisiana Folklore Miscellany* 6, no. 2 (1986–87): 35–43.

"La Festa di San Giuseppe in Sicilia." Accessed February 6, 2009, http://www.sicilyland.it/festa_san_giuseppe_sicilia.htm.

Field, Carol. 1997. "San Giuseppe." In *Celebrating Italy: The Tastes and Traditions of Italy as Revealed Through its Feasts, Festivals, and Sumptuous Foods,* 392–407. New York: Harper–Collins.

Gatto, Marianna. 2009. *Los Angeles's Little Italy.* San Francisco: Arcadia.

Giallombardo, Fatima. 1990 (1981). *La festa di San Giuseppe in Sicilia* (The feast of St. Joseph in Sicily), vol. 2 of *Archivio delle tradizioni popolari siciliane* (Archive of Sicilian folk traditions). Palermo: Folkstudio. First published in *Archivio delle tradizioni popolari siciliane* 5, Palermo: Folkstudio.

González, Maria Cristina. 2003. "Ethnography as Spiritual Practice: A Change in the Taken for Granted (or an Epistemological Break with Science)." In *Studies in Language and Social Interaction: In honor of Robert Hopper*, edited by Phillip J. Glenn, Curtis D. LeBaron, and Jenny Mandelbaum, 493–506. Mahwah, NJ: Erlbaum.

Herman Clapp, Joanna. 2009. "My Homer." In *Oral History, Oral Culture and Italian Americans*, edited by Luisa Del Giudice, 183–91. New York: Palgrave Macmillan.

IOHI, Italian Oral History Institute Collections. 1994–2007. UCLA Ethnomusicology Archive, Los Angeles. See Field Recordings, below. Finding aid: http://content.cdlib.org/view?docId=kt7870289c&chunk.id=dsc-1.2.6&brand=oac.

Italian Treasury: Puglia: The Salento (CD). 2003. Alan Lomax Collection. New York: Rounder Records.

"List of Viceroys of Sicily." Accessed February 22, 2009, http://en.wikipedia.org/wiki/List_of_Spanish_Viceroys_of_Sicily.

Lomax, Alan, and Luigi Chiriatti, eds. 2006. *Alan Lomax in Salento: Le fotografie del 1954.* Texts by Alan Lomax, Luigi Chiriatti, Luisa Del Giudice, Anna Lomax Wood, Goffredo Plastino, Sergio Torsello. Calimera, Lecce: Edizioni Kurumuny.

Mintz, Sidney W. 1986. *Sweetness and Power: The Place of Sugar in Modern History.* New York: Penguin.

Montanari, Massimo. 2000 (1996). "Introduction: Food Models and Cultural Identity." In *Food: A Culinary History (European Perspectives)*, edited by Jean-Louis Flandrin and Massimo Montanari. English translation by Albert Sonnenfeld. New York: Columbia University Press.

Myers, Ched. 2002. *The Biblical Vision of Sabbath Economics.* Washington, DC: Church of the Saviour.

Pendergrass, Jennifer. 1999. "Sicilian Festivals in Los Angeles." Unpublished student essay and sound recording. See Buscemi Carlson (1999) in Field Recordings, below.

Pitrè, Giuseppe. 1969 (1900). *Spettacoli e feste popolari siciliane* (Spectacle and folk feasts in Sicily). Bologna: Forni Editore.

Ruffino, Giovanni. 1995. *I pani di Pasqua in Sicilia: Un saggio di geografia linguistica e etnografica* (Easter breads in Sicily: A geo-linguistic and ethnographic essay), 2 vols. Palermo: Centro di Studi Filologici e Linguistici Siciliani, Istituto di Filologia e Linguistica, Facoltà di Lettere e Filosofia (Center for Sicilian Philological and Linguistic Studies, Institute of Philology and Linguistics, Faculty of Letters and Philosophy).

"San Giuseppe: Padre putativo" (St. Joseph as putative father). Accessed June 14, 2022, http://it.wikipedia.org/wiki/Giuseppe_%28padre_putativo_di_Ges%C3%B9%29#column-one.

Saxon, Lyle. 1945. "Saint Joseph's Day," and "Saint Rosalia's Day." In *Gumbo Ya-Ya: A Collection of Louisana Folk Tales*, edited by Lyle Saxon, Edward Dreyer, and Robert Tallant, 93-106 and 107-20. Boston: Houghton Mifflin.

Sciorra, Joseph. 1993. "Multivocality and Vernacular Architecture: The Our Lady of Mount Carmel Grotto in Rosebank, Staten Island." In *Studies in Italian American Folklore,* edited by Luisa Del Giudice, 203–243. Logan, UT: Utah University Press.

Sciorra, Joseph. 2001. "Imagined Places, Fragile Landscapes: Italian American Presepi (Nativity Crèches) in New York City." *The Italian American Review: A Social Science Journal of the Italian American Experience* 8, no. 2: 141–73.

Sciorra, Joseph. 2007. "Gramsci's presepio." In *Occhio Contro Occhio* (blog). Accessed June 13, 2022, http://www.i-italy.org/bloggers/981/gramsci-s-presepio.

Sisters of St. Joseph. 1985. *Viva San Giuseppe: A guide for Saint Joseph Altars.* New Orleans: St. Joseph Guild.

Speroni, Charles. 1940. "The Observance of Saint Joseph's Day Among the Sicilians of Southern California." In *Southern Folklore Quarterly* 4, no. 3: 135–9.

Stramare, Tarcisio. 1993. *San Giuseppe (nella Storia della Salvezza)* (St. Joseph [in the history of Salvation]). Torino: Editrice Elle Di Ci.

"Le tavole di San Giuseppe" (St. Joseph's Tables). Accessed February 6, 2009, http://www.otrantopoint.com/tavole_san_giuseppe.html.

"Tavole di San Giuseppe." Accessed February 6, 2009, http://it.wikipedia.org/wiki/Tavole_di_San_Giuseppe#column-one.

Texas Tavola: A Taste of Sicily in the Lone Star State (film), 2007, 34 mins., directed by Circe Sturm and Randolph Lewis.

Turley, Erika. 1999. "Religious Experience among Sicilian Women in San Pedro." Student paper, including audio tapes, photographs, saints' cards, and 2 audio cassettes. See Orlando (1999) in Field Recordings, below.

Turner, Kay, and Suzanne Seriff. 1987. "'Giving an Altar': The Ideology of Reproduction in a St. Joseph's Day Feast." *Journal of American Folklore* 100, no. 398: 446–60.

Uccello, Antonino. 1976. "La cena di San Giuseppe" (The St. Joseph's dinner). In *Pani e dolci di Sicilia* (The breads and sweets of Sicily). Palermo: Sellerio, 73–81.

"Un paese in festa (Valguarnera)" (Feast in town). n.d. Accessed February 6, 2009, http://www.festasangiuseppe.it/.

Varvaro, Alberto, and Rosanna Sornicola. 1986. *Vocabolario etimologico siciliano* (Etymological dictionary of Sicilian). Palermo: Centro di Studi Filologici e Linguistici Siciliani.

Villaseñor Black, Charlene. 2006. *Creating the Cult of St. Joseph: Art and Gender in the Spanish Empire.* Princeton: Princeton University Press.

The Virtual St. Joseph Altar (website, blog). Evann Duplantier, developer. Accessed June 20, 2022, https://virtualstjosephaltar.com/.

Vocabolario siciliano. 1977. Vol. 5. Edited by Giorgio Piccitto, Giovanni Tropea, Salvatore Trovato. Catania-Palermo: Centro di Studi Filologici e Linguistici Siciliani.

FIELD RECORDINGS IN THE ITALIAN ORAL HISTORY INSTITUTE (IOHI) COLLECTIONS, UCLA ETHNOMUSICOLOGY ARCHIVES

Buscemi Carlson home, *St. Joseph's Day Table,* videographer: Ken Carlson, Downey, CA, March 18, 1987; home VHS videotape.

Buscemi Carlson home, *St. Joseph's Day Table,* videographer: Ken Carlson; Downey, CA, n.d.; home VHS videotape.

Buscemi Carlson, Virginia, interview by Luisa Del Giudice, Downey, CA, May 30, 1990; audiotape.

Buscemi Carlson, Virginia, interview by Luisa Del Giudice, Downey, CA, October 2, 1995; audiotape.

Buscemi Carlson, Virginia, interview by Jennifer Pendergrass, Downey, CA, June 14, 1999; audiotape. See Pendergrass 1999.

Casa Italiana, *St. Joseph's Day Table*, Los Angeles, CA, videographer: Steve Weimeyer, March 18, 1995; VHS videotape.

Casa Italiana, *Celebrazione di San Giuseppe Dinner Dance*, n.d., Los Angeles, CA; videotape.

Mistretta Family. 1998. Chants for St. Joseph, recorded by Kenneth Scambray in March, Upland, CA, audiotape.

Mistretta Family. 1998. St. Joseph's Day Chants, recorded by Kenneth Scambray in March, Upland; videotape.

Orlando, Rosalia, Giuseppa La Fata, and Paolina Manzella. 1999. Interview by Erika Turley on June 8, San Pedro, CA; two 90-minute audiotapes. See Turley, 1999.

Pisano, Fr. Andrew, Vita Gracchiolo, Maria and AgostinoVaccaro. 1995. Interviews by Luisa Del Giudice on March 17, San Pedro, CA; audiotape.

Pisano, Fr. Andrew, Joseph També, and women singing novena, private *St. Joseph's Table*, mass, and blessing, n.d., San Pedro, Los Angeles, CA; videotape.

St. Joseph's Church, *St. Joseph's Day Table*, videographer: Ken Carlson, Los Angeles, CA, March 18, 1990; VHS videotape.

Vaccaro home, *St. Joseph's Day Table*, San Pedro, CA, March 17, 1995; videotape.

Figure 3.1: Saint's niche on altar at Casa Italiana (St. Peter's Italian Church, Downtown Los Angeles) with dollar bill donations attached to a sash. Note the pasta which often substitutes golden sheaves of wheat.

Figure 3.2: Maria and Agostino Vaccaro, in front of their home altar in San Pedro (1990). The Vaccaros had given a St. Joseph's Table for over 25 years.

Figure 3.3: The Vaccaro altar in a typical three-tiered arrangement with the Eucharistic elements for the mass, preceding the blessing of the table.

Figure 3.4: Father Pisano, the priest responsible for introducing the public St. Joseph's Table to Los Angeles through the Italian Catholic Federation, is here blessing the Vaccaro table.

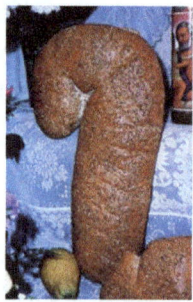

Figure 3.5: Braided votive bread for Joseph in the shape of a staff (*vastuni* < It. *bastone*). Breads for Christ are in the shape of a cross or crown, while a palm frond is reserved for Mary. From the Vaccaro altar.

Figure 3.6: Breads as *emblemata*, the implements of the Passion (reproduced in the 1998 program brochure for the Hammer Museum table; from Uccello 1976).

Figure 3.7: Cardoons, other vegetables, and a Christmas *panettone*.

Figure 3.8: Palm Sunday and Easter symbols are also sometimes found on St. Joseph's Tables, given the calendrical proximity of the two: woven palms, sugar lambs, breads with eggs embedded in them.

Figure 3.9: *Fichi d'India* (prickly or cactus pears). Cactus pears, *il carretto siciliano* (a painted Sicilian cart and horse), and the sound of *the scacciapensieri* (the Jew's/jaw's harp) are primary emblems of *Sicilianita*, or Sicilian identity.

Figures 3.10: Fish (a symbol of Christ) is a main feature of this mid-Lenten tradition (cf. the medieval battle between meat and fish during Carnival and Lent; Del Giudice, Chapter 1 this volume). Displayed here is a whole salmon provided by noted Sicilian chef, Celestino Drago. More humble fried fresh sardines, the staple catch of Sicilian fishermen in San Pedro for generations, might also be included.

Figure 3.11   Figure 3.12

Figures 3.11–3.12: Detail: cornucopias of vegetable and fruit *primizie* (first fruits of spring) including fresh fava beans. Dried fava beans are obligatory on a St. Joseph's table. Note the fishing boat that is especially representative of this community of Sicilian fishermen.

Figure 3.13: Increasingly, elaborate bakers' cakes in honor of St. Joseph (often given by other patron saint's societies) are commissioned by guilds and societies for the table. St. Peter's Italian Church is home to many (predominantly Pugliese) patron saint societies. Sweets have come to predominate on the tables, including store-bought cookies and even Christmas *panettone*, possibly because they can be preserved for longer periods of time without spoiling.

Figure 3.14: Vita Gracchiolo†, bearer of Sicilian religious oral traditions, periodically rallying the participants with "*Viva Gesù, Maria, Giuseppe, evviva!*"

Figure 3.15: Children in Italian costume for the ethnic display at the San Pedro St. Joseph's Day procession around the church street block. The distance in years seems to have increased their numbers.

Figure 3.16

Figure 3.17

Figure 3.16–3.17: Processing behind the St. Joseph's Society's banner, around Mary Star of the Sea Church. Note the Croatian and Filipino society banners in the 2009 procession. The Mexican Guadalupe banner followed thereafter but is not pictured here.

Figure 3.18: Founding women of Mary Star of the Sea Church's St. Joseph's Society, San Pedro. From left to right: Giusenie Dukie, Nunzia d'Orio, Paolina Manzella, Rosaria Lo Grande, Giuseppa La Fata (cf. Turley 1999). The Society celebrated its twenty-fifth year in 1998. Rosalia Manzella Orlando, whose mother was one of the founders of the St. Joseph's Society, has continued the tradition into the next generation. Rosalia is still coordinating the festivities at Mary Star of the Sea Church. Photograph courtesy of Rosalia Manzella Orlando

Figure 3.19: Virginia Buscemi Carlson†, next to the Table she and Sam Perricone gave at St. Joseph Church, 1989. This was the first table I encountered in my research.

Figure 3.20

Figure 3.20–3.22: Table co-curated by Virginia Buscemi Carlson† and Luisa Del Giudice at the UCLA Armand Hammer Museum, 1998.

Figure 3.21: Detail: The mid-Lenten St. Joseph's Tables feature vegetables such as stuffed artichokes and *frittate* of all sorts, often garnished with wild fennel. Eggplant, cardoons, favas, peppers, and a variety of other colorful vegetables and fruits are also common.

Figure 3.22: Father Buccheri, on the right, blessed the table at the 1998 UCLA Arm and Hammer Museum. He was accompanied by women of the St. Joseph's Society of San Pedro (partly out of view), who sang songs in honor of St. Joseph amidst the general public.

Figure 3.23: The "saints" are seated directly at the table in the church hall at Mary Star of the Sea Church, San Pedro.

Figure 3.24: In Sicily, a palm frond or olive branch over the door signaled to the village that a family was opening its doors to the community (from Giallombardo [1981] 1990, 51, fig. 31).

Figure 3.25: A bread roll, orange or lemon, and a fava bean given to guests were sometimes used as talismans to ward off hunger, storms, and so forth. Among New Orleans African Americans, they were known as lucky beans.

Figure 3.26: At this Casa Italiana table in 2005, the *giardini* became an entire carpet of grass.

Figure 3.27: Pins, artifacts (and homemade sweets) for sale at Mary Star of the Sea Church (San Pedro, March 15, 2009).

Figure 3.28: A communal meal forms a normal part of giving a table. After the food has been blessed and the saints have eaten, all are invited to partake of a "poor man's meal." Here the main dish is *pasta e ceci* (pasta with garbanzo beans soup), although in the home of the Vaccaros, many more dishes are added to the menu to be enjoyed by close friends and families. In San Pedro, fried calamari (certainly not a "poor man's" food) are typically served. The food in the Vaccaro home is laid out in the garage and on kitchen counters, while the altar is in the living room.

Figure 3.29: The banquet hall of Casa Italiana is ready to receive a steady stream of pilgrims, rich and poor alike, to enjoy a pasta-based meal. Other items of food (e.g., cannoli and other baked specialties) are sold to raise funds.

Figure 3.30: Sam Perricone† (of Sam Perricone Citrus, Inc.), a generous devotee of St. Joseph, gave a table for many years in his Downtown restaurant before creating tables with Virginia Buscemi Carlson at St. Joseph Church in East Los Angeles.

4. Ischian Cultural Sites on the San Pedro, California, Map

In 1989, I was commissioned to map the Italian community of Los Angeles for the Department of Cultural Affairs' Folk and Traditional Arts Program.[1] City officials wanted to know who and where the somewhat "invisible" Italians were in this sprawling city.[2] That "Preliminary Survey of Italian Folklife in Los Angeles" (1990)—which documented the many and diverse Italian communities' social and ceremonial life, associations, foodways, markets, traditional arts, games—has since metamorphosed into www.ItalianLosAngeles.org, a project of the Italian Oral History Institute (IOHI), conducted in collaboration with UCLA students and community volunteers.[3]

The internal chronology of this essay has not been updated, for the most part, and reflects the dates and cited references of the original publication.

1   This essay was first published in *Pè terre assaje luntane: L'Emigrzione Ischitana verso le Americhe* (Napoli: Associazione Ischitani nel Mondo, September 2007). Unless otherwise noted, English translations and photography are by me.

2   Extensive research on the historic Italian community has been conducted by then-CSUN professor, Gloria Ricci Lothrop (December 30, 1934–February 2, 2015) and published in her monograph *Italians of Los Angeles*, 2003. Her research helped fuel the Italian community's effort to reclaim the Historic Italian Hall in the heart of the Pueblo de Los Angeles Historic Monument, beginning in 1990. The Historic Italian Hall Foundation was incorporated in 1993 and evolved into the Italian American Museum of Los Angeles (IAMLA), https://www.iamla.org/. For a more extensive bibliography, see "Further Readings: Italians of Southern California," www.ItalianLosAngeles.org.

3   In the several courses on Italian folk and immigrant culture I taught at UCLA from 1996–2001, students were required to conduct fieldwork in the community in order that they understand the varieties of Italian experience in Los Angeles and how people actually lived (or didn't live) out their Italian heritage. Several students were inevitably encouraged to explore Italian life in San Pedro. The range of research topics included, for example, women's religious life, fishermen's festivals, the A-1 market, Italian folk art, and so forth. Indeed, the IOHI was a direct outcome of

It was then that I came to learn of two Italian island communities living in San Pedro, California, (the Port of Los Angeles): those originating in Ischia and those from Sicily. By unofficial accounts, the Italians of San Pedro number in the tens of thousands (anywhere from 25,000 to 40,000), while the official number, according to Councilwoman Janice Hahn's district office, is closer to 5,000.[4] But what of the Ischian (It. *Ischitano)* subset of that Italian presence?

I have written elsewhere of the importance of oral historical research in the writing of Italian immigrant history and therefore will not elaborate here (cf. Del Giudice 2001b; 2007; 2009). This brief essay, based on the IOHI Collections (now in the UCLA Ethnomusicology Archive, Los Angeles), adds its modest contribution to that effort as it presents cullings from fieldwork in the San Pedro community. What follows, therefore, are a few Ischian cultural sites on the Los Angeles map that touch upon foodways (e.g., A-1 Imported Groceries and Deli, Marabella Vineyard Co.), religious and civic celebrations (patron saint feast days at Mary Star of the Sea Church, the Fisherman's Fiesta [*sic*]), and folk art (e.g., the Boccanfuso *presepio*, or nativity scene).

While the city's Downtown sites—the heart of the Pueblo de Los Angeles Historic Monument (e.g., Historic Italian Hall), and east, out toward Lincoln Heights (e.g., St. Peter's Italian Church,

---

my teaching and inevitably went beyond academia and into the public sector as a nonprofit institution. It was such research projects that lead to the idea of founding a public nonprofit institution devoted to Italian oral historical research—since so little of this sort of research is ever supported by university Italian departments and similar cultural entities. The Italian Oral History Institute, a unique institution which bridged academic and public sectors, was active until 2007, and produced many conferences/festivals for both academics and a general audience. It also focused on bringing together combined community and university efforts to create a "virtual piazza" in its Web site, www.ItalianLosAngeles.org—where all aspects of the community could be made visible to itself and to the non-Italian public as well. Major divides that exist in the reality of relationships between Italians and Italian Americans, between regional Italians, and so forth, could be somehow minimized through this strategy of allowing every voice to be heard. [Editor's note: The website has since been archived and is no longer active.]

4   Carmela Funiciello's honorary mayoral campaign in San Pedro stated that there are 30,000 Ischians in San Pedro, perhaps further inflating the claims of the Ischian demographic presence.

Casa Italiana)—constitute the historic Little Italy,[5] in some respects, it is San Pedro that represents our more traditional and *de facto* Little Italy today, being somewhat insular (true to its island heritages) and where Italians still actually live. Ethnic clustering was here fostered for a unique reason. San Pedro is still geographically and administratively somewhat discrete, and until quite recently, occupationally compact. As Los Angeles's port, longshoremen and fishermen predominated there. And Italians, first Ischian, then Sicilians[6] (along with Croatians from the Dalmatian coast), dominated all aspects of the once-vibrant fishing industry, now fairly collapsed (Parsons 2003)—even though they left barely a trace in the Los Angeles Maritime Museum until recently!

San Pedro Italians and Los Angeles Italians may see themselves as separate communities: San Pedro as a compact and perhaps culturally conservative "urban village," while St. Peter's Church and Casa Italiana function as the center for larger-scale Italian social events, gathering in the community from far and wide. Indeed, illustrating this divide was news that, although the effort to make the Historic Italian Hall the focal museum for the entire Italian community had been underway for over a decade, a separate effort to found a museum of immigration was being promoted by Italians in San Pedro.[7]

San Pedro has few formal Italian American associations, and even fewer town and regional clubs. The Ischians, however, have gravitated toward the Italian Catholic Federation through their parish churches, while the Sicilians are represented in greater numbers in the Italian American Club and in the Trappeto (province of Palermo, Sicily) Club. Community celebrations, frequently promoted by such associations,

---

5   See n.2, sup. However, resident Italian Americans have now become rare in that area.

6   Ricci Lothrop mentions that Ischians and Sicilians began arriving in the early migrations of the late nineteenth century: "The second half of the nineteenth century witnessed the influx of Piedmontese vintners and a few Tuscan entrepreneurs, along with a cluster of fishermen from Ischia and Sicily, constituting a trans-migrant vanguard to the Pacific coast." Parsons puts the Ischians as having arrived first, joined by Sicilians after WWI.

7   More recently though, that effort has been directed toward developing Piazza Miramare within San Pedro's newly designated Little Italy District. Groundbreaking for the Piazza occurred in October 2022.

form an important vehicle for the continuity of traditional life. One of the most significant for local Italians in Los Angeles and San Pedro, still today, is the presentation of St. Joseph's Day Tables, held on and around March 19 each year.[8] Among the more fully articulated of these (involving a procession and pageant) occurs at Mary Star of the Sea Church (formerly at Ninth and Center Streets, and since 1958, at Seventh and Meyler) [Figure 4.1], itself a gathering place for most Italian religious festivities in San Pedro. Because this festivity (brought to the United States by Sicilians) occurs during Lent, fish is a key ingredient on these food altars offered as a communal banquet for the poor. Therefore, the fishermen of San Pedro, including those of Ischian descent, have played a key role in these celebrations by contributing fish specialties to the communal feast, as has, of course, the St. Joseph's Guild, founded in 1973 and largely made up of Sicilian women, which organizes the annual feast.

While the Sicilians celebrate the patron saint days of St. Joseph and St. Rosalia, the Ischians celebrate the Feast of San Giovan Giuseppe della Croce (St. John Joseph of the Cross, apparently born and died on the island of Ischia, August 15, 1654–March 5, 1739) in the manner in which it is still carried out annually in Ischia Ponte. It is a movable feast traditionally held during the first week of September. The strong Ischian presence at the church—whose patron saint, the Madonna of the Sea (*Maria Stella Maris*), has watched over the lives of fishermen from the top of the church for generations—is also enshrined in stained glass on its south wall [Figure 4.2]. Some aspects of fishermen's ritual celebrations have been transmitted in San Pedro for generations. In decades past, for instance, the Fisherman's Fiesta was a major expression of the San Pedro Italian community's traditional culture.[9] The first was held March 26, 1938, and thereafter in September, attached to the sardine season. A detailed account can be found in Charles

8   In 1989, I began documenting St. Joseph's Tables for the Cultural Affairs Department of Los Angeles and, in 1998, co-curated (with Virginia Buscemi Carlson) a table for the Armand Hammer Museum of Art and Cultural Center. (See: Del Giudice 2010, ch. 3 this volume.)

9   NB, the Hispanic *fiesta* has been absorbed for over a century into California English, especially to launch and publicize local events.

Speroni's 1955 article on California's fishermen's festivals. These and similar findings, supplemented with more recent oral research (cf. Seefeldt 2001), narrate the earlier, more compact fishing community then largely living around the wharf, which managed the three-day festivity itself. The celebration included many traditional elements such as the blessing of the fleet, decorated purse seiners processing at sea, the statue of the Madonna carried to the wharf by six skippers, a wreath thrown into the water, food booths, boat rides, and so forth.

But San Pedro's fishing identity has clearly been in crisis since the mid-1980s. With the waning industry, the celebration became a more generic festival to celebrate the city itself, and was renamed the San Pedro Festival. Once the fishing industry declined, the participation of fishing families also declined, and the festival was transformed. In recent years efforts have been underway to revive the Fiesta— although it is questionable what the place of fishing families within the celebration is to be.[10] St. Peter's (San Pietro), too, has emerged as a saint's day celebration with fishing reminiscences, if one is to judge from the decorated boat Santa Rita in procession at the Sunday, June 29, 2003, Mary Star of the Sea festivity. St. Peter was, after all, a Galilean fisherman (and fisher of men).

But there are few fishermen still fishing these coastal waters. One of the last of the sardine fishermen was Vince Lauro, skipper of the Endurance, who happens to be of Ischian descent with many generations of seafarers in his blood (cf. Parsons 2003). He still shouts "Molla!" (Italian for "Let it go") to spur his crew into action. He recounts the ups and downs of tracking the *sardinops sagax*, the "wily sardine," the recent resurgence of local sardine populations (which periodically simply vanish, sometimes "for decades at a time),[11]" and sadly reflects

---

10   Issues of liability that have precluded fishermen from offering boat rides to the public, and the bitterness of the fishing community over the fate of its industry, have perhaps made the mood less than celebratory for actual fishermen (cf. Seefeldt).

11   "In the early part of the 20th century, sardines were so plentiful there seemed to be no bottom to the supply. In 1937, California fishermen caught more than 700,000 tons. A little more than a decade later, the fish began to disappear and, by the mid-1960s, the total catch for the entire West Coast was less than 1,000 tons. Just as folks were beginning to talk about sardines being fished to the brink

on how today, "it's the fishermen who are nearly extinct."[12]

But Ischian occupational and cultural identity in San Pedro is not only sea based. For instance, the original owner of A–1 Imported Groceries and Deli, at 348 West Eighth Street, at the corner of Eighth and Mesa, and his successor were Ischia-born, as are many of their clients. Among these was centenarian Fernando Di Bernardo, fisherman, deceased at the age of 105. Di Bernardo, who was a loyal customer of the Marabella Vineyard Co.[13] next door, continued to make wine in his garage for over 50 years.[14] When I interviewed Di Bernardo in the

of extinction, they returned. . . . Despite all of the fish's unpredictable comings and goings, sardines helped build San Pedro. The Yugoslavs from the Dalmatian Coast and Italians from the southern island of Ischia founded the fishery at the turn of the last century with their innovative purse seine nets, and to this day they dominate the fleet. . . . The consensus among fishermen seems to be that their industry can't last another 10 years [writing in 2003]. The fact that fishermen were saying that 20 years ago (and probably with more justification) does not disprove their argument. . . . The San Pedro fishing fleet, which numbered nearly 500 boats in 1937, is down to fewer than two dozen today. Of the 16 canneries that once occupied San Pedro and neighboring Terminal Island, none are left. The last closed in 2001. Most of the work has fled to low-wage countries, first to American Samoa, Puerto Rico, and the Philippines, and now to Malaysia. . . . 'I'm the last of it. I've got two sons and no way are they going into the industry,' says Lauro" (Parsons 2003).

12   "The processing company to which Lauro sells his catch, State Fish, is headed by Vanessa DeLuca, the third generation of her family in the industry. Her 105-year-old grandfather, Ferdinando di Bernardo, is still giving advice" (Parsons 2003). On di Bernardo, see n.13.

13   At the time of the original writing, Tony Marabella still sold wine presses, mosto, and supplies for home winemaking as the only wine supplier left in San Pedro. He made wine the old way, and his rhythms were seasonal: he sold in the Fall, and farmed 200 acres in Rancho Cucamonga the rest of the year. His shop was open Fridays and Saturdays only. Marabella is still in business.

14   I first became aware of Di Bernardo in a *Los Angeles Times* article on home winemaking written by Stolberg in 1990 and interviewed him myself shortly after. Stolberg writes: "Ferdinando Di Bernardo is one of Marabella's steady customers. The 92-year-old retired fisherman, who has been making wine in his garage for as long as he can remember, buys 50 gallons of grape juice from Marabella every year. This annual exchange, which the two men have repeated for at least 40 years, is more than a simple business transaction. It helps keep a dying tradition alive." Ferdinando Di Bernardo recounted to me his own traditional uses of wine: in daily family meals, for large for family gatherings, and how he has never been drunk in his life. Unusual for California, local Italians built their

early 1990s, I was struck by his archaic dialect,[15] and reflected on my ability to follow it. We were both, each in our own way, immigrant linguistic museums. My 1950s' vintage Terracinese dialect (on the mainland just north of Ischia) remained—and remains—lively in my own immigrant family as I grew up in Toronto, Canada.

In 1932, Frank Matera†, originally from Ischia via New York,[16] opened a grape and grape juice supply company (now known as Marabella Vineyard Co., owned by Tony Marabella, and the last one left in San Pedro [Figures 4.3–4.5]). In 1947, as an expansion of the grape and wine trade, Matera opened A-1 next door [Figure 4.6]. (A visual cue to his Ischian heritage is found in the mural of Ischia Porto behind the cash register [Figure 4.7].) The grapes came first, the fruits, vegetables, and meats followed. The gregarious and polyglot owner could speak to his diverse European customers in their own languages.[17] Emiddio Ungaro,[18] the next owner of the market [until 2021], remembered the market's glory days, when it truly was a vibrant community meeting point in the 1960s and 1970s, as a youth growing up in San Pedro. His own family's routine was to do general shopping on Friday nights, and then shop for Italian products (cold cuts, bread, meats, etc.) on Saturday mornings, the traditional shopping day. He remembered other weekly rituals of the more compact ethnic community of his childhood: picnics in Avril Park, strolls after church along the waterfront in Ports

---

homes with cellars, to accommodate their stock of wine. On the role of wine and wine cellars in immigrant culture, see Del Giudice 2001a, ch. 2 this volume.

15　Di Bernardo's dialect (and thence origin) was mistakenly identified as Sicilian by a researcher in the Library of Congress special project, *Italians in the West*, conducted in San Pedro in the early 1990s.

16　This pattern was not uncommon: arrival in New York and a second migration farther West. This migration pattern is also recorded by UCLA student Abbatiello, whose grandmother, Raffaela Di Meglio Abbatiello, tells of her own mother (Carmela Monti), born in Ischia (Porto), October 16, 1900 (See Abbatiello 1996). San Pedro seemed to them to closely resemble Ischia (the seaside, its weather, and so forth). These life stories focus on beliefs, the relationship between New York and San Pedro, and the more tolerant social climate of Southern California.

17　Frank's nickname was "Bullshit" (and the market was known as "The Bullshits"), no doubt earned by virtue of his talkative streak!

18　May 18, 1958–October 31, 2021.

of Call Village to buy pizza at Mamma's Restaurant or pastries—part of the traditional Sunday outing, *la passeggiata della domenica*. Ungaro began working long but happy hours at the market as a box boy at the age of 15, where Frank was as much a father figure as an employer. The market became the focus of Ungaro's entire life as he worked his way up to partial owner (buying a 25 percent share from Frank in 1986), and then sole proprietor in 1997 when, after Frank's retirement, his son, Anthony, sold Ungaro the remaining 75 percent of the business. Emiddio Ungaro [Figure 4.8] was born in Ischia, the son of Rosario Ungaro (b. May 17, 1926; d. February 29, 2004) and Libera Di Massa (b. Febraury 4, 1934). His father had immigrated in 1956 to New York, returned to Ischia in '58 to marry, then left to join relatives in a fishing business in San Pedro that did not work out.

Emiddio left Italy for San Pedro at the age of two with his mother in 1960, and there met his father for the first time. In the 1960s, Rosario and his brother, Mario, bought, reburbished, and sold houses until Mario, Emiddio's uncle, packed up his family and returned to Ischia in the mid-1960s. Rosario returned to the shipyards until his retirement, at which point he became Emiddio's "number one PR man," spending his days in the market where many *paesani* would pass through. Market and family have been Emiddio's entire life. He worked long hours, took little time off for any sort of recreation, but then had to find creative ways to supplement and diversify his small-scale operation through wholesaling and catering. By the mid-1980s, with the decline of the fishing industry, the market too started to see fewer Italians, as many moved away. Competition from big-box stores such as Costco, together with a lack of ethnic loyalty in younger Italian shoppers,[19] made it increasingly difficult to survive. In fact, the market was largely patronized by the older Italian and European community of San Pedro, and obviously still functioned, to some degree, as something of a piazza for this generation. Ungaro maintained that the market's uniqueness is that it did not compromise its cheerful, personalized, family-oriented atmosphere and hasn't changed in decades (its customers

---

19 "It's almost as though they've cursed you," laments Ungaro. I suspect that at work here is also a dose of familiar Italian *invidia* or envy. "They don't understand," continues Ungaro, "the hard work it took to get here."

don't want it to). Ironically though, what makes it a unique magnet will also put it out of business, he surmised.

The preservation of ethnic foodways requires primary materials; hence the importance of Italian grocers and delis, wine suppliers, and home gardens in immigrant lives. San Pedro's geography and climate must have struck many Ischians as familiar and benign, permitting undisturbed the continued growth of grapes, figs, lemons, and vegetables, as they had done in Ischia. Further, proximity to the sea provided the other ingredients needed for traditional dishes *alla pescatora* in their predominantly fish-based Mediterranean diet. There was even mention of an itinerant fish retailer in the community—reminiscent of the traditional *venditore ambulante*—Andrea Briguglio, who delivered fresh fish to one's door. If preferred however, one could go straight to the docks for the Saturday morning fish market.

Grocery stores were indeed among the first businesses opened in early Italian immigrant settlements, providing the staples of Italian cuisine. Until the mid-1980s and the advent of more readily available Italian products in mainstream supermarkets, farmers' markets, and specialty stores (e.g., fresh pasta, olive oil, balsamic vinegar, *prosciutto*, *mozzarella*, *rucola*, *finocchio*, *radicchio*, *polenta*, etc.), pilgrimages to these earlier Italian markets were indispensable. These traditional markets still provide a sensible and more affordable alternative to the Italian food "boutiques" for their affluent Italophile clientele. Rather than prestige import labels, one is more likely to find local and Italian *American* products. Many of the older markets have sought to respond to the current popularity of Italian cuisine with increasing numbers of Italy-direct imports in their inventories. Markets remote from high-end customers, such as A-1, must rather adapt to a mixed-ethnic community by stocking products for local Croatians and Latinos, in addition to economy-minded Italians. Over the decade following my first visits to the area, I had created my own family rituals around these food pilgrimages to San Pedro. I returned to San Pedro whenever I needed to relive or confirm my own childhood market recollections.[20]

---

20   Saturday morning in Toronto was market day for our family as well; my mother and sisters would walk to the Italian market, order our groceries, including fresh *mortadella*, *panini*, and when they were available, striped black and white Mediterranean snails (from Spain).

Simultaneously, I had added an important food gathering experience to the mix: collecting what I presumed to be Mediterranean snails in the proximity of the scent of sea air and sweet fennel.[21] In order to approximate Toronto and Terracina experiences for my own daughters, as well as for visiting family and friends (both from Italy and Canada), such expeditions became existentially necessary. For my father, a fisherman in his pre-immigration Terracina days, buying fish straight from the fishermen and communing with them at the docks was palpably uplifting for him when he visited from Toronto. In San Pedro, we found echoes or evocations of familiar Italian life on the Pacific shore.

My own ritual consisted of driving the Harbor Freeway south to San Pedro, preferably on a Saturday morning, and going directly to A-1, where we purchased fresh *panini, melanzane sott'aceto, affettati.* We also did our grocery shopping: fresh meats from the butcher's counter, still individually cut (*fettine di vitello, salsicce*), greens such as *rapini* (Terracinese=*broccoletti*), *scarola, finocchio,* and sometimes artichokes, canned tuna, pasta products and polenta, and newly discovered frozen *sfogliatelle,* which we would later bake at home for special dinner guests [Figures 4.9–4.10]. On one occasion, when I couldn't seem to locate the pastries, someone shouted out to Joe in colorful *Italiese*: "Hey Joe, get the *sfugghis!*"—which has since become a family joke. Finding an ocean view in Angel's Gate Park, we would assemble to eat *panini,* reenacting *scampagnate* (picnics in the open) of past times. Snail gathering followed (at a location to remain anonymous), then a visit to St. Mary Star of the Sea, and a coastal drive home, stopping for espresso at Italianate Malaga Cove with its Giambologna fountain.

But found reveries of an immigrant aside, as an ethnographer and as a founding member of the Los Angeles Convivium of Slow Food, I was immediately and professionally concerned with A-1 and with Marabella's. It was the market's and vintner's role in the preservation of

---

21   I have not been able to confirm which ethnic group is responsible for having introduced them into the local ecology but I suspect (or like to imagine) it may have been some nostalgic Ischians for whom snails were as much a coveted delicacy as they were for my family. The distinct black and white snails indeed were very familiar to me, as they resembled those I had gathered in Terracina, and are unlike those found elsewhere in Southern California [Figures 11–12].

traditional foodways, and the fact that they provided a centripetal force for the fragmenting community, that prompted me to create a Slow Food program around these sites in 2001, replicating my own family experiences for the benefit of local Slow Food members [Figures 4.11–4.12]. It also seemed an oddly appropriate one, given the association's emblem: the snail (see www.slowfood.it)—but a *sciammaruga* to me. I guided the group on gathering, purging, cooking, and eating Roman-style *lumache* (or *sciammarughe*, as they are known in Terracinese), the latter steps all under the watchful guise of then *Los Angeles Times* food editor, Russ Parsons, and his photographer.[22] Traditional Italian markets in immigrant communities served more than just physiological needs, however: they were community gathering places and thus often formed a surrogate *piazza*. Here Italians could meet friends and *paesani* (fellow townspeople), exchange news, and speak some Italian. Therefore, as a community site, A-1 also became an important place from which fieldwork could be launched for other oral history projects. During one of those Saturday morning pilgrimages to A-1, and while casually speaking Italian to my daughter, a woman by the name of Filomena Boccanfuso began telling me about her husband, of a *presepio* he had built and how it now filled an entire backroom. I took down her telephone number and promised to return. As it turned out instead, years later two Italian UCLA students, Consuelo Griggio and Michela Merlo, both temporarily in Los Angeles, volunteered as IOHI researchers in 2004 and it was they who visited the Boccanfuso household.

Italians, of course, have a centuries-old artisan and handcraft tradition that embraces a variety of media. Many of these are alive and well, while others have waned. Italian men have held key roles in the building trades, and because family and home are among an Italian's greatest treasures, these tradesmen invest family foyer with great love, effort, and expense (Del Giudice 1994; Sciorra 2015). Once-common embellishments took the form of yard fountains

---

22   These photos never were published in the Food section of the newspaper, I suspect because the *Times* might have received many disgusted emails and letters from a general public unfamiliar with Italian snail culture, and who generally considered snails to be garden pests. Escargots are marketable, Italian *lumache* are not. Indeed, few friends nor even *compaesani* have ever shared in these down-home food rituals in my home.

and statuary, decorative wrought iron, and so forth. Some are more utilitarian, such as a home-built outdoor oven or barbecue, fruit and vegetable gardens—labors of love created with one's own hands and serving specific cultural needs.

One widely practiced form of Italian folk art is the annual crafting of a Christmas nativity scene or crèche (a *presepio* or *presepe*). Though found all over the Italian peninsula, the *presepio* reaches its grandest form in the Naples, Campania area.[23] Thus it remains one of the stronger, more resistant traditions transmitted by immigrants (cf. Sciorra 2001, 2015, 2022).

Boccanfuso, a skilled carpenter from Ischia who lived in San Pedro for over 40 years, continued in this trade, also embellishing his own home with handmade doors, tables, and cabinetry until his retirement. He then turned his full attention to building his *presepio*. In the late 1990s, childhood memories of island village life started haunting Boccanfuso and a nostalgia for past traditions inspired his recreation of an important memory. The stable and manger evolved into a village; the village grew as figurines collected from here and there or donated by friends were added, "until the village began to contain miniature villages within itself" and became a permanent rather than seasonal fixture. A visit to the *presepio* by an Ischian bishop remained a satisfying memory to the Boccanfusos. This is how Griggio and Merlo describe the crèche:

> The light and softly corrugated eucalyptus bark Mr. Boccanfuso used profusely as a foundation for the scene gives it an eerie appearance, reminiscent of a Californian desert, which well combines an Italian tradition with the local geography!" . . . The more you look at it, the more scenes you discover—for example, a New York-style Christmas scene, or some wolves climbing up the rocky walls, obviously looking for sheep, . . . [commingled with] some exquisite English porcelain dolls [Figure 4.13–4.15].

Longing for the village of one's past and evocations of such landscapes have inspired many an immigrant, particularly among older generations

---

23   The Museo e Gallerie Nazionali di Capodimonte in Naples has numerous examples of *presepi*.

of men. After all, many were builders. This impulse to recreate long-lost and even imagined landscapes in later life has produced some unparalleled examples of folk art. It was true for Baldassari Forestieri's *Underground Gardens*, north of Fresno, as well as for Sabato Rodia's *Watts Towers* in Los Angeles (cf. Scambray 2001; Del Giudice 2014).

Since the late 1980s, the "Preliminary Survey" has evolved into a website on the Italians in Los Angeles. Much has changed, of course, as the local Italian community has indeed become more visible and has received much public recognition, thanks to a variety of initiatives promoted by Italians themselves—some in conjunction with civic authorities.[24] Furthermore, recent trends focusing on naming discrete ethnic groups and neighborhoods on the cityscape, has resulted, for instance, in San Pedro receiving a "Via Italia" sign in 2004, just in front of the Italian American Club meeting hall [Figure 4.16]. And on Wednesday November 8, 2006, in the City Hall Rotunda, Ischia was officially named a sister city to San Pedro/Los Angeles.[25]

WORKS CITED

Abbatiello, Franca. 1996. "Life Stories of Carmela DiMeglio and Raffaela Abbatiello," Unpublished UCLA student manuscript, June 7, 1996. Includes recording, transcript, photographs. IOHI Collections, UCLA Ethnomusicology Archive.

---

24 E.g., the Historic Italian Hall opened as the Italian American Museum of Los Angeles (IAMLA) in 2016; the San Gennaro Foundation; the Italian Oral History Institute's launching of the Italian Los Angeles Web site in 2005, and its festival on the community itself, *Italian Los Angeles: Celebrating Italian Life, Local History and the Arts in Southern California* (curated by the author); the project coordinated by Alessandro Trojani on *Italians in the Gold Rush and Beyond*; together with the efforts of Italian authorities (e.g., the Italian Consulate, the Istituto Italiano di Cultura, etc.), and municipal agencies (e.g., Los Angeles Department of Cultural Affairs). Many more milestones for the local Italian community have been achieved since.

25 Ischian Carmela Funiciello campaigned for the title of honorary mayor of San Pedro, and although unsuccessful, her campaign hinged on the important presence of immigrants within the community.

Del Giudice, Luisa. 1990. "Preliminary Survey of Italian Folklife in Los Angeles" for the Folk and Traditional Arts Program, Department of Cultural Affairs, City of Los Angeles. (See www.ItalianLosAngeles.org.)

Del Giudice, Luisa. 1994. "The 'Archvilla': An Italian Canadian Architectural Archetype." In *Studies in Italian American Folklore*, edited by Luisa Del Giudice, 53–105. Logan: University of Utah Press, 1994.

Del Giudice, Luisa. 2001a. "Wine Makes Good Blood: Wine Culture among Toronto Italians." Chapter 2, this volume. First published in *Ethnologies* 23, no. 1: 1–27.

Del Giudice, Luisa, ed. 2001b. "Mountains of Cheese and Rivers of Wine: *Paesi di Cuccagna* and Other Gastronomic Utopias." Chapter 1 this volume. First published in *Imagined States: National Identity, Utopia, and Longing in Oral Cultures*, edited by Luisa Del Giudice and Gerald Porter, 11–63. Logan: Utah State University Press, 2001.

Del Giudice, Luisa. 2005. *Italian Los Angeles: Italian Resource Guide* (website). Los Angeles: Italian Oral History Institute (IOHI). www.ItalianLosAngeles.org.

Del Giudice, Luisa. 2009. "Speaking Memory: Oral History, Oral Culture and Italians in America." In *Oral History, Oral Culture and Italian Americans* (selected papers from the 38th AIHA annual meeting, Los Angeles, 2005), edited by Luisa Del Giudice. New York: Palgrave Macmillan.

Del Giudice, Luisa. 2010. "Oral History, Oral Culture and Italian American Studies." In *Teaching Italian American Literature, Film, and Popular Culture,* edited by Edvige Giunta and Kathleen Zamboni McCormick, 160–167. San Francisco: Modern Language Association.

Del Giudice, Luisa, ed. 2014. *Sabato Rodia's Towers in Watts: Art, Migrations, Development.* New York: Fordham University Press.

Griggio, Consuelo, and Michela Merlo. 2004. "It's always Christmas at the Boccanfuso household: a grandiose Nativity Scene village is a well-kept secret in the heart of San Pedro." Unpublished UCLA student manuscript and media. IOHI Collections, UCLA Ethnomusicology Archive.

Lothrop, Gloria Ricci. 2003. *Italians of Los Angeles*. Los Angeles: Historical Society of Southern California.

Mahon, Rachel. 2001. "Role of an Italian Market in Los Angeles: A-1 Imported Groceries." Unpublished UCLA student manuscript, IOHI Collections, UCLA Ethnomusicology Archive. Includes 10 black-and-white prints (with negatives); 25 color slides; 10 color prints (with slides).

Parsons, Russ. 2003. "Chasing the Wild Past: Off San Pedro's Coast (A small fleet is back catching sardines the way fishermen did generations ago)." *Los Angeles Times*, October 15, F1.

Scambray, Kenneth. 2001. "Creative Responses to the Italian Immigrant Experience in California: Baldassare Forestiere's Underground Gardens and Simon Rodia's Watts Towers." *Italian American Review* 8, no. 2: 113–140. John Calandra Italian American Institute, SUNY, New York.

Sciorra, Joseph. 2001. "Imagined Places, Fragile Landscapes: Italian American Presepi (nativity crèches) in New York City," *Italian American Review* 8, no. 2: 141–173. John Calandra Institute, SUNY, New York.

Sciorra, Joseph. 2015. *Built with Faith: Italian American Imagination and Catholic Material Culture in New York City*. Knoxville: University of Tennessee Press.

Sciorra. Joseph. 2022. "The Cultural Politics of the *Presepio*: Autoethnography, Artistry, and Protest from the Italian American Imaginarium." In *La stanza degli specchi: Impegno politico-culturale e diaspora Italiana* (The hall of mirrors: cultural-political engagement in the Italian diaspora), ed. by Katia Ballacchino and Luisa Del Giudice, special issue of *Voci*, Winter 2022: 118–141.

Seefeldt, Monica. 2001. "Fishermen's Festival: San Pedro, California." Unpublished UCLA student manuscript, March 16, 2001. IOHI Collections, UCLA Ethnomusicology Archive. Includes typescript, attachments, release form, photographs, two ninety-minute audio cassettes.

Speroni, Charles. 1955. "California's Fishermen's Festivals." *Western Folklore* 14, no. 2, April.

Stolberg, Sheryl. 1990. "Drinking In the Past: San Pedro Merchant Carries On Old World Winemaking Traditions." *Los Angeles Times*, February 15, 1.

Figure 4.1: Mary Star of the Sea Church, San Pedro.

Figure 4.2: A tribute to Ischia in stained glass on the South wall of the church.

Figure 4.3: Tony Marabella's son, crushing grapes.

Figure 4.4

Figure 4.5

Figure 4.4: Tony Marabella with son and grandchildren. Figure 4.5: Inside Marabella's winemaking supply shop. Photograph by Ulf Wallin

Figure 4.6: A–1, 348 W. Eighth Street, at the corner of Eighth and So. Mesa Street.

Figure 4.7: Mural, depicting the port of Ischia, the birthplace of A–1 market's original owner, Frank Matera

Figure 4.8: Emiddio Ungaro†, owner of A–1.

Figure 4.9   Figure 4.10

Figure 4.9: Typical variety of breads in Italian American markets.Photograph by Rachel Mahon. Figure 4.10: Saturday morning Italian customers at the meat counter.

Figure 4.11: The Slow Food San Pedro program participants in front of Marabella Vineyard Co., nextdoor to A–1.

Figure 4.12: Black and white snail on fennel plant. Photograph by Ulf Wallin

Figure 4.13: Mr. and Mrs. Boccanfuso, San Pedro, in front of their *presepio*. Photograph by Consuelo Griggio and Michela Merlo

Figure 4.14

Figure 4.15

Figure 4.14–4.15: Details of Boccanfuso *presepio*. Photographs by Consuelo Griggio and Michela Merlo

Figure 4.16: "Via Italia," San Pedro, designated in 2004.

5. Pasta

Ground grain of the wheat plant (genus *Triticum*; family *Gramineae* or grass), native to Eurasia, forms the fundamental component of commercial *pasta*, the generic term for what the United States Federal Standards of Identity (1989) call *macaroni products*.[1] Italian commercial dried pasta traditionally combines durum wheat (*Triticum durum*, hard wheat, or semolina, its coarsely ground endosperm) and water into a large number of shapes and sizes. Soft or common wheat (*Triticum vulgare*) is used for homemade or "fresh" pasta (which often contains egg, and sometimes oil and salt), as well as for bread and pastries. These are the two most important wheat grains in the Mediterranean diet.

Pasta is a versatile, nutritious, economical, thus democratic, and increasingly international food. In past times, it was fried and sweetened with honey, or tossed with *garum* (fish paste) by the ancient Romans. Or it might have been boiled, or baked in rich pies, called *timballi*, that defied Renaissance sumptuary laws. Today, pasta is usually boiled to a slightly chewy, resistant consistency (*al dente*), and dressed with a variety of sauces, eaten in soup, or baked. The oldest, most traditional Italian condiment from the thirteenth to the nineteenth centuries consisted of butter and cheese (with sugar, cinnamon, or other spices); pasta was also boiled in meat broths. Only since the 1830s was it combined with the now familiar tomato sauce. In the course of its history, pasta has been both a luxury and, only recently (since the nineteenth century), a popular food.

As late as the 1960s, the people of northern Italy normally ate risotto, polenta, and egg pasta, while southerners ate mostly bread and pasta—just as, in terms of fats, butter versus oil divided the cooler

---

1   This essay first appeared in Solomon H. Katz and William Woys Weaver, eds., *Encyclopedia of Food and Culture* (New York: Charles Scribner's Sons, 2003), 46–52. The encyclopedia format did not allow for citations; instead a bibliography was included (called "Works Consulted" herein). Photographs and translations are mine.

north from the warm south. The eventual leveling of traditional foodways has made pasta a truly national food. However, this Italian first course (*primo*) has been adapted to main dish, side dish, salad, and even dessert in its diverse cultural naturalizations.

HISTORY: DOUGH VERSUS PASTA

It is vital to distinguish between two classes of pasta—freshly made (normally with egg, sometimes without) and dried—in order to make sense of its history. The most ancient form of pasta is flattened dough (Italian *sfoglia*) from which many fresh pasta forms have evolved. Cereal-derived foods, based on whole, crushed, or finely ground grains, have been common to the Mediterranean for several millennia, taking the primitive form of mush (for example, Roman *puls*). Dough might be kneaded and shaped, and then fried, roasted, baked, or boiled. When it was flattened into a thin sheet and cut into strips, then boiled, a proto-pasta was created. This final step in the process appears to have created the archetypical category known today as "pasta."

Because a flour dough base is common to both pasta and bread, the histories of these foods have been merged and blurred. Although pasta may seem a simpler food, bread has held a more central place in the Mediterranean and Italian diet and worldview. Were historians to agree upon a common categorization of pasta, based on ingredients and cooking method (boiling in liquid), it might facilitate a clearer distinction between pasta and other forms of dough-based foods.

TERMINOLOGY

Dough for boiling evolved into a variety of shapes. The original form appears to have been string-shaped, thread-shaped, worm-shaped, or ribbon-shaped—that is, long and thin, flat or round, as the earliest terms attest. For example, Latin *lásanum* (earthenware pot, from Greek *lásanon*, "three-footed pot") blended with *láganum* (a long strip of thin, rolled dough), whence *lasagne*, a plural form in standard Italian. Still today, in Neapolitan or Calabrian dialect, a rolling pin is known as a *laganatura*. Other terms include Latin *tracta* (a long piece of dough; literally, "drawn out"), Arabic *itrija* (string-shaped dough, whence southern Italian *trii* or *tria*, and Spanish *aletria*), Italian *vermicelli*, and later, *spaghetti, tagliatelle*, and *fettuccine*. Other early forms of pasta were created from small bits of rolled dough (Latin *lixulae*; Italian *gnocco*, "knuckle") or stuffed dough (*ravioli*). Standard Italian *maccherone* and dialectal Italian *maccarone* (the source of English "macaroni"), an early synonym of *gnocco*, is said to derive from the Indo-European verbal root *mak* ("to knead with force," whence Italian *ammaccare* "to crush"; e.g., *macco,* a fava bean purée); if so, it testifies to the force required to knead and shape durum wheat dough.

But even the earliest Italian terms for pasta present wide regional variation. Indeed, Italian pasta history has been vexed, enlivened, and bedeviled by profound lexical specificity. One outwardly identical term may designate different things, historically and geographically. For instance, *maccarone*, from its first citation in the twelfth century, has referred to short dry pasta (twelfth century and twentieth century), long dry pasta (southern Italy, eighteenth through the twentieth centuries), long fresh pasta (regional Italian), *gnocchi* (fourteenth through the seventeenth centuries), and even *ravioli*. And it is not clear whether *lasagne* (*lágana*), widely used by the thirteenth century, were not more like fritters (similar to today's Carnival sweets: *cenci, bugie, chiacchiere*) than boiled dough.

Pasta means "paste, dough, batter" in Italian. An earlier, now obsolete term was "alimentary paste," a loan translation from Italian *pasta alimentare.* Today, a lexical shift makes "pasta" the generic term for which all others stand as subsets, and "macaroni" (Italian *maccherone/ maccaroni*) now refers to hollow, short dry pasta, with a few shape exceptions surviving as regional homemade specialties in southern Italy.

ORIGINS: EAST OR WEST

Spontaneously invented forms of pasta existed simultaneously in various parts of the world—East and West—a clear case of polygenesis. Even a cursory look at this basic starch in the food systems of China and Italy, for instance, makes this parallel development obvious. While certain similarities may be surprising (noodles = *tagliatelle*; wonton = *ravioli*), the differences are no less so. Pasta is eaten by a variety of peoples but in significantly different ways.

The innovative leap—and the part of pasta's history that is more closely associated with Italy—is the revolution that *dry* pasta entailed in conservation, economy, and diffusion. This process was established by the twelfth century in the Sicilian–Arab world. Thus, only in Italy (and a few parts of Asia) did pasta become so central to diet and cuisine, and such a diversified food. Further, Italy must be credited with pasta's global diffusion.

HISTORICAL LANDMARK VERSUS LEGEND

A few landmarks are fixed points in an otherwise fluctuating ocean of pasta history. Alongside such documentation, however, exists a substantial body of pasta mythology, the most notable involving the vexed question of Marco Polo's supposed introduction of Chinese noodles to Italy, likely attributable not to the *Milione* itself (which, however, mentions noodles made from the sago palm tree enjoyed by Polo in Fanfur, likely Sumatra [Rustichello and Polo ca.1298–99]), but to the October 10, 1929, issue of *The Macaroni Journal* (publication of the National Association of Pasta Makers), featuring "A Saga of Cathay." This legend tells of the encounter of a sailor named "Spaghetti" with a Chinese maiden preparing a strange dish of boiled strands of dough, and of how he divulges this secret to the West. The story was evidently an effort to create a plausible link between the presence of noodles in China's more ancient civilization (documented during the Shang dynasty, 1700–1100 BCE) and the predominantly Italian identity of pasta in the modern world.

Polygenesis is not a concept that is easily grasped or generally appealing. Italians had been making, consuming, even exporting pasta before Polo's return in 1292, as the earliest known document, a Genovese testament predating Polo's return by at least twelve years, clearly attests. Evidence from the *Milione* further suggests that Polo considered the sago variety a type of pasta, which presupposes the existence of, and his familiarity with, pasta as a food. Other data confirms the parallel development of this food in the West.

ETRUSCAN AND ROMAN

The Etruscan tomb, La Tomba dei Rilievi in Cerveteri, fourth century BCE, provides iconographic evidence: a woman in the act of rolling out dough, accompanied by familiar implements (a rolling pin, sack of flour, water container, knife), although it is not clear how the flattened dough might have been prepared. Horace (*Satires* VI 35 BCE, book 1, line 115) mentions the comfort of his simple dish of chickpeas, leeks, and *lágana*, whence Salentine *ciceri e tria*, still eaten today. Cicero also speaks of these long strips of thin, rolled dough made with water and flour. Apicius, in *De re coquinaria* (fifth century, book IV, chapter 2), describes *lágana* fried in oil and tossed with pepper and (that all-purpose Roman condiment) *garum*—a dish of which Petronius's character, parvenu host Trimalchio (in the *Satyricon*), was particularly fond—and *tractae* (evidently dried durum pasta) for thickening broth. Apicius also elaborates on a rich, layered *lágana* dish involving meats, fish sauce, and spices.

ARAB SICILIAN GEOGRAPHER

The first clear Italian reference to dried—hence preservable—pasta and to a pasta industry comes from Arab Sicily. In 1138, a Moroccan geographer, Muhammad ibn Muhammad al-Idrīsī, was commissioned by Roger II, the Norman king of Sicily, to survey his kingdom. In his 1154 codex, he describes the vast fields, many mills, and farms at Tràbia (30 kilometers from Palermo), where a string-like pasta (referred to by its Arabic name, *itrija*) was produced and exported in "shiploads" to Calabria and to other parts of the Muslim and Christian worlds. The pasta was evidently dry, and a large-scale operation is being described. Although no generic term, hence no notion of pasta, existed in Arab gastronomy at this time, Arabs knew of this dried convenience food—particularly useful for long caravan rides, and later, to seafaring Genovese and Sicilian sailors. Beginning in the twelfth century, in fact, Genovese merchants became agents of Sicilian pasta's northward diffusion. By the fourteenth century, they began producing and selling *vermicelli* and other pasta *di Genova*—so that Genoa became, after Sicily, one of the earliest production centers in Italy.

GENOVESE BARREL OF *MACCHERONI*

In the bequest of a soldier, Ponzio Bastone, written by notary Ugolino Scarpa (February 2, 1279), a *bariscella plena de macaronis*, a small barrel of dried pasta, is listed. This earliest attestation of the term *macaroni* is important for three reasons: It suggests the value of the food product (that is, worthy of being listed in a will); that it was indeed dry pasta (since it was conserved in a barrel); and that it was, by this date, known as a generic term (as pasta is today).

GASTRONOMIC UTOPIAS: *CUCCAGNA*

In the mythic land of plenty, known to the Italians as *il paese di Cuccagna* and in medieval Europe as Cockaigne, there was a very peculiar mountain. The Italian version of the myth was first described by Boccaccio (1353 *Decameron*, VIII, 3). In this gastronomic utopia, which he calls Bengodi, a cauldron sits on top of a Parmigiano-cheese mountain and continuously spews forth *maccheroni* and ravioli which roll down the mountain's side, land in a rich capon broth, and are free for the taking by the poltroons (see chapter 1, this volume). Such macaroni, however, were evidently synonymous with *gnocchi*, chestnut-sized or larger balls of flour dough (not potato), often pictured as served on a skewer. This shape accounts for the ease with which they could roll down the *Cuccagna* mountain.

THE MACCHERONIC MUSE

Since pasta has inspired myth, legend, literature, art, film, and graphic design, its history ought to take into account historical data as much as its presence in cultural history, for it has a long oral as well as written tradition. Its creation myths have involved the noblest of gods in the Roman pantheon, emperors, and magicians; pasta miracles have promoted worthy candidates to sainthood (for example, St. William the Hermit turned dirt-filled ravioli into a delicious dish); folk narratives often feature magic (pasta) pots; traveler's tales tell of marvelous and strange pasta dishes (for example, Marco Polo); and street theater masks—and actual Neapolitans—have made a public spectacle of pasta. The maccheronic muse has also inspired carnivalesque literature, theater, song, odes, proverbs, and more.

Pasta gave its name to a linguistic/literary phenomenon known as "maccheronic poetry," peaking in the fifteenth century. It was a pastiche of Latin and vernacular Italian, frequently producing a comic effect by borrowing a vernacular term that reflected the rustics, who, in turn were referred to by the gross and simple food they ate, *maccherone* or *gnocco* (noodle-head), and who spoke no Latin, the language of culture. The most notable example of this tradition is the maccheronic poet, Teofilo Folengo (alias Merlin Cocai), author of the mock-heroic epic *Baldus*, in which pasta-maker muses reside on Mount Cockaigne, and whose genius is attributed to the consumption of *maccheroni* and *lasagne*.

EIGHTEENTH-CENTURY NAPLES
AS PASTA CAPITAL

Naples began to import pasta from Sicily at the end of the fifteenth century, but it was not until the eighteenth century that Naples became the emblematic capital of pasta, and the city's representative was the *commedia dell'arte* character, half-starved Pulcinella, who on stage was always eating or talking about macaroni. By 1785 there were 280 pasta shops in Naples. Pasta became a street food and its most devoted consumers were street people—*lazzaroni*—as seen in myriad popular prints of the time, where they are characteristically portrayed holding the long strands, dressed with Romano cheese, with their fingers, and at arms length sliding them, often unchewed, down the gullet. Indeed, so unique was this spectacle that it became a must-see tourist attraction, and gentlemen on the grand tour often ordered up a plate of pasta for a *lazzarone*, just to see it performed.

IMMIGRANTS AND PASTA

Neapolitans and other southern Italians were critical to pasta's diffusion throughout the world. For it was as much immigration—and the majority of immigrants were in fact, Neapolitan and southern—as technological advances and transatlantic trade that brought pasta to the world's attention. Along with the wave of late-nineteenth-century immigrants came shiploads of spaghetti in blue wrap (for example, Napoli Bella and Vesuvio brands), olive oil, and condensed tomato paste. Americans first considered these inedible foreign foods and tried to reform the newcomers' diet, but spaghetti won out and eventually became American, not merely ethnic, fare. Italian immigrants were to introduce many other cultures to pasta wherever they settled.

Although Thomas Jefferson, much interested in macaroni and pasta technology, brought cases of the foodstuff to America in 1786 (and later had a pasta machine shipped to him from Campania), it was not until 1848 that it began to be produced commercially in America. The World War I years and the interruption of pasta imports from overseas gave rise to an expanded pasta industry in the United States, as many Italian American pasta importers became manufacturers through small family operations, many of which still exist. Prohibition may have given pasta a boost as well, since it seemed a logical accompaniment to speakeasy wine. In the expanding pasta industry of the 1930s, pasta ceased to be merely Italian and became an American food.

PASTA AS EMBLEM

Ethnic stereotyping frequently makes reference to food. Italians have long been associated with pasta, and Italians from different regions represent themselves by the type of pasta they eat. In England, from approximately 1750 to 1850, a "macaroni" referred to a foppish Englishman, a dandy, who affected foreign (Italian) style by overdressing, wearing a preposterous wig (for example, "Yankee Doodle Dandy" who "stuck a feather in his hat and called it macaroni"; or the London gentleman's club, the Macaroni Club), and perhaps eating foreign foods. On the negative side, a cultured Italian might have referred to a simpleton or country bumpkin as a *gnocco, maccarone,* or *spaghetto.* Sicilians—later Neapolitans—were derogatorily labeled *mangiamaccheroni* (macaroni-eaters) by Italians farther north. Americans have referred to Italians as "Spaghetti Benders." And Marinetti's Futurist Manifesto did not help matters when it declared war on traditional foods, especially pasta, a food which, the avant-garde insisted, promoted moral and physical laxity. The ideal, evidently, was the Germanic meat-eater, a virile warrior race. Italians ignored the Futurists' cultural violence. Instead, Mussolini waged a battle for wheat (*battaglia del grano*) in an attempt to make Italy wheat sufficient. The vastly increased wheat acreage had the effect of shifting the epicenter of production northward (pasta producers included Agnesi in Oneglia, Buitoni in San Sepolcro, Barilla in Parma), thereby ending the dominance of Naples by the 1940s.

Many legendary Italian pasta-eaters have helped raise the image of this food: Rossini, Caruso, and Sophia Loren, who famously said: "Everything you see I owe to spaghetti." Pasta iconography, old and new, traces its presence in cultural history, from early popular prints of *Cuccagna* or of Neapolitan pasta-eaters, to pasta advertisements, packaging, and film (for example, Charlie Chaplin in *City Lights,* Disney's *The Lady and the Tramp*), and in Italy, Totò—all of which molded pasta's image for millions.

COMMERCIAL PASTA: FROM ARTISAN GUILDS
TO MULTINATIONALS

From the fourteenth to the sixteenth centuries, pasta became well established all over Italy. Pasta makers became so numerous that they formed corporations and guilds, largely to protect their interests against competing guilds (for example, bakers). These guilds were in Florence (*lasagnari*), 1337; Genoa, 1574; Savona (*fidelari*), 1577; Naples (*vermicellari, pastai*), 1579; Palermo, 1665; Rome, 1642.

It is in the passage to dried pasta that the quantum historic leap is achieved and pasta commerce begins, the earliest record of which goes back to medieval Arabs and Sicilians. In more recent times, increasingly efficient technology relating to the basic phases in pasta production—kneading, pressing, extruding, cutting, and drying—together with improved distribution networks and power sources (electricity), have led to an enormous increase in production and consumption. Indeed, by the mid-twentieth century, commercial pasta had truly become a universal food for all classes.

Large-scale pasta production first flourished in coastal areas (Palermo, Genoa, later Naples) where plenty of sun and alternating warm and cool sea breezes allowed for outdoor drying—the most critical part of the process—and also made shipping easy. Like laundry, spaghetti was hung to dry on outdoor lines and became part of the Neapolitan folkloric milieu. Pasta brands from Gragnano and Torre Annunziata, where warm Vesuvian air and cool sea breezes created perfect drying conditions, became renowned. Once artificial drying technology was devised, however, manufacturing was freed from such climatic considerations.

Other technological milestones included mechanical kneaders, continuous-feed presses, even refinements of the fork. Cesare Spadaccini of Naples invented the first mechanical kneader to replace feet (although this was not developed), as well as a four-prong shortened fork to make spaghetti twirling easier and its consumption possible at the Neapolitan court of Ferdinand II (circa 1840). But it was a spate of mostly nineteenth-century inventions that revolutionized the industry: for example, Féreol Sandragné's prototype of the continuous-feed machine, and the "Marsigliese," a mechanical sieve that could sort crushed grain.

Early artisans' guilds and small family-run businesses have largely given way to multinational giants who count pasta manufacturing among their diversified holdings and enjoy large market shares of a lucrative, expanding global market. Some of these companies are the following: Borden (largest pasta producer in the United States, sole US distributor for De Cecco since 1988, and head of an empire of small, regional companies); Philip Morris (parent company of General Foods, acquired Kraft in 1988); Nestlé (acquired Buitoni in 1988); Hershey's; Campbell's; and Lipton.[2]

WHEAT

Sicily and southern Italy—ancient Rome's, then Italy's, breadbasket— was an early source of durum wheat for Italian pasta, which, since 1967, is the only legally-mandated grain allowed for this food. While Italians came to produce and consume the world's largest quantities of pasta outside Asia (over fifty pounds per capita in 1988), Italy's capacity to produce wheat is easily overwhelmed. In the nineteenth century, other sources were added. Genovese merchants imported the best Kubanka wheat (up to 19 percent protein), grown in the fertile black earth of Taganrog, Crimea, on the Black Sea. But famines, revolution, and genocide had destroyed this mythic Russian wheat by the 1920s and 1930s, apparently forever. North American wheat from Manitoba and North Dakota filled the vacuum. American durum wheat production— which, in turn, boosted the American pasta industry—was largely due to the efforts of one man. Mark Carleton, an agronomist for the United States Dept. of Agriculture and an expert in plant pathology, went to Russia in 1898 looking for rust-resistant wheat and, upon returning, converted farmers, milling companies, chemists, and hotel and restaurant cooks, to durum wheat.

---

2   The commercial landscape, of course, has changed since the original publication of this essay.

PASTA TYPOLOGY: CUTTING
THE LINGUISTIC DOUGH

Estimates of the number of pasta shapes range from 600 to 1000. Pasta atlases are only recently beginning to appear. The sheer volume of regional, traditional, and also industrial and historical types—although only a fraction of them remain in common use—makes this task a daunting one. Some of the earliest terms refer to length and thinness; for example: Arabic *itrija* and *sev* or *seviyan* (from Hindi *sevika* "thread"), Italian *vermicelli* ("small worms"; originally, finger-length), and later, Italian *spaghetti* (from *spago* "string"). Other terms refer to the dough and to shaping techniques that involve cutting (Italian *tagliatelle,* from *tagliare* "to cut"), rolling, or stamping. Greatest variation occurs in commercial, not homemade pasta, for the obvious reason that industrial dies have made such innovations possible.

A RAVIOLO BY OTHER NAMES

The language of pasta (as of music) is Italian. Much of its rich lexicon is attributable to the richness of the Italian language itself. There are suffixes, given in their plural forms here, that can reduce its dimensions (*-elli, -etti, -ini, -otti,* as in *ravioli/ravioletti* and *tortelli/tortellini*), or increase its dimensions (*-oni,* as in *ravioloni, tortelloni*), or subtly grade it by increasing width (*tagliolini > fettuccine > tagliatelle > pappardelle > lasagne*). There is also rich regional variation [Figure 5.1]. For example, the case for filled pasta (of which Emilia-Romagna is the heartland) is known as *casoncelli* (*cansonsei*) in Bergamo, *tortelli* in Emilia-Romagna, *agnolotti* in Piedmont, *pansoti* in Liguria, *cappelletti* or *ravioli* in central Italy. As for the most common homemade ribbon-shaped egg pasta, *tagliatelle* are also known (with slight variation in size) as *fettuccine, lasagnette, trenette* [Figures 5.2-5.3].

Still today, a marked distinction exists between egg-based fresh pasta, a special, often festive food, and dried commercial pasta, daily fare. But Italians also divide pasta as follows: pasta in clear broth (*pastina in brodo*); pasta in heartier vegetable soup (*minestra,* whence *minestrone*); dried pasta drained and served with a sauce (*pasta asciutta*); and baked pasta (*pasta al forno*; for example, *lasagne, timballo, pasticcio*).

Pasta typologies might further be ordered according to varying criteria: method or place of preparation (home, restaurant, factory); grain type (soft, durum, whole, alternative); calendrical occurrences (festive versus penitent pasta, for example; with and without meat sauce or eggs); Italian versus non-Italian or emigrant pasta (for example, Italian American spaghetti and meatballs); and finally, pasta morphology. Pasta can even be classified according to consumer profile, age, cultural background, and health concerns. For instance, adult pasta differs from children's varieties: there is Italian nursery food, *pastina in brodo* ("tiny pasta in clear broth"); American macaroni and cheese and canned dinosaur or alphabet pasta; and pasta on toast for the British. Special pastas have been developed for the wheat intolerant; and gourmet pastas are aimed at the high-end market. Homemade pasta can be further classified according to the instrument used: rolling pin versus pasta maker or small press (for example, a *torchietto* for extruding *bigoli* in the Veneto); a "comb" or *pettine* (for example, for *garganelli* in Romagna); a zither-like instrument, known as a *chitarra* (guitar), over which thin dough is stretched and rolled to produce thin strands (for example, for *tonnarelli*, resembling square spaghetti, in the Abruzzo); a long metal rod or *ferro* (for long *maccheroni* in Calabria, Puglia, Sicily).

Then there is morphology—long versus short, smooth versus ribbed, hollow versus filled, straight versus fluted. The myriad shapes draw from many semantic areas—human, natural, and even divine. There are helixes, tubes, shells, pearls, nests, worms, butterflies, snails, birds, stars, moons, waves, threads, ribbons, bowties, even "priest-stranglers" (*strozza-* or *strangolapreti*). Paternosters and avemarias (resembling rosary beads), and other shapes inspired by politics (*garibaldini, mafalde, tripoline, assabesi, abissini*), are no longer made. But innovation continues, even though some shapes prove to be mere fads (for example, radiators, UFOs).

With the myriad and continuously evolving forms of pasta available to any cook, matching pasta type to sauce, determining pasta to sauce ratio, and knowing the correct cooking time are subtle areas of pasta connoisseurship, traditional for Italians but learned by others (although traditional canons are shifting even in Italy). In a fifteenth-century cookbook, *De honesta voluptate ac valetudine* (Of honest pleasure and well-being), Bartolomeo Sacchi (pseudonym Plàtina; ca. 1470–75) cautioned that pasta should be cooked "for as long as it takes to say three paternosters"—a short amount of time, even for fresh pasta.

TRENDS

Pasta trends take place within wider social and nutritional contexts. There has been a move toward whole foods and alternative grains such as corn, buckwheat, and spelt. Innovative ingredients—some restaurant-driven—include colored pasta (tomato, herb, beet, mushroom, shrimp, even chocolate) and novelty-stuffed pasta (seafood, artichoke, dried tomato). There has also been a trend toward fusion cuisines, for example, blending East and West. New health guidelines advise lower fat, higher fiber, greater vegetarianism, less processing. The American trend toward greater convenience favors ready-cooked, frozen, microwaveable, and cold-serve pastas, although the Slow Food movement began countering this trend in the new millennium. Americans are becoming more sophisticated in regard to better quality products, taste, nutritional value, authenticity, seasonality, and the artisan tradition.

NUTRITIONAL VALUE: FAT OR SKINNY?

Pasta's fortunes have fluctuated over its long history: it has been considered both a luxury food (in the sixteenth century Neapolitan authorities prohibited its consumption in times of famine or scarcity of wheat), and a vernacular staple. Commonly perceived as a poor man's food at the beginning of the twentieth century, pasta began, with the support of nutritionists extolling the virtues of the Mediterranean diet in the 1970s, to experience a rehabilitation. New nutrition guidelines (and the food chart reformulated in the 1990s) recommended less protein, less saturated animal fat, more fiber, and more complex carbohydrates. Pasta, therefore, is now recognized to be a healthy food.

It is also a highly versatile, immediately satisfying food, recommended for athletes ("carbo-loading" sustains energy before strenuous sports), and even for refined palates.

Vegetables, lean meats, or fish, combined with good quality (even enriched or whole wheat) pasta, makes an excellent, balanced meal. Components of pasta include moisture (water), energy, protein, fat, carbohydrates, and ash. According to the United States Department of Agriculture bulletin ([1989] website 2018), nutrient values for one cup of wheat spaghetti (two ounces uncooked) are approximately seven to fourteen grams of protein, thirty-nine grams of carbohydrates, and when enriched, it provides calcium, phosphorus, iron, potassium, thiamine, riboflavin, and niacin. The caloric value of one cup of cooked pasta is approximately 190 calories (if al dente) and 155 (if tender) (1989).

WORKS CONSULTED

Agnesi, Eva, Giuseppe Giarmoleo, and Vincenzo Agnesi. *E tempo di pasta* [*Time for Pasta*]. Rome: Museo Nazionale delle Paste Alimentari, 1998.

Alberini, Massimo. Introduction to *Pasta & Pizza*, by Anna Martini. Milan: Mondadori, 1974.

Alberini, Massimo. *Maccheroni e spaghetti: storia, letteratura, aneddoti, 1244–1994* (Macaroni and spaghetti: history, literature, anecdotes). Casale Monferrato (AL): Piemme, 1994.

Alberini, Massimo. *Storia della cucina italiana* (History of Italian cuisine). Casale Monferrato (AL): Piemme, 1992.

al-Idrīsī, Muhammad ibn Muhammad. *Kitāb nuzhat al-mushtāq fī ikhtirāq al-āfāq* (*The Pleasure Excursion of One Who Is Eager to Traverse the Regions of the World* [title translation: Britannica]). Also known as *Kitā Rujār*, or *Al-Kitāb al-Rujārī* (Roger's book). 1138.

Apicius. *De re coquinaria,* book IV, chapter 2. 5th C. See the English translation by Joseph Dommers Vehling. *Cookery and Dining*

in Imperial Rome. Project Gutenberg, 2009. https://www.
gutenberg.org/cache/epub/29728/pg29728-images.html.

"A Saga of Cathay," attributed to Keystone Macaroni Manufacturing
Company (1928) in *The Macaroni Journal* of the National
Association of Pasta Makers (now National Pasta Association)
11, no. 6 (October 10, 1929): 32–34. https://ilovepasta.org/wp-
content/uploads/macaroni/1929%2010%20OCTOBER%20
-%20The%20New%20Macaroni%20Journal.pdf.

Bastone, Ponzio, and Ugolino Scarpa, notary. February 2, 1279.
Bastone's will, Historical Archives of Genoa.

Boccaccio, Giovanni. "Calandrino, a fool's tale," *Decameron*, Day
VIII, story 3, 1353.

"Contre Marco Polo: Une histoire comparée des pâtes alimentaires"
(Against Marco Polo: a comparative history of pasta). In
Médiévales 16–17 (1989): 27–100.

Cùnsolo, Felice. *Il libro dei maccheroni* (The macaroni book). Milan:
Mondadori, 1979.

Davidson, Alan. "Pasta." In *The Oxford Companion to Food.* Oxford:
Oxford University Press, 1999, 580–584.

Del Conte, Anna. *Portrait of Pasta.* New York: Paddington Press, 1976.

Del Giudice, Luisa. "Mountains of Cheese and Rivers of Wine: *Paesi
di Cuccagna* and other Gastronomic Utopias." Chapter 1, this
volume. First published in *Imagined States: National Identity,
Utopia, and Longing in Oral Cultures*, edited by Luisa Del
Giudice and Gerald Porter. Logan: Utah State University
Press, 2001.

Hazan, Giuliano. *The Classic Pasta Cookbook.* Sydney, Australia: RD
Press, 1993.

Horace. *Satires* VI, book l, line 115. 35 BCE.

Lawson, Nigella. *Il museo immaginario della pasta / The "Musee
Imaginaire" of Pasta* (bilingual). Turin, Italy: Allemandi, 1995.

Medagliani, Eugenio. *Pastario, ovvero, Atlante delle paste alimentari italiane : primo tentativo di catalogazione delle paste alimentari italiane* (Pastarium, or The Italian pasta atlas: a first attempt toward an Italian pasta catalog), 3rd edition. Lodi, Italy: Bibliotheca Culinaria, 1997.

Montanari, Massimo. "Macaroni Eaters." In *The Culture of Food*. Oxford: Blackwell, 1996, 140–148. Translated from *La fame e l'abbondanza: Storia dell'alimentazione in Europa*. Bari: Laterza, 1993.

Morelli, Alfredo. *In principio era la sfoglia: storia della pasta* (In the beginning there was *sfoglia*: the history of pasta). Pinerolo, Italy: Chiriotti Editori, 1991.

Prezzolini, Giuseppe. *A History of Spaghetti Eating and Cooking for: Spaghetti Dinner*. New York: Abelard-Schuman, 1955.

Prezzolini, Giuseppe. *Maccheroni & C.,* 2nd edition. Milan, Italy: Longanesi, 1957.

Rizzi, Silvio, and Tan Lee Leng. *The Pasta Bible*. New York: Penguin Studio, 1996.

Rustichello da Pisa and Marco Polo. *Livre des Merveilles du Monde* (Book of the marvels of the world) or *Devisement du Monde* (Description of the world) (Franco-Venetian); commonly called *Il Milione* (Italian) and *The Travels of Marco Polo* (English). Ca. 1298–1299.

Sacchi, Bartolomeo (pseud. Plàtina). *De honesta voluptate ac valetudine* (Of honest pleasure and well-being). Ca. 1470–1475. A 1480 edition is reproduced at https://www.loc.gov/item/85664760/.

United States Department of Agriculture, Federal Standards of Identity. 1989. *Composition of Foods: Cereal grains and Pasta: Raw, Processed, Prepared*. Washington, DC: U.S. Government Printing Office. See also Code of Federal Regulations for Specific Standardized Macaroni Products. 1977. https://www.ecfr.gov/current/title-21/part-139/subpart-B. For a more recent version, see also United States Department of Agriculture.

"Food Data Central: Pasta, dry, enriched." 2018. https://fdc.
nal.usda.gov/fdc-app.html#/food-details/169736/nutrients.

The U.S. Pasta Market: A Business Information Report, Business Trend
Analysts: Commack, NY, 1991.

Valli, Carlo. *Pasta nostra quotidiana: viaggio intorno alla pasta* (Our daily
pasta: journeying around pasta). Padua, Italy: MEB, 1991.

Figure 5.1: Handmade *tortellini*, a meat- and cheese-filled, fresh egg-pasta variety, a specialty of the Emilia Romagna region.

Figure 5.2   Figure 5.3

Figures 5.2–5.3: Special-occasion egg pasta for *fettuccine* (long strips), from the author's Lazio region. 5.2 shows machine-rolled sheets of dough drying, before they are machine-cut, while in 5.3 the dough has been hand-rolled with a long rolling pin (*mattarello*), and hand-cut.

6. Feeding the Poor— Welcoming the Stranger: The Watts Towers Common Ground Initiative and St. Joseph's Communal Tables in Watts

The Watts Towers narrative is as much the story of a man and his artistic obsession as it is about citizen action and art in community.[1] It also tells how an artwork, located in a place of poverty, such as Watts (Los Angeles, California), has come to find itself at the crossroads of community development efforts. *Sabato Rodia's Towers in Watts: Art, Migrations, Development* (Del Giudice 2014) more extensively treats

1   This essay was first published in Regina F. Bendix and Michaela Fenske, eds., *Politische Mahlzeiten / Political Meals.* German translation of the introduction by John Bendix. Berlin: Wissenschaftsforum Kulinaristik, 2014. Chapters in English or German as originally written. Unless otherwise noted, all photographs are mine.

I wish to express my heartfelt thanks to all who contributed to making the Communal Tables in Watts program possible (as well as to all partners in the Watts Towers Common Ground Initiative). All donors, individual and institutional, are named at http://wattstowerscommonground.org/festival_food.html. I especially thank (once stranger and now friend), Rosie Lee Hooks, director of the Watts Towers Arts Center, for her abiding support for the various Watts Towers-related projects I have proposed over the years. None would have been possible had she not said yes. Many personal and community rewards have come about because of it. Thank you to UCLA students Claire Lavagnino and Melina Madrigal, ever willing to lend a hand. And to my own family, Edward, Elena, Giulia, and Mattia, who not only did some heavy lifting, but baked bread, ladled soup, and kept me sane throughout "just one more program," I say: I am truly blessed.

these interrelated topics, and contextualizes this essay, which instead will shift the focus to how a program on food, art, and the Sicilian St. Joseph's tradition, "Communal Tables: Practicing Hospitality, Sustainability," sought to address larger political and economic issues facing Watts, namely those relating to poverty, migration, and common ground—themes embedded in the Watts Towers themselves.

The extraordinary and unusual work of art known as the Watts Towers, an assemblage of bits of tile, glass, pottery, seashells (a National Historic Landmark), was built as a labor of love, for over three decades, beginning in the early 1920s, by a solitary immigrant worker, Sabato (Sam, Simon) Rodia. Rodia's Towers are located at the heart of Watts, an area whose very name has become emblematic of poverty, urban blight, and violence since the Watts Riots/Rebellion of 1965. Soon after Rodia walked away from his Towers in 1954, they were "discovered" by a small band of concerned citizens (later incorporated as the Committee for Simon Rodia's Towers in Watts [CSRTW]), who saved them from a city demolition order in 1959, and thereby became involved in a decades-long effort to conserve their physical integrity and to promote art in community through the creation of the Watts Towers Arts Center (WTAC). Controversy continues to swirl around the Towers—most recently, as plans for enhancing the campus have raised questions about what forms of development are appropriate. Changing political regimes, the economic recession, and demographic shifts, are all contributing to the transformation of Watts, and thus are having an impact on the Watts Towers as well.[2]

The Watts Towers Common Ground Initiative: Art, Migrations, Development sought to address multiple goals along a continuum from the Watts Towers–Watts Towers Arts Center–Watts community.[3] Conferences, exhibitions, performances, and tours were aimed at refocusing local, national, and international attention on the monument, the better to study, present, and celebrate Sabato Rodia and

---

2   This essay cannot provide more than a passing summary of the historic narrative which is better told elsewhere: e.g., Goldstone and Paquin Goldstone 1997 and Del Giudice 2014 (also providing an extensive bibliography for further study).

3   Website: http://wattstowerscommonground.org/ (accessed March 3, 2014).

his Towers in Watts—with a newly added emphasis on the migration context/subtext. The Initiative's first task was to bridge divides and to gather together diverse communities around this common cause. But the Initiative also represented a form of ethnographic practice which I had come to embrace personally: that is, to apply academic and field learning more responsibly in the world, seeking to help resolve *real-life* problems. As the coordinator of the Initiative, I resolved to ensure that theory and praxis, contemplation and action, intersected, thereby also engaging issues that went beyond the Towers and the specific context of Watts. That is, sociopolitical concerns could be embraced simultaneously, and in one place, along with an academic, artistic enterprise, by sponsoring conferences and public programs.

Some of those larger issues (all painfully affecting Watts itself) engaged such facts as these: one in six Americans go hungry; the economic, social, and political divide between rich and poor continues to grow (now known as the 1 percent and 99 percent); immigration reform remains largely ignored or worse, provoking a xenophobic backlash; a living wage is on the radar of few politicians. The Initiative's concluding communal-table food program therefore was a direct response to pressing needs—albeit in a ritualized mode (the St. Joseph's altar, pageant, and banquet), but which did not ignore the actual filling of Watts food pantries. But before describing this food program, some historical background seems in order.

Upon saving the Towers from obliteration, the CSRTW was immediately challenged by this question: how could they be so concerned with the work of art while ignoring human suffering in the community in which it was located? Did the Uptown art lovers have any true knowledge of Downtown social and economic realities?[4] Of course, because many among the Towers' defenders were also politically progressive, they naturally gravitated toward and helped advocate for human and civil rights for communities such as Watts. The Committee

---

4   The Watts Towers as an artwork, more or less, seem to have represented the interests of an educated, progressive, outsider elite (municipal, national, and international), while the Arts Center which the CSRTW created for the community, gathered together the local community of need as beneficiary of their efforts. Today, the situation has evolved and it is the local community and the WTAC that see themselves as the de facto guardians of the Watts Towers.

(not without heated debate) stepped up to the challenge by creating the Watts Towers Arts Center and offering free arts education for local youth. It was also anticipated that, by educating the community about the arts and fostering creativity, the center would also create a local base fully capable of valuing and defending the art treasure in its midst. In time it also became clearer that by investing in human artistic development locally, economic betterment might follow. Indeed, by degrees, but steadily, the circle of support rallying around the Towers and its Arts Center, widened to embrace Watts residents themselves—many of whom recalled contributing materials to "old man Rodia's" Towers as they watched them rise. The WTAC, as it came under the directorship of prominent African American artists, increasingly galvanized gallery activities and exhibitions, and took charge of teaching and related public programs aimed at addressing African American self-representation, attracting artists, musicians, and poets, and instituting major festivals such as the Watts Towers Simon Rodia Jazz Festival (begun in 1978) and the Watts Towers Day of the Drum Festival (in 1981). Thus, the Towers campus became and continues to stand as a significant cultural institution on the map of Black Los Angeles.

I began learning about the Watts Towers and its communities through several Italian public programs and private research projects in which I had become involved, beginning in 2003, with the organization of the Italian Oral History Institute's 2005 festival: Italian Los Angeles: Celebrating Italian Life, Local History, and the Arts in Southern California. While helping to organize two Watts Towers conferences (University of Genova 2009 and UCLA 2010), I also began researching historical archival materials regarding the Watts Towers in UCLA Library's Special Collections. Through these years of activity in and around the monument, I became more acutely aware that the thorny questions of insider/outsider, of who were the stakeholders in the campus, and of who ought guide its development efforts, persisted. Various historic and more recent fault lines seemed to divide communities of interest around the artwork. But it also became ever clearer that Los Angeles itself was a patchwork of many historically overlapping cartographies and sites to which various ethnic communities laid claim. Rodia's Towers in Watts were no different.

Since Rodia's times, Watts continued to "welcome strangers"—often the most marginalized newcomers to America and to the Southwest. Rodia indeed, had moved to a community where Japanese, African Americans (many from Louisiana and the rural South), southern Europeans, Mexicans, and others lived side by side. The war effort shifted this demographic mix, as significant numbers of African Americans came to Watts to take jobs in war-related industries. The shutting down of these industries, a rerouting of transportation hubs, and other factors led to social and economic decline in post-War Watts, and thus ultimately to the Watts Riots/Rebellion in 1965. More recently, in the 1970s and 80's, Watts saw another demographic shift as Latin Americans began displacing African Americans. Therefore, Watts' identity has continued to evolve, from multiethnic and multiracial origins, to predominantly African American, and now to increasingly Latino.

The migration context for the Watts Towers therefore, was present from the very start. It encompassed not only the artist who created them, but the shifting community of Watts itself, the community for whom the Arts Center was created. The Watts Towers Common Ground Initiative attempted to recognize this complex mix and to help foster common ground, most notably in its culminating program. The goal was to ensure that literally all be seated at the same table. Hadn't food always represented a vehicle for sharing good will across ethnic boundaries among Americans?

The "Communal Tables" program combined two of my own local historical and ethnographic research interests: "Sicilian St. Joseph's Day Tables in Los Angeles: Feeding the Poor, Welcoming the Stranger" (Del Giudice 2010, ch. 3 this volume), together with the Italian cultural and historic contexts of the Watts Towers in "Sabato Rodia's Towers in Watts: Art, Migration, and Italian Imaginaries" (in Del Giudice 2014). It was also a way of bringing two communities, geographically and politically contingent, closer together—two communities which, as it happened, both come under the same civic jurisdiction: San Pedro and Watts. Had no one (not even the local councilperson's office) previously considered this possibility? For instance, the Sicilian St. Joseph's Table tradition had for decades been practiced by the Sicilian fisherman of Los Angeles's port city, San Pedro, and one of its major tables in the entire Southland took place at Mary Star of the Sea Church in that community. The Italian immigrant, Sabato Rodia, who had moved to nearby Watts, frequently visited the Long Beach sea communities in search of usable shoreline treasures, and created an artwork that was deeply embedded in Italian South Central culture and immigrant history. Both San Pedro and Watts therefore were significant and contiguous sites on any map of Italian Los Angeles.

It was my ethnographic and oral historical field research in the Italian immigrant communities of Los Angeles that had suggested the historic, cultural, and geographic possibility of bringing the two together; my perspective and experience as a public sector folklorist that assured me it could be done. But it was my growing commitment to social advocacy (e.g., food justice, immigration reform), that convinced me it should be done. And so I embarked on actually creating a St. Joseph's Table (with all the fixings) in Watts—where, *nota bene*, there was no Italian community [Figure 6.1].

The primary goal of any St. Joseph's Table, of course, is to feed the poor and welcome the stranger. Among Sicilian Americans it had also become a means of commemorating their own historical hardships as migrants, and of giving thanks for overcoming them (e.g., a "Sicilian Thanksgiving"). Its dynamics inherently addressed many of the issues and challenges facing our own Initiative. Its component parts included: a decorative altar reproducing abundance, a pageant dramatizing the saintly migrants (Mary, Joseph, Jesus) in search of hospitality, and the welcoming of strangers. Thereupon, the communal banquet that followed was an open table, extending hospitality to all. The tradition entails the begging of food and the redistribution of it to those most in need. Our food program sought to weave a circle elegantly around Watts Towers–Watts Towers Arts Center–Watts Community, and thereby to demonstrate one way care of one another might be achieved, while underscoring the *tangible* needs for food and shelter combined with the *intangible* needs for art and an inclusive sense of community.

But where in Watts should a table be created? Partners of the Initiative in Watts led me to St. Lawrence of Brindisi Church (founded by Capuchin Franciscans from Ireland in the early 1920s). Indeed, it seemed an appropriate venue, given that Franciscans have traditionally been devoted to the poor—among them, the disenfranchised, the homeless, and the displaced. (The fact that it bore the name of an Italian saint from Brindisi, in southern Italy, also seemed a good omen and a sign of welcome.) The parish staff and priests knew nothing about the Sicilian tradition but graciously welcomed us to install one in the church. I soon discovered that the parish itself reflected Watts in transition: the ratio of Latinos to African Americans had become roughly 9:1, and the church administrators seemed keenly aware of the need for integrating communities. Icons inside the church, and on the long mural in the parking lot outside, reflected both communities. On the one hand, were depictions of Our Lady of Guadalupe, Cesar Chavez, Bishop Oscar Romero, while on the other, the Knights of Peter Claver (the largest African American Catholic fraternal organization in the US),[5] as well as significant African American community members of the local parish. Symbolic representation here seemed vital. Could such boundary crossings within the church be heightened by the symbolic action of a communal table?

What place could a Sicilian St. Joseph's Table occupy within this referentially complex scenario—while still remaining grounded in Rodia's Towers in Watts? How could it be integrated into this parish? And more importantly: would anyone come? Cultural (and linguistic) translations were in order. A text (with illustrations) outlining the Sicilian tradition, together with the full three-day program on March 18–20, 2011,[6] were published in the parish bulletin in English and Spanish. These were kept on hand next to our food altar. And I explained to parish school children what we

---

5   The 16th C. Catalan Jesuit was a missionary in New Spain shortly after slavery had been instituted by King Ferdinand. He became the patron saint of slaves and minister to African Americans. The Order was founded in Mobile, Alabama and is presently headquartered in New Orleans, http://en.wikipedia. org/wiki/Peter_Claver (accessed May 10, 2013).

6   St. Joseph's feast day is March 19 which, in Italy, is also Father's Day.

were doing. But to make the entire food program viable I would need to appeal to donors outside Watts. We mounted a PR campaign on radio, social media, and the newsletters of the Italian Consulate, the Accademia Italiana della Cucina, Los Angeles chapter (which I headed at the time), and all Initiative partners, to solicit tangible support. Our major "on the ground" collaboration in Watts came from the Watts Towers Arts Center and its director, Rosie Lee Hooks. The program included three days of viewing of the altar, a pageant, and the blessing of the altar; a tour of "Mudtown Farms" (Watts Labor Community Action Committee [WLCAC]), a food sustainability project by Janine Watkins; illustrated lectures on St. Joseph, San Giuseppe, San José by Charlene Villaseñor Black, Professor of Art History and Chicana/o Studies at UCLA ("The Cult of St. Joseph in Mexico and the Hispanic World"), and by me ("Rituals of Charity and Abundance: The Sicilian St. Joseph's Day Table in Los Angeles, A Feast for Our Times"). The most ambitious part of the program however, was the communal banquet on the final day of the program, Sunday, March 20. Volunteers helped set up, cook, serve, and clean up. Despite the rain (a rare occurrence in Southern California), we fed approximately 500 under a canopy that the parish had set up [Figure 6.2].

The focus of the Sicilian tradition directly addresses hunger, poverty, homelessness, and redistribution of resources. These form its core. How one transforms an ethnically specific into a cross-cultural event seemed secondary. One overriding question was what to retain and what to leave aside from the Sicilian tradition, especially as related to foods and the pageant. For instance, as a Lenten festivity, a pasta with fish (*pasta con le sarde*) is traditionally served at a Sicilian St. Joseph's banquet, followed by fish, salad, and citrus. But *pasta e fagioli* (Italian bean soup) was also a good option and worked especially well in this community, since beans are a staple of Latin American foodways.

Just what were we to do however, about the pageant of "the saints"—the wayfaring Mary, Joseph, Jesus—and how would their "Flight into Egypt" procession be conducted? That reenactment is either eliminated from the festivity today, or else relegated to the youth—perhaps since it identified the poorest members of the community, who traditionally filled the role, and thus presents some shadow of stigma. Yet, precisely as a dramatization of the search for hospitable shelter, it seemed to me a core theme of any St. Joseph's Table in Watts, given the vast influx of new migrants and the growing numbers of homeless among the long-standing residents. Given the real-life drama of begging and poverty on the streets of Watts every day, the quest for shelter and sustenance did not seem so far removed. Further, knocking on doors for hospitality, the search for a "home," forms a central tenant of many current migrants' wanderings, as well as figuring in the reality of the homeless literally outside the church's doors. In earlier times, the pageant carried special meaning for Sicilian Americans who were fleeing the poorest region of Italy in the late nineteenth century mass migrations and even today, commemorates a time when they, as immigrants and strangers, needed to be welcomed. (Such cultural memories of migration must be one of the reasons the table tradition has survived so well among Sicilians in America.) As our reenactment played out, our "saints" were actual immigrant members of the parish, chosen by the church itself. The pageant took place on a Friday evening. Musical accompaniment (perhaps recalling a Las Posadas tradition),[7] although not requested, was spontaneously added, and a festive procession followed the saints to the main doors of the church as they knocked to be let in. For Rosie and for me, opening the doors, welcoming all to enter, and then leading the saints down the aisle and to the St. Joseph's side altar, was one of the most poignant moments of the entire three-day event [Figure 6.3]. After an impromptu sermon by the visiting priest, who blessed the altar, we two distributed bread rolls to the packed church, and the parishioners were invited, along with their friends and families, to return for the Sunday banquet.

---

7   Similar traditions, of course, were known to these ethnic Catholics. Mexicans also practiced devotion through food altars, as well as reenacted the Flight into Egypt in the Christmas Las Posadas tradition. And, at least for some of the African American parishioners, the St. Joseph's Table might have harkened back to parishes of remoter origin in Louisiana, where several Spiritualist churches also created St. Joseph's Tables, learned from their Sicilian neighbors in that state (cf. Estes 1986–87, 1987).

The altar itself was assembled inside the church in a side niche, left of the main altar (not in the church hall or basement, as is frequently the case), which limited its size. The fact that it was placed in a Marian niche (without forethought—it was the only available space available) resulted in the face of Mary overlooking—almost hovering—over husband and child! I certainly did not object. Space limitations also entailed an "essentialization" of the altar. It was pared down to core elements: bread, garlands, citrus, flowers, and little else. The usual cornucopias were reduced to a few baskets of vegetables, placed on the floor, at the altar's base; nor could there be a sequence of dish upon dish of cooked vegetables, fish, cakes—staples on public St. Joseph's Day Tables (e.g., St. Mary Star of the Sea Church in San Pedro; or the Casa Italiana at St. Peter's Italian Church, in Downtown Los Angeles). Indeed, our program presented an altar while almost eliminating the table. Our more humble table, less a groaning board and more a minimal, iconic Italian dinner table (placed between the St. Joseph altar and the "Big Table"—the main altar of the Church) with familiar, more domestic versions of the Christian rite: homemade loaves of bread and a flask of red wine, on a blue and white checkered tablecloth, and Italian-style place settings of flat and pasta plates, napkins, and traditional, small wine glasses—all from my home and reminiscent of my own immigrant family table [Figure 6.4]. Nearer the communion rail were baskets of bread, including a decorative flat bread depicting the Watts Towers but labeled with their name as inscribed by Rodia: "Nuestro Pueblo" [Figure 6.5]. Despite its condensed size, the altar nonetheless radiated a sense of abundance and resplendence, as it was densely adorned with decorative and fanciful breads [Figure 6.6], interspersed with citrus on a background of greenery. Artfulness and art were at the very center of our altar, not only through its design (thanks to the combined efforts of many hands, a close examination of historic bibliographic sources, and the talents of artists at the WTAC), but in the visual links to the Watts Towers, including a miniature of the Watts Towers themselves, created by Charles Dickson, and placed on the altar [Figure 6.7]. Care was lavished on the choice of all forms of adornment—from the sculpted breads, the garlands of fruit, and flowers, to the embroidered linens, ceramics, and basketry.

Who was responsible for this work? The St. Joseph's Day altar and table were created with and between communities. The altar was built and adorned in collaboration with the director and artists of the Watts Towers Arts Center. I learned to make, and with family and friends, produced the artistic breads hanging from the garlands. The ritual braided breads (and all breads to be distributed during the banquet) were baked and donated by renowned Los Angeles Sicilian chef, Celestino Drago. Donations of citrus and greenery came from a variety of sources, including residents of Watts. Foods for the communal banquet were donated by Celestino Drago, Sam Perricone Citrus Co., Food Forward, and Evan Kleiman. Evan Kleiman, Los Angeles chef, founder of Slow Food Los Angeles, and radio host of "Good Food," presided over the cauldron of bubbling soup. The meal was served by many volunteers, including UCLA students and Kleiman's radio audience [Figure 6.8]. Financial assistance for the entire effort came, in large measure, from individual donors in the Italian community of Los Angeles (including the Consul General of Italy in Los Angeles, Nicola Faganello, who also personally assisted at the communal banquet in Watts), St. Alban's Episcopal Church, and other charitable organizations. All monetary donations ($3,000) were translated into food certificates redeemable at the local supermarket in Watts, and entrusted for distribution to the parish, the Watts Senior Citizen Center, and the Watts Towers Arts Center. Food donations were equally divided as well.

What was political about this meal? Calling public attention to the plight of the poor is itself a radical political act in America today. The mainstream media devotes little attention to the issue of poverty, partly because the poor have little effect on policy and are low on the nation's list of priorities (in an increasingly corporatized political system). The extremely poor, even the moderately so, and the homeless, now in ever-increasing numbers since the financial recession (but also present before), require advocates on all fronts. Every day, we are challenged to reassert the concept of a common good into our national discourse, but the notion itself seems to be meeting fierce resistance. Instead, the displaced—economic refugees (immigrants), whether documented or undocumented, as well as others on the economic margins—are willfully criminalized. Immigration reform recedes from our collective will. And new Jim Crow legislation threatens to reverse progress on the human rights front (cf. Alexander 2010). Programs instituted to aid the poorest (many instituted immediately after the Great Depression) are mercilessly slashed, while affordable healthcare for all has proved a bitter battle. The spectacle of itinerants in this most transient of cities—knocking on doors, seeking to belong, asking for the barest of necessities (food to eat, a place of shelter)—is everywhere. Hospitality is hard to come by these days.

A historic perspective helps us understand repeating cycles of migration (internal and global)—from nineteenth century Europeans to twentieth century Dust Bowlers, Africans from the American South, the post-War westward movements, to twenty-first century Latinos from Mexico, Central and South America, and more recent tides of political refugees from East Africa and Southeast Asia. Most often, they leave their homes in response to specific economic, social, and political disasters. Migrants and refugees continue to search out hospitable places of opportunity, even as their global movements produce corresponding rising tides of xenophobia.

Rodia himself, among that earliest immigrant wave from an impoverished central-southern region of Italy (Campania), was subject to its sting. He was keenly aware and vocal about the needs of the working man, the deep divide between "the boss(es)" and the poor, about exclusion and ethnic hostilities. The artist transformed these experiences into his great opus, the Watts Towers, and they provide critical keys to understanding the perennial mystery about what they are, why he built them. He named his constructed complex Nuestro Pueblo (Our Town/Our People), and although we cannot know precisely what he meant to convey in this name, we can surmise that it represented an act of inclusion (*nuestro*) he might have hoped for himself, in a not always hospitable land. "I build the tower, people like, everybody come," he is heard saying in the film documentary, *I Build the Tower* (Landler and Byer 2006). The Towers attempt to bind the collectivity together around a thing of beauty, love, and celebration. His was a gratuitous gift to the community, an invitation for all to partake—indeed, something of an open communal table: the radical inclusivity of an open communal table is a radical political ideal.

Today, those living on the social margins fill the streets of Watts and places like Watts all over the country, but often seem to be invisible, strangers in our midst. In a city as diffuse as Los Angeles, fragmented into socioeconomic enclaves, it is easy to ignore such places. And yet, I am convinced that we must intentionally seek them out, cross over into landscapes where we have never been, and initiate dialogs we rarely have, in order to create a more civilized society through partnerships of human solidarity. How else can we help all achieve basic needs such as food security, health, education, as well as the creative means toward self-expression through the arts? How many human treasures among us are waiting to be enabled and released, ready to enrich the collective? No one should be forced to beg to meet needs of body and soul. Sometimes such needs brilliantly combine. The St. Joseph's tradition might represent one such instance where art, feasting, and community are literally embodied.

The Watts Towers Common Ground Initiative itself began around a (political) meal. Many strangers were invited to sit around my dinner table, colleagues at UCLA, as well as several key Watts and Watts Towers stakeholders, to share a simple meal and to discuss whether we might begin the process at all. I needed to know whether the collected company wanted to be in dialog and what might be accomplished by it. Would we academics, activists, and others (a sort of extension of the original CSRTW perhaps) be viewed as outsiders in Watts? What was being asked of us and by us? And what would it really take to create common ground around the Watts Towers? We awaited with bated breath to hear—especially from members of the Watts community—whether we should continue. Timothy and Janine Watkins, of the Watts Labor Community Action Committee (WLCAC), which had been leading development efforts in Watts since the 1960s, were most vocal in raising issues of concern but their carefully considered *yes* signaled that we could at least try to achieve something together. Certainly, a willingness to listen, the practice of honesty and respect, were necessary points of departure. As was the recognition that the Watts Towers, its Arts Center, and Watts were inextricably linked in the view of local advocates. We were alerted to the fact that collaborative efforts between such unequal partners, between privileged Westsiders and communities of extreme poverty such as Watts, required great care and sensitivity. Divergent goals, cultural models, even language, threatened definitive breaks (even among organizers) at times, but dialog helped us work beyond them. We faced our fears, bumped up against community boundaries, and came to some form of (always and necessarily) partial understanding.

Constant vigilance and consultation were required throughout the process. I had much to learn. For example, I became (not immediately) aware that even the Initiative's meager resources needed to be shared.[8] As did our moral support for issues which affected the Watts Towers, the Arts Center, and Watts (e.g., support for arts funding at the WTAC, resistance to the privatization of the WTAC, and to a skateboard park on the campus).[9] It also became apparent to me that border crossings should occur in both directions, that we must provide opportunities for communities to listen to the other, for Watts to be represented in Westwood, and for Westwood to go to Watts. And so followed an exchange of programs, as well as an understanding that the support would continue after the immediate conference and festival came to a close. Indeed, support for programs at the Watts Towers continued to be forthcoming from the Italian Cultural Institute and the Consulate

---

8   The repeated request by the WTAC director to all audiences to "leave something behind" sensitized me to the economic issues attendant to the Initiative. Not just intangible but tangible good must accrue to the community. Therefore, I decided to engage a local graphic designer to design the flyer (i.e., Willie Middlebrook). And whereas speakers were not paid to present at the conference, we made a special exception for the Artists in Conversation Panel, as well as the Watts Prophet, who were at least modestly compensated for their time. Further, we did not hold all activities in Westwood (UCLA or the Italian Cultural Institute), but determined that part of the conference activities should take place in Watts (at the Watts Labor Community Action Committee) where lunch would be prepared by their employees (and compensated by attendees). This also provided the opportunity to visit not only the Towers but the remarkable Civil Rights Museum while in Watts.

9   A Facebook page (Watts Towers Common Ground Initiative), a direct outcome of the Initiative, has become the vehicle for the communication of many of these concerns which continue to arise, as well as publicity for programs and issues relating to the campus.

General of Italy in Los Angeles for many years thereafter. It remains to be seen whether a *lasting* partnership has been forged.

To conclude: the Initiative sought to demonstrate tangibly how to achieve common ground through geographic boundary crossings, open forums, and joint programs, including communal tables. In some small measure, I believe we achieved some important goals, among them, providing a tangible example of how a common good could be reached.

WORKS CITED

Alexander, Michelle. 2010. *The New Jim Crow: Mass Incarceration in the Age of Colorblindness.* New York: The New Press.

Del Giudice, Luisa. 2010. "Rituals of Charity and Abundance: Sicilian St. Joseph's Tables and Feeding the Poor in Los Angeles." Chapter 3 this volume. First published in *California Italian Studies* 1, no. 2.

Del Giudice, Luisa. 2014. *Sabato Rodia's Towers in Watts: Art, Migrations, Development.* New York: Fordham University Press.

Estes, David C. 1986–87. "St. Joseph's Day in New Orleans: Contemporary Urban Varieties of an Ethnic Festival." In *Louisiana Folklore Miscellany* 6, no. 2: 35–43.

Estes, David C. 1987. "Across Ethnic Boundaries: St. Joseph's Day in a New Orleans Afro-American Spiritual Church." *Mississippi Folklore Register* 21, nos. 1–2: 9–22.

Goldstone, Bud, and Arloa Paquin Goldstone. 1997. *The Los Angeles Watts Towers.* Los Angeles: Getty Conservation Institute and J. Paul Getty Museum.

Landler, Edward, and Brad Byer. 2006. *I Build the Tower.* Los Angeles: Bench Movies; feature-length documentary film.

Figure 6.1: The St Joseph's Day Altar and Table, co-curated by Luisa Del Giudice and Rosie Lee Hooks, and assembled by Watts Towers Arts Center artists, friends, and family. The altar was assembled in the Marian niche, left of the main altar, in St. Lawrence of Brindisi Church, Watts.

Figure 6.2: Communal table, under a canopy to protect from the rain.

Figure 6.3: The "saints" knocking at the door of St. Lawrence of Brindisi Church, asking to be let in.

Figure 6.4: A simple dinner table with bread and wine set in the Italian manner, to the left of the main altar at St. Lawrence of Brindisi Church.

Figure 6.5: A replica in bread of Nuestro Pueblo (the Watts Towers), made by Elena and Giulia Tuttle, the author's daughters.

Figure 6.6: Artistic breads made with Nancy Romero, ready to be integrated into the altar, festooned with greenery and citrus.

Figure 6.7: WTAC artist Charles Dickson's sculpture of Watts Towers on the St. Joseph's Table.

Figure 6.8: St. Joseph's Day Table volunteers, including UCLA students, KCRW's *Good Food* host, Evan Kleiman, and members of the *Good Food* radio audience, Italian Consul Nicola Faganello, WTAC director and co-curator, Rosie Lee Hooks, and Watts Towers Common Ground Initiative coordinator, Luisa Del Giudice, and others.

7. Treasure from Trees: Gold and Liquid Gold in the Oral and Archaeological Traditions around Horace's Sabine Villa in Licenza, Italy

PRELIMINARIES

I have great affection for the olive.[1] Given its symbolic density and versatility, the olive—tree, fruit, and final by-product—represent many of my own activities rather well; thus, I made it a personal icon on my website (www.luisadg.org) [Figure 7.1]. For me, it symbolizes activities that involve Italian food (e.g., serving as the Los Angeles Delegate for the Italian Academy of Cuisine);[2] Mediterranean folk culture (e.g., acting as co-convener of the Mediterranean Studies Section of the American Folklore Society,' formerly the Italian Section);[3] organizing cultural programs, festivals, academic conferences, and publications on Mediterranean culture (e.g., Del Giudice and Van Deusen 2005

---

1   This essay derives from research published in Frischer, Crawford, De Simone, *The Horace's Villa Project: 1997–2003* (Del Giudice 2006), and a version of this paper as read at the conference held at the University of Toronto on "Olive Oil Culture in the Mediterranean," November 10–11, 2011. I wish to thank the editors for permission to reproduce parts of that published paper and illustrations here. All photography is mine. Unless otherwise noted, translations are also mine.

2   I was Delegato for the *Accademia Italiana della Cucina* from 2010–2012.

3   I convened the Italian Section from 1988–1995, then the Mediterranean Section (co-convened for the last couple of years, with Sabina Magliocco) from 2007–2011.

[Figure 7.2]; Essential Salento: Festival of Salentine Culture, Los Angeles, 1998); extending figurative olive branches in peace and social-action projects (some of them involving food justice: e.g., "Rituals of Charity and Abundance: Sicilian St. Joseph's Tables and Feeding the Poor in Los Angeles" Chapter 6 this volume); and finally, organizing spiritual retreats [Figures 7.3–7.4], social actions, and global justice initiatives. The metaphoric olive integrates all of them.

But I suspect it is also the olive's firmly rooted place in the Italian peasant imaginary and in cultural tradition which has made it especially appealing to me. Like other Italian immigrants, I attempt to cultivate a few olives and re-create landscapes of memory in hospitable California, "the Mediterranean on the Pacific." Olives have become an integral part of our landscape as well, thanks to the early Spanish padres, and today, they are a major industry in our state. However, other more tenacious Italian immigrants, such as Sam Pantaleo—originally from Bari and living in Richmond Hill, Ontario, Canada—do so in decidedly *un*-Mediterranean environments. His trees produce only a handful of olives (high yield is not the point), but like his lemons and figs [Figures 7.5–7.7], these trees are iconic and satisfy deep psychological needs. Given Canada's less than favorable climate (recalling that extreme and prolonged cold is the olive's greatest enemy), Sam produces rare, near-miraculous natural treasures. Many have noted the vital importance of gardens in immigrant lives (for example, Grillo's 2010 film, *Terra sogna terra / Earth Dream Earth* or Klindienst's book, *The Earth Knows My Name*, 2006).

The venerable olive tree, however, is in a class of its own. It was sacred to the Romans who forbade its use in domestic fires, reserving it for devotional altars, and who transmitted some of its ritual uses through Christian rites (e.g., on Palm Sunday, also known as *domenica dell'oliva* [Olive Sunday], or in the sacrament of Extreme Unction, anointing this life's last passage). Homer was one of the first recorded to call olive oil "liquid gold."[4] For peasants, *oil*, which has salience over

---

4 This metaphor occurs in *The Odyssey*, where Nausicaa welcomes Ulysses, presenting as a beggar-stranger, by giving him a flask of olive oil with which he anoints his body after his bath. The beggar is thereby dignified and transformed— just as precious gold, laid over silver, renders it more precious. "God sends the

tree and fruit, was truly precious—certainly as precious as the golden egg of fairytale tradition (cf. Del Giudice 2001, ch. 1 this volume).[5] Indeed, oil represented a prized, focal end product that concentrated the fruit of many trees through much physical labor. Since only a few liters could be derived from each tree, each drop was treasured. It was central in the domestic economy and carefully guarded; it was one of the few high-calorie foods in a fat- and protein-poor diet, adding essential flavor[6] to the otherwise simple, bland foods such as vegetables and bread, and thus a fundamental element in the Mediterranean Diet. Further, it was a key ingredient in the domestic pharmacopoeia

---

stranger and the beggar man, we gladly give, not much, but what we can. . . . They brought Odysseus to a sheltered place as the princess, Nausicaa told them to do. They laid a wrap beside him and a tunic, and gave him the golden flask of olive oil and bade him go into the river for his bath. . . . When he had washed all clean and rubbed himself with olive oil and put on the clothes which the princess had provided, Athena daughter of Zeus made him taller and stronger to look at. . . . as when a plating of gold is laid over silver by some clever craftsman, who has learnt all the secrets of his art from Hephaistos and Pallas Athena, and knows how to make works full of grace, so Athena covered his head and shoulders with beauty" (Homer [8th–7th century BCE] 1919). See also the artwork of Sarah Naomi Holt, who explores this notion of Homer's liquid gold in her art. www.nomiart.com/portfolio/the-harvest-of-homers-liquid-gold/.

5   I thank my husband, Edward F. Tuttle, linguist-dialectologist, for first bringing to my attention the salience of olive oil over olive in the Italo-Romance dialects. I further investigated, culling relevant material among the proverbs of Rossi-Ferrini 1931 and Giusti (1853) 1911. Tuttle notes that broad-scale agribusiness already in Roman times favored wine and oil: both *golden*, as the final concentration of invested-labor value in a relatively stable, reduced-volume form, which thus admitted of easier distribution to the most lucrative markets. Such prominence finds echoes in folk speech, to judge by dialectal extensions of the Latin word OLEU, the *oil* root, into the etymological descendants of *olive tree*. E.g., Calabrian, Apulian, and Campanian variants of *aghiastru* (for olive tree) seems to be a convergence of golden with *olio* (OLEUM), its final by-product, so that "golden oil" came to have greater salience than its source (the root-word OLIVA/O); see Padula-Trumper 2001, 70. Cf. Meyer-Lubke 1935 (6054 *oleum* and 6056ss *oliva*): while most all the Latin-descended Romance languages had an orally transmitted local heir to OLEUM (*oglio*, *ogio*, etc.), as attested in Medieval documents, it was widely supplanted in Italo-Romance by the semi-learned *olio* of Latinate notarial business contracts, medical recipes, and so forth.

6   "*Olio, aceto, pepe e sale, sarebbe buono uno stivale*" (Of oil, vinegar, pepper, and salt, it would be good to have a boot-full; that is, one can never have enough; Giusti [1853] 1911, 312).

and in magic and healing practices (e.g., "*olio di lucerna, ogni mal governa*" [(lamp) oil heals every ailment]; Giusti [1853] 1911, 292).[7]

Consider a few proverbs from Italian oral tradition, speaking to the olive's high economic value as well as symbolic meaning: "*mercante di vino, mercante poverino; mercante d'olio, mercante d'oro*" (wine merchant, poor merchant; oil merchant, gold merchant; Fresta 1991) or "*olio, ferro e sale, mercanzia reale*" (oil, iron and salt, royal merchandise; Giusti [1853] 1911, 71). "*Macari la rigina, si cala pri l'oliva*" (the olive is so precious that even a queen would bend down to gather its fruits; Rossi-Ferrini 1931, 134). And many are the proverbs which treat the optimal care required in olive cultivation, methods of processing, and so forth: for example, "*la prima raccolta è d'oro, la seconda d'argento, la terza non val niente*" (the first harvest is gold, the second silver, the third worthless; Rossi-Ferrini, 133)—that is, optimal yields are normally produced in a cycle of every third year; "*chi vuol tutte le olive, non ha tutto l'olio*" (he who wants all the olives, cannot have all the oil)—that is, waiting until all the olives become perfectly ripe, means that some will be lost. Or, inversely, patience in waiting for ripeness (a later harvest), produces optimal yields: "*l'oliva quantu cchiù ppenni, tantu cchiù rrenni*" (the longer the olive hangs on the tree, the more [oil] it yields; Piccitto and Tropea 1990, vol. 3, 401). Luckily, the olive grows even in inhospitable terrain, is capable of surviving decades of neglect, and of being recaptured from the wilderness and made productive by radical pruning (above) and lavish fertilization (below): "*agli olivi, un pazzo da capo, un savio da piè*" (for the olive tree, a mad man above, a wise man below; Rossi-Ferrini 1931, 131). The olive was generally perceived to be of great antiquity and generational depth: e.g., "*vigna piantata da me / moro da mio padre / olivo da mio nonno*" (vines planted by me / mulberrry by my father / olive by my grandfather; Fresta 1991). Indeed, olive groves have formed an integral part of Mediterranean landscapes for millennia, and not infrequently still cohabitate with ruins of ancient civilizations, at times nearly coeval with them (e.g., Plato's Olive Tree in Athens; or the great gnarly

---

7 E.g., a common evil eye "diagnostic" consisted of putting a few drops of oil in a dish of water and examining if, or how much, it scattered, thereby discerning whether the evil eye had been cast and how recently.

millennial trees of Magna Grecia, the "Silent Sentinels" photographed by Salentine photographer Fernando Bevilacqua in Southern Puglia).[8] Claims have been made for exceptional, surviving olive trees ranging from 2,000–3,000 years old.

BACKGROUND AND INTRODUCTION

In 2000, I was invited by Bernard Frischer (then UCLA Classicist, and director of the Horace's Villa Project at the American Academy in Rome; Frischer, Crawford, De Simone 2006) to carry out an oral history investigation in Licenza, the presumed location of Horace's Sabine country villa. The farm in Digentia (present-day Licenza) was a gift from his patron, Maecenas, circa 33 BCE, and was to serve as a source of income to raise him from penury, the better to pursue poetry. My goal was to discover the place and meaning of this archaeological site in local oral tradition. I conducted two brief fieldwork trips there in the spring and summer of 2001. The following essay, based on that research, considers this ancient, agricultural landscape in the Sabine hill country east of Rome.

---

8   The author co-curated a photographic exhibition of Bevilaqua's Salentine landscapes in *the deep murmur . . . il sibilo lungo* (October 18–25, 1998, at the Istituto Italiano di Cultura, Los Angeles), within Essential Salento: Festival of Salentine Culture. The term comes from a passage by Antonio Verri (a poet, advocate, and inspiration to many contemporary Salentine artists and writers, who died an untimely death in the late 1990's): "*Cambia, cambierà di molto il volto della campagna, degli aggregati umani, di interi paesi . . . quel che non cambierà mai sarà l'idea del dialogo con la terra che l'uomo ha stabilito dal tempo dei tempi, il grosso respiro, il sibilo lungo che si può udire solo di mattina, mirando nella vastità dei campi, con accanto sentinelle silenziose gli alberi d'argento . . .*" [It changes, it will change much, the face of the land, of gathered humanity, of entire towns . . . what will never change is the idea of dialoguing with the earth, that humanity has established from time immemorial, the long breath, *the deep murmur* which can be heard only in the early morning, while looking out over the vast fields, while standing next to the silver trees, the silent sentinels . . .]. There are many current initiatives in the Salento to help save their olive trees, some quite ancient.

FOLKLORE AND ARCHAEOLOGY

Although folklore and archaeology once shared in a mutual search for antiquities (oral—songs and narrative—in the first case, physical artifacts in the second), the disciplines parted ways long ago (cf. Del Giudice 2006). Folklore's stance vis-à-vis archaeology might be viewed as analogous to the peasant, shepherd, or brigand vignettes often gracing a landscape painting's corners (see early paintings of the Licenza Valley by Jakob Philipp Hackert, J. Hullmandel, and John Smith [Figures 7.8–7.10] vs. a view of Licenza today [Figure 7.11]; Margozzi 2000, 10), that is, as charming accessories, giving a sense of scale and local color, and creating the illusion that human groupings (*personaggi di contorno*) were part and parcel of an ancient and *unchanged* natural landscape—a fallacy, of course [Figure 7.12]. Yet, recent trends in archaeology (e.g., Gazin-Schwartz and Holtorf 1999) suggest a rapprochement between the disciplines, as archaeologists are called to explore "complementary landscape histories" (Brown and Bowen 1999, 255), a site's "cultural value," and the multiple meanings attributed to monuments through time.[9] Here, folklore can help "in understanding not only what happened and when, but how events were experienced by people participating in them and remembered by their descendants."[10] Indeed, my work attempted to bring those at the margins of the canvas into greater relief by focusing on the evolving cultural meanings that seem to intersect with Horace's Villa in local tradition, specifically by examining perceptions of landscape and concepts of treasure.

---

9   "Cultural value accrues from the study of the changing meanings of monuments through the ages" (Burström, Winberg, and Zachrisson 1996, 10). "Today [however], there is gradual recognition that all meanings that have been ascribed to ancient monuments contribute to their cultural value. This realization motivates a renewed archaeological interest in folklore" (Burström 1999, 35).

10   And folklore may also help explain "how these memories influenced the creation, preservation, and destruction of monuments in landscapes" (Gazin-Schwartz and Holtorf 1999, 3).

LANDSCAPES

A consideration of the land is critical to any discussion of the importance of the villa to Horace himself; it was a source of inspiration (and income)—a bucolic refuge for a world-weary man of letters.[11] Today, it is central to ecologists and cultural heritage managers, as the villa comes to be integrated within a nature conservancy, Parco Regionale Naturale dei Monti Lucretili, along a broader antiquities trail [Figures 7.13–7.15].

Land draws together archaeologist and peasant: both dig dirt, handle stone, rebuild walls, and carefully study terrain. But what makes field stones conceptually distinct from artifacts, or dry stone terracing distinct from those of a villa's garden walls? [Figure 7.16] Topography plays a key role in archaeological site identification (through oral, literary, and visual sources, and direct observation), even though nature and humanity may alter a site's contours across time. For peasants, land is the very stuff of life. Thus, they give human scale to the land as they shape it by clearing, terracing, grazing, plowing, dividing, and sometimes altering or damaging the historic site through agricultural work. At other times however, it may be the peasant's intimate knowledge of seasonality, local history, fauna and flora, and topographic memory that informs the archaeologist's project. In their spadework, farmers have frequently uncovered artifacts and clues directly useful to archaeologists. Conversely, in this instance, the land on which the rustic Roman villa sits has produced food century after century. Around Horace's Villa, even in an earlier period when an agro-pastoral life was economically viable, only olive trees, hardy spelt (ancient *farro*, now being revived), a few vineyards, and chestnut trees seemed to survive on this craggy land, meager even for a shepherd's needs. We note, for instance, the current mixed use of this land, where sheep graze among the olives, along the edge of an encroaching wilderness [Figure 7.17].

---

11   Horace, himself, describes his simple, olive-based diet: "*Me pascunt olivae, me cichorea levesque malvae*" (As for me, olives, dandelion greens, and mallow provide sustenance; Horace, *Odes* 1.31.15, ca. 30 BCE).

TREASURE AS METAPHOR

Treasure has proven a surprisingly versatile metaphor for interpreting various discourses that revolve around Horace's Villa. For example, the hunt for treasure is not only a common folk narrative motif, but early folklorists and archaeologists often referred to their delving in terms of discovering gems of the past (e.g., folktales or Roman statuary). Folklorists speak about tradition bearers as "living cultural treasures." And finally, there are the *fiscal* treasuries of public administrations. Such wealth of interpretive possibilities prompts a weaving together of historical narratives, oral memories, archaeology, and economic development. Yet, it also suggests potential for contested meanings, since peasants, archaeologists, antique dealers, treasure hunters, and public administrators all have differing notions of *treasure*. An overview of the site and its surrounding area provides some sense of the overlapping narratives at play here where a plaque calling attention to its presence in ancient Roman history, within discourses of Christian piety (such as the roadside shrine), as well as its integration into an eco-recreationalist nature trail. We also note the villa's association with foreigners, initially with English and Germans on the Grand Tour; today with American scholars, such as the fellows and visiting scholars of the American Academy in Rome [Figure 7.18–7.19].

ARCHAEOLOGY AND ORAL TRADITION

Let us now examine how oral tradition may express a local perspective on these issues—even if sometimes obliquely. I have grouped local narratives into three types: 1. treasure tales concerning brigands, hideouts, and gold; 2. meta-archaeological tales, or what I call "exercises in oral archaeology," such as "The Villa Buried Under the Chestnut Grove," which tries to account for the disappearance of an entire villa in a landslide, or "Artifacts in the Wilderness," an anecdote that tells of inscribed tablets lost on an overgrown country path; and 3. Horace's Villa narratives, which explicitly make reference to the site (e.g., recounting Horace's amorous exploits and secret trysts with a local peasant, Meneghetta, via underground tunnel). In this essay I will focus only on treasure tales.[12]

TREASURE

Commonly in many rural areas of preunification Italy, banditry was rampant, pre-banking practices the norm, and the landscape was strewn with ruins, so buried-treasure tales were bound to flourish. This was true in all of central Italy, including Licenza.[13] Gold was said to be found at the base of venerable trees (or even inside hollowed-out trees), or in caves. Sometimes, secret stashes were revealed by the deceased in dreams. Imagined treasure dotting the land was rarely retrieved however: secrecy betrayed, mismanaged spells and instructions, or supernatural guardians often put the gold just beyond reach. Oral narrative scholarship agrees that traditional treasure tales have much to do with the concept of "limited good." That is, in the static, closed economy of the peasant, it is perceived that if you get more, the group is getting less; hence, only an extraordinary occurrence, such as luck or theft, can expand such limitations.

Two tales recorded in the Licenza repertoire tell of (or conversely, conceal) treasure. They refer to the land surrounding the villa and both speak of brigands:

1. "Molten Gold" (Narrator 1, Female)

My mother told me about the treasure from a tree in the vicinity of the Castagneto where the mountain came down, directly above the Villa. In the mountains there, it was raining one day, and so a bandit, under a half-hollowed-out tree, lit a fire to warm himself. He saw something running down. Hidden in the trunk of this tree was gold, which melted.

12 For a more complete discussion of the oral narrative tradition in Licenza, including additional narratives relating to the Villa, see Del Giudice 2006.

13 Thompson 1932–1936.

2. "Treasure by the Waterfall" (Narrator 2, male)

There were many stories told about treasure and not just there, but near the waterfall as well, at Vigna della Corte. My paternal grandfather never told anyone else, but he had a lot of trust in me, and so he told me. I'm remembering it now but I have never told anyone before. There was a fig tree and there should be a hidden treasure there. I tried repeatedly to buy that land but was never able to. I never told anyone. My grandfather told me this when he died.[14] . . . I'm only telling it now for the first time. He said that someone in prison had given him this information. Is it still there? I don't know. Maybe, but I never really looked.

The Tale Not Told (Narrator 1, female)

But the most intriguing treasure tale encountered was the tale *not* told by the first narrator the second time around. While in a first, unguarded encounter, the woman told the story of the molten gold and of hidden treasures, upon reconsideration, and likely due to family pressure, she presumably feigned forgetfulness during a second encounter. Perhaps she feared that such tales would prompt unwanted probing into her family's life and economic status, thereby provoking envy. Treasure seekers and the invidious, after all, could do harm. As though to underscore the border between civil and illicit discourse, only outside any publically scrutable location, in the anonymous countryside itself, had the narrator consented to speak.

---

14 Note that this family secret is transmitted only *in extremis*, from the grandfather's deathbed.

INTERPRETING NARRATIVES

First, we note the proximity of the tales' settings to Horace's Villa, an area presumably perceived to be of great antiquity (although only excavated in the 1930s) and clearly outside the town's confines. Only in the realm of the wild, dangerous, hidden, illicit, or supernatural could treasure be located.

Second, such tales speak to land ownership: that is, desirable land seen as containing hidden treasure, or the fear of potential treasure seekers trespassing on one's private property. The molten gold (or "treasure within the tree") narrative, however, seems to offer the most interesting interpretive possibility of all. In its close association of treasure and tree, the narrative seems to indicate that it was the very tree itself (the ancient olive) and the liquid gold it produces that ought to be considered precious—literally and figuratively. Indeed, for centuries the greatest treasure on the agricultural landscape *was* that form of "liquid gold," olive oil, for which Licenza was renowned.

The tales speak to land issues (man vs. nature) in other ways as well: in "The Villa Buried under the Chestnut Grove," or in "The Artifact Found Among the Brambles" (a narrative not included here), the wilderness seems to be swallowing traces of man's work, ancient and more recent. That is, both the memory of ancient civilization (in the form of a villa or inscribed stone), as well as the peasants' careful agricultural work on the landscape (fields, paths), are being slowly obliterated by a common enemy: both risk being swallowed by the encroaching *macchia* or wilderness, the protection of which is actually the goal of competing ecotourism.[15] Indeed, with widespread emigration during the 1970s, the wilderness has been slowly reclaiming the Licenza Valley. Along with the intentional reversion of the land to wilderness, in the form of a regional park, it is not surprising that the few remaining *contadini* lament the fact that wild beasts and rapacious birds (*l'aquila*

---

15   However, in the opinion of Mary Fort, a local resident (now deceased), the paradox is that humans created the wilderness by using local resources to the point of deforestation. It may also have resulted from inheritance practices of dividing plots equally among children in large families, so that plots became smaller and smaller in time, resulting in a marginal economic interest in cultivating so few trees.

reale, or golden eagle) are privileged over fields, domesticated animals, and agro-pastoral life. Heritage managers might be advised to better take the land's actual human history into consideration. Both the villa and the park, therefore, are perceived by the locals as foreign (culturally and literally) to local traditions and concerns.

GUARDIAN OF THE TREASURE

Every treasure must have its guardian. In the case of Horace's Villa [Figures 7.20–7.24], that guardian was Giuseppe Rinaldi, the site's custodian poet from the mid-1960s to the late 1970s [Figure 7.25–7.26]. (When I met him he was in his late 80's and has since passed away.) In Rinaldi there was a curious and unusual meeting of distant worlds, where ancient Classical poet meets oral folk poet and archaeology intersects peasant tradition. Fifteen solitary years on the site bound him deeply to that place. Rinaldi lived, breathed, and dreamed the villa. He was, as he stated polemically, *un vero custode* (a true custodian)—an actual curator it would seem, caring for the physical site with a peasant's sensitivity to land management,[16] fencing off the grounds to keep out animals, tending plants and trees, and slowly reclaiming the fruit-bearing trees from the wilderness (loquat, pear, pomegranate, walnut, apple). Much as archaeologists themselves recover sites of human activity from the wilderness, one might add. He worked from sunrise to sunset (*dall'alba al tramonto*), rain or shine, all year round, still wedded to an old-world work ethic (when one did not count hours, he noted).

On walks through the imagined villa, conversing with the Poet, he mused about its natural beauty and tranquility. He composed poetry of the land, odes to humble plants—rosemary, a vine, a rose—to his mind, all worthy of poetic attention, as well as odes to the villa itself,

---

16 While a night custodian for 25 years at the Baths of Diocletian, Rinaldi took holidays in winter to coincide with the olive harvest. While working at Horace's Villa, beginning in the mid-1960s (for about 15 years), he continued to tend his 140 olive trees, waking at 4:00 a.m., arriving in his grove near Roccagiovine by 6:00 a.m., and thereafter beginning his workday at the Villa, which lasted until sundown.

to Horace, and about his encounters with scholarly and other visitors. The more he learned about Horace—from disparate sources, including visiting Classicists and archaeologists—the more Rinaldi began to narrate *his* Poet and *his* Villa, selectively merging his few literary and historic facts into an idealized whole. His mission was to pass on his own passion for Horace and the site to anyone who would listen. It was as a guide that Rinaldi truly came into his own, enjoying the thrill of performance, regaling tourists with his poetry.[17]

By listening to, recording, and transcribing Rinaldi's own words, I hoped to bring at least one of those figures from the canvas margins into greater focus and to the attention of the site's scholars. Perhaps archaeologists can learn from those who live with monuments, care for them, and have their own unique way of narrating them. In a more accessible idiom, informed by a folk perspective, mediators such as Rinaldi have even proven capable of eloquently communicating to a wider audience a sense of wonder and profound respect for ancient rural landscapes such as those around Horace's Villa. Here, through inversion and complementarity, we may consider how the archaeological site is situated *in* the world of agrarian labor, among those who have tilled that soil for millennia, both producing liquid gold from its trees and spinning tales of gold in an oral repository of local memory.

WORKS CITED

Brown, Martin, and Pat Bowen. 1999. "The Last Refuge of the Faeries: Archaeology and Folklore in East Sussex." In *Archaeology and Folklore*, edited by Amy Gazin-Schwartz and Cornelius Holtorf. New York: Routledge.

Burström, Mats. 1999. "Focusing on Time: Disciplining Archaeology in Sweden." In *Archaeology and Folklore*, edited by Amy Gazin-Schwartz and Cornelius Holtorf. New York: Routledge.

Burström, Mats, Björn Winberg, and Torun Zachrisson. 1996. *Fornlämningar och folkminnen*. Stockholm: Riksantikvarieämbetet.

---

17 For Rinaldi's poetic texts, see Del Giudice 2006.

Del Giudice, Luisa. 2001. "Mountains of Cheese and Rivers of Wine: *Paesi di Cuccagna* and other Gastronomic Utopias." Chapter 1 in this volume. First published in *Imagined States: Nationalism, Utopia, and Longing in Oral Cultures,* edited by Luisa Del Giudice and Gerald Porter, 11–63. Logan: Utah State University Press.

Del Giudice, Luisa. 2006. "Interpreting Treasure: Oral Tradition, Archaeology and Horace's Villa." In *The Horace's Villa Project: 1997–2003,* edited by Bernard Frischer, Jane Crawford, and Monica De Simone, Vol. 1, E6, 345–64; Vol. 2, illustrations, 951–56. Oxford, UK: Archaeopress.

Del Giudice, Luisa, and Nancy Elizabeth Van Deusen, eds. 2005. *Performing Ecstasies: Music, Dance, and Ritual in the Mediterranean.* Ottawa: Institute for Medieval Music, Claremont Cultural Studies–Musicological Studies. Papers, program, and photographs from the conference and festival organized in Los Angeles by the Italian Oral History Institute in conjunction with Istituto Italiano di Cultura in October 2000.

Fresta, Mariano. 1991. "L'olio nei proverbi e nelle tradizioni popolari" (Oil in proverbs and folk tradition). http://www.proverbi.info/proverbi/proverbi-italiani/olive-olio/ (accessed November 1, 2011).

Frischer, Bernard, Jane Crawford, and Monica De Simone, eds. 2006. *The Horace's Villa Project: 1997–2003*, 2 vols. Oxford, UK: Archaeopress.

Gazin-Schwartz, Amy, and Cornelius Holtorf, eds. 1999. *Archaeology and Folklore.* New York: Routledge.

Giusti, Giuseppe. (1853) 1911. *Raccolta di proverbi toscani*, compiled 1847–1852. Florence: F. Le Monnier. Reprint, Florence: A. Salani.

Grillo, Lucia, producer-director. 2010. *Terra sogna terra / Earth Dream Earth,* New York: Calabrisella Films. https://www.calabrisellafilms.com/filmmaker-musicvideos.

Homer. (8th–7th century BC) 1919. The Odyssey 6, line 211. English Translation by A.T. Murray, PhD, in two volumes. Cambridge, MA: Harvard University Press. Archived at https://www.perseus.tufts.edu/hopper/text?doc=Perseus%3Atext%3A1999.01.0136%3Abook%3D6%3Acard%3D211.

Horace. ca. 30 BCE. *Odes* 1.31.15.

Klindienst, Patricia. 2006. *Earth Knows My Name: Food, Culture, and Sustainability in the Gardens of Ethnic Americans*. Boston: Beacon Press.

Margozzi, Mariastella. 2000. *Verso la casa di campagna di Orazio: viaggio pittorico erudito di Jacob Philipp Hackert* (Towards Horace's country house: Jacob Philipp Hackert's erudite pictorial journey). Palombara Sabina, Rome: Parco Naturale Regionale dei Monti Lucretili.

Meyer-Lübke, Wilhelm. 1935. *Romanisches etymologisches Wörterbuch*. Heidelberg: Heidelberg University Publishing, winter.

Padula, Vincenzo, and John Trumper. 2001. *Vocabolario Calabro: Laboratorio Del Dizionario Etimologico Calabrese* (DEC). Rome: Editori Laterza.

Piccitto, Giorgio, and Giovanni Tropea. 1990. *Vocabolario siciliano* (Sicilian dictionary), 4 vols. Palermo: Centro di Studi Filologici e Linguistici Siciliani.

Rossi-Ferrini, Ugo. 1931. *Proverbi agricoli* (Agricultural proverbs). Florence: I Fermenti.

Thompson, Stith. 1932–1936. *Motif-Index of Folk Literature*, 6 vols. Bloomington: Indiana University.

Figure 7.1: The olive has become a personal icon on www.luisadg. org. Detail, photograph by Diana Lundin: http://www.dianalundin. com/#. Website design by Joy Deborah Robison.

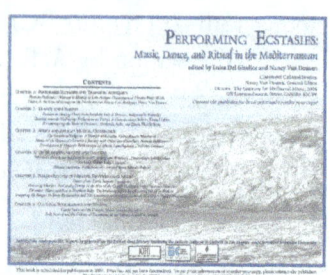

Figure 7.2: *Performing Ecstasies: Music, Dance and Ritual in the Mediterranean,* Los Angeles, encompassed a conference and festival in 2000 and a publication in 2005.

Figure 7.3

Figure 7.4

Figure 7.3–7.4: Roots and Fruits: An Olive Harvest Retreat was a women's spirituality retreat in the Sierran foothills of central California.

Figure 7.5

Figure 7.6

Figure 7.7

Figures 7.5–7.7: Sam Pantaleo's olive trees, lemons, and figs growing in his Richmond Hill, Ontario, backyard in November 2011.

Figure 7.8

Figure 7.9

Figure 7.10

Figures 7.8–7.10: Jacob Philip Hackert (1737–1807), *Views of the Licenza Valley: View of Licenza; View of Mandela; View of the Fonte Bello*, three of a series of 10 landscape views painted in 1780, also issued as a set of engravings; C. J. Hullmandel (1789–1850), *View of Licenza near Horace's Villa* (ca. 1820); John Smith, *View of Horace's Villa* (London, 1816).

Figure 7.11: Licenza at a distance, as it was in 2001.

Figure 7.12: Peasants on donkeys may still grace the landscape but are not unchanged since ancient times.

Figure 7.13: An historic marker indicates the way to Horace's Villa.

Figure 7.14

Figure 7.15

Figures 7.14–7.15: The Trinity roadside shrine (constructed in 1996) first greets the tourist taking the road up to Horace's Villa.

Figure 7.16: Recent stone terracing is sometimes difficult to distinguish chronologically from more ancient stone walls.

Figure 7.17: Olives, wild trees, and animals coexist in an agricultural landscape being reclaimed by wilderness

Figure 7.18

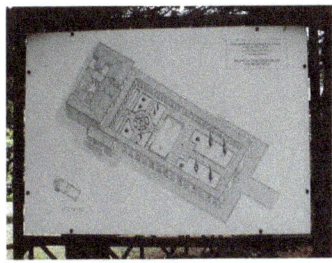

Figure 7.19

Figures 7.18–7.19: Signage at the Villa's entrance and an isometric representation of the Villa call attention to the foreign element associated with this site: the American Academy in Rome.

Figure 7.20

Figure 7.21

Figure 7.22

Figure 7.23

Figure 7.24

Figures 7.20–7.24: Remains of the Villa.

Figure 7.25: Giuseppe Rinaldi†, custodian poet of Horace's Villa, during a guided tour of the villa on May 2, 2001, 9:30 a.m.

Index

A

A-1 Imported Groceries and Deli,
16–17, 25, 30, 174n3, 175,
179–80, 182–84, *190–91*

abbonanza mantra, 9, 14, 41n12,
58n32, 98–99, 106, 148n44
See abundance

abundance: 9–11, 14–15, 17–19,
21, 58, 98–99
vs. enough, 14–6, 18–22,
156, 231, 253
generosity/sharing, 11, 14–15,
18–23, 51, 116, 121, 135,
149–54, *172–73*, 216
in immigrant life/worldview,
8, 11, 23, 54–58, 60
vs. over-abundance, 17–19,
21, 24, 93, 95, 106, 154
vs. scarcity, 9–10, 15, 19–22,
28–33, 35, 54–55, 98,
106, 116, 147, 197–98
well-being, 15, 19–21, 57
See also food; *Paese di
Cuccagna*; hunger;
justice; St. Joseph's

Accademia Italian della Cucina
(AIC), 24, 219, 229n2

Addis Ababa University, Ethiopia, 22

America [Canada and/or United
States]
Anglo-American asceticism, 37n8

America, *cont.*
hunger/poverty in, 22, 154, 222
as *il Paese di Cuccagna*, 10–11,
22, 37, 49, 54–58, 261
in folk narratives, 37, 57–59
See cuccagna, economics;
hunger; migration

B

"Big Rock Candy Mountain, The"
(song), 37

Bizzotto, Fr. Giovanni, 153n50

Boccanfuso, Filomena, 185, *192*

Brer Rabbit, 37–38, *78*

Buccheri, Fr. Vincenzo, 116, *171*

Buscemi Carlson, Virginia (St.
Joseph's), 115, 124n16, 132,
140, 146n43, 153, *170*

C

cantina (wine cellar), Toronto, 10,
12, 18, 25, 88–114, *113–14*
descriptions of 96–7
food or wine (his and hers),
103–6
significance, 98–99, 106–107
wineries, 100–101, 103, *114*

NOTE: NUMBERS IN ITALICS REFER TO PAGES WITH ILLUSTRATIONS.

Carnival, 45n18, 46–47, 49–51, 53, 56, *76*, *80*, 105, 136, 149n45, *168*, 195, 199

Casa Italiana, 118, 120n10, 134, 146, 153, *166, 172–73*, 176, 221

Cecchinato, Loredana (Osteria Mamma), 24

celebrations, 11, 12, 18, 48, 50, 92, 104–105, 107, 118, 128, 134, 182
  See Del Giudice, St. Joseph's

Committee for Simon Rodia's Towers in Watts (CSRTW), 213–14, 224

COVID-19 pandemic, 15–16, 257

Cuccagna (see *Paese di Cuccagna*)

D

Del Giudice family
  Alberto (father), 9, 10, 13–15, 17–18, 61, 88–90, 92–93, 95n6, 98–99, 101, 102n21, 104, 109–10, 183
  cantina, 10, 12, 18, 98–99, 101, 106–108
  emigration, 9–10
  foods/wild foods, 10, 12–13, 17–18, 61, 197–98
  gardens, 13, 89
  life in Terracina, 9, 14, 16–17, 61, 89–90, 98, 100, 106, 183
  life in Toronto, 21, 58–59, 61, 88–89, 10–14, 18, 20, 62, 92, 96, 101, 104 (see also *cantina*, wine)

Del Giudice family, *cont.*
  Mother (Liliana), 9–10, 14, 18, 20, 61, 100, 182
  Poldi, Giuseppe (brother-in-law) and Otello (nephew), *29*, 109
  sisters (Claudia, Franca, Irene), 20, 182
  war stories, 9, 61

Del Giudice, Luisa
  advocacy, 23, 25
  ethnography as spiritual practice, 155–57, 230, *244*
  food memories, 12–14, 16–18, 101, 107, 110
  hospitality, conviviality, 14–17, 23, *32*, 61
  professional activities, 21, 23–25, 33n1, 61–62, 88n2, 89, 115n1, 117–18, 174n1, 186n1, 212n1, 229–30, 233, *244*, 254
  See also justice

Del Giudice–Tuttle family, 16
  Edward Tuttle (husband), 231n5
  Elena (daughter), 31, 227
  food traditions, *27–32*, 197–98
  gardens, 15, *28*
  Giulia (daughter), 31, *227*
  recreating Terracina/Toronto activities, 16–17, *29*, 183
  special foods, 16–17, *27, 32*, 106n26

di Bernardo, Ferdinando, 186–87

Disney Enterprises, Walt Disney, 37–38, 78, 201

E

economics, 21–22, 56, 144,
178n11, 201, 214–16, 222–
23, 231
economic refugees, 9, 57, 142
the economic boom/the
Italian miracle, 60
Sabbath economics, 20–22,
229–31
wealth, 45, 54, 56, 144–5
ethnography of compassion, 117

F

Fincher, Rev. Michael, 19
food
abbondanza vs. sufficiency, 9,
11, 15, 17, 19, 140n33
bread, elemental food, 15,
17, 19, 22, 34, 39, 48,
108n28, 119, 138–40
as cultural activity, 17, 23, 62,
93, 102, 108, 109, 135
See also St. Joseph's Tables
in Cuccagna, 11, 13, 33–34,
50–52, 170–78, 37
diet, 10, 17–18, 37–38,
40–41, 59–60, 108–9,
120–21, 124, 125,
206–7, 231
food justice, 21–24, 149–50
health, mental and physical,
14–15, 15, 17–18, 21,
35n5, 40, 57, 60, 62, 89,
99, 108, 197–98, 232
See also wine: health

food, cont.
in imagery: cultural,
theological, 35, 37, 40
in immigrant culture/
worldview, 25, 59, 62,
89, 93, 150
immigrants, associated with
foods, 59, 144
nature's abundance, 14–16,
183–84
politics, 23, 214, 216,
222–26
production/distribution,
60, 144–45, 182, 200,
202–3, 206, 211
ritual foods, 10, 119–121,
122n13, 130, 219, 230
stereotyping with foods, 61,
108, 199, 201
See abundance; foraging;
hospitality; hunger;
justice; St. Joseph's;
trauma
foods and foodways
abbendata (grilling event),
16, 29
American durum wheat, 211
Carciofi alla romana (Roman-
style artichokes), 27
casatella (coffee, marsala,
ricotta pie), 27
ceccamariti/ceccamarini/
struffoli (pastry), 27
ciambelle (wine cookies), 10,
27, 108, 110, 124
foraging for wild foods, 13–
15, 59, 183–84
gnocchi, 38
hearth cooking, 16, 29, 197–98

foods and foodways, *cont.*
    holiday foods, 107, 110
    Italian foods in America, *191*, 200, 207
    octopus, 30
    provisioning food, 9–10, 16, 61, 97, 183
    snails, 12–16, *29*, 97, 99, 109, 190, *198*, 259
    wine as food staple, 88–89, 91, 95
    See A-1; *cantina* (wine cellar); gardens; Ischians; Marabella; pasta; St. Joseph's Tables
Forestieri, Baldassari, 186

G

gardens, 10–11, 13, 15–6, 28, 60, 98, 182, 185, 230
gastronomic utopias, 11, 25, 33–87, 35, 37
generosity/sharing, 18–23, 60, 117, 198
    See also abundance.
Gracchiolo, Vita (St. Joseph's), 122, 128n21, *169*

H

Historic Italian Hall, 118, 174n2, 175–76, 186
Hooks, Rosie Lee, 219, *227–28*
    See also Watts Towers; Watts Towers Art Center

Horace's Sabine Villa, 222–43, *245–48*
    folklore vs. archeology, 234–36, 240–241
    Horace, 233, 235–37
    landscape, 230, 232–35, 239–40
    farmers, local, 235, 237–38, 239–40
    narratives, 230–231, 234, 236–41
    Rinaldi, Giuseppe (custodian), 240–241
    treasure metaphor, 230–231, 234, 236–39
hospitality, 11, 14, 17, 23, *32*, 116, 139n31, 140–141, 143, 151n2, 216–17
hunger/poverty 9, 22–23, 25, 35–37, 39–40, 55, 58–62, 99, 106, 116, 140n34, 142, 150n46, 151, *172*, 214, 219, 253, 229–31
    fear of, 21, 99

I

il Tranese, Giovanni, 34, 44, *74*
immigrants
    reception, 23, 142
    immigration, 9–10, 23, 45, 151–52, 200, 222–23
    immigration reform, 214, 217
    worldview, 9–11, 14, 18, 36–37
    See celebrations; food; foods/ foodways; migration; wine
Ischians in San Pedro (Los Angeles), 16, 122, 134, 171–89, 176–77, *190–2*

Ischians in San Pedro, *cont.*
    See A-1; Marabella; Mary Star
        of the Sea; St. Joseph's
Istituto Italiano di Cultura (Italian
    Cultural Institute), 21, 116
Italian American Museum of Los
    Angeles (IAMLA), 118, 122,
    174n2
Italian diaspora, 9–11, 23, 61,
    100, 101, 120, 127, 134–36,
    140, 143, 155, 196, 258, 262
Italian Oral History Institute
    (IOHI), 24, 117n3, 118n7,
    122n15, 128n21, 130, 174–
    75, 184, 186n24, 215, 250
Italians in Brazil, 99n14, 131n23,
    134
Italians in Los Angeles, 11, 23,
    106n26, 116–18, 121,
    122n14, 123n15, 124n16,
    128n21, 130–33, 145,
    153n51, 174n2, 176–177,
    180, 186
Italian Los Angeles (website), 117–
    18, 186n24, 215, 217
    Italian cultural/social
        organizations, 134, 153,
        166, 176, 186
Italy
    as *il Paese di Cuccagna*
        (1960s), 60
    Italian diaspora, 9, 10, 118
    as Land of Hunger, 253
    World War I, 200
    World War II, 9, 90
    See economics, migration

J

Joseph, Saint
    cult of, history, 123–30
    diverse attributes/supplicants,
        127–29, 142n37
    Eastern Church influences,
        125–28
    Madonna–Child narrative,
        inversion, 124
    patriarch, 116, 123, 128, 132,
        142
    Spanish influences, 123,
        125nn18–20, 127, 141,
        218n5
    St. Joseph Society, 121–23,
        141, *169–70,* 177
    See St. Joseph's
justice: food, social, economic,
    21–23, 25, 46, 136, 149–50,
    155, 217 224, 230, 252
    advocacy, 21, 25, 117, 217

L

Los Angeles Cultural Affairs
    Dept., 117

M

Magliocco, Sabina, 24n3, 229n3
Mary, Saint, 119, 124–25, 126,
    127–28, 130
Mary Star of the Sea Church,
    116, 121, 134n27, 123n15,
    142n38, 146, *170–72,* 175,

Mary Star of the Sea, *cont.*
177–78, 183, *190*, 217, 221
Marabella Vineyard Company,
16n2, 54–55, 175, 179–80,
183–84, *190–91*
Migration, 9, 37, 116, 118, 143–44,
155–56, 176n6, 180n16, 212–
14, 216, 220, 223, 239, 253

O

olives, olive oil, tree, 25, *28*, *30*,
37, 60–1, 91, 100, 109, 139,
141, 154, *171*, 182, 200,
229–33, 235, 239, 240n16,
244, *247*

P

Paese di Cuccagna (Land of
Cockaigne), 25, 33–73,
74–87
America as, 11
cultural variants, 34–35,
37–38, 43, 49
games, 6, 36n6, 54
gastronomic utopia, 11, 25,
34–38
iconography, 11–3, 17, 34–
35, 37, 43, 49, 198
as imagined state, 36, 43, 49,
57, *76*
immigrant life, correlation
with, 58, 62–63
the lie, 54–55, 57–59
macchine della Cuccagna
(Cuccagna machines),

Paese di Cuccagna, cont.
51, 53, *82–87*
mythology/metaphor, 11, 13,
25, 35–37, 57, 62–63, 89
Oral traditions, 33–34, 36–8,
55, 57–58, 78, 143, 199,
201
prints/broadsides, 33–34, 37,
42–43, *74–86*, 201
in propaganda literature, 56,
58
social class, 36, 40–2, 45–47,
59
social movements, 45
street performers/literature,
34, 36, 38–39, 41–42,
44–45, 47, 62, 122
subversion of social/
theological values, 35,
37, 39, 45–46
paradise, etymology, 35
travel tale, 56–57
Roverso Mondo (Upside-Down/
Topsy-Turvy World), 43,
55–56, *79*, 151
See abundance, America, hunger
pasta, 17, *32*, 193–211
in *Cucagna* imagery, 13, 17, 49
diet and health, 60, 205–7
history of, 25, 193–97, 199
homemade, 9, 32, 182
and politics, 201
cooked, 97n11, 122, 124,
140–41, 197–98, 205–6
production/distribution, *30*,
182, 196–98, 200–3
in popular culture, 18, 199, 201
types & shapes, 11, 112, 193–
95, 197, 204–6, *211*

Pisano, Fr. Andrew, 134, 135n27, 146, *166*

Pueblo de Los Angeles Historic Monument, 118

R

Ricci Lothrop, Gloria (historian), 117–18

Rodia, Sabato/Sam/Simon, 186, 212–18, 221

I Build the Tower (film), 223

S

Sabbath economics, *see* economics

San Pedro (Los Angeles)
    fishing community/industry, 17, 122, 134, *168*, 174–79, 181–83, 214,
    food forays to, 16, 182–83, 197–98
    Italians in, 174n3, 175
    See Ischians; St. Joseph's; Sicilians

Sicilians in So. California, 25, 115–17, 122, 128n21, 130–34, 153n51, 176–77
    See San Pedro, St. Joseph's

Simplicity Movement, 161

Sisters of St. Joseph, 143

Slow Food, 15, 24, 61, 191, 214, 229

social justice, 21–22, 229–33, 24, 117, 233, 224

St. Alban's Episcopal Church, Westwood, 18, 222

St. Joseph's Tables/Alters, 116–17, 121, 136–38, *166, 170–71,* 212–28
    Holy Family, 119, 121, 123, 130, 131n23, 138, 149–50, *171,* 219
    in Italy, 130–34, 141, 147–48, *171*
    in Los Angeles, 118–22, 130, 134, 146
    in New Orleans, 135–36, *172*
    in North America, 134
    novenas (song), 122, 124n16, 128,
    other ethnicities, inclusion, 143n40, 150n47, 152–58, 218, 220
    pageant/procession, 121–22, 140–41, 150, *169–71,* 219–22
    pre-/non-Christian rituals, similar, 147–49
    private devotional tables, 146
    public tables, 121–22, 146, 153, *168–73,* 221
    ritual foods, 119–21, 134, 138–41, 148–49, *166–169, 170–72,* 177
    Sicilian American tradition, 117, 120–21, 128n21, 155
    symbolism/meaning, 116, 137–45, 151, *167–68,* 217
    gender roles, 124
    See also food; Ischians; Joseph; Mary; Mary Star of the Sea; Sicilians

St. Lawrence of Brindisi Church, 218, *227*, 252

St. Peter's Italian Church, 118, 134n27, 153, *166*, *169*, 175–76, 178, 221

T

taverns in folk culture, 96n7

Terracina, Latina, Italy, 90, 105, 129n22, 180

    foods, 14, 16–17, *27–29*, 107

    World War II stories, 9, 29

    See also Del Giudice

Texas Tavola (film), 134

Toronto, Ontario

    immigrant life in, 10, 16, 20, 61, 89

    Italian community, 8, 11, 58

    See also *cantina,* Del Giudice, wine culture

trauma, 14–15, 20, 22–23, 47n21, 60–62

travel tales, 57, 143

U

Underground Gardens, 186

V

Vaccaro, Maria, and Agostino, 124n26, 128n21, 146, *166*, 172

W

Watts (Los Angeles), 25, 213–20, 222, 224–25

Watts Towers, 25, 212–13, 214n4, 215, 216, 221, 223–25, *227–28*

Watts Towers Art Center (WTAC), 213, 214n4, 215–16, 219, 221–22, 224–25, *227–28*

Watts Towers Common Ground Initiative, 23, 156, 212–26, *227–28*

Watts Labor Community Action Committee (WLCAC), 224

wine culture, 9, 11, 25, 93, 88–114

    expositions, 24

    and foodways, 88–89, 94

    games, 104

    in gastronomic utopia myths, 34

    gender disparities, 89, 95–96 102–6

    health, 13, 62, 88–93, 95, 102–3, 108–10

    home winemaking, 10–11, 98–99, 100–4, 109–10, *114*, *190*

    symbolism, 89–82, 88–89, 91–92, 94–95, 99, 103–5

    taverns, 96n7

    See also *cantina*

Wine cellar. See *cantina*

wineries, 16, 100–03, *114*, 175, 179–80, *190–1*

Acknowledgments

The accumulated gratitude for this volume goes back decades—some of it well-aged, mentioned in the essays as they were originally published—and some of my gratitude is more recent. There were years, after I announced in one essay after another that *In Search of Abundance* was "forthcoming," when I honestly felt like a liar, that I should stop saying it, that it might never happen. And yet, ironically, food writings were among my best known, collegially appreciated, and original contributions to the field of Italian and diaspora studies. But they sat, the last on my priority list for re-publication. Even when I rallied my flagging energies and gathered these essays in a folder labeled "Abundance," that folder waited about nine years to be dusted off. I thank my friends for pushing me toward a reckoning. It is not easy for me to return to my writings, once they have been published. Several colleagues though had been reminding me of this unpaid debt recently, and finally I agreed that it was something I really *must* do. So, during our second COVID year, I resolved to do it.

But it was only when I asked my good friend, Shan Emanuelli, family friend, former-Italian Oral History Institute Executive Board member, and professional editor, whether she would consider helping me assemble this volume, and she said yes, that it suddenly became feasible. Checking references, writing for renewed permissions, and the nuts and bolts of unifying a style sheet among diverse formatting were tasks that I simply was not willing to accomplish on my own. And so Shan's affirmative response meant that *In Search of Abundance* could now be in your hands! Immeasurable gratitude to you, Shan.

I also thank Anthony Tamburri, Dean of the John D. Calandra Institute, friend, colleague, and co-editor of Bordighera Press, for offering to publish this volume. Without that offer, this—my second volume with Bordighera Press—would simply not have been published, because I no longer had the patience for the glacial timelines of university presses. Nonetheless, I thank those presses for their permission to republish essays and to the various owners of visual materials to reproduce illustrations a second time around: Gale, Utah State UP, *California Italian Studies, Ethnologies.*

The biggest debt of gratitude, though, goes to my family of origin and their deeply food-centered ways, for without their food and cultural knowledge, I would not have learned to treasure food processes, culture, and memories nearly as much as I do. The traditions continue, albeit transformed. To the Del Giudice ancestors, grape farmers in Terracina, and to my father, grape farmer and professional fisherman before he became a house painter in Toronto, I honor your hardworking, millennial ways as some of the most archaic and essential work done by humankind throughout history. I also thank my sister Claudia for her persistence in keeping many food traditions alive—including a tenacious bond with the concept, and act, of creating abundance. To Claudia, so much a kindred spirit, with her concern for hospitality, family, and the convivial sharing of food, I say thank you. She has been the fiercely loyal Mother to us all—to her family, to our families, to parents and grandchildren—comforting, nurturing, embodying family memory, remembering the original meaning of *festa,* as well as the precious recipes that make feasting traditional. To my brother-in-law Mimmo Galletta, Claudia's husband, a Toronto-based Calabrian gardener like no other I know (see Del Giudice 2022); to sisters (Franca, Irene) and daughters (Elena, Giulia) for whom food-centered activities are as important as they are to me. I thank Franca and her family in Terracina, who introduced me to the star-filled nights of snail gathering among the olive trees with a flashlight. To my Venetian son-in-law, Mattia Bastasin, who is as food-centric as any in my family, and who has taken to our foodways. Without family (and friends) around a table to enjoy the primal experience of the convivial meal, life would be impoverished indeed.

There are those who I have thanked in various publications either for helping to improve my writing, or who have shared their knowledge through fieldwork, or who find themselves within these pages. To the Sicilian community of Los Angeles specifically: thank you for helping me understand the deeper meanings of St. Joseph's Tables. *Grazie infinite.* Foremost among them are Virginia Buscemi Carlson† and Rosalia Orlando. To my friends, artists, and colleagues at the Watts Towers Arts Center, especially Rosie Lee Hooks, goes my respect, for their unfailing support and their work of making the table assembled at St. Lawrence of Brindisi Church in Watts the memorable and beautiful event it was. Those events represent some of the proudest moments of my professional and activist life. Thank you.

Finally, I thank my many Facebook friends and food fans who egg me on, encouraging me to cook, bake, garden, blog, film, write, and present! With all the food photography, the talk of food preparation, and all my food portraits (as I like to call them): my face to face encounters with the beauty of the food, I've given you all the food talk I had to give. Images of market stalls full of crisp chard, plump garden tomatoes still on the vine, sheets of freshly-rolled pasta drying, gleaming jars of kumquat marmalade—these are among my favorites. My FB albums now stand as meticulously documented testimony of so much baking, cooking, gardening, processing, making of pastas, bread, and drinks, to help you (and me) replicate some of these treasures in the future. Many are treasured family-based recipes and foodways, while others are the result of creative experimentation. I have shared what I had and what I knew enthusiastically. And you are right to point out to me that food has been a core of my identity. Why else would my own personal website (www.luisadg.org) feature food, as baskets of just-gathered olives from our Sierran trees?

I have written elsewhere that my theology is food-centric: I have always believed in hospitality as a deeply sacred act and convivial meals as a social good (even though my approach to food itself has evolved over the years). Today, it is less about entertaining friends and colleagues with lavish meals, and more about directly feeding the poor and welcoming the stranger in food justice actions. Perhaps, I no longer feel compelled toward food performance. I no longer participate in food organizations, nor write about food, per se. I am here merely wrapping up lose ends. Frankly, it is time for me to close the refrigerator door.

The fact is, I no longer feel that once all-consuming need to seek abundance. My endless involvement with food matters is also somewhat over. The sense of scarcity is gone and I finally know that I've had enough, done enough, planned, written, achieved enough. I am enough. I have documented the historic meaning of that search for abundance that has so marked our family (and many others like it). That part of our family history, so tightly linked to migration, with its natural tendency toward material betterment, achievement, and consumption, seems to have played itself out, has been superseded, is gone. Indeed, it seemed to have led to a dead end, to clogged arteries, and to cluttered houses; it may even have killed a family member or two. The dreamed-of Land of Plenty, *Cuccagna* (=America or Canada or Australia), functioned as a mythic, inverse mirror to their Land of Hunger (Italy)—which they successfully fled. Now, I wish to live in the Land of Enough. My transformed meaning of abundance, as I understand it today, is simply to achieve "the fullness of life and love"—a full heart, rather than a fuller stomach. As it turns out, food was only one ingredient in that recipe.

WORK CITED

Del Giudice, Luisa. 2022. "Mimmo's Garden." *Ovunque Siamo* (Summer), https://ovunquesiamoweb.com/archive/summer-2022/luisa-del-giudice/.

About the Author

LUISA DEL GIUDICE, Ph.D. was born in Terracina (Latina), emigrated to Toronto in 1956, and has lived in Los Angeles since 1981. She is an Independent Scholar, has taught at various universities, and was Founder-Director of the Italian Oral History Institute in Los Angeles. She is internationally known for her work on Italian and Italian diaspora ethnology, folklore, and oral history. As an academic, public folklorist, and community activist, she has bridged many roles and audiences. She has edited numerous volumes, among which are: *Sabato Rodia's Towers in Watts: Art, Migrations, Development* (Fordham UP, 2014); *On Second Thought: Learned Women Reflect on Profession, Community, Purpose* (The University of Utah Press, 2017); *Triangulations Within the Italy-Canada-USA Borderlands* (Bordighera Press, 2020). In 2008, she was named an honorary Fellow of the American Folklore Society and Cavaliere by the Italian Republic. www.luisadg.org

Saggistica

Taking its name from the Italian—meaning essay, essay writing, or nonfiction—
Saggistica is dedicated to essay writing in its many forms, from the polemic and
personal to the scholarly.

Vito Zagarrio
> *The "Un-Happy Ending": Re-viewing The Cinema of Frank Capra.* 2011.
> ISBN 978-1-59954-005-4. Volume 1.

Paolo A. Giordano, Editor
> *The Hyphenate Writer and The Legacy of Exile.* 2010. ISBN 978-1-59954-
> 007-8. Volume 2.

Dennis Barone
> *America / Trattabili.* 2011. ISBN 978-1-59954-018-4. Volume 3.

Fred L. Gardaphè
> *The Art of Reading Italian Americana.* 2011. ISBN 978-1-59954-019-1.
> Volume 4.

Anthony Julian Tamburri
> *Re-viewing Italian Americana: Generalities and Specificities on Cinema.*
> 2011. ISBN 978-1-59954-020-7. Volume 5.

Sheryl Lynn Postman
> *An Italian Writer's Journey through American Realities: Giose Rimanelli's*
> *English Novels. "The most tormented decade of America: the 60s."* 2011.
> ISBN 978-1-59954-034-4. Volume 6.

Luigi Fontanella
> *Migrating Words: Italian Writers in the United States.* 2012. ISBN 978-1-
> 59954-041-2. Volume 7.

Peter Covino & Dennis Barone, Editors
> *Essays on Italian American Literature and Culture.* 2012. ISBN 978-1-
> 59954-035-1. Volume 8.

Gianfranco Viesti
> *Italy at the Crossroads.* 2012. ISBN 978-1-59954-071-9. Volume 9.

Peter Carravetta, Editor
> *Discourse Boundary Creation (LOGOS TOPOS POIESIS): A Festschrift*
> *in Honor of Paolo Valesio.* 2012. ISBN 978-1-59954-036-8. Volume 10.

Antonio Vitti and Anthony Julian Tamburri, Editors
Europe, Italy, and the Mediterranean. 2012. ISBN 978-1-59954-073-3.
Volume 11.

Vincenzo Scotti
Pax Mafiosa or War: Twenty Years after the Palermo Massacres. 2012. ISBN
978-1-59954-074-0. Volume 12.

Anthony Julian Tamburri, Editor
Meditations on Identity. Meditazioni su identità. ISBN 978-1-59954-
082-5. Volume 13.

Peter Carravetta, Editor
*Theater of the Mind, Stage of History. A Festschrift in Honor of Mario
Mignone.* ISBN 978-1-59954-083-2. Volume 14.

Lorenzo Del Boca
*Italy's Lies. Debunking History's Lies So That Italy Might Become A "Normal
Country"* ISBN 978-1-59954-084-9. Volume 15.

George Guida
*Spectacles of Themselves. Essays in Italian American Popular Culture and
Literature.* ISBN 978-1-59954-090-0. Volume 16.

Antonio Vitti and Anthony Julian Tamburri, Editors
Mare Nostrum: prospettive di un dialogo tra alterità e mediterraneità. ISBN
978-1-59954-100-6. Volume 17.

Patrizia Salvetti
Rope and Soap. Lynchings of Italians in the United States. ISBN 978-1-
59954-101-3. Volume 18.

Sheryl Lynn Postman and Anthony Julian Tamburri, Editors
Re-reading Rimanelli in America: Six Decades in the United States. ISBN
978-1-59954-102-0. Volume 19.

Pasquale Verdicchio
Bound by Distance. Rethinking Nationalism Through the Italian Diaspora.
ISBN 978-1-59954-103-7. Volume 20.

Peter Carravetta
After Identity. Migration, Critique, Italian American Culture. ISBN 978-
1-59954-072-6. Volume 21.

Antonio Vitti and Anthony Julian Tamburri, Editors
The Mediterranean As Seen by Insiders and Outsiders. ISBN 978-1-59954-107-5. Volume 22.

Eugenio Ragni
After Identity. Migration, Critique, Italian American Culture. ISBN 978-1-59954-109-9. Volume 23.

Quinto Antonelli
Intimate History of the Great War: Letters, Diaries, and Memoirs from Soldiers on the Front. ISBN 978-1-59954-111-2. Volume 24.

Antonio Vitti and Anthony Julian Tamburri, Editors
The Mediterranean Dreamed and Lived by Insiders and Outsiders. ISBN 978-1-59954-115-0. Volume 25.

Sabrina Vellucci and Carla Francellini, Editors
Re-Mapping Italian America: Places, Cultures, Identities. ISBN 978-1-59954-116-7. Volume 26.

Stephen J. Belluscio
Garibaldi M. Lapolla: A Study of His Novels. ISBN 978-1-59954-125-9. Volume 27.

Antonio Vitti and Anthony Julian Tamburri, Editors
The Representation of the Mediterranean World by Insiders and Outsiders. ISBN 978-1-59954-113-6. Volume 28.

Philip Balma and Giovanni Spani, Editors
Translating for (and from) The Italian Screen: Dubbing and Subtitles. ISBN 978-1-59954-141-9. Volume 29.

Antonio Vitti and Anthony Julian Tamburri, Editors
The Representation of the Mediterranean World by Insiders and Outsiders. ISBN 978-1-59954-142-6. Volume 30.

Anthony Julian Tamburri, Editor
Interrogations into Italian-American Studies. The Francesco and Mary Giambelli Foundation Lectures. ISBN 978-1-59954-143-3. Volume 31.

Susanna Nanni and Sabrina Vellucci, Editors
Circolazione di idee e di persone: Integrazione ed esclusione tra Europa e Americhe. ISBN 978-1-59954-155-6. Volume 33.

Sian Gibby, Joseph Sciorra, and Anthony Julian Tamburri, Editors
This Hope Sustains the Scholar: Essays in Tribute to the Work of Robert Viscusi. ISBN 978-1-59954-167-9. Volume 34.

Antonio Vitti and Anthony Julian Tamburri, Editors
Mediterranean Encounters and Clashes. Incontri e scontri mediterranei. ISBN 978-1-59954-171-6. Volume 35.

Wendy Pojmann
Espresso. The Art and Soul of Italy. ISBN 978-1-59954-168-6. Volume 36.

Paolo Giordano and Anthony Julian Tamburri, Editors
Il miglior fabbro. Essays in Honor of Joseph Tusiani. ISBN 978-1-59954-184-6. Volume 37

Antonio Vitti and Anthony Julian Tamburri, Editors
Mediterranean Encounters and Legacies. Incontri e lasciti mediterranei. ISBN 978-1-59954-142-6. Volume 38.

Antonio Vitti and Anthony Julian Tamburri, Editors
The Mediterranean As Seen by Insiders and Outsiders. ISBN 978-1-59954-107-5. Volume 22.

Eugenio Ragni
After Identity. Migration, Critique, Italian American Culture. ISBN 978-1-59954-109-9. Volume 23.

Quinto Antonelli
Intimate History of the Great War: Letters, Diaries, and Memoirs from Soldiers on the Front. ISBN 978-1-59954-111-2. Volume 24.

Antonio Vitti and Anthony Julian Tamburri, Editors
The Mediterranean Dreamed and Lived by Insiders and Outsiders. ISBN 978-1-59954-115-0. Volume 25.

Sabrina Vellucci and Carla Francellini, Editors
Re-Mapping Italian America: Places, Cultures, Identities. ISBN 978-1-59954-116-7. Volume 26.

Stephen J. Belluscio
Garibaldi M. Lapolla: A Study of His Novels. ISBN 978-1-59954-125-9. Volume 27.

Antonio Vitti and Anthony Julian Tamburri, Editors
The Representation of the Mediterranean World by Insiders and Outsiders. ISBN 978-1-59954-113-6. Volume 28.

Philip Balma and Giovanni Spani, Editors
Translating for (and from) The Italian Screen: Dubbing and Subtitles. ISBN 978-1-59954-141-9. Volume 29.

Antonio Vitti and Anthony Julian Tamburri, Editors
The Representation of the Mediterranean World by Insiders and Outsiders. ISBN 978-1-59954-142-6. Volume 30.

Anthony Julian Tamburri, Editor
Interrogations into Italian-American Studies. The Francesco and Mary Giambelli Foundation Lectures. ISBN 978-1-59954-143-3. Volume 31.

Susanna Nanni and Sabrina Vellucci, Editors
Circolazione di idee e di persone: Integrazione ed esclusione tra Europa e Americhe. ISBN 978-1-59954-155-6. Volume 33.

Sian Gibby, Joseph Sciorra, and Anthony Julian Tamburri, Editors
  This Hope Sustains the Scholar: Essays in Tribute to the Work of Robert Viscusi.
  ISBN 978-1-59954-167-9. Volume 34.

Antonio Vitti and Anthony Julian Tamburri, Editors
  Mediterranean Encounters and Clashes. Incontri e scontri mediterranei.
  ISBN 978-1-59954-171-6. Volume 35.

Wendy Pojmann
  Espresso. The Art and Soul of Italy. ISBN 978-1-59954-168-6.
  Volume 36.

Paolo Giordano and Anthony Julian Tamburri, Editors
  Il miglior fabbro. Essays in Honor of Joseph Tusiani. ISBN 978-1-59954-
  184-6. Volume 37

Antonio Vitti and Anthony Julian Tamburri, Editors
  Mediterranean Encounters and Legacies. Incontri e lasciti mediterranei.
  ISBN 978-1-59954-142-6. Volume 38.

www.ingramcontent.com/pod-product-compliance
Lightning Source LLC
Chambersburg PA
CBHW050339030726
47503CB00008B/2519